The Riven Realm

Nigel Tranter

CORONET BOOKS
Hodder and Stoughton

Copyright © 1984 by Nigel Tranter

First published in Great Britain in 1984
by Hodder and Stoughton Limited

Coronet edition 1987

British Library C.I.P.

Tranter, Nigel
 Riven realm.
 I. Title
 823'.912[F]   PR6070.R34

 ISBN 0 340 40571 6

Printed and bound in Great Britain for
Hodder and Stoughton Paperbacks, a
division of Hodder and Stoughton Ltd.,
Mill Road, Dunton Green, Sevenoaks,
Kent (Editorial Office: 47 Bedford
Square, London, WC1B 3DP) by
Cox & Wyman Ltd., Reading.

THE RIVEN REALM

Sorry the nation where a babe is king, runs the old saying, and surely never was its truth more directly demonstrated than in Scotland after its most grievous disaster, Flodden Field. It was a shattered realm, the power-hungry waiting like jackals to assail the kingdom. Douglases, Hamiltons, Stewarts, Homes, even Holy Church and Henry VIII of England seeking to gain by conquest, assassination, intrigue and bribery, overlordship of the northern kingdom.

Against this background, Nigel Tranter tells the tale of two main characters, both named David – David Lindsay of the Mount, later famed as the author of the celebrated *Three Estates*; and David Beaton, who was to become the second most execrated name in Scottish history. They became friends at the University of St. Andrews and met again later when their paths crossed in unforeseen ways. Both their names became famous – or infamous – to mark Scottish history for evermore.

In the first of a trilogy of novels, sixteenth century power politics and brinkmanship are drawn in bright stark colours by a master Scottish storyteller.

Principal Characters

IN ORDER OF APPEARANCE

DAVID LINDSAY: Usher and Procurator to infant Prince of Scotland. Son of Sir David Lindsay of Garleton.

MASTER JOHN INGLIS: Abbot of Culross. Assistant tutor to the Prince.

MIRREN LIVINGSTONE: A mistress of King James the Fourth of Scots.

MASTER WILLIAM ELPHINSTONE: Bishop of Aberdeen and Lord Privy Seal.

JAMES THE FOURTH: King of Scots.

MARGARET TUDOR: Queen of above. Sister of Henry the Eighth of England.

JAMES STEWART: Prince of Scotland and Duke of Rothesay. Infant son of King.

SIR DAVID LINDSAY OF GARLETON: East Lothian laird and former warrior.

LADY ISABELLA LINDSAY: Wife of Lord Lindsay of the Byres.

KATE LINDSAY: Daughter of above.

ARCHIBALD DOUGLAS, MASTER OF ANGUS: Great noble. Later 6th Earl of Angus.

MASTER JAMES BEATON: Archbishop of Glasgow and Chancellor of the Realm.

ALEXANDER, 3RD LORD HOME: Lord Chamberlain. Great Border noble.

SIR ARCHIBALD DOUGLAS OF KILSPINDIE: Known as Greysteel. Uncle of Angus.

MASTER GAVIN DOUGLAS: Brother of above. Provost of St Giles. Poet.

MASTER GAVIN DUNBAR: Tutor to James the Fifth. Poet.

JAMES HAMILTON, EARL OF ARRAN: Lord High Admiral. Cousin of the King.

ANTOINE DE LA BASTIE: French envoy and noted soldier.

PATRICK, 4TH LORD LINDSAY OF THE BYRES: Kate's father.

DAVID BEATON: Lay Rector of Campsie. Nephew of Archbishop Beaton.

JOHN STEWART, DUKE OF ALBANY: Cousin of the King and French citizen.

WILLIAM KEITH, EARL MARISCHAL: Great noble.

MARION OGILVY: Daughter of 3rd Lord Ogilvy of Airlie.

SIR JAMES HAMILTON OF FINNART: Illegitimate son of Arran. Known as The Bastard of Arran.

ARCHIBALD, 3RD EARL OF ARGYLL: Lord Justice General. Chief of Clan Campbell.

MASTER WILLIAM DOUGLAS: Abbot of Holyrood. Another uncle of Angus.

1

The square-faced young man with the darkly humorous eyes nudged with his elbow his companion standing beside him, and jerked his head half-right, grinning, towards where Mirren Livingstone, the King's newest young lady, was intently inspecting herself inside her notably low-necked gown and scratching comprehensively at the same time—activity calculated to engender interesting speculation in any male worthy of the name. His friend began to smile, then changed to a head-shaking frown. After all, John Inglis was a cleric, Abbot of Culross no less, despite comparative youth, and they were in church, St Michael's by the Palace, at Linlithgow, no place for levity, especially on this solemn occasion. He lowered his head again, presumably in prayer, while the choir of singing boys continued to render sweet background music suitable for a monarch at his devotions.

His younger companion, David Lindsay, maintained his not-too-obvious vigil on Mirren Livingstone, whom he rather admired—at a distance, naturally—whilst dutifully keeping his eye on his beloved King James. The monarch, fourth of his name, knelt at a reading-desk, the only kneeling figure in the crowded south transept of St Michael's, before the altar of St Katherine, where Bishop Elphinstone of Aberdeen was conducting Vespers, a special service. All others must stand. James was a notably pious prince—in a practical way, of course, which would not restrict his other interests. He was here to pray for the success of his forthcoming great venture against his wretched brother-in-law, Henry Tudor, eighth of that name on the English throne. It was St Christopher's Day, 25th July, 1513.

The Queen was noticeably not present.

David Lindsay was not in a particularly worshipful frame of mind, apart altogether from Mirren Livingstone, mainly because he was being expressly excluded from the King's notable adventure. He had pleaded to be taken, along with all the flower of Scotland's chivalry. But James had been adamant. Davie's place was with the little Prince, he had insisted. He was his appointed Gentleman and Procurator, and his place was at the child's side, the heir to the throne. There would be opportunities in plenty for armed prowess and glory, later, never fear. So attendance at this special service was scarcely relevant for him.

Wondering what Mirren would be up to whilst the King was away—since he could hardly take her with him—movement caught David's roving eye. From an archway of the transept, to the right of St Katherine's altar, a figure emerged, a strange, an extraordinary figure. It was that of a tall old man, upright, dignified, with long white hair, parted at the forehead, falling down below the shoulders, dressed in a blue robe tied with a linen girdle, walking with a long white stick like a shepherd's crook. Ignoring the bishop, priests and acolytes at the altar, this apparition came slowly across the chancel, in majestic fashion, seeming almost to glide, towards the head-bowed King. David stared, and not only David. The choir's singing faltered momentarily.

The eye-catching figure moved directly over to the monarch at his faldstool and there stood. James looked up, eyes widening.

Strongly, sternly, the old man spoke, loudly enough to be heard above the singing and chanting.

"Sire—I am sent to warn you. Not to proceed with your present undertaking. You hear? Not to proceed. For if you do, it shall not fare well with either yourself or those who go with you."

He paused, as the King eyed him, astonished.

"Further," he went on, "it has been enjoined on me to bid you shun the familiar society and counsels of women, lest they occasion your disgrace and destruction. Hear you, I say."

"Save us—who a' God's name are you? What . . . ?" It is safe to say that James Stewart had never before been addressed thus.

The other dismissed the question with a wave of the hand. "Heed!" was all he said, but dramatically, and with another jab of his pointing finger, passed on.

The monarch lifted to his feet in a single movement, for he was a very fit man for his forty years although beginning to thicken at the waist. "Wait! Stop! Stop, you!" he commanded.

The oddity paid no heed.

David Lindsay moved sideways and thrust out a hand to detain the old man, but he eluded his grasp and pressed on into the crowd behind, which swallowed him up.

Gazing after him, the King shook his head. "A madman! Or a spectre—which?" he demanded, of no one in particular.

And no one answered, even though it was a royal demand.

"Davie—fetch him for me."

Young Lindsay turned and pushed his way into the throng which filled the side-chapel—lords, lairds, courtiers, soldiers and their women. But they were so close-packed that his progress was slow and, despite the remarkable impact of the strange figure, no sign of it was now evident in the crush.

Urgently David worked through and out of the transept into the main nave of the great church, much less crowded here, although worship was proceeding in some fashion before some others of the two dozen altars therein. Still there was no stranger to be seen. He went to the tall west doorway, to stare out. Nothing. The curiosity seemed to have disappeared into thin air.

Back at the King's side, David had to confess his failure. James, who had exchanged worship for discussion and debate, was surrounded now by a group of his lords, all very vocal although the service was still proceeding up at the altar. At the young man's announcement that there was no trace of the interloper, Andrew, Lord Gray, Justiciary, declared that it was, as he had said, a spectre, a bogle, sent by the Prince of Darkness himself, others agreeing. How else had he won into the church unchallenged and out again? He was from the Other World, clearly, a messenger, a wraith . . .

James frowned, hitching at his waist, a habitual gesture when in doubt or unease, adjusting the lie of the chain which he had worn next to his skin since the day twenty-five years ago when he had looked down on the dead body of his father, the hapless James the Third, and recognised how he, the fifteen-year-old son, had been used by unscrupulous nobles to bring his sire to this grievous pass, and took the chain, a mere harness chain, as reminder of his vow of remorse. That it was the same Lord Gray, old now, who had finished off his injured father with a dirk, on that occasion after the Battle of Sauchieburn, might have added some significance to this present, possibly fateful, interlude.

"You, Davie Lindsay—you were close to this, this creature," the King charged. "And you, Abbot. How say you? Was he honest man, however insolent? Or spirit, phantom, good or ill?"

David shook his head. "I know not, Sire. How can I tell? I have never seen a phantom. He seemed but man to me, although strange. And yet . . ."

"Yet, what, man—what?"

"I thought to grasp him, Highness, as he passed. As you bade. But . . . touched nothing! And then I went after him. But he disappeared. Gone. I, I do not know . . ."

"And you, Abbot John?"

"I would not venture an opinion, Your Grace. I saw nothing to have me think that he was other than an old man, probably deranged in his wits. But—who knows?"

"Aye. Mirren—how say you? You were nearby, also."

The young woman, red-haired, full-lipped, full-bosomed and lively—James had a weakness for redheads—came forward. "I say that he was wraith, Sire. None other would dare to speak you so. Sent to warn you against this invasion. I pray Your Grace to take heed . . ."

"Aye—we all know *your* wishes in the matter, lass!" the King said, with a half-smile. "Some others wish it, too, if for different reasons! But whether Heaven or Hell are so concerned is less certain."

"But you will pay heed, Sire?"

"We shall see . . ." James turned to face the altar, where the venerable Bishop Elphinstone made belated recognition of the fact that his congregation was scarcely with him in worship any longer by winding up the service quickly and signing for the choristers to do likewise. He came hobbling down to the royal group.

"Your Grace is pleased to dispense with further seeking of God's blessing?" he reproved.

"Scarce pleased, old friend. Say provoked. You saw this, this visitant?"

"I saw another old man pass me, who might be more

lacking his wits than even your servant, Sire! Was that sufficient to interrupt this holy office?"

"He miscalled the King. Spoke against this great endeavour. Threatened ill," the Earl of Atholl asserted. "Would you have such go unheeded, Sir Priest?"

"I think to heed Almighty God the more, in this house of His," Elphinstone said simply. His was a fine face, although lined and worn, with the noble features of a saintly yet practical philosopher, who had held the highest offices in the land, including that of Chancellor or chief minister; James's early mentor, who should have been Archbishop of St Andrews and Primate—only the King's own illegitimate seventeen-year-old son, Alexander Stewart, had been given that position.

"Aye, well—enough of this meantime," the monarch said. "Back to the palace. My belly rumbles, spectre or none! Come, Mirren . . ."

Leaving the Bishop to unrobe, they all moved from the church and crossed the mound above Linlithgow Loch, which it shared with the handsome brownstone palace.

At the meal which followed, in the great first-floor banqueting-hall, the talk, needless to say, was all of the apparition and what it might signify—the story, naturally, growing with the telling. Only a few who had been nearby had actually heard the words spoken, of course, so that there was considerable scope for the imagination. David and Abbot John—who was the young Prince's appointed tutor, although at only seventeen months not much tutoring was yet being attempted—discussed the matter back and forth, and although they came to no definite conclusions, certain indications were established for further debate.

It is to be doubted whether any similar progress was being achieved up at the dais-table, or at least at its centre, where the King and Queen scarcely exchanged a word; the French ambassador, on James's other side, had not been present in church and was besides a military man and unlikely to concern himself with metaphysics.

James Stewart and his wife were hardly the best of friends. Married for ten years now, they both bored and were bored with each other. On his part this was little to be wondered at, for he liked vivacious and attractive women, and Henry the Eighth's sister was neither. Margaret Tudor was plump, dumpy and somewhat moon-faced, without personal grace, and although still only twenty-two years old already looked almost middle-aged. Yet she was notoriously highly sexed and her little pig-like eyes, so like her brother's, were shrewd enough and missed little. She was probably the least popular queen-consort Scotland had ever had, and knew it—no pleasant situation for any woman. Their marriage, when she was only twelve, at Henry's urging, had done little to interrupt James's long succession of mistresses. Her own amorous adventures had to be less explicit.

When the Queen and her ladies retired and the men were getting down to serious drinking, a page came down from the dais-table to inform David and John Inglis that the King would speak with them, and to await him at Queen Joanna's Bower in the park, presently. James was abstemious about liquor, whatever else, and frequently left his hard-drinking lords to get on with it whilst he sought a different kind of solace.

The two younger men wandered out into the fine July evening. Of all the palaces of Scotland, Linlithgow was the most picturesquely sited, embosomed in low green hills, with the long, narrow curving town on the south side and the fine broad loch on the north, palace and church sharing the ridge between. With the last of the sunset staining sky and water crimson, black and palest green to the north-west, and drawing long purple shadows out of every fold and hollow of the hills, it was pleasant there amidst the last of the darting swallows and the dusk-flighting duck as the friends walked down to the summer-house known as Queen Joanna's Bower, after Joan Beaufort, wife of James the First.

They were not there long before they saw the vigorous figure of James Stewart come striding downhill, alone.

"Here comes the finest king Scotland has had since my noble namesake, David the First," Lindsay observed, "the Bruce excepted."

"You still say that?" his companion charged, smiling. "After his refusal to take you on this great venture of his? Wise as I would say he is, in that!"

"Yes. He has his reasons, no doubt—although I wish that he had not."

The King beckoned them out. "Come—we shall walk around the loch. No long ears there! And I can do with

12

stretching my legs. Too much sitting and talk in the rule of a nation!" Ever straightforward, James came at once to the point. "This at Vespers. What do you make of it all? You were both close by me. And you both have sound wits, or I would not have chosen you to watch over my young son. You have had time to consider it. How think you?"

The others glanced at each other. Inglis spoke. "We do not think that it was any spectre, Sire."

"No? Nor do I. But—why?"

"Would a spectre lean upon a stick, Your Grace?" David asked.

"Ha! A fair point. Anything else?"

"Would a spectre have entered the chapel from the main church and crossed the aisle thereafter, to you? Would one not rather have materialised directly before Your Grace?"

"Perhaps. I am not wise in the ways of phantoms."

"Nor are we, Sire," Inglis hastened to declare. "If such there be."

"You think that doubtful?"

"With respect, Sire—yes."

"Yet Holy Church speaks much of the spirits of the departed and the like."

"But not as coming to haunt men on earth, Highness. Only as existing in the hereafter."

"Indeed. I bow to your superior knowledge, Abbot John. So—if this was no spectre, what was it?"

"Possibly a seer, Your Grace. Some eremite or holy man believing that he has the sight and can foretell the future. There are some who so conceive, I understand."

"Possibly, yes. I had so considered. Crazed or otherwise."

"I do not think that he was crazed, Sire," David said.

"No? Why?"

"Because of what he said in the second place. The first, about doom and scaith, could have been the babblings of a crazed man. But the second was different, quite. About, about . . ." David looked embarrassed. ". . . this of women, Sire. I misremember the words. But it was to do with shunning familiar women. Something of that."

"I heard," James said grimly. "What of it?"

"That is not, I think, what a seer or a crazed religious would have said. That was a different matter, no prediction but a rebuke, a challenge. That was . . . different."

"So-o-o! There, now, we have shrewd thinking! I had not perceived the difference. Yes, you are right. That was no message from the Other World, nor yet the dreams of a crazed seer. Those were the words of a man with a purpose. But, why? Who was he?"

"Does it matter *who* he was, Sire? That old man. A mummer, perhaps, a play-actor. Rather, who sent him?"

James nodded. "No doubt you are right again, Davie. Where did you win the head on those young shoulders?"

"It is none so remarkable, Highness. Who mislikes both your venture into England, and your, your interest in other women, sufficiently to have contrived this?" David's slight catch of breath at his emphasis on the word "other" betrayed his fear that he might have gone too far.

The King paused in his walking to eye him searchingly. "You mean the Queen, man?"

"Your pardon, Sire—but who else has such good reason? Leastways such *strong* reasons."

James hitched at that chain of his. "True. But . . . would she do this? So fell a device?"

Neither of his companions ventured to answer that.

"It could be," he went on slowly. "In truth she has done all that she can do to halt this project. No doubt at her brother's behest. This could be a last attempt. And she much dislikes the Queen of France's fair words in sending me her glove, and to venture three steps into England for love of her."

This great expedition was being undertaken at the urgent request of King Louis of France under the mutual-aid provisions of the Auld Alliance, whereby Scotland and France had long sought to contain English aggression against either by agreeing each to stage an invasion, south or north, if the other was menaced. Henry was at present engaged in the attempted conquest of Guienne; and James, who had suffered much at his brother-in-law's hands, was only too pleased to accede.

David had a notion that the Queen's objection to familiar women would be apt to be centred nearer home than Versailles, but he did not say so.

"The English were ever great on play-acting, mummery and masques," he mentioned.

"Aye. This could be West's device." Dr West was the

English ambassador. "Although Her Grace has the wits to have thought it up for herself!"

"Will you heed it, Sire?" Inglis wondered.

"I will not. All is prepared. Arran, the admiral, has already sailed from the Clyde with my fleet. Home, with his Borderers, is probing into Northumberland. It is too late to turn back now—even if I could. I go to Edinburgh in two days. And we march some days later."

There was silence for a while as they walked on.

"You will cherish my son for me, while I am gone," the King went on presently, in a different tone of voice. "There are ever ill-intentioned folk in this kingdom, as in any other, who would grasp the heir to the throne if they could, to use him to advance themselves. And I do not trust Henry's ambassador, West. So keep ever close to the lad. I chose you two carefully. You can call on any of my royal guard left behind, at need."

"The Prince is safe with us, Sire," David assured.

They were almost back at the palace when James added his second injunction—and it was clearly to David that he gave it. "Look after Mirren when I am gone," he said briefly, and waved them away.

It was two weeks later, in fact, when David Lindsay and John Inglis stood on the vantage point of the Borestane Knowe and gazed out over the Burgh-muir of Edinburgh, spellbound by the sight. It is safe to say that never had that lofty and extensive moor above the city, traditional mustering place for Scotland's armies as it was, seen such a sight as this. Near and far, from the town walls right to the very slopes of the Braid Hills two miles away, the concourse stretched, not in any wide-scattered dispersal but in close-marshalled, serried and orderly ranks, as far as eye could see, the sunlight gleaming on steel and blazoning the colours of a thousand banners and standards which fluttered in the breeze, the steam of scores of thousands of horses raising a sort of mist above all, the encampment of baggage-wagons, ox-carts and weapon-sleds itself larger than the city below. Men said that there were one hundred thousand gathered there—and although that was probably an exaggeration, even half that number would be a greater army than ever Scotland had gathered before in her long story of warfare and strife. None other than James the Fourth, the most popular monarch ever the land had had, *could* have assembled this enormous host from every corner of his kingdom, from the distant Hebrides to the Mull of Galloway, from Sutherland and Ross to the Borders, the manpower of a score of earldoms, a hundred baronies, thirteen bishoprics and two score Highland clans, townsfolk of every burgh in the land. Great armies had marched from here a many, down the centuries, but never anything like this.

The knoll where the young men stood with their charges was like a small island in the sea of glitter and colour, and itself a crowded island, tight-packed and even more colourful than the rest under its forest of waving lordly pennons and escutcheons and tossing plumes, for here waited the principal nobility of the realm who were not for the moment heading up their armed strength, the officers of state and the leaders of Holy Church. In this galaxy of earls and bishops and lords, Lindsay and the Abbot would have merited no least place—save that they escorted two charges, or three, the seventeen-months James, Prince of Scotland and Duke of Rothesay and his nurse the Lady Erskine, and Mirren Livingstone. The Queen was not present, having remained at Linlithgow.

Young James was a chubby and cheerful infant, well-made and restless—which, considering his present seat on David's broad shoulder, where he could view all, brought its problems. He chortled and pointed, laughed and dribbled and beat on his Procurator's bare head, to emphasise his satisfaction with all the prospect. Mirren, perhaps unsuitably, clutched an arm each of the young men, also exclaiming at all she saw. Lady Erskine was more discreet.

A curious, creaking, groaning, rumbling noise turned all heads northwards, city-wards, but the crowds and the falling level of the land hid the cause, and speculation was superseded by the return to the Borestane Knowe of the tight little group of horsemen under the great Lion Standard of Scotland, spurring from the other direction. Reining up before them, the King raised his hand high.

"All is well," he cried. "The South Galloway folk have arrived. And the Arran Hamiltons. We now but await the cannon."

"We hear it now, I think, Sire," George Douglas, Master of Angus, called. "Listen!"

"Aye. They are slow, cannot be other. We shall see them come, then march." James made a splendid figure, in black gold-inlaid half-armour over scarlet and cloth-of-gold doublet and doeskin breeches, with thigh-length riding boots, a purple fur-trimmed cloak flung back from his shoulder. But, as usual, his head was bare, only a simple gold circlet at his brow restraining the long thick auburn hair which fell to his shoulders.

He dismounted, throwing his reins to an esquire and striding up to take his son from David, to toss the gurgling child into the air and catch him, laughing.

"Hey, Jamie Stewart! Ho, Jamie Stewart!" he shouted. "Here's to you, and here's to your sire and here's to this fine realm of ours! Yours, one day! See you yon Lion ramping there?" And he pointed up to the great red and gold tressured banner, held aloft and flapping above the royal charger by his standard-bearer, Scrymgeour of Dudhope. "True Thomas said: 'When Alba's Lion throats a roar; wise men run to bolt their door!' That Lion is throating a big roar this day—and you are hearing it, Jamie. Pray others will also—but scarce in time to bolt their doors! Eh, my lords?"

There was a roar of approval from the ranked nobles. But not from them all. A harsh, rasping voice spoke.

"*I* say, see that your Lion doesna choke on this meal you seek to give it! Or it will no' roar again for long enough!"

There was a shocked hush at that, and then a storm of protest which drowned out even the rumbling, clanking noise.

James raised one eyebrow towards the old man. "You belled the cat one time, Archie Douglas," he said, mildly enough. "But you'll not bell the Lion so easy!"

A shout of mirth greeted this sally. Archibald Douglas, fifth Earl of Angus, had been known as Bell-the-Cat ever since, thirty years before, he had disposed of the man Cochrane and others of the late James the Third's odd minions, by the simple expedient of hanging them from Lauder Brig.

The Earl, head of the great Red Douglas house, irascible always, scowled and, since even he could scarcely challenge his sovereign-lord, rounded on the others instead. "Laugh,

17

dizzards!" he cried. "Laugh whilst you may! For, by the powers, you may not have much longer for laughing if you proceed with this folly. Have you considered what you do? You challenge England's might, in war. How many of you ken what war is? You are bairns in the business—bairns! But Henry's lords are old in war—his father saw to that, in his French campaigns. How many of you have ever drawn sword in battle? You are but tourney fighters! I tell you, this will be no tourney!"

The laughter changed to growling. Even the speaker's eldest son and heir, George, the Master, joined in the hostility. "Too late for doubts now, my lord," he called, embarrassed. "When has Douglas ever been afraid to hazard a toss? Is not this the greatest might our land has ever mounted? And our cause just?"

"Cause! *Whose* cause, fool? Louis of France's cause, not ours. All this, to save Louis! What has Louis of France ever done for Scotland?"

"The Auld Alliance . . ."

"The Alliance is all one-sided. What do we gain?"

"Honour, at least!" somebody shouted.

"Honour! I would choose to die for more than honour! Are all summoned here, my lord King, to die for honour? Whose honour? Last night there was another summons, I am told. Not to flourish empty honour, but to compear before the Throne of Darkness within forty days! On the commands of the Prince of Darkness himself. If you do not turn back. And he named many by name—you, Atholl! And you, Argyll. And you, Glencairn. And Bothwell. Aye, and you Cassillis. And Lyle . . . !" Angus's pointing finger jabbed at the owner of each proud title, under their heraldic banners.

There was a shocked silence as he continued with his grim roll-call. All there had heard how, at midnight a bare twelve hours before, a disembodied voice had sounded at the Mercat Cross of Edinburgh announcing that Pluto hereby required all the earls, lords, barons, gentlemen and sundry burgesses of the city to appear before his master, King of the Underworld, within forty days, under pain of disobedience, designating many of the foremost names in the land, as a consequence of this present expedition.

James frowned. "I say whoever contrived yonder

mummery at Linlithgow, with its mouthings, contrived last night's play-acting also," he said, shortly. "Speak no more of King Henry's friends' inventions, my lord!"

"Such calling up of the powers of darkness is evil and should be cast from our minds," another old voice asserted, that of Bishop Elphinstone. "But I much urge Your Grace nevertheless to consider well your intentions, in this venture. Already you have despatched your fleet to France's aid and to threaten the English coasts. And sent my lord of Home and his mosstroopers into England. I pray you to be content, Sire, to take this great array only as far as Tweed and there rest, on your own side of the Border. Posing sufficient threat to King Henry, without leaving your own territory. The English will well perceive the danger, never fear, and will be as greatly concerned as if you had crossed into their land. But you will have remained on your own soil, as you have all right to do, and no men's lives endangered. Wait this side of Tweed, my lord King—in the name of Holy Church, I beseech you."

As murmurs arose for and against this course, there was a diversion, from behind the King this time, where a gallant youth leapt down from one of the fine horses beneath the standard and strode over to take the infant prince from his father's arms in familiar fashion.

"Come, rascal—to your gossip, Alex," he exclaimed. "And let us tell these greybeards that Holy Church can speak with other voice than trembling caution when the cause is just! I say, enough of gloomy doubts and fears. Let us be doing and on our way! And Saint Andrew of Scotland himself will loud out-voice all these quavering ancients!" This was Alexander Stewart, James's seventeen-year-old son by Marion Boyd, his first mistress, Archbishop of St Andrews and Primate of the Church—even though the only hint of episcopacy about him today was the mitre painted on his gleaming half armour. He bounced his small half-brother about vigorously, apparently to the satisfaction of both.

The cheers which greeted this spirited intervention indicated general support.

The King waved a hand for quiet. "I have heard all, and shall consider all," he said. "But meantime we have this host to set in motion. Here come the cannon, at last. We shall see them past and then be on our way."

He had to shout that, for the rumbling, squealing and growling noise was now so loud as to drown all else. The cause of it all was becoming evident, a vast ponderous cavalcade of horsemen, oxen, artillery, wagons and marchers, half a mile long, before which all the serried ranks of the assembled host had to draw aside, however difficult this was. First came a splendidly mounted figure in emblazoned full armour and nodding plumes, under the three black cinquefoils on white, the banner of Lord Borthwick, Hereditary Master Gunner of the realm; and behind came his sons, vassals and followers. Then trundled his famous Seven Sisters, Scotland's greatest cannon, normally kept at Edinburgh Castle, massive monsters each drawn by a score of plodding oxen, their protesting wheels and axles setting up most of the screeching din, added to by the shouts of the drivers and the cracking of their long whips. Behind were ten lesser pieces, similarly ox-drawn. Then innumerable wagons, carts and sleds carrying the cannonballs, powder-casks and other necessary stores. Finally came a succession of hay-wains, laden with the thousands of eighteen-foot pikes which King Louis had sent from France as his contribution to the invasion, looked at distinctly askance by most Scots although allegedly good for keeping attacking swordsmen at more than arm's length. Over four hundred oxen were required to draw all this cumbersome weapon train, such as no Scots army previously had fielded.

As Lord Borthwick came level with the King, he signed for his banner to be dipped in salutation and raised a hand high, James acknowledging. He did not pause, for once that lumbering cavalcade ground to a halt it would take a deal of starting again. It had fifty miles to go to Tweed and would be lucky to cover it in five days.

Now the royal party stirred, most there eager to be on their way. Alexander Stewart gave the young Prince back to David Lindsay, and the King came to kiss the child goodbye.

"You will see well to this one, Davie," he charged. "He is fell precious. None other near the throne save my cousin Albany in France. Those in Henry's pay will seek to grasp him if they can. And the Queen . . . less than single-minded! See to it."

"With my life, Sire."

"Aye." James turned to Mirren. "So, lass—it is farewell, for this present." He reached into his breeches pocket and brought out a jewelled pendant on a gold chain, rubies glowing richly red. "Here is a keepsake to mind me by while I am gone. These two will look after you," and he gestured to Lindsay and the Abbot. He gave her a smacking kiss, slapped her round bottom and made for his horse. In front of all that company even the non-hypocritical James Stewart had to be casual about his ladies. But he looked back before he mounted. "You said that you were going to Garleton, Davie? Take them with you, I think—both. It might be best, meantime."

"If you wish, Sire . . ."

With the monarch in the saddle and reining round, his herald-trumpeter blew a resounding flourish, and the leadership group was on its way, the nobles and bishops swinging into jostling place behind, flags waving, plumes tossing, armour clanking, harness jingling, a brave sight. Not all there went, to be sure, some few remaining to gaze after the departing company, Bishop Elphinstone, Lord Privy Seal, amongst them, and a proportion of the royal guard— but it was noteworthy that the old Earl of Angus, despite his strictures, rode with the King. The Bishop shook his white head sorrowfully.

David Lindsay, holding the Prince, looked from his friend to the two women, and shrugged. "It seems that we *all* go to Garleton. Why, think you?"

"*I* do not, that is sure," Lady Erskine said decidedly. "And the Queen will expect the Prince back at Linlithgow, forthwith."

"His Grace's command was clear," the Abbot pointed out.

"Not for me. I take my orders from the Queen, now. And I am the child's nurse and keeper."

David eyed her thoughtfully, learning so soon something of the burden of reponsibility and difficulty his liege-lord had laid on his shoulders. "The King's express command must prevail," he asserted. "I am his appointed Procurator for the Prince. He goes to Garleton, with me. As does Mistress Livingstone. Your ladyship must do as you see fit."

"I return to the Queen, then. To inform Her Grace of this . . . this folly. The child needs a woman's care, and should come with me."

"*I* will see to the Prince's needs," Mirren put in.

"I said a woman's care—not a whore's!" Lady Erskine said, and turned her back.

The young men exchanged glances.

"Come, then—let us be on our way," David announced, hurriedly. "We have fifteen miles and more to ride. Mirren—which is your horse . . . ?" And, lower-voiced, he added. "What my father will say to this, the good Lord knows!"

2

Garleton Castle sat snugly beneath the quite steep escarpment of the green Garleton Hills, at the head of its fair hanging valley between the vales of Tyne and Peffer, in East Lothian. It was a pleasant, peaceful place, no mighty fortalice, but sufficiently strong for protective purposes, with its tower, turrets, parapets and shot-holes, its position strong too, as witnessed by the ancient Pictish fort which occupied the rocky spur immediately above. Garleton had been a Lindsay possession for almost four hundred years, ever since in the twelfth century Sir William de Lindsay had wed the Dunbar heiress of Luffness, the great castle and estate two miles to the north, on the shores of Aberlady Bay, and became baron thereof, with this Garleton, Byres, Athelstaneford and much else. Here David had been born and would one day be laird—although for official occasions he was styled Lindsay of the Mount, from a smaller property he had inherited, in Fife, from his mother.

The little company, eight strong, clattered into the courtyard filled with the long shadows of the sinking sun, the small Prince jouncing about in front of David's saddle but making no complaint, indeed almost asleep despite the motion. With the father he had he was much used to horseback travel. They had adopted the King's suggestion and brought along four members of the royal guard as escort.

As David set the toddler down on the yard flagstones and turned to aid Mirren to dismount, a large, burly man of middle years appeared within the arched doorway of the main keep, beneath the coloured heraldic panel with the carven Lindsay arms, the blue and white chequy-fesse on red.

"What a God's name is this, Davie Lindsay?" this individual demanded, in something of a bellow. "You'll no' tell me you've fathered a bairn this age without me kenning! I'll no' believe it!'

"No, sir—no, no!" David disclaimed protestingly. "This is the Prince. Young James, Prince of Scotland. The heir."

"Sakes—here? The Prince? Why? What's to do?"

"The King's command. I will tell you. He is gone to England . . ."

"All the world kens that, boy! I have sent eight stout lads for him. With the Byres' tail. Patrick's gone himself, with his three sons. Would God I could ha' gone myself, but this leg . . . But—no' yourself, it seems, Davie? *You* havena gone!"

"His Grace decided otherwise." That was short. David turned to the others. "This is my father, Sir David, of Garleton. Here is Master John Inglis, Abbot of Culross, of whom I have spoken. Tutor to the Prince. And . . ."

"Aye—and the lassie? You'll no' tell me that you've brought a woman home, at long last? After all your daffery and dalliance? Boy, at your age, I was wed four years, and you were older than this princeling!"

"No doubt, Father. But this lady is Mistress Mirren, kin to my Lord Livingstone. She is a, a friend of the King. He has placed her in my, in *our* care, meantime . . ."

"Ha—is that the way of it? His Grace had ever a guid eye for a horse, a hound and a woman—whoever he had to wed! You should learn frae him, Davie! Forby, mind, I wonder he trusts you with this one!"

His son cleared his throat—as he frequently had to do in Sir David's company. "Mistress Mirren will be tired. We have ridden straight from the Burghmuir of Edinburgh. And the child needing his bed. And feeding, first . . ."

"Aye, to be sure. Bring them in—and welcome. You'll no'want the lady in your own bedchamber, then—nor yet the Abbot's? We'll have to see what we can do . . ."

Mirren giggled, as servitors came to take the horses, the men-at-arms were led to the kitchen premises in the lean-to buildings of the courtyard, and Sir David limpingly conducted his guests into the main keep and up the twisting turnpike stairway to the hall and private quarters. Perhaps because of his bad leg, he found it necessary to grasp the young woman's quite sturdy person round the waist to aid in the ascent, his son sighing behind, but not in surprise.

Later, with young James fed and put down to sleep, the

others sat at table in the hall and discussed the day's events. Sir David lived alone at Garleton these days, a widower for many years now, and his other son and two daughters married and away.

This son was particularly interested in why the King should have deemed it advisable that he brought the little Prince here to Garleton instead of taking him back to Linlithgow Palace. They had puzzled over this as they rode, and come up with no adequate answer.

"He must believe the bairn in danger," the laird said. "He doesna trust that Queen of his—and I blame him not! She is more Henry Tudor's sister than James Stewart's wife!"

"But the Prince will have to go back to his mother sooner or later. We cannot keep him here. Forby, she'll send for him, for sure. We have no authority to hold him here, or otherwhere. He merely said to guard him well. And later, added to bring him here meantime."

"Aye. Then he must have feared some early attempt on the bairn. If Henry's friends could take and hold the heir to the throne, hide him away somewhere, then they have a notable grip on the King. They could force him to turn back on this invasion, perhaps. Every child-king or prince in this Scotland has been grasped or threatened thus—this King Jamie himself. He weel kens the danger. And what better time to grasp at the bairn than now, when none would look for it? When in the care of but yourselves? Before he's back to the safety of yon Linlithgow."

"Then it might not be the Queen at all that the King fears?"

"He said something of Her Grace being less than single-minded," John Inglis pointed out.

"If he feared something of this sort, then why did he bring the boy to Edinburgh? Why not leave him safely at Linlithgow? Or send him to Stirling Castle, where he would be safer still?"

"Who knows, lad. But he would have much on his mind with this great venture to prepare. And he may indeed mistrust Margaret Tudor. The Queen did not come to Edinburgh with him? No—then that might be it. He might not wish to leave the bairn alone, with her."

"He says that Dean West has the Queen in his pocket," Mirren Livingstone made her first contribution. "He much mistrusts the Dean." Nicholas West, Dean of Windsor, was English resident at the Court of Scotland.

"A slimy toad!" Sir David commented. "I've heard that he has the same pocket full of gold, to bribe any who will enrol in Henry's service. And such are no' that hard to find, I fear, where gold is on offer! Aye—and what better time to grasp the Prince, when most leal men are away with the King?"

They digested that thoughtfully, with their cold venison.

"What are we to do, then?" David demanded, presently. "We cannot keep the lad here, over long. Or we ourselves could be thought to have abducted him! The Queen will send for him."

"The good Bishop Elphinstone would hear the King tell you to bring the Prince to Garleton," the Abbot reminded. "He will let it be known that all is in order."

"True. But that would not prevent the Queen sending here. And with His Grace gone, she will now rule the land, not Bishop Elphinstone. Forby, she does not love *him*, either."

"You can but wait, then, to see what transpires," his father said. "And in a day or two, perhaps, send our Abbot friend here to Bishop Elphinstone for his guidance. He is an honest man, and wiser than most. And Privy Seal, forby. He will best advise."

That seemed fair counsel, and they left it there.

David saw Mirren to her room door, presently, and there she seemed reluctant to say goodnight.

"Davie—what is to become of me?" she asked, clutching his arm.

"Why, lass—you will do well enough," he assured.

"Are you sure? *What* am I to do? Where can I go?"

"Go? You have your quarters in Linlithgow. And when the King comes back, all will be as it was."

"The King may not come back."

"Wheesht, Mirren—what way is that to talk?"

"He may not! It is war he goes to. And I am afraid of the Queen!"

That admittedly was not something which could just be laughed away. Margaret Tudor was not the woman to look kindly on a husband's mistress.

"What of your home? Your father's house?"

"My father is dead. There is only my mother and three sisters at Dechmont. They could not save me from the Queen. Nor, nor I think, would wish to!"

"M'mm. And the Lord Livingstone?"

"My uncle is gone with the King. With all his strength."

David frowned. "You can bide here meantime, lass. Never fear—all will be well." Feeling protective, he put an arm round her—he was his father's son, after all. And she responded, pressing her ripely rounded warmth against him.

Somewhat hastily he disengaged. "I . . . ah . . . fear nothing!" he told her. "Goodnight, Mirren—sleep well . . ."

He left her, to mount the stair higher to his own chamber.

They waited a few days before Abbot John went off to consult Bishop Elphinstone, pleasant enough days, with Sir David and little Jamie Stewart getting on notably well together, the child being friendly and easy-going by nature and little trouble to anyone. Which left David free to conduct his friend round the neighbourhood and show him what was to be seen—for John Inglis came from Ayrshire and did not know Haddingtonshire or East Lothian. And inevitably Mirren was apt to come along too, being a little bit chary of being left alone with the laird—in which the son scarcely blamed her—and as inevitably her red-headed good looks, generous endowments and unmistakably approachable character, drew considerable comment and interest. And since it was neither convenient nor suitable to declare to all and sundry that this was the King's present mistress; and since even with the prevailing state of the clergy, with concubines commonplace, it could not be assumed that she was Abbot John's paramour, it was generally taken for granted that she was David's lady, and congratulations were apt to be the order of the day. Which, embarrassing as it was at first—to David, for Mirren was not readily embarrassed—became in time so normal that the embarrassment wore off and was replaced by a sort of mutual and secret amusement, which engendered its own intimacy.

That it was largely female neighbours and friends who jumped to these conclusions added its own dimension to the situation, for the fact was that the countryside, hereabouts at any rate, was largely denuded of its menfolk, so successful had been the King's call to his standard. Every castle, tower and lairdship in that fair county between the Lammermuir Hills and the sea, appeared to have sent most of its manpower on the great adventure, save for the ancient and decrepit—this, of course, by no means diminishing David's own need for explanation as to his non-inclusion.

He had another subject of challenge to counter, in which the other two could nowise come to his rescue—poetry. For David Lindsay was a poet, of sorts, had been since his student days at St Andrews, and had something of a local reputation to sustain, however inadequate he knew his verse to be—and of course used to it being overshadowed by the offerings of the famous William Dunbar and Gavin Douglas, both of whom, oddly enough, hailed from this same county. But the fact was that he had written not a word since he had been summoned, over a year before, to take up this appointment with the infant Prince, his new life at court quite absorbing all his attentions and interests—this despite having previously started on what, in his folly, he had already informed folk was to be a major work and to which he had even presumed to give a title—*The Dream*. Oddly, it was his father who was mainly responsible for bruiting this abroad. The Lindsays had always been fighters, soldiers, as had Sir David himself—his damaged leg was a relic of warfare in King James's Highland campaign—and he was much tickled that the line had at last produced what he referred to as a man of letters, although of course he would have been the first to object strongly if this literary inclination had tended to lead to any lack of manly vigour and spirit in his son.

David himself had said little about this interest of his, latterly—indeed, Mirren knew nothing of it and even Inglis took it to have been a passing youthful concern not engaged in since student days at St Andrews where they had first met. But any secrecy was forfeited when, on the third day at Garleton, they paid a visit to the Byres.

This strangely named property was the next estate west-wards, below the green Garleton Hills; indeed, originally, Garleton Castle and demesne had been part of this larger barony, the full name of which was Byres of Garleton. But locally it was known merely as the Byres; and when that branch of the chiefly house at Luffness, now Earls of Crawford, themselves became sufficiently renowned in war and statecraft to be given a lordship of parliament, they deliberately elected to use the title of Lord Lindsay of the Byres. So that, although there were one thousand and one byres in Scotland, every farm having its cowshed so named, there was only the one Byres with a capital B. The present Patrick, fourth Lord Lindsay of the Byres, with all three of his sons gone adventuring with the King, was a far-out kinsman of David's, the first of Garleton being a younger son of the first of the Byres.

They were well received, for this house—despite its name a larger and finer castle than Garleton, and standing within a handsome, high-walled garden—had been a second home for David ever since his mother had died when he was but a boy. He had always called Lady Lindsay Aunt Isabella.

"I am thankful to see at least two sensible young men who have not gone off in this madness of the King's!" she greeted, kissing David warmly after the introductions, a big, strong woman, still handsome. "It has been long since we saw you, David."

"Two years, yes. I have been away with the King's Grace the length and breadth of the land. And last time I was here, you were from home."

"You enjoy the King's service?" It had been largely through the Lord Lindsay's influence that David had won his position with the Prince.

"Indeed, yes. It is good. Because the Prince is so young, I am much with the King himself. He is kind to me. Even though he did not take me with him to England."

"You wished to go? The more fool you!"

"All are going, why not I? The King needs everyone . . ."

"And none left to see to all he leaves behind? James has a realm to rule. Even he could not be so foolish . . ."

"Davie—oh, Davie!" The cry turned him round. A girl had appeared within the hall doorway, gazing great-eyed. She held out her hands towards him and then came running.

David was staring, too, as well he might. "Kate!" he got out. "It's Kate!"

Then she had hurled herself into his arms in headlong, impetuous joy. "At last, at last!" she cried.

"Kate—behave you! You are not a child now, remember," her mother said, but smiling.

The girl ignored her. "Davie—so long! Why? Why did you never come?"

"I, I have been occupied, Kate. Throng with affairs. Busy. Going hither and yon. I am Prince Jamie's Procurator. I, I . . ."

"I know, I know. But you were only at Linlithgow and Stirling . . ."

"And Falkland and Kincardine, at Dumbarton, even Inverness. The King is never in one place for long, lass. And takes his young son, to show to all—the heir." Gently he put her from him, but only to arm's length, where he held her young loveliness. "Lord, Kate—you have . . . changed!"

"I have *not!*" Impulsively she shook her dark head. "*You* may have done. I think that you were unkind. Never to come."

"Heed her not, Davie," the Lady Lindsay advised. "She is but growing up. A process which can be trying. For all!"

He wagged his head. "No, no—not that." But it was that, of course. Kate Lindsay was indeed growing up, and most dramatically. A gawky, angular thirteen-year-old when last he had seen her, now at fifteen she had changed almost out of recognition, become a young woman and a beauty, features firmed and bloomed, person filled out and developing into promising excellence. Dark-haired, dark-eyed, clear-skinned, vivacious, eager, she was no longer the child he had known and looked on almost as a sister.

"Growing up, I see, yes. And I like what I see!" he said.

"You have waited sufficiently long to see it! But, now that you *have* come, you have brought . . . others!"

"Ah, yes. This is Mistress Mirren Livingstone of Dechmont. And the Abbot John of Culross. Friends."

The girl dipped a curtsy towards them, deep enough to be slightly mocking, towards Mirren at least. "Friends of Davie Lindsay's *must* be friends of mine!" she declared, eyes flashing.

"The Abbot is Prince Jamie's tutor," he explained. "And Mistress Mirren is at the King's court."

"Indeed. Have you finished my poem? *Katie Lindsay's Confession?*"

"Ah, no. No, I fear not. I, ah, have not been writing poetry, Kate. So much to do . . ."

"But it was nearly finished. And you promised!"

"I am sorry. But my life now is not helpful to writing poetry, I fear. All bustle and company and travel. Too many people coming and going . . ."

"Too many people, yes!" she agreed, looking daggers.

"Kate—fetch our guests wine and cake," her mother ordered briskly.

"I did not know that you were a poet, Davie," Mirren said.

"Nor am I," he disclaimed. "I used to scribble the occasional verse. Nothing of any real worth."

"That is not true," Kate threw back, from the doorway. "He wrote much that is fine, splendid. *The Dream* is great poetry." She slammed the door behind her.

"So you kept it up," John Inglis observed. "I said that you should. What is this of a dream? Some major work?"

"No, no. Just a few notions and observations. On a—a theme. Nothing of moment."

"I would wish to see it, nevertheless . . ."

"Davie is too modest," their hostess asserted. "Much of his work is very fine—although I know little about poetry. But—I like it. As do many."

"I always said that he had promise. At college . . ."

When Kate brought them the wine, oatcakes and honey, David had managed to get them off the subject of poetry. But that young creature was not to be balked.

"See," she said, "I have here my copy of the *Confession* you wrote out for me," and she drew out from her burgeoning bosom, now just large enough to contain it, a rather grubby wad of folded paper which she thrust at him. "Now you can complete it, Davie Lindsay."

He took it, warm from her person. "It is scarce worth it, lass."

"If it was worth starting, it is worth finishing. For me, Davie."

"Very well . . ."

"I will hold him to it," the Abbot promised, smiling.

After that, Kate was all sweetness and charm, even to Mirren. When the visitors left, she declared that she would come over to Garleton the following day to make the acquaintance of the young Prince.

31

That evening, Abbot John took the many pages of *The Dream* to bed with him, with a candle. And a little later, David saw Mirren to her room door again, to say goodnight.

"The lassie Kate is a lively one!" she declared. "She did not love me, I think."

"You must not heed her, Mirren. She is young and grown headstrong, it seems. She was not so before. I have known her all her life."

"And been fond of her, it seems."

"Why, yes. Almost like her older brother—although she has brothers of her own. We are cousins, of a sort, after all."

"She sees you as no brother, that one, Davie! And she is going to be very beautiful."

"She is greatly altered, yes. In looks, as in, er, behaviour. I scarcely knew her. In but two years."

"This poem she covets? About herself?"

"In some fashion, yes . . ." Something between a grunt and a snort came from the next room where the laird slept, door open, and lowered David's voice to a whisper. "A childish thing just, suitable for a bairn. I am no true poet."

Whispering in turn, she drew him into her room—for it would be a pity to wake Sir David, if he was indeed asleep. "Why did you never tell me? Does the King know of it? Abbot John thinks that you are good. This poetry. Will you make a poem about me, Davie?"

"M'mm. Well—I am truly not writing poetry at this present, any more, Mirren . . ."

"But you *can*. Am I not good enough, fair enough? Will you not do it? Just a little one? For me . . . ?" She was close, and came closer, gazing up into his eyes, a most natural-born and unashamed wanton. And he, to be sure, was no monk. As her thrusting breasts brushed against him, he put an arm around her, pulled her closer still, and their lips met. She was wholehearted and generous about that, too.

But quickly his conscience got the better of him. After all, she was the King's woman and he the King's servant. This would not do. She was in his care. Almost roughly he pushed her from him.

"No, we must not," he jerked. "This is folly! Worse!"

"Is it? I do not think that James would mind," she whispered. "He is open-handed. In all things."

"Nevertheless . . ." He shook his head. "I will write you a verse. Goodnight, Mirren." He hurried off.

It took him some time to sleep.

In the morning, John Inglis was loud in his praises over *The Dream*, however unresponsive and preoccupied the author. Mirren was her usual uncomplicated self. Poetry, David thought, and indicated, was an unsuitable subject for the breakfast table.

Kate turned up thereafter, in excellent spirits, and made a great fuss over the little Prince, Jamie loving it. Soon she was announcing that she would come each day to look after the child whilst he remained at Garleton. None ventured to say her nay.

The next day Abbot John set off for Linlithgow and Bishop Elphinstone.

With his friend gone and the Prince being more than well looked after by Sir David and Kate, David and Mirren were more and more alone in each other's company, and inevitably the pressure grew. Mirren probably could not help herself, and seemed to make little attempt to do so. David was both mightily exercised and sorely tried. He took occasional refuge in his upper chamber, which opened on to the parapet-walk of the keep, ostensibly to write poetry, which required much privacy.

This was only a moderately successful device, for although it kept Mirren at a distance it had little such effect on Kate, who of course was almost as much at home at Garleton as was David at the Byres. Moreover, the parapet-walk round the tower's wallhead was a favourite viewpoint for young James, from whence he could survey all the countryside around, croodle at the pigeons and watch the darting swallows. Not infrequently, then, the poet had company after all.

At least this had the effect of getting Kate's *Confession* completed sooner than would otherwise have been the case, to the girl's satisfaction. She, of course, promptly showed it off to Mirren—which produced a different variety of pressure on the versifier.

It was five days before Abbot John got back. He had had to go all the way to Stirling to find the Bishop, although the Queen was still at Linlithgow. Margaret Tudor and William Elphinstone failed to get on; and Stirling, to be sure, was the true seat of government, Linlithgow being merely a royal residence and, moreover, the Queen's own jointure-house, settled on her at her marriage.

The gist of John's report was this. The Queen was displeased at her son being taken to Garleton; but the Bishop had told her that this was at the King's express command. She had done nothing about it, as yet, but Elphinstone judged that it was only a question of time before she sent for the boy. His advice was that they should not wait for this, but return to Linlithgow fairly soon, for there was no point in causing unnecessary unpleasantness. On the other hand, the King's fears for the Prince's safety probably were not wholly ill-founded and further precautions should be taken. There could well be others than Margaret Tudor who had their eyes on the heir to the throne. The Bishop would advise the Queen, in his capacity as temporary chief minister—Archbishop Beaton, the Chancellor, was with the King—that the Prince should be brought to Stirling Castle, for greater security. He would get the Privy Council, or the rump of it left behind, to make this official policy. Then the Queen could scarcely refuse. Young James would surely be safe in Stirling Castle, the strongest fortress in the land.

This all seemed reasonable and wise. It was decided to take the Bishop's advice and return to Linlithgow shortly, and then on to Stirling. Mirren was less than enthusiastic, preferring to have remained at Garleton until the King came back; and for once Kate was in full agreement. The laird also declared that Garleton would be a duller place without them.

All were reluctant to go, in fact.

3

The appalling, unbelievable news reached Linlithgow just three days after their return. It was utter and complete disaster for Scotland. The King was dead. Slain in battle, most of his lords with him, and untold thousands of his ordinary folk. Even his son, the seventeen-year-old Archbishop.

The scale of the catastrophe was beyond all comprehension—twelve earls, two bishops, fifteen lords, innumerable knights, lairds and chiefs of name died with their sovereign lord, together with most of the greatest and most illustrious army the land had ever fielded, cut down in utter bloody ruin, mountains of dead, and the King fallen eventually himself on top of one of these mountains.

His realm reeled.

It had happened, apparently, not far into England, at a place high above the Till valley called Flodden Edge, a strong position which the Scots had occupied but which James had abandoned, allegedly to meet the English army under Surrey on more equal terms. This sounded the completest folly, but James was chivalrously inclined and the entire expedition was a chivalrous gesture towards France and her Queen. At any rate, the entire Scots host had dismounted, leaving their scores of thousands of horses there on the high ground, and charged down the steep escarpment to the waiting English below. And there those eighteen-foot pikes, sent by King Louis of France, had begun the disaster, causing men to trip and stumble and fall in the downhill rush, shafts snapping, jagging, wounding. And into this headlong chaos the disciplined, ranked English bowmen had rained their arrows in unceasing thousands, so that even before true battle could be joined the Scots had lost large numbers and confusion reigned. Thereafter, typically, the dashing James had led like a captain of foot rather than a general, in the very forefront, sword tireless; and one by one his lords and knights and clerics had died around him, the royal standard falling and rising again above him, held up successively by a score of hands. Just when the King, wounded many times, had finally been struck down, reports did not say; but night had descended on continuing carnage and fight—but in the morning only the slain remained on Flodden's field. The pride of Scotland was laid low.

The effect of these fearful tidings was indescribable, the reaction shattering, people just incapable of accepting the magnitude of the calamity. There was scarcely a home in the land unscathed, whole villages had lost their menfolk, many burghs their provosts and magistrates, including Edinburgh itself. And almost the entire government and leadership of the nation had fallen with its monarch. Never, in a thousand years of history, had anything like this befallen.

Linlithgow, and no doubt Stirling too, was as stunned as the rest—except for the Queen, that is. Margaret Tudor gave no impression of being stunned—on the contrary, she had never seemed so vigorous and decisive. If she grieved for her husband, she showed little outward sign of it, apart from ordering court mourning. She took charge—and admittedly it was necessary that someone should do so.

One of her first acts was to send for David and John, to fetch her son to her, from their wing of the palace. Two days before, she had given them a vehement dressing-down for taking the Prince away without her knowledge or permission—to which they could only say that it was done on the King's command. Her displeasure had been pronounced, but against the monarch's authority it had had to be muted. Now that situation no longer pertained.

They found her in a private anteroom of her bedchamber, with a young man of high colour and hot eyes, whom they knew to be Archibald Douglas, son of the Master of Angus and grandson of old Bell-the-Cat, the Earl. Young James eyed his mother doubtfully. She held out her hand to him.

"Come, James," she said, smiling.

Perhaps he was not used to that smile, for he hesitated, and David gave him a little push.

It was unfortunate that there was a bearskin rug on that anteroom floor, over which the toddler caught his feet and fell his length. He was none the worse, indeed chuckled cheerfully as he picked himself up—but promptly his expression switched to alarm at the outbreak of hot words his small mishap produced.

"How dare you, sirrah—to strike the King's Grace!" the Queen exclaimed.

"Oaf—keep your hands to yourself!" the young Douglas jerked, jumping to his feet. He strode over to the boy. "Sire—all is well. Heed him not. Come to Her Grace."

The boy looked him up and down, made a face, and turned to run back to David.

This unfortunate contretemps produced a rather difficult pause.

"Your Grace sent for us," Abbot John said, diplomatically.

"Yes. I require your heedful attention," the Queen asserted, frowning. She was a plump woman, with a round face, heavy-lidded eyes and a long nose, and displayed a lot of bosom. Those eyes were shrewd, calculating. "All is now changed. I have no reason to consider you suitable persons to be so close to the King's Grace."

This seemed a strange announcement, at this stage, until David's mind adjusted to the fact that it was not her late husband to whom the Queen referred but to her little son who was now, to be sure, King James the Fifth. This would take some getting used to. They waited.

"I have many more pressing matters to deal with and put in order than choosing others to take your places," she went on, in her clipped English voice. "So, for this present, you will continue to minister to my son, but you will do so in a very much more respectful way and in entire obedience to my wishes and commands. He is the King's Grace, and will be treated as such, under *my* authority. Is that understood?"

They bowed to that.

"Meantime, you will prepare His Grace, his person and effects, for travel. The court moves to Stirling tomorrow. Lady Erskine has already gone there to prepare suitable quarters in the castle. You will be ready to ride at sun-up. His Grace will ride with the Master of Angus, here."

"Yes, Madam." So Archie Douglas was now being styled the Master. That could only mean that his father, the Master and heir to the Angus earldom, was another of the battle's casualties.

"That is all. You may retire."

Again they bowed. "And His Grace . . . ?" David asked.

"What of him?"

"Is he to remain?"

"Take him with you."

So much for the King of Scots.

As the two young men backed out, their charge running ahead thankfully, they were halted at the door.

"Lindsay—the woman Livingstone," that imperious voice said. "I understand that she was with you at Garleton? Get rid of her!"

As they returned through the palace corridors, they sought to digest all this.

"It seems that our services are not much longer to be required," David commented. "Young Jamie, I fear, is in for change. And not going to like it, King or none."

"Poor laddie! It is hard on him. Not only to lose his father, whom he loved, but . . . all this! I can go back to my abbey and you to your Garleton and your poetry. But for young James . . . ! He hardly knows his mother. And clearly mislikes that Douglas. Nor do I blame him for it. He is a hard one that, I judge. It seems that he is close to the Queen."

"Yes, I had heard some hint of this."

"He is married, is he not? Although young. Younger than the Queen, I think."

"Married to Patrick Hepburn's daughter, the Earl of Bothwell. Married very young. She is frail, it is said. I have never seen her at court. And he will require no frail woman, that one, I swear!"

"Perhaps. And he will be Earl of Angus, one day, head of the Douglases. If he is not, already."

"No—the Queen called him the Master. So his father must have died. But not the old Earl." They had reached their own very modest accommodation, near the servants' wing. "It is strange to think that this bairn is the King of Scots. And in these humble quarters!"

"No longer after today, since we move to Stirling. Davie—what is to be done about Mirren Livingstone?"

"Lord knows! It was difficult enough before. But now that the King is dead . . . ! Yet, he told me to look after her. And I promised."

"I heard, yes. You must do what you can for her. But, Davie—do not wed her! She is attractive, yes. Generous and good company. But—do not think to carry out the King's charge by wedding her."

"I had no such intention, I assure you!" David said shortly.

"Perhaps not. But *she* might have!"

David looked at his friend strangely. "What makes you say that? Since when has the Abbot of Culross become so informed in the ways of women?"

"Being in holy orders does not make me blind nor witless, man! Mirren is fond of you, and now needs a protector. Aid her as much as you can—but do not wed her. She would not make the wife for you."

"You are very sure."

"I am, yes."

They left it at that. But that evening David went down to the house that King James had found Mirren in Linlithgow town, near to St Lazarus Well.

She greeted him joyfully. Since the news had come of the King's death, she had remained indoors, shut up for fear of the Queen's spite. David came as a deliverer.

In the circumstances, he found it difficult to deliver his message, at least, with her arms around him and her lips on his own.

"I thought that you would never come, Davie," she declared, between kisses. "I have been cooped like a hen in a yard! Oh, it is so good to see you!"

"And you. But . . ." He got no further.

"I have missed you, Davie. So greatly. After all our time together."

"It is only two days, lass . . ."

"It seems eternity!" In his arms, or he in hers, she was all but imperceptibly leading him towards an open door. He was fairly sure that it was her bedroom.

"The Queen sent for us, the Abbot and myself . . ." he got out.

"Do not speak of that evil woman. I hate her!"

"More to the point, lass—she hates *you*!"

"I know it. But not tonight, Davie. You have come. That is what signifies, for this present. And we are alone."

"We shall have to consider it, sooner or later, Mirren," he said, rather feebly. He was ever loth to offend a friendly lady; and Mirren was something rather special.

Within the bedchamber, she detached herself—but only to stand back and look him up and down. "You want me, Davie?" she demanded—although it was much more a statement than a question. "I think that you have always wanted me? As I have wanted you. And, now that James has gone, we can have each other!" She made it sound entirely simple and suitable. To emphasise the point she began to untie the strings of her bodice. No churl, after a moment or two David moved to help her.

No great assistance was required in fact, for her clothing seemed to be fairly loosely attached and largely fell off of its own accord, so that in almost less time than it takes to tell she was standing in a froth of lace and undress. Naked, she was a gladsome sight, strikingly yet satisfyingly made, full-breasted, with large, dark aureolas, a belly frankly round over a fiery-red triangle, and ample buttocks and thighs. Like many titian-haired women, her skin was startlingly white and fine. She stood, arms akimbo, at ease, proud of her body, obviously waiting to see its effect upon him.

He feared that he must appear all too appreciative in one respect, and found nothing to say in another.

She laughed. "Come, Davie—do not say that I strike you dumb! You have seen women so before, I swear!"

"Not . . . like you!" he got out.

"Ah! That, now, is better! Kind. You . . . improve." She held out her hands. "Come—I shall aid *you*!"

"No need . . ." he declared, beginning to unbutton his doublet; but she moved in nevertheless, thereby complicating the business although engendering a certain hilarity, especially when it came to his lower parts. It was in high spirits, then, rather than in high passion, that they tumbled on to the bed.

Once there, however, there was no giggling fumbling. Mirren was clearly expert and David not without experience—he could scarcely have made his year's tour of Europe, after university, without learning certain skills. They found each other's rhythm with minimum delay.

Although the man was sufficiently masculine, the woman's need seemed to be the greater, and, if anything, she took the lead. Her hands active, stroking, feeling, gripping, the insistence of her body did not fail to inflame him, although even so she retained the initiative. Her person was smoothly hot, save for her breasts which were strangely cool against him, in itself arousing. Tongue as active as the rest of her, she took him with her into physical ecstasy. It occurred to him, fleetingly, at some stage, to perceive why King James, so knowledgeable about women, had found this one so greatly to his taste. Also to wonder if Mirren was right in assuming that her late master would not grudge this so swift consolation after his tragic demise. But present imperatives did not allow such considerations to preoccupy him for long.

When they were both sated and lay back, it still seemed no appropriate time to broach the subject of the Queen's command. Especially as after only a brief interval, Mirren was employing her considerable dexterity to ensure a repetition of the engagement.

When that too was over, rather more prolonged delight, the hour was growing late and David, a little concerned now over a possible interrogation by Abbot John, made his excuses—although Mirren undoubtedly would have liked him to stay the night. She did not help him on with his clothing, but lay back on the bed watching, all spread and open invitation in the candle-light.

"This of the Queen," he jerked, more roughly than he knew. "We must speak of it. She ordered us to—to get rid of you!"

She shrugged white shoulders. "So?"

"She meant it, Mirren. She is a hard woman. And she now has almost complete power in this land."

"So you are to get rid of me! Where, Davie? What is to be done with me?"

He shook his head. "I wish that I knew. You cannot remain here, I fear. Although the court goes to Stirling in the morning, Linlithgow remains the Queen's own property. She would not overlook you, here."

"Then where am I to go?"

"Can you not just go home? To Dechmont."

"No. I will not go there. My mother will have none of me. Since I . . . went with the King. She names me strumpet, and worse. I cannot go home."

"You will have other kin that you might go to?"

"None. None that would have me. Where do you go, Davie? Can you not take me with you?"

41

"How can I, lass? We will be at Stirling, with the court. Looking after young James still, now the King. It may not be for long, for the Queen does not love us, either. But meantime . . ." He stared at her. "There must be somewhere that you can go?"

"I have no money. How can I go anywhere? Of myself? I have some trinkets which James gave me, but I would not wish to sell them."

"No. I understand that." He paused. "See you—how would it serve if you were to go to Garleton? Back to my father? He would look after you, to be sure. Meantime. He liked you."

"To Garleton? Why, yes—yes, that would be good. Would he have me? And you? You would come?"

"When I could, yes—when I could."

"Oh, Davie—that would be good . . ."

So it was arranged. David would provide a horse, a pack-horse and a groom to escort her to Garleton the next day—and he prayed that his father would find it in him to co-operate.

It was, in fact, long after sun-up before the royal party was ready to move off westwards from Linlithgow, quite a large cavalcade. After handing over a very reluctant small monarch to the haughty Master of Angus, David and the Abbot retired to a much more humble place in the company, to await the Queen's appearance and a start.

There they came across an East Lothian acquaintance, Robert Seton, one of the Queen's pages and grandson of the third lord of that name. A wounded brother had just won back from the defeat at Flodden Edge, telling of the Lord Seton's death, amongst the others. He was able to provide further details of the disaster. It seemed that considerable blame was being attached by the survivors to the Lord Home, who had had command of the cavalry wing of the Scots left, largely Border mosstroopers who were never to be parted from their horses, and which the King had used as a flanking force when all the rest were charging downhill dismounted. It seemed that Lord Home in fact won his encounter with the English right, but then, instead of swinging round behind the enemy rear as required, had gone chasing off after the fleeing English cavalry, deep into the Cheviot foothills, and was seen no more in the battle. This failure undoubtedly contributed much to the eventual Scots defeat.

Then there was the ineffectiveness of the vaunted Scots artillery, stuck up there on the high ground and unable to depress their great muzzles sufficiently to fire down upon the English ranked below, in dire impotence.

Further news was that there had been an angry scene between the King and the old Earl of Angus before the battle was joined, Bell-the-Cat objecting strongly, vehemently, to the abandonment of the strong position on the ridge, declaring it to be romantic folly, and announcing that he and his would have none of it. His son, the Master, however, had taken a different view, accepting the royal decision, and the Douglas armed host had followed his lead, not the old man's. So the Earl had thereupon left them all and ridden off alone, asserting that his liege-lord and son were fools both. It was said that he had since gone in sorrow to the Priory of Whithorn, in Galloway, to end his days—whereas, of course, the Master had ended *his* there and then by dying beside his monarch.

Robert Seton, in fact, proved to be quite a mine of information, as presently they forded Avon, heading for Falkirk and the Carron, on their twenty-mile journey to Stirling. He had been sent by the Queen the day before to Edinburgh Castle, with orders for the garrison there, and had found the city in a state bordering on panic, its provost, dean-of-guild and many of its magistrates lost, and everyone in expectation of early attack by the triumphant English. The citizenry, even women and children, were already being driven into building a great new extension to the city wall, for better defence, houses being knocked down to provide the necessary stone swiftly; and the castle itself was being stocked up with provisions in preparation for siege, its garrison bewailing the loss of its cannon. All Lothian, in fact, was in dread, for having lost much of its manpower the land lay wide open to invasion by Surrey's victorious army.

David, for one, wondered whether, instead of thus heading westwards for Stirling, he ought not to be hastening in the other direction, for Garleton, and his own home area, to help in its defence? Indeed, he asked himself just what he might have sent Mirren into? And, to tell truth, worried still more about young Kate.

Seton, being a page in the Queen's entourage, was also knowledgeable on the present governmental situation, and young enough to be proud to demonstrate the fact. It seemed that this move to Stirling was primarily at the Privy Council's urging, led by Bishop Elphinstone—although the real Chancellor, Archbishop James Beaton of Glasgow, was now said to be there, having wisely escorted the army only as far as Tweed before turning back. The Queen might well have arranged to go to Stirling anyway, of course. They would be as secure there as anywhere in the southern half of Scotland; and could always disappear into the nearby Highland wilderness if the invaders should indeed get that far—something which had been done times without number in the nation's past. A parliament had been called, for ten days hence, to decide on the measures necessary for the realm's defence and rule in this dire situation—called in the young King's name, of course. Normally parliaments required forty days' notice of calling, to allow commissioners to attend from the farthest corners of the kingdom; but such time just could not be spared on this occasion, with invasion threatened and chaos at home. So this would be a very small gathering inevitably, however important, what with the short notice and so many of the nation's leaders dead or missing. Young Seton feared that it would be largely composed of churchmen, God help Scotland! Belatedly he remembered Abbot John's cloth, and made excuse to ride off in others' company.

Deliberately that royal column made as little fuss and display as possible, in the circumstances, with none of the usual panoply of standards, banners, heralds and musicians. What the Queen's own sentiments might be was not to be known, her situation now being quite extraordinarily transformed from heretofore. With the loss of her husband, suddenly she was focus of all attention, not only in that she held the infant monarch, in whose name all must be done, but in that she was the King of England's sister, with all that implied in present circumstances. Before, she might have been at the centre of intrigues against the King, or at least his policies towards England, at the behest of Dean West, the English ambassador, or of various power factions amongst the nobility; now she was openly in command of the situation—although parliament might modify that; also she might be in a position to temper the harshness of Henry's victorious forces. Probably a parliament was the last thing that she wanted; but its calling, in a national emergency, was a constitutional right which she could not gainsay.

It was afternoon before they sighted Stirling from the high ground above the Bannock Burn, the dramatic citadel on its lofty rock towering above the huddled town amongst the great silver loops and meanders of the River Forth before it reached its estuary, with all the blue ramparts of the Highlands behind, one of the fairest and most significant vistas in the land. It took them more than another hour to reach it, however, encircling the skirts of the great Tor Wood and avoiding the wetlands below St Ninians.

The cavalcade thereafter wound its way up through the steeply climbing narrow streets, where folk came out to stare in silence, to the tourney ground extending before the lowermost castle gate and drawbridge. Here a welcoming party was assembled to greet them, with the keys of Scotland's strongest fortress. Robert, fourth Lord Erskine, who claimed to be rightful Earl of Mar, was the Keeper; but he had gone to England with his sovereign and none knew whether or not he had survived. But his young son, John, Master of Erskine, came to present the keys to the infant monarch, accompanied by his mother, Isabella, Lady Erskine—who, of course, had been the Prince's nurse. James had travelled all the way, not very happily, alternately in front of the Master of Angus's saddle, that of his mother, or that of Gavin Douglas, the Master's uncle who was Provost of the Collegiate Church of St Giles, Edinburgh, and a noted poet. Apparently the child had slept fitfully but frequently demanded to be returned to the company of Da, as he called David Lindsay. He was now ordered by the Queen to touch the keys held out to him, and then handed over to Lady Erskine, briefly shown off to the waiting and bowing notables and then whisked off through the portcullis gateway into the castle outer bailey.

Standing beside old Bishop Elphinstone was another and much more richly dressed cleric, a stoutly built, florid and heavy-jowled man, of a dissipated appearance but shrewd and watchful expression, James Beaton, Archbishop and Chancellor of the realm. As senior in both Church and State he greeted the Queen in the name of all, in flowery language but much as he might have recited a litany, with a minimum of feeling behind his words, even whilst remarking on her loss, and the nation's, in the dread death of the King's Grace that was. Margaret Tudor was known to dislike James Beaton even more than she disliked William Elphinstone. David had been a fellow student at St Andrews of the Chancellor's brilliant nephew, David Beaton, who was now making a name for himself at the French court.

The Queen nodded, almost curtly, and forestalled any further speech-making by announcing flatly that she was wearied with travel, in her present state, and would seek her chamber forthwith.

All hastily changed their stance and attitude, to draw aside, bending the head and knee, so that she might ride on inside, after her son.

The great hilltop citadel made a strong but less than comfortable refuge for the court. The Keeper's House, of course, was reserved for the Queen and those closest to her, and, since it was anyway the Lady Erskine's normal residence, she and young James were permitted to occupy a corner of it. The Chancellor, Bishop Elphinstone, and the other Privy Councillors, were already installed in the best of the remaining accommodation, so that the rest of the new arrivals, however illustrious, had to make do with whatever they could find. David and the Abbot rated very low on this scale, and ended up roosting in a mere cellar attached to a powder magazine near the Overport Battery. They hoped that they would not be therein for long; but at least they had it to themselves, preferable to lying on the floor of the great cold Parliament Hall, the fate of most of the Linlithgow party.

In the days that followed, frustrating as they were for active young men, in cramped quarters, with insufficient to do, at least they learned more of the Flodden tragedy and its immediate aftermath. Foremost was the intriguing story that the King had gone into battle without his famous chain. Apparently, dallying at Ford Castle, some miles north of Flodden, waiting for the English army to put in an appearance, he had found convenient solace with Lady Heron thereof—whose husband, incidentally, was a prisoner in Fast Castle, one of the Lord Home's strongholds, on account of cross-Border raiding. And Lady Heron, it seemed, had found the chain round the King's loins uncomfortable, and persuaded him to take it off—the first reported occasion of such nicety, although David for one wondered what Mirren would say to that? At any rate, whether from forgetfulness or otherwise, James had left his chain at Ford, when called to leave in a hurry—and there was no lack of folk to declare that this was behind the débâcle, the royal vow broken. Others recollected the apparition at St Michael's Church, Linlithgow, warning against meddling with strange women.

There was the information, also, from an escaped captive of the English army, that terrible as the disaster had been, it was not all quite so clear-cut as at first thought. It seemed that at nightfall, the Earl of Surrey, the English commander, had still been sufficiently uncertain of the outcome to gather, when darkness precluded further fighting, forty of his captains, and berate them soundly for their tactical failures, a worried and angry man. But when morning dawned and revealed only the Scots dead, including the King and most of his nobility, left lying on the field, Surrey changed his tune to the extent of actually knighting the said forty captains for their military excellence.

The arrival of Lord Home at Stirling, on the fifth day, created something of a to-do, especially as he came, if not exactly cock-a-hoop, at least well satisfied with himself, as the only commander on the Scots side to have won his own part of the battle, apparently quite unaware that he was being blamed for much of the disaster by failing to turn the main enemy's flank and assail his rear, instead of chasing off after the fleeing cavalry. He was hot in defence of his own course, and scornful against stay-at-home strategists. And since he was Lord Chamberlain, and had brought a tail of two hundred Border mosstroopers with him to Stirling, the criticism became muted. Scotland was going to need all such in its present state.

The details of the casualties were gradually becoming known. The Earls of Argyll, Atholl, Bothwell, Caithness, Cassillis, Crawford, Erroll, Glencairn, Lennox, Montrose, Morton and Rothes were all dead, as were the Archbishop of St Andrews and the Bishops of the Isles and of Caithness and the mitred Abbots of Kilwinning and Inchaffray. So many lords that none could name them all, but including the Lord Erskine, Keeper here; also the chiefs of clans from the Highlands, James having been perhaps the only Scots monarch who could have got these to come and fight for him since Bruce the hero king. As for knights, lairds and gentry, these were beyond all numbering; and the common folk in their thousands. Even the French ambassador, de la Motte, was amongst the slain.

The parliament to follow would not be much larger than a normal meeting of the Privy Council.

That parliament, held on 21st September, two weeks after Flodden field, was unusual in other than its scanty numbers. Taking place in the castle's Parliament Hall, cleared of its lodgers for the occasion, on the motion of the Chancellor it went into temporary recess almost as soon as it was convened.

Those attending, with more spectators than commissioners, even so by no means filling the hall, stood for the flourish of trumpets and the entry of the young monarch, led in between the Queen and the Master of Angus, the little boy being deposited on the high throne—on which he promptly stood rather than sat—whilst his mother occupied a lesser throne at his side and Archibald Douglas stood behind. In the Scottish parliament, it was necessary for the monarch to be present in person; otherwise it was no true parliament, only a convention of the Three Estates of lords, shire representatives and churchmen, and could not pass effective legislation. The Chancellor chaired the deliberations but the King presided, and could intervene, join in the debate and close the sitting at will.

Bowing to the throne, Archbishop Beaton made his announcement that, in accordance with ancient procedures this was a proper assembly of the high court of parliament, in the presence of and by the authority of their undoubted liege-lord, James, fifth of his name, by God's grace High King of Scots. However, in order that the parliament's due authority should be effective beyond the least doubt, it was considered advisable, in the present grievous circumstances in which they forgathered, that the monarch's position should be established beyond all possible doubt. Therefore it had been decided that a coronation ceremony should take place forthwith, in the Chapel Royal, whereafter the parliament would be resumed. It was usual, of course, for the coronation to be held at Scone. But this was not obligatory, and in the circumstances the Chapel Royal here would serve. Was this the will of the parliament here assembled?

No contrary voice was raised.

So a temporary adjournment was proclaimed, and all filed out of the hall, behind the royal party, to a different level of the rock-top fortress where the Chapel Royal was situated, no large edifice, so that it was perhaps as well that numbers were so low, otherwise all would not have won into the church. John Inglis, as Abbot of Culross, could have probably claimed a place up in the chancel, but nobody had asked him and he preferred to squeeze in at the back with David.

There followed probably the briefest coronation ceremony that Scotland had ever known, not only on account of the need for haste but because so many who should have taken part were just not present. There was no Lord Lyon King of Arms to pronounce the monarch's undoubted right and genealogy back into the mists of antiquity; no representative of the MacDuff line to act as Inaugurator and bear the crown; no High Constable to carry the sword of state; no hereditary bearers of sceptre, orb and spurs. Home, as Chamberlain, had to shoulder responsibility for most of this aspect of the proceedings, appointing such deputies as he thought fit. There was no lack of ecclesiastics, at least, for the most significant part of the ceremonial.

In the absence of the Primate the only other archbishop, Beaton, with the Abbot of Scone, conducted the service with a minimum of fuss, as though to get all over as quickly as possible, for he was no ritualist. Young James, on whose behaviour so much depended, was remarkably patient for most of the time, although he yawned a lot, fidgeted and stared around him. But by the time that they got to the actual crowning—which was difficult anyway, with the crown far too large to be actually placed on his small head, having instead to be held over him while the necessary pronouncements were intoned—the boy had had enough, and made it sufficiently plain, to the disruption of the proceedings. The Queen came forward to try to soothe him; and when that failed, adopted a sterner stance, actually shaking the monarchial arm in exasperation. This produced a spirited reaction of tiny fists, and when the Master of

Angus moved in with a strong arm, he was met by a howl of fury. James jumped down from the coronation chair, to glare around him, seemingly preparatory to bolting.

In these alarming circumstances, Margaret Tudor did probably all that remained open to her. Presumably from her lofty position up near the high altar, she had seen David and John take their places at the back. Now she looked searchingly in that direction and extending her arm, jabbed an imperious finger towards them, twice, ending in a beckoning gesture.

Distinctly embarrassed, the two young men pushed their way forward through the crush.

They were just in time, with James, having discerned a vestry doorway nearby, about to make a dash therefor.

"Jamie, lad—Jamie!" David called, on impulse. "Wait, Jamie—it is Da."

The boy turned. "Da!" he exclaimed. "Da!" and rushed to hurl himself at his friend.

Not a few folk sighed with relief.

Taking the child's chubby hand, David led him back to the Archbishop. "Not long now, Jamie," he said, low-voiced. "Just a little longer. Be good. You will do very well. Abbot John and I will stay with you. Just a little more . . ."

Doubtfully, clutching his protectors' hands on either side tightly, the King of Scots allowed himself to be taken to the coronation chair and sat thereon. One on either side of it, the young men stood. Ignored, the Queen and the Master returned to their places.

Thankfully, Beaton resumed his delivery, hastening now to get it over and done with. Abbot John thus had his part in the coronation, after all.

The Archbishop finished, a fanfare of trumpets proclaimed the fact that Scotland again had a crowned king. Then there was a hiatus. The clergy formed up to lead the procession back to Parliament Hall. But none could leave, of course, before the monarch. And James clung to David and John, and scowled at everybody else.

After a few moments the Queen, frowning, had to accept the situation. "Escort His Grace to the Hall," she directed abruptly.

So, at the head of all, the boy and the two young men wound their way back.

In the hall, infant majesty was not to be left without his accustomed guardians again; and to save another scene erupting, the Queen signed for them to remain standing behind the throne. Young James, to be sure, was not normally like this; but he had never had much to do with his mother, being very much his father's boy. Now he stood on his throne, back to the assembly, and grinned and made faces at his chosen companions. The Master of Angus stood behind the Queen's chair, muttering.

Chancellor Beaton, content that it was all no worse, reconvened the session.

He began by fairly briefly summarising the situation in which the kingdom found itself, and emphasising its desperate straits in the loss of its beloved monarch and so many of the nation's best, in lords, church and people. He did not require to stress the heavy duty which lay upon them all in this hall, those left to carry the burden of state, with the land reeling, open to invasion, and so much of its might gone. But this must be no session of lamentation, he emphasised. They had no time nor occasion for that; nor was it the spirit which Scotland required this day. Resolute action the nation demanded of them all, from highest to lowest—let none forget it.

He went on to indicate the proposed agenda. First and foremost there must be the matter of the continuing rule and governance of the realm under His Grace, since he was a minor—the question of regency. Also decision as to the succession to the throne, now urgent, with a child monarch. Then there was the filling of offices of state under the crown, so many of which were now vacant, so that the due responsibility for the direction of the kingdom would be apportioned, especially the defence of the realm and the maintenance of the law and public order. Much else would demand their attention, but these were the principal immediate issues for decision—and would more than suffice for this day. Was it agreed that they dealt first with the vital matter of rule and the care and destination of the crown?

None could deny that this was the first priority, since all authority stemmed from the crown—and the said crown was at the moment playing happily enough with the two carved and rampant lions which decorated the back of the throne, David Lindsay endeavouring to keep the royal oohs and ahs and chuckles at as low a key as possible.

The Archbishop had scarcely got his question out before the Queen spoke—and thus early in the proceedings demonstrated something of the problems before that assembly. For in theory she had no authority to raise her voice. There was no place for a queen-consort or queen-mother in the Scots parliament other than as a mere spectator sitting beside her royal spouse or son.

"My lord Chancellor," she said, in that clipped, assured English voice. "I have a statement to make, relevant to my royal son, the King's Grace, and to the succession. I am three months pregnant by my late husband. I expect to bear his child until the month of April next."

This, needless to say, created no little stir in the company, for it is probable that none had really considered this possibility, James and his wife having gone more and more their own ways for some time now. Margaret had borne him two children before this young Jamie, both of whom had died in months. Having at length produced a healthy male heir, it had not been anticipated that she would have risked more.

The significance of this announcement at least provided an excuse for the Chancellor not having to point out that Her Grace was out of order in addressing the parliament.

However, she went on. "I further must state that in the matter of rule and governance, I cannot consider the appointment of any soever, other than myself, to act in my royal son's name. Let this be understood by all."

If the first announcement intrigued the assembly, this bombshell stunned it. Margaret Tudor was highly un-popular throughout the land. Moreover no woman had ever been regent or held supreme power in Scotland—which traditionally required a very strong hand at the helm. Yet here was this Englishwoman as good as claiming that position.

In the appalled silence, with even the normally authoritative Archbishop at a loss for words, another voice spoke up, jerkily forceful and self-assertive, that of Archibald Douglas, from his position behind the Queen.

"I hereby propose and nominate the Queen's Grace to be Regent of this kingdom during the minority of the King's Grace," he declared.

This time there was no awkward hush. Shouts of dissent arose all over the hall.

The Chancellor could deal with this, at least. "Master of Angus," he said severely. "I must remind you that you have no warrant to speak nor make any motion before this parliament. You are not a lord of parliament as yet, nor the commissioner of any shire, nor yet, so far as I know, a representative of Holy Church!"

"I speak, sir, as the head of the house of Douglas!" the young man cried hotly. "Is Douglas to have no voice in the affairs of this realm? My father is dead. My grandsire, the Earl, is retired to a monastery. Who says that I shall not speak for Douglas?"

At that challenge there was uproar in the hall, so that David had to soothe the young James, alarmed at the noise and passion aroused. The Douglases were the most powerful family in Scotland, and the richest, with wide ramifications, more so than the royal line of Stewart itself. Inevitably they had enemies, many resenting their influence. On the other hand they had friends and hangers-on; and there were not a few present in similar position to the Master, heirs of line, unsure whether their fathers, uncles, brothers lived yet or no, and so of their own situation; or kin of fallen shire commissioners, who felt that they should be filling their places in this meagre parliament. In the confusion and shouting, old Bishop Elphinstone rose to his feet and raised a hand. Seeing it Beaton banged his gavel, no doubt thankfully, and bellowed for silence for the Lord Privy Seal.

William Elphinstone was undoubtedly the most respected man in the land, former Chancellor, founder of Aberdeen University, historian, former tutor, friend and confidant of the late King. He had no difficulty in obtaining a hearing.

"My lord Chancellor," he said, his eighty-two-year-old voice surprisingly strong. "I have here something which much bears on this present situation and which should help us in our decisions." He waved a paper in the air. "It is the testament of our late and much loved liege-lord James, whom God cherish in a better land than this Scotland, and where I look forward to joining him before long! His Grace left it in my keeping, as his confessor and friend." He looked over at the Queen. "Amongst other matters which I shall, to be sure, convey to the proper quarters, His Grace has written that, should aught ill befall him, he leaves his son and heir in the hands of the Queen's Grace for his care and protection, as tutrix and guardian—but only for so long as she does not remarry. Should Her Grace indeed remarry, then the young monarch is to be transformed into the care and keeping of whoever is appointed Regent of the kingdom." The Bishop sat down.

Again the assembly sat silenced—save for the child concerned, who chortled on, now playing with the tassels of Abbot John's girdle. But as men took in the implications of this revelation, a stir arose and eager discussion amongst delegates. And not only delegates and men. The only woman present turned in her chair and spoke urgently to the Master of Angus, upset most evident.

Beaton allowed the gathering its head for a few moments, and then claimed order with his gavel. "We have to thank my lord Bishop for his contribution to this discussion," he said. "No doubt the Privy Council will examine this document fully in due course, with action in view. We all know the Lord Privy Seal sufficiently well to be assured that this testament of our late liege-lord is a true and honest one. And we are, to be sure, bound to heed its directions in our decisions. From what has been told us, it seems clear that our newly crowned monarch is to remain in the care and keeping of the Queen's Grace meantime. But this applies to the King's royal person, not to the kingdom. In this testament King James speaks of a Regent, to whom His present Grace would be entrusted in the event of the remarriage of the Queen-Mother. So clearly these cannot be one and the same person. In other words, a Regent to rule the realm in the King's name is required, other than the Queen-Mother. So that, even if the Master of Angus had warrant to move his motion, such motion must fall."

Cheers were raised throughout the hall.

Margaret Tudor sat forward in her chair. Her eyes were not such as could blaze, but the smouldering anger in them was not to be hidden.

"Sir Chancellor," she exclaimed, "not so fast! This is not to be borne! I should have been informed of this testament, my own husband's will—if it is indeed honest in truth, which remains to be proven. I shall, you may rest assured, keep and guard my son—and let none think to ordain otherwise! But, of this of rule and regency, I deny what you may, sir. Nothing in what was reported could exclude me from the regency. Bishop Elphinstone said 'whoever is appointed Regent of the kingdom'. *Whoever!* There is nothing there to say that such Regent shall not be myself."

Into the murmurings, Beaton spoke. "Madam—your royal son could not be transferred from yourself to yourself! *Transferred* is the word. My lord Bishop—I take it that this is indeed the word used by our late liege-lord? In his testament?"

"It is, yes. Transferred to whoever is appointed."

"And you would agree that this must mean that whoever is appointed could not be Her Grace the Queen-Mother?"

"Clearly so, my lord Chancellor. Such was His Grace's intention."

"I deny that!" Archibald Douglas shouted. "This is but clerkly play with words! *Whoever* is appointed does not rule out the Queen's Grace."

"Master of Angus—you have no voice in this parliament!" the Archbishop thundered.

"But *I* have!" another voice spoke up strongly, that of a namesake indeed, Sir Archibald Douglas of Kilspindie, commonly known as Greysteel, fourth son of Bell-the-Cat and commissioner for the shire of Haddington. "And I agree with my nephew, the Master. Nothing in what has been said can debar Queen Margaret from the regency. I so move. Move that this parliament appoints Her Grace as Regent."

"And I second. Who better than our young King's lady-mother? And sister of His Grace of England—and so more able than any other to protect this realm from English spite." That was said in the mellifluous tones of the brother of the previous speaker, Gavin Douglas the poet who, as Provost of the Collegiate Church of St Giles, the capital's principal church, ranked with the mitred abbots and had a seat in parliament.

The house of Douglas was making its position plain.

For good measure, Margaret Tudor went on. "The good Master Gavin is right. In this pass, this kingdom requires above all else the goodwill of my royal brother, Henry. Can any deny it? And can any deny, likewise, that I, the King of

England's sister, am the most like to obtain goodwill from him? Could any other Regent so claim?"

There was silence at that, for a moment or two, before the Lord Home raised his voice. "My lord Chancellor, the King of England's goodwill towards this realm has scarcely been evident hitherto! He has claimed, before many, and to our late King's especial envoy, that *he* was Lord Paramount of Scotland, that he was the very owner of Scotland indeed, his very words. And that the late James only held it of his, Henry's, homage! All know of this, this insolent and vaunty boasting. Are we to believe that with Henry's royal sister here ruling the land in her son's name, the Leopard of England will then become a cooing dove? Rather, I say, he would roar the fiercer! He would take over the realm!"

The shout of support for Home spoke for itself, and did much to reinstate the Chamberlain in esteem.

But the Queen was not finished yet. She raised that minatory finger of hers, to point. "Has my lord of Home overlooked the fact that all is changed? With regard to England. Now that my husband is dead. Before, my royal brother feared James's enmity and spleen—and with reason, as witness this late wicked invasion of England, resulting in such dolour. But now the King of Scots, my son here, is no threat to Henry, and must remain none. So long as he is not, Henry, who is fully occupied in France, will not trouble him, or his realm. *I* can best ensure that." She paused significantly. "And not only not trouble him, but indeed cherish him and his kingdom. For my son is now heir-presumptive to the throne of England! Have none realised it?"

By the gasps and exclamations it was evident that few, if any, had. But it was true, of course. Henry, although married for four years to Catherine of Aragon, was childless, brotherless, Margaret his only sister, and young Jamie his only nephew. There was no one else. If Henry, battling in France, should fall, like his late brother-in-law, this child now behind his throne with his friends, not on it, was next in line for the crown of England. Belated recognition, and the implications, left the company bemused.

Not all of it, however. Bishop Elphinstone rose and spoke into the chatter. "This situation, which some of us have foreseen, must be considered in our decisions," he said calmly. "But with great respect for the Queen's Grace, I do not think that it indicates that King Henry will look more kindly on Scotland. On the contrary, my lord Chancellor, I would say that he will be the more like to seek to grasp Scotland, and probably its young King with it, since he arrogantly claims this realm as his. And so to have his heir in his own keeping. This I believe will be his attitude, not kindly concern. And if so, a woman, and his sister, ruling Scotland, would be as good as an invitation to him to come and take what he wants. I . . ." Cheers drowned out the rest.

Beaton took over. "I have a motion before this parliament, proposed by Sir Archibald Douglas of Kilspindie and seconded by his brother, the Provost Gavin, that Her Grace the Queen-Mother should be Regent of this realm as well as guardian and tutrix of the child King. Before any vote is taken, however, it is my duty as Chancellor to point out that it has always been the custom and tradition of this kingdom, from earliest times, to appoint a near *male* kinsman of the monarch to be Regent during a minority. I do not say that this is incumbent upon us, but it is the custom, on the understanding that the realm requires a strong man's hand in such situation. Are there any other motions before we come to a conclusion on the matter?"

Half a dozen men were on their feet at once. The Chancellor gave precedence to Lord Home.

"I move as amendment that John, Duke of Albany, full cousin of our late King, be appointed Regent," the Chamberlain said. "As well as the closest male kin, he is powerful, Admiral of France, and in kinship by marriage with the King of France. Albany, I say."

There were cries for and against. John Stewart was the son of Alexander, Duke of Albany, who had been younger brother to James the Third and who, after trying to supplant his weak brother on the throne, had had to flee to France, where he had married one of the greatest heiresses, the daughter of the Comte de Boulogne; and this John was the son, a *grand seigneur* of France and to all intents a Frenchman, unable, it was said, to speak a word of English, much less Scots. Nevertheless, he was undoubtedly the nearest male relation to young James, and was known to be highly regarded in his adoptive country.

"I support that nomination," Andrew Forman, Bishop of Moray declared.

"We have, then, John, Duke of Albany proposed and seconded as Regent, instead of Her Grace," Beaton said. "Is there any other nomination?"

"Yes, my lord—I nominate James Hamilton, Earl of Arran, Lord High Admiral." This was another cleric on his feet, and a notable one, John Hepburn, Prior of St Andrews and brother of the Earl of Bothwell, who was one of the fallen at Flodden. An able, not to say unscrupulous and ambitious churchman, although only a prior, his was a position of great influence, for he had long managed the metropolitan see, first for the late King's younger brother and then for his illegitimate son, neither true clerics and uninterested in the archepiscopate save for its powers and revenues. Many bishops were less important. "My lord of Arran is grandson of King James the Second, Lieutenant-General of this realm and Warden of the Marches. He, at least, can speak our tongue! I propose the Earl of Arran for Regent."

"No!" That was Home again, coldly. "How could we trust James Hamilton? Has he not already cost this kingdom dear? Where is he now? None know, for sure. I say that Arran as Regent would be a disaster. I move that he be not considered."

There was uproar in the hall, some shouting that it was not only Arran who had cost the kingdom dear.

"But I second Prior John's nomination!" the Bishop of Dunkeld cried into the hubbub.

"And I Home's!" the Lord Saltoun barked.

Beaton was in a quandary. He rapped on his desk. "I have two new motions, making four in all. I am uncertain whether the Lord Home's second motion is competent, moving that the Prior John's be not considered—when itself is a competent motion. What is the will of the house in this matter?"

"Chancellor," Home insisted, "how can we consider the appointment of Arran? He may not even be alive! Our late monarch sent him, in command of the realm's fleet, to assail the English west coast and so to aid in His Grace's venture. This, weeks ago. He was to distract the English forces. But he did not do so. He sailed off from the Clyde to attack *Ireland* in some ploy of his own—God knows what! None know where he now is, or our ships. Some say that he has sailed them to France. How could this realm consider such a, a weathercock as its Regent?" The Earl of Arran had divorced Home's sister four years earlier.

"Nor Albany either!" the Queen-Mother put in tartly. "A prancing Frenchman!"

The Douglases cheered, the Hamiltons shook their fists and most of the company appeared to be on their feet.

James, King of Scots, not liking the noise, made a dart for the open dais door behind the throne, and out, Lindsay in pursuit.

It was not like James Beaton to be found at a loss, tough character as he was. He looked about him now, almost helplessly, banging for quiet but uncertain what to do with it when he got it.

Again it was William Elphinstone, former Chancellor, who came to his aid, when he could make himself heard. "I suggest, my lord Archbishop, that you should adjourn this sitting. That tempers may abate. We have all heard sufficient to cause us most seriously to think. Better that all should do so with cool heads. Tomorrow will serve us well enough to nominate a Regent, be it the Duke of Albany, the Earl of Arran, or Her Grace." He paused, before going on with a faint smile. "Forby, our liege-lord appears to have put any further debate out of order by abandoning the session!"

Thankfully Beaton nodded. "I accept that as good advice. Tomorrow, then, my lords. At noon." He turned and bowed to the Queen. "After Your Grace . . ."

Margaret Tudor rose and swept out of the hall without a glance at anyone, Archibald Douglas hurrying after. They passed her son, on all fours in the passage outside, equally without glance or pause.

As thankfully as the Chancellor, his two partisans picked up their charge and hurried him off to their quarters.

4

David Lindsay, for one, was well content to obtain his further information about the doings of that momentous parliament at second hand. For, sensibly, the Chancellor and Privy Council contrived a constitutional device whereby the monarch's necessary presence could be presumed, by the substitution of a high commissioner sitting in the royal name. By general agreement Bishop Elphinstone was appointed such commissioner. This spared all concerned, young James from prolonged boredom, the assembly from being at the mercy of an eighteen-month-old child's whims, and David and John from embarrassing attendance. The Queen-Mother's reaction went undisclosed, since she was not consulted—but she continued to attend the sessions.

Instead of listening to speeches, arguments, accusations and proposals, whilst the future of the nation was decided, the two young men and the little boy then entertained themselves as best they might. They were commanded not to leave the security of the fortress; but this was less cramping than they might have feared. Stirling Castle was a hilltop citadel, and within its perimeter walling much space was enclosed, at varying levels, by no means all, or even most, of the area built up with towers, bartizans, parapet-walks, barracks, storehouses, kitchens and the like. There was room for archery butts, a quoiting pitch, a bowling green, even a menagerie, although this was presently untenanted save by a couple of Muscovy bears, trained for dancing but now fat and sleepy. Not only on the rock summit, but part-way down the precipitous sides, were grassy ledges and terraces, with steps cut for access, utilised for gardens and recreational pursuits. In especial, some way down the north-east flank but still within the walling, was a remarkable feature, more than any shelf this, poised dizzily between the plain and the soaring turrets, an irregularly shaped plot of ground amounting to a few acres, which could actually be tilled, and whereon were pastured two or three tethered cows to provide milk for the garrison. This was humorously known as the croft of Ballengeich, and was a favourite venue, for there was a steep and fairly smooth grass slope down to it, much appreciated for the sport of hurly-hackit, a grass-sledging activity. This was played by sliding down the hill on the skulls of cows or oxen, steering by means of the up-curling horns, the name coming from hurl, the Scots for ride or glide, and haukie, the term for a white-headed cow. Spirited competitions and races could be held at this, with attempts to cannon into and unseat opponents adding to the excitement.

This became one of young James's favourite pastimes, at first seated in the lap of one or other of his escorts, later pick-a-back clinging to the shoulders, and finally alone on his own small calf's skull, quite fearless despite all the bumps and spills. He, and for that matter his two attendants, found this a deal better than attending parliaments—even though Abbot John did not like to be seen engaging in the sport, conceiving it to be inconsistent with his abbatial dignity—but, as David pointed out, he was only a titular Abbot, not a true one, any more than the late Alexander Stewart had been a true Archbishop, installed by influence and receiving most of the revenues, but not concerned with the religious and monastic responsibilities. Culross Abbey and its affairs were professionally managed by a genuine prior, and John's commitments were covered by two or three brief visits there each year. Such were the convenient arrangements of Holy Church in this early sixteenth century.

All the monarch's time, of course, was not spent sliding down hills and toiling up again, feeding already overfed bears, playing quoits and bowls and clambering about that rocky plateau. Quite frequently it rained and they had to be indoors; and at the Queen's command some sort of attempts had to be made at lessons and training, although James was much too young for any real schooling. John did his best, as tutor, but it was really only behaviour and manners which could be inculcated at this stage. David, for his part, being musically inclined, played lute and harp and taught the boy songs and ballads and to love words.

Despite enforced proximity in the restrictions of the castle, they saw little of the Queen-Mother and her party.

Bishop Elphinstone, however, took a great interest in the child, and from him they learned the gist of what went on at the parliamentary sessions, slow to progress as these proved to be. The regency question was in abeyance meantime, a large majority having agreed to send to the Duke of Albany, in France, to seek his acceptance of the position. If refused, the Earl of Arran was to be approached—if he could be found. Meantime, a triumvirate of the Privy Council—the Chancellor, Home as Chamberlain, and himself as Privy Seal—were to exercise the regency authority. It seemed that the Queen-Mother's candidacy never really had a chance, only the Douglas faction supporting it.

An equally vexed question appeared to have been that of the Primacy of Holy Church, the appointment to the archbishopric of St Andrews, left vacant by young Alexander. This was most important, given the influence of the Church, especially in present circumstances with the King a minor and so many of the heads of families and the baronage likewise suddenly under full age. The urgency of this appointment was emphasised by the report that King Henry had petitioned the Pope to demote the archbishopric from metropolitan status and place it, and Scotland, under the ecclesiastical jurisdiction of the Archbishop of York, in his campaign to bring Scotland under English control. An embassage was being sent to Rome to counter this; but it revealed the lengths to which Henry would go.

Elphinstone himself had been the almost unanimous choice, it appeared, for the Primacy; but reluctantly he had declined. He explained to the young men that to have accepted would have been folly, and worse. He was much too old. A man in his eighties should be considering the next world, not embarking on a most testing and demanding new responsibility. It would mean a new appointment in a year or two. A much younger and more vigorous man was required in this situation. Admittedly his refusal would entail much bickering and competition amongst other contenders, which was unfortunate. There were three principal candidates—Provost Gavin, the Douglas nominee; Prior John Hepburn, who had in fact been administrating the archdiocese for Alex Stewart; and Bishop Andrew Forman of Moray, a most able cleric. The Queen, of course, supported Gavin Douglas; but parliament was almost equally divided between the other two.

David, for one, wondered why parliament had anything

to do with the election of an Archbishop? Surely this was the business of the Church itself? To which the old man replied that it should indeed be so. But that for long the crown had usurped the Church's privilege in nominating incumbents for high ecclesiastical offices to the Pope for consecration; and now, with the crown in a child's hands and no Regent yet, parliament considered that it must be involved, with so much depending on the appointment. Personally, Elphinstone believed that Forman would be the best choice, a Bishop already and an experienced cleric, and was so advising the Pope. But both the Douglases and the Hepburns were strong, with the armed might of their earldoms behind them, and might could prevail. Such was the plight of Christ's Church.

For the rest, the parliamentary news was more constructive. Many necessary appointments had been made to positions vital for governance—justiciarships, sheriffdoms, keeperships of royal castles, captains of ports, marchwardenships and the like. Inevitably the great families gobbled up most of these; but to be sure they had the power to enforce their authority, once appointed, which was also necessary. The secret was to maintain a nice balance between the Douglases, Hepburns, Homes, Stewarts, Kennedys and the rest—aye, and the Lindsays also—so that none grew over-powerful. That was ever the aim of domestic statecraft.

As for the nation's situation, happily full-scale invasion had not developed, as yet. Henry required more troops in France, so Surrey had turned the main army southwards again, for embarkation into ships at Tyne and Humber. Also, the Welsh had taken the opportunity to rise, as so often, and forces were needed to contain them. But Lord Dacre, the English Chief Warden of the Marches, had been given orders to raid and devastate as far into Scotland as he could; and, of course, the south of the country was wide open to his savagery. Towns, villages, abbeys, churches, lairdships, were going up in flames, and terrible things done to the people. The Lord Home had been appointed Chief Marches Warden and charged with somehow halting Dacre. But it would be no easy task.

The day after the parliament ended and the commissioners and lords temporal and spiritual had in the main left Stirling, came the news that other than parliamentary decisions still counted in Scotland. The Douglases had attacked and taken St Andrews Castle, the seat of the archbishops, by armed force. The poet Provost Gavin and his brother Greysteel were now in firm possession, indicating that there were more ways than one of seeking high office in the Church, and that literary leanings need be no bar to such preferment. The Master of Angus was still at Stirling with the Queen-Mother; no criticism of the action emanated from the royal quarters. Clearly it had been carefully timed, so that parliamentary criticism would not be forthcoming either.

The Chancellor and Privy Council were angry, and William Elphinstone grieved—but none was really surprised. This had been the pattern in Scotland for all too long. The late King's strong hand had restrained such activities by the powerful nobles; but it was almost too much to hope for, that, his hand removed, they would not revert. The need for a Regent, and a strong one, was the more evident.

Then, just over a week later, there were further tidings from Fife. The Hepburns under Prior John and his nephew, the new Earl of Bothwell, had assailed St Andrews, town and castle, in great strength and managed to retake both, driving out the Douglases with considerable losses. There was major upset in the Queen-Mother's quarters at Stirling, and the Master of Angus departed eastwards in haste, trumpeting calls for an immediate muster of all Douglas power. Civil war could be in sight, to add to all Scotland's other troubles. The Privy Council, sending out urgent orders for peace and observance of the law, considered recalling Lord Home from the Borderland, the only experienced military leader left in the Lowlands, to try to deal with this situation; but decided that, on balance, Lord Dacre's English raiders were the greater menace at the moment. What the Master of Angus's neglected wife, back at Tantallon in East Lothian, thought about all this was anybody's guess; she was a Hepburn, sister of the new Earl of Bothwell.

Fortunately, the Douglas might always took some time to marshal, being so widely dispersed over the country, men having to march from as far apart as Galloway in the south-west and the Mearns in the north-east, something that the Hepburns would have reckoned on. Also, they had suffered large losses at Flodden, which was bound to have its effect upon a call-to-arms so soon after. This gave time for the Hepburns likewise to summon their full strength, nothing like so great as that of Douglas but more concentrated, in Lothian; also they could call upon more allies, all who feared and resented Douglas. It also gave time for a courier to arrive from Rome, with the word that Pope Leo the Tenth had appointed Bishop Forman of Moray to be the Archbishop of St Andrews, as advised by Elphinstone; and not only so, but as a notable snub to the King of England, had emphasised the full metropolitan status of the Scots archdiocese and even given the hint that a cardinal's hat might possibly be forthcoming for the new Primate. Not only that, but he appointed him Legate, with power to regulate the benefices of Scotland in the papal name.

This development effectively threw a douche of cold water on the Douglas-Hepburn flare-up, since neither could very well continue to contest it once the Vatican decision was made. But of course such powerful and jealous competitors were not to be called off without some compensation. The new Archbishop Forman was, however, a realist, and, in conjunction with Home, came to an arrangement with the Hepburns whereby Prior John, still in possession at St Andrews, was to retain most of the revenues of the see meantime, and also to get Forman's own newly vacated bishopric of Moray, whilst the Prior's nephew received the rich Home Priory of Coldinghame. This, of course, infuriated the Douglases, but also had the effect of further isolating them. And the ousted Provost Gavin was astutely ambushed by the minions of Home, who hated all Douglases, and thereafter clapped prisoner in the Sea Tower of the very St Andrews Castle in which he had recently been lording it—and where, as it was said, he could write poetry to his heart's content.

The Douglas cause was thus in some disarray, for the Provost Gavin could be used as a hostage. Moreover, at this juncture, the voice of old Bell-the-Cat was belatedly raised, from his sanctuary at Whithorn in Galloway, declaring that no more Douglas blood was to be spilled in unprofitable adventures whilst he remained Earl of Angus. So the Master, his grandson, returned to Stirling in nail-biting rage and disappointment. With Margaret Tudor now in mid-pregnancy, it was doubtful whether he even obtained much consolation from that quarter.

All this much interested but did not greatly affect David and John—although, not being enamoured of Archibald Douglas, they were not greatly grieved at his misfortunes. What did concern them, however, was the arrival on the scene of a new tutor for the infant King—as though, at his present age, Abbot John was not more than adequate. But Queen Margaret had not forgotten her announcement, that day before they all came to Stirling, that she did not consider them suitable persons to attend on the King's Grace and that she would, presently, look for others. Since then, to be sure, she had discovered that young James was not to be parted from his friends without dire consequences in his behaviour, highly embarrassing. So, as attendants, they remained. But to assert her authority, a senior figure was to be put over them. She chose Master Gavin Dunbar, a chaplain, nephew of the Archdeacon of St Andrews, another Gavin Dunbar, who was a supporter of Gavin Douglas now incarcerated in St Andrews Castle. As well as having the same Christian name as the would-be Primate this Gavin was also a poet, although a less successful one. Indeed, his lack of success in his career generally, thus far, had been marked, despite illustrious family connections, for he was kin to the most noted poet of all, William Dunbar, who had written so flatteringly of Margaret Tudor in *The Thistle and the Rose*—which was probably why she chose this kinsman to be her son's tutor, even though, as far as the Church hierarchy went, he was actually junior to Abbot John. For all that, the newcomer did not appear to be very grateful for this appointment, clearly considering himself worthy of very much higher office than any mere tutorship, even to his monarch.

So Gavin Dunbar came to Stirling. He proved to be no very striking personality, a studious, bumbling sort of man, somewhat older than Lindsay and Inglis, and with a very considerable chip on his shoulder. But, after the first day or two, the others came to the conclusion that their new senior, properly handled, ought not to prove any great problem to them. For one thing, he was not very fond of children, and recognising that James was far too young for the sort of erudition he was qualified to impart, left the boy largely to his juniors, whilst he pursued his own affairs and studies.

So James now had three tutorial guides and not sufficient

work for one. David, in especial, of a vigorous and restless nature, found life less than satisfying, despite his fondness for his young charge. His thoughts tended more often than not to drift eastwards towards Garleton.

It was with something like stimulation, then, that he greeted developments on the national scene, which at least had the effect of stirring up life for all at Stirling Castle. Three ships from France arrived at Dumbarton, on the Clyde, Scots ships, even though a very small part of the fine fleet which had left the same port under Arran some months before. They brought the said James Hamilton, Earl of Arran, and a most notable Frenchman, Antoine D'Arcie, Sieur de la Bastie, as envoy for the Duke of Albany; and these two, with a considerable and gallant company, came hotfoot to Stirling in mid-November.

They made a brilliant and colourful pair, although so very different in character, both handsome, dashing, voluble and over-dressed by Scots standards, and both in their mid-forties. But there the resemblance ended. Arran was flamboyant, mercurial, rash, having a large way with him—as perhaps befitted Scotland's Lord High Admiral and third in line for the throne, his grandmother having been a sister of James the Third. De la Bastie, although sufficiently lively, was a much more solid individual, without being in the least stolid, one of the most renowned chivalric figures in Christendom, famed for his knightly prowess, much admired by the late King James as a man after his own heart. He came to announce that John, Duke of Albany was prepared to consider the call to the regency but that it must be understood that he could not come to Scotland immediately. He was a French citizen, High Admiral of France indeed, and his country was at war with England. King Louis could by no means sanction his departure at this present stage. But if it was still desired, he would come when possible.

This created problems and considerable discussion. The nation needed authoritative direction *now*, not in the vague future. On the other hand, Albany remained the most obvious choice as Regent. Now that the second choice, Arran, had arrived, the discussion was the more to the point, not to say heated.

First and foremost, James Hamilton had some explaining

to do—and did not greatly impress by his explanations. He declared that he had decided that the best way to aid the Scots invasion had been not to assail the English coastline but to attack them where they were most vulnerable, in Ireland, with the object of drawing off forces from England itself, which his fleet could then attack whilst making the sea crossing. He had therefore landed his own three thousand troops in Ulster and attacked the main English stronghold there, Carrickfergus, whilst the fleet patrolled the narrow seas. His siege of Carrickfergus had been crowned with success and they had captured a great deal of booty—which he had apparently despatched back to his own town and seat of Hamilton in Lanarkshire, via the port of Ayr. Unfortunately, the mainland English had failed to send any reinforcements to Ulster—at least none that his ships had intercepted—and after waiting for some time, he had re-embarked his troops and sailed on southwards, to menace the English west coasts, as arranged. The enemy had not risen to this challenge however, so he had thought it best not to turn back for Scotland but to sail on to France, there to seek either to bring a French army back to Scotland to aid King James, or to encourage the French themselves to stage an attack on south-west England. King Louis had been slow to make up his mind, and while they waited, news came of the disaster of Flodden Edge. So it was too late for any French intervention, with James dead. Then the invitation to Albany had arrived from Scotland, and he had decided to return, with Albany's envoy, de la Bastie.

This sorry catalogue was received at Stirling with some scepticism. Any number of questions presented themselves—in particular, where was the rest of the fleet of thirteen fine vessels, and the three thousand troops Arran had set out with? They were told, in offhand fashion, that the French were a notably parsimonious people and that three thousand men took a deal of provisioning and quartering, so that funds had to be found to pay for them. The only means of paying was in the ships themselves, so they had been forced to sell some to Louis, including the *Great Michael* itself, for forty thousand francs.

Appalled at this, for the *Great Michael* had been the late James's pride and joy, symbol of Scotland's rise to be a maritime power, his hearers had been only very slightly mollified by Arran's assurance that he had gained considerable benefits for Scotland in his French visit, especially the concession that the Auld Alliance provisions should be renewed and that all Scots resident in France should have equal rights with French citizens, and that trade between the two countries should be free of restrictions.

These crumbs of comfort were scarcely sufficient to raise cheers. The Arran-for-Regent faction wilted noticeably.

Nevertheless the regency problem remained. Something would have to be done, or the Queen-Mother would assume the regency almost by default. The urgency became even more apparent when, presently, news came from Whithorn that old Bell-the-Cat had died, and his grandson, the Master, was now Earl of Angus and undisputed head of the most powerful family in the land. Allied with Queen Margaret and her custody of the infant monarch, this was a situation which the Privy Council viewed with the utmost alarm.

It was decided that Albany should be considered, and proclaimed, Regent-elect; and in his absence a council-of-regency should be established to wield supreme authority—this to consist of the Chancellor, the Primate and Bishop Elphinstone; and to balance the three churchmen, the Lord Home, and for the looks of the thing, Arran. Also, to avoid, if possible, outright warfare, the young Angus was invited to join, in the confidence that he could always be outvoted by five to one.

It was not a satisfactory solution, but probably the best that could be contrived in the circumstances. That Yuletide, at Stirling as elsewhere throughout Scotland, was probably the grimmest since Wallace and Bruce and the Wars of Independence—especially as it was desperately cold and wet, and with so many breadwinners gone the harvest had been grievously poor and famine stalked the land. And at Stirling, Bishop Elphinstone was obviously failing in health.

If none of these problems affected the young King of Scots, the same could not be said for his guardians. David and John, along with others in the know, well recognised that it was only a question of time, and no long time at that, until there was dire trouble in the nation. And once the campaigning season started again, with better weather, the English would be here in strength, for sure . . .

5

It was early March before David's distinctly pent-up feelings obtained any real relief, welcome indeed even though the occasion was to say the least ominous as far as the national scene was concerned. He was sent for one day to Bishop Elphinstone's quarters in the castle, out of which the Lord Privy Seal had seldom stirred throughout that dire winter. Indeed David had not seen him for some weeks, and was shocked at the changed appearance of the old man, so bent and frail was he, in his bed-robe, and parchment-white as to features. Archbishop Beaton was with him.

"Davie," Elphinstone said, voice thinner than heretofore, "my lord Archbishop and I have a task for you. Believing you to be the best, probably, to undertake it. Knowing that you are to be trusted—as, I fear, not all here are now. But first, we must know whether you are free to undertake it. With respect to our young liege-lord's care and service?"

"Can you leave him, safely?" Beaton added, more bluntly.

"The King? Surely, my lords. If you mean, for an interval? Not . . . altogether?"

"No, no—only for a short spell, lad," the older man assured. "A week or two. You are James's usher and keeper. More important, his favourite companion. We must know whether His Grace will be well enough, with you gone? He must not be distressed or difficult. Or else his royal mother may take the opportunity to remove him into her own keeping, and that of . . . others. Which would be unfortunate, as you will appreciate."

"My lord of Angus? Yes—I understand. But—His Grace will be very well so long as Abbot John remains with him, I think, my lords. Also, to be sure, there is Master Dunbar . . ."

"Aye, we know of Dunbar!" the Archbishop said briefly. "And place scant trust in him. But John Inglis will keep the child content? This is important."

"Surely, my lord. His Grace is very fond of the Abbot."

"That is well. See you, Lindsay—you are from the shire

of Haddington, and will know it all well. Know its folk, and be known. And, we believe, be trusted. Your father's name is esteemed. We have an errand for you, in East Lothian and the Merse. One which must remain secret."

"Secret . . . ?"

"Privy, at least, Davie," Elphinstone explained. "We need to know certain informations. Without seeming to be enquiring too openly. You, coming from Garleton, and with your Lindsay lands in those parts, can visit there, travel through that land, talk with folk, and none will think it strange. Most others here could not do so. You could learn for us much that we require to know. For the realm's weal."

David waited, more than interested.

"It is Angus. And Home," Beaton, who never had any use for diplomatic and tactful approaches, declared.

"But . . ."

"We are concerned over my lord of Angus and what he may be plotting," Elphinstone went on patiently, holding his chest as though in pain. "You will know that the Queen-Mother is in constant touch with her brother, King Henry of England, through the Lord Dacre, the English Warden of the Marches . . . ?"

"You mean . . . ? He who is devastating the Borderland? Slaying and burning! Our fiercest enemy . . . ?"

"The same, Davie. We have known of this from the start. Dean West of Windsor, Henry's envoy to this court, has the right to send despatches to his master, and does so through Dacre. Queen Margaret does the same, and although this is not correct, we have not protested. But, recently, one of West's couriers fell into Armstrong hands—as you will know, the Armstrongs are perhaps the most practised thieves on the Border, and are waging hottest war against Dacre, in this pass. They should not have assailed the English envoy's courier—but they did. How they used him they have not disclosed. But they took his letters, and read them. And believing that they concerned the safety of the realm, they sent them to the Chancellor. We have, of course, returned them to Dean West, with apologies. But . . ."

"We read them first," the Archbishop said grimly. "And the Queen-Mother's letter commends Angus to Henry and says that he awaits his further instructions and thanks him for his latest payment."

"Lord!" David gasped. "Angus, in Henry's pay?"

"The Tudor will buy any he may, man. So—we had the next courier intercepted. Discreetly, mind. Got him drunken as he journeyed south, in the hospice of the Red Friars at Soutra. Had the priest in charge there steam open the sealed letters, read them, and reseal them, so that naught was known of it. And the later letter implicated *Home*."

"But . . . but, my lord, Home and Douglas have ever been at enmity. They would never work together. Lord Home aided the Hepburns to oust the Douglases from St Andrews. And he was ever strong against the English. He is our Warden of the Marches . . . !"

"When the Archbishop says that the Lord Home was implicated, he means only that his name was mentioned in Nicholas West's letter as possibly worthy of Henry's approach," Elphinstone said. "He writes that Home resents my lord of Arran, who has slighted him, it seems. Also that he had recently visited Tantallon, Angus's stronghold on your Lothian coast. There may be no ill in it. But we require to know. These three, Angus, Home and Arran are all on the present Commission of Regency. If there is treachery, plotting, we have to learn of it. So we want you to go, secretly, to sound out the land. Douglas controls most of the Lothian coast and Home that of the Merse, right to the Border. *You* can move there without being suspect. For there are Lindsay lands there also . . ."

"Dunbar," Beaton interjected. "We want, in especial, Dunbar and its castle considered. Its state now. It could be useful."

"Dunbar is the only stronghold between Angus's Tantallon and Home's Dunglass," the older prelate pointed out. "Since the Dunbar family was brought low, it has been forfeited to the crown. But the late King did little with it. And since it was largely Douglas who brought the Dunbars down, Douglas may now be holding it. We have to know this. And its state for defence and warfare. Master William Dunbar here would have been the best to send there—but he is the Queen-Mother's man and we dare not trust him."

"We wish to know all concerning Dunbar. How many men are required to garrison it? What is its state? What cannon it has and how many? Who commands there? All," Beaton asserted emphatically. "We may have to use Dunbar.

Not only to check Tantallon and Dunglass but because it commands the mouth of the Forth. If Henry sent up a fleet . . ."

"But, my lords—I am no soldier!" David exclaimed. "I know nothing of cannon and fortress defences and garrisons. Nor of the armed strengths of Douglas and Home in Lothian and the Merse. I am not the man you require . . ."

"We know that," the Archbishop interrupted. "You will have one with you who well understands all such matters. But knows not the country."

"Davie—we are going to send Sir Anthony, the Sieur de la Bastie, with you. He is a great knight, a noted commander and a close friend of the Duke of Albany. He is a most useful man. He will survey the land and advise us on matters military. And he is wholly to be trusted. You and he will do very well together. For he writes poetry, also!"

Embarrassed, David shook his head. "I but scratch and scribble, my lord." He paused. "But—the Queen, in all this? Will she agree that I go? Leave His Grace?"

"We shall see that she does. You are the King's servant, not hers."

"We shall tell her that you have the Regency Council's permission, Davie. That you have private matters to attend to at your home. Her Grace will care nothing, I think—for if I mistake not, she loves you little better than she loves me!" Elphinstone attempted a laugh, but it was beyond him, for obviously he was tiring grievously.

Perceiving it, Beaton waved David away. "Tomorrow, then, Lindsay . . ."

So, early next morning, without risking a scene by taking leave of young James, David, de la Bastie, and two of the Archbishop's men as escort, rode quietly out of the citadel and Stirling, the first time David had left the town in almost six months—so that, despite the secret and possibly even dangerous nature of his mission, he felt almost like singing aloud in his sense of freedom from constriction. He was, admittedly, a little bit in awe of the Sieur de la Bastie, with his Christendom-wide reputation for gallantry and daring, champion of tourneys innumerable, and accomplished envoy to many courts. But Antoine, as he asked to be called, was as unassuming and as easy to get on with as he was handsome and personable, with no least condescension towards the younger man, so that very quickly David was on good terms with him. It helped that he had discarded his magnificent clothing for much more modest garb and rusty half armour, in the interests of anonymity, and might have been any small laird—although an unusually good-looking one.

They chatted companionably as they rode eastwards, for Antoine, having visited Scotland twice previously, spoke fair if accented English, the accent partly Scots. David learned much about the Duke of Albany, how highly he was esteemed in France, how rich and influential, how he kept his own court, almost to rival that of King Louis, and how notable a sacrifice all this would be to leave and come to Scotland. Although far too courteous to say so, the Frenchman might inadvertently have given just a hint that he too perhaps was making some sacrifice in visiting this strange northern and war-torn land, threatened with further strife.

How threatened it was was vividly brought home to them at Edinburgh, which they reached well before dusk of a windy March day to find the city gates already about to be shut and barred for the night and the walls manned by the vastly increased and volunteer town-guard, with beacons ready to be lit at quite close intervals along the perimeter. Indeed, the travellers, small party as they made, had some difficulty in gaining entrance to the city, so suspicious of strangers were the guards. David's assertion that he was a kinsman of the Lord Lindsay of the Byres, who was well-known in Edinburgh, however, got them in. They had not ridden far into the narrow street of the West Port when they heard the gates clang shut behind them. The feeling of being beleaguered was very strong.

That night, in an alehouse of the Grassmarket, the talk around them was all of an English raiding force at Peebles, on the upper Tweed, only a score of miles to the south, and of the stories of rapine, slaughter and savagery being perpetrated there. The difference in attitude and atmosphere from that of Stirling, thirty-five miles to the north-west, was very noticeable.

It was only a further sixteen miles due eastwards, fording the Esk at Musselburgh, to Garleton—and once beyond that ancient town, also in a state of wary preparedness, strangely enough there was much less feeling of tension and threat in the countryside, Antoine remarking on it. He asked if this could be because they were now entering Douglas country; and David had to admit just the possibility that this might have something to do with it.

Their unexpected arrival at Garleton Castle produced joy but just a little embarrassment also, when it became clear that Mirren had now moved into Sir David's bedchamber and was more or less acting mistress of the house. David was scarcely surprised and not really upset, although his father tried, not very successfully, to explain it all away by asserting that he had not been very well of late and Mirren, kindly nursing him, had found it convenient to be near at hand. His son gravely hoped that the laird would soon be restored to his normal robust health.

Despite all this, Mirren was most evidently quite bowled over by the Sieur Antoine, all but drooling over his brilliantly well-favoured and assured person. David found her, presently, removing her things back from his father's bed-chamber to that which she had occupied previously, and knew a little sympathy for his lame and elderly sire.

He learned that his brother, Alexander, who had been with the King's army in Lord Lindsay's following, had been wounded at Flodden, like his chief, left for dead by the English, but had survived, again like his chief, managed to get back across the Tweed, and after being succoured for weeks in a shepherd's cothouse near Birgham, had eventually found his way home. That home was at the Barony, a subsidiary Lindsay property high on the East Garleton Hill behind the castle, only a mile or so away but hundreds of feet higher. David, of course, felt duty-bound to go at once to visit his brother.

He had never been very close to Alexander, a strange and moody young man who resented the fact that David, only a year older, was not only the heir but had been left also the smaller estate of The Mount, in Fife, by their mother, whilst he had to be content with this crow's-nest of a place on the top of a hill. It was not only that, for they had never got on well, Alexander being very much a physical character, de-lighting even as a boy in fisticuffs and fighting, in demon-strating his prowess in outdoor sports and pursuits where muscle rather than wits were called for, and despising David, even before he began to write poetry, for his love of music and balladry. *He* had not gone to St Andrews University, nor on the year-long continental tour thereafter—he would have hated both, but nevertheless found these a further cause for grudge. He had married the daughter of a small local laird whom he had got with child; and although David felt sorry for her and did not dislike her, they had little in common.

So he rode up to the Barony, was well enough received by Jean his sister-in-law, but only surlily welcomed by Alexander, whom he found emaciated and obviously still suffering from the effects of his wound. He did not actually say that David had failed in his duty by not being with the invading Scots army, but that was implied, and no explanation that it was by royal command impressed.

David did not stay long, but learned some further details of the battle at Flodden Edge and the mismanagement thereof. His brother blamed King James for his chivalric folly, of course, but reserved his principal condemnation for Home and Huntly with the cavalry wing, and those damnable French pikes. He also scoffed at the prized artillery as a useless encumbrance and declared that the English bowmen were the real victors of the struggle, standing well back out of danger, slaughtering at their leisure, and never having to be within striking distance of naked steel. The cavalry wing, to be sure, should have swung round after its breakthrough and rolled up those archers from the rear . . .

David left his brother to his resentments, and spurred downhill again towards a more pleasurably anticipated meeting—at the castle of the Byres. It was known that Lord Lindsay, wounded likewise, had won home; and Bishop Elphinstone had given David a message to deliver to him. But much as he approved of his chief and kinsman, and of his Aunt Isabella, he had to admit to himself that it was Kate whom he was mainly looking forward to seeing again, the transformed Kate who had been so much in his thoughts these last months.

He found Patrick, fourth Lord, lacking an arm, which had had to be amputated after the battle, gangrenous, superintending the excavation of a new well in the walled pleasance of the castle, a high-coloured, slender man of middle years, fine features rather unbalanced by a great beak of a nose. When he recognised David, he greeted him with his accustomed sardonic smile, waving his remaining arm.

"See who comes!" he cried. "Our sovereign-lord's stay and support! I wonder that you honour this humble house, Davie lad!" That was not said unkindly.

"Your arm, my lord! I did not know. I—I am sorry."

"So am I, lad—so am I! But I might have been a deal sorrier! I was more fortunate than most. What, God help us, is an arm or two? Where have you come from? Stirling? You are not dismissed? Lost your fine place?"

"No. I am on a—a mission. In these parts."

"A mission? On whose behalf? That woman . . . ?"

"No, no. The Queen would never send *me* on any mission. It is Bishop Elphinstone and the Chancellor. They require information. About the Douglases. And others. They also send a message to yourself. They ask that you come to Stirling. Say that such as yourself are much needed there. In the realm's service."

"They do? And how am I to serve the realm, Davie? Part crippled!"

"They did not say. But it will be your counsel that they seek. They are notably short of honest lords! I expect that they want you on the Privy Council."

"Well, we shall see. So you want to enquire into the Douglases? You must needs be careful on that ploy, Davie! What do you want to know?"

David explained the situation. The Lord Patrick was particularly interested to hear of the Sieur de la Bastie's involvement, of whom he had heard great things. He seemed more intrigued by this than by the object of the mission. On the subject of the Douglases, he quite often saw Greysteel and Douglas of Longniddry, near neighbours both; and had heard they had been visiting Tantallon together more than once recently—which looked as though something was being hatched. As to Home, he had heard nothing; but assumed him to be loyal and no friend of Douglas, now or ever. He blamed him for the Flodden business, of course.

It was at this stage that David, looking up, perceived Kate watching them from the garden gateway. How long she might have been there he did not know. No running to hurl herself upon him on this occasion, just this quiet scrutiny. Typically, he was the more eager to detach himself from her father and hurry to her.

The older man saw the direction of his gaze, and smiled. "There is someone who will offer a young man more pleasure than talking to an *old* man about the Douglases! She speaks of you, often."

"I will go to her, sir . . ."

She still waited for him there—and he told himself that he had never seen anyone more lovely, more so even than last time, more graceful, further developed—developed sufficiently, presumably, to preclude impetuous welcomes.

"Kate!" he exclaimed. "How good you are to see! A joy! I have missed you."

"Have you, Davie?" She sounded interested rather than ecstatic.

"Indeed, yes. It has seemed a long time."

"Not so long as before. But six months."

"So—you counted them!" He grinned. "I came so soon as I could."

"Yes. You are so important a man, now! Keeper of the King's Grace, no less! We are fortunate even to see you at all!"

"Your father said something the same! Do I hear some question in your voice, Kate?"

"Why, no. Who would question the King's keeper? Save perhaps, the King!"

"Keeper is scarcely right, lass. Procurator and Usher—these I am, to our young lord. Am I to have a kiss, Kate?"

"If you wish." She held up her face to him. His arms and lips were perhaps a little more enthusiastic than cousinly, but she did not draw back, indeed responded to some degree, before recollecting her now sixteen years and their burden of responsibility, and detached herself. "Court ways!" she got out, a little breathlessly.

He shook his head, ruefully. "Scarce that, lass. Just affection. And esteem."

She turned away. "Have you written any more poetry? Or are you still too full of busyness?"

"A little—only a little." He hesitated, always embarrassed by his versifying. "I am put off it, somewhat, you see. There are too many poets at Stirling. Gavin Douglas is close to the Queen. And now a youth called John Bellenden has arrived. It is strange. It was the late King who liked poets, not Margaret Tudor who, I think, cares nothing for

78

poetry. Yet they gather at court. And do not love each other! I am something off poetry!"

"That is foolish. And wrong. When you have the gift. You could write a poem about the young King—since few can know him better. Do none of your fine court ladies presently inspire you?"

"They never did. Besides, there are few ladies at Stirling. Queen Margaret does not like other women around her, preferring men. Especially Douglases! Indeed the citadel is starved of women . . ."

"Well, your Mistress Livingstone is not like to go back, I think! She is too snug with Sir David, now! I hope that you are not jealous? Of your own father!"

"Lord, Kate—do not talk that way! Mirren means little to me. Or—she is a friend of course, but only that. The King, the *late* King, charged me to look after her. And the Queen-Mother mislikes her. So I sent her here . . ."

Lady Lindsay called to them from a castle doorway and relieved David of his prickly problem for the moment.

The Sieur Antoine was a much safer and surer subject of conversation, and David made the most of it thereafter—although hoping, at the back of his mind, that he was not overdoing it as far as Kate was concerned; the Frenchman might make all too great an impression on that burgeoning young female. When he left, in the gloaming, he was committed to bringing de la Bastie to see them all at the Byres very soon, whether or not that was wise.

Kate saw him to his horse, and her farewell embrace was sufficiently encouraging to send him homewards in a warm glow despite the chill air off the Norse Sea.

Next day the four men rode eastwards, out of the hanging valley of Garleton and down the fertile Vale of Peffer, past Athelstaneford, where Scotland had acquired Saint Andrew as patron saint, past the Pictish symbol stone at Prora, in which Antoine was much interested, and round the southern base of the conical green height of North Berwick Law, where David pointed to the ramparts of a Pictish fort on the summit. The Frenchman was much intrigued by the Picts and their traces, for he was from Brittany himself and the Bretons were traditionally of the same early Celtic stock as the Cruithne—it was the Romans who had called them

Picts because they used a pictorial rather than a written language. But all this concern for the past did not preoccupy their minds to the exclusion of their present task, and as they approached the Tantallon area they grew more wary.

Tantallon Castle, the principal stronghold of the Red Douglas earldom of Angus, was perched on an immensely strong and striking clifftop site three miles east of North Berwick town, a huge place, practically impregnable, of rose-red stone keep and flanking towers, linked by lofty curtain walls topped by parapet-walks, the whole protected from landward by a series of deep moats and dry ditches designed and placed so as to keep any besieging cannon well beyond range of the castle itself. The plan was highly unusual, the towers and curtain walling being in fact little more than a high defensive screen cutting off a thrusting headland from which the cliffs fell sheerly hundreds of feet to the boiling tides; so that behind this great fortress wall what amounted to a township of subsidiary and lean-to buildings could cluster secure, unassailable from land or water. The mighty rock known as the Craig of Bass soared abruptly from the sea two miles offshore, completing a dramatic scene which had Antoine whistling his admiration as they viewed it all from an inland vantage point.

They dared not approach the castle itself, of course; but it had a quite sizeable castleton nearby of cothouses and cabins, even a hostelry, for retainers, servants, farm folk and the trains of visiting lords. To this David reckoned that they might risk a call—but left behind their two escorts as too obviously men-at-arms. Also their half armour.

Their arrival in what was really a village appeared to occasion no great interest, certainly no disquiet, and they found their way to the alehouse where three or four men were drinking. David accounted for himself as a cattle dealer from Leith and his companion as a Low Countries merchant and importer, interested in the trade of salted herring. They were making for Dunbar town, where they understood that the fisherfolk salted and smoked much of their catch. Was there anywhere else on this coast where they might try for regular supplies of barrelled herring, to be exported from Leith?

This, with drinks bought all round, initiated a lively discussion. North Berwick, apparently, was no use, its harbour drying out at low water and so unable to take the larger fishing craft necessary to catch the deep-water herring. The same applied to almost all this shallow sandy Lothian coast until Dunbar. Further south, the Merse coast was better for the herring, with fishing communities at Dunglass, Bilsdean, Pease Cove, Redheuch, St Abbs Haven and Eyemouth. Whether they salted their herring in these havens their informants could not tell them.

But the Merse was Home country, was it not, David pointed out. And the Homes had the name for being difficult folk, Border reivers and lairdly thieves. Was it safe to take their Netherlands friend into such country, especially in present circumstances, with the English raiding over the border?

This leading question elicited a useful crop of responses. The Homes were rogues and scoundrels truly, and usually in a state of war with Douglas. But matters were different at the moment—although how long this would last, none knew. There was a sort of truce for some reason. Indeed, the Lord Home himself had been here, at the castle, only two weeks before, with his kin of Wedderburn and Blackadder, to meet Greysteel of Kilspindie and other Douglas lairds; and it was said that the Douglases could now ride through the Merse unharmed. Whether this would apply to a Leith cattle dealer and a Low Country merchant was another matter. But they could always say that they rode under Douglas protection.

Much appreciative of this kindly suggestion, David ordered more ale. This excellent idea might save them from the Homes, he agreed. But what of the English? Once past Dunbar it was a mere thirty miles to the border at Berwick, was it not? Too near possible raiding Englishry for comfort?

It was the alehouse keeper himself, drawn into the discussion and drinking with them, who answered that one. The English were not raiding Douglas territory, having too much respect for their new Earl who had the Queen in his pocket, the English King's sister. And he had heard that part of the deal with Home was that the English would also avoid Home lands. So the travellers ought to be safe from them too, meantime, if they claimed Douglas or Home protection. Humble folk like themselves had to make use of the great ones' ploys as best they could, to their own advantage!

Heartily agreeing with these sentiments, the visitors expressed admiration and astonishment that the Earl of Angus, great lord as he was, could be said to have the Queen-Mother in his pocket. Was she not reputed to be a hard and strong woman? Surely their friend was mistaken in this matter?

Not so, the other asserted. All men knew how far ben Angus was with the Englishwoman. Indeed, it was said that he would *marry* her, presently. When his present wife died.

David stared. How could that be, he wondered? The Lady Margaret Hepburn—or now, the Countess of Angus—was quite young, was she not? Little older than the Earl Archibald himself.

The lady ailed, he was told shortly. And one of the others, silent hitherto, barking a laugh, added that she ailed indeed—helped on, it was reckoned, aye, helped on! This dire suggestion produced an uncomfortable pause, and then disclaimers and argument, the alehouse keeper declaring that gossip about poison was but the idle chatter of castle servants and not to be bruited abroad, whilst the individual who had suggested it asserted that it was more than gossip, that he had it from one of the kitchen wenches who saw the lady's food prepared.

This indiscreet loquacity producing disapproval amongst the others, and a noticeable change of atmosphere, the enquirers recognised that it was probably time that they departed. One last point David raised—who was now in charge at Dunbar Castle? If they were to do business there, it might be as well to know. He was told, as though he ought to have known it, that of course Sir William Douglas had been master at Dunbar for long, brother of the late Master and of Greysteel.

Provided with considerable food for thought, the visitors made their way back to the two Archbishop's men-at-arms, left in hiding in woodland, before heading on southwards for the Tyne estuary and Dunbar.

Assessing the information thus gained—if it was to be believed—they reckoned that they had made a fair start. It looked as though there was indeed some rather alarming link-up between the long-time enemy clans of Douglas and Home, and with ominous English associations, the more dire in that Lord Home was chief Scots Warden of the

Marches, and that he and Angus were both on the Regency Council. So Elphinstone's and the Chancellor's fears, however aroused, appeared to have some basis. As to the suggestion that Angus was indeed contemplating actual marriage with the Queen-Mother, this seemed scarcely credible, as did the talk of poison for his unfortunate countess. According to the late King's testament, Margaret would lose all control of her son, and any power in the land with it, if she remarried. Surely, unscrupulous as she was, she would not be so foolish?

Although Dunbar was a mere seven miles from Tantallon as the crow flew, the great tidal bay and estuary of Tynemouth had to be circumnavigated by travellers, so that it was nearer a dozen miles, and sundown, before they reached the town. And again the escort, insisted on by Beaton, proved something of a nuisance, for ordinary traders and merchants did not normally go so protected. However, Dunbar was quite a large community, with a number of inns and hostelries, and they were able to deposit their escort in one such whilst they patronised another down near the harbour.

If Tantallon had been an impressive strength, Dunbar Castle was no less so, and although very dissimilar, likewise unique in Scotland, for which it was known as one of the 'keys of the kingdom'. For it was erected, not on any clifftop, but on a number of stacks of naked rock rising out of the sea, its towers limited in size and shape by these rock platforms but linked together by bridge-like covered corridors of masonry above the tide, in extraordinary fashion, so that it sprawled and clung and soared into the waves, completely controlling the narrow entrance to the quite large harbour. It had been besieged times without number, being on the principal invasion route from the border, the most famous occasion when Black Agnes, Countess of Dunbar, had defied a large English army for months in 1339. It had yielded more than once but never been actually taken by force of arms.

It was too late for Antoine to try to assess its military state and capabilities that evening, one of his main tasks; but they were able to glean a fair amount of information in the inn, from fishermen and others, whilst supposedly enquiring about the herring trade. They learned that although in theory a royal castle since the Dunbars were put down it had been firmly in Douglas hands for some years now, Sir William, brother of Greysteel, having some fifty men garrisoning it, with a number of cannon. They took toll of every fishing boat's catch before allowing the craft into the harbour, to the great resentment of the community, then sold the fish back to the merchants and salters. David pricked up his ears at this, perceiving a possible excuse for making an approach to the castle direct. They had to be careful, of course, not to get too deeply committed to this herring business or they might have difficulty in extricating themselves.

On the morrow, then, after visiting some of the smokehouses and salteries, they approached the castle itself, a cautious approach, as it had to be, over a drawbridge above the swirling water to a gatehouse guarded by lounging retainers who were anything but respectful but who eventually, after suitable inducement, consented to escort them over another inner drawbridge to the first tower where they were left while someone more able to talk business was fetched. Meanwhile, Antoine's eyes were busy indeed, assessing, memorising.

Presently a burly individual appeared, all bushy red beard and hair, announcing that he was under-steward here and what did they want? David explained. He had heard that the castle had at its disposal quite large quantities of fish, and wondered if a deal might be done, for their mutual benefit? If the castle were to sell the fish direct to himself and his Netherlands friend here, instead of to local merchants, cargoes of it could be sailed up-Forth daily to Salt Preston, near Musselburgh, where were the salt-pans, thus saving two journeys—the salt being brought here to Dunbar and the salt-fish taken back for export at Leith. For a regular supply, this would enable them to pay a higher price than the Dunbar merchants could afford. Would they consider it?

The under-steward scratched amongst his beard and said that they had better go and see the steward.

So they threaded some of the vaulted corridor-bridges of that extraordinary stronghold, the Frenchman noting all. The steward, one Robert Douglas, young for the position and therefore probably an illegitimate son of Sir William, listened to it all again, arrogantly unimpressed at first but growing interested—too much so presently, so that David began to worry about extricating himself from this tissue of falsehood. But eventually the other declared that he would have to consult Sir William, who was away at present; and thankfully David agreed that they should come back on another occasion. They made their escape, Antoine reasonably content that he had seen enough to make a useful report on the strength of the place.

After that they were in rather a hurry to get out of Dunbar before people began putting two and two together.

Dunglass was their next objective, only eight miles south of Dunbar but in markedly different country, as though emphasising the contrasts between Douglas and Home, between Lothian and the Merse. Here the sandy beaches and fertile fields gave place to rocks and reefs and ravines, to beetling precipices and secret wooded denes, where the Borderland hills came abruptly down to the sea, wild country which had Antoine shaking his handsome head. There were little fishing communities tucked away in hidden creeks and coves, but all too small for any pretence at commercial fish buying. So the cattle dealing aspect was now to be emphasised, with Antoine interested in hides for export.

Dunglass Castle was much smaller than either Tantallon or Dunbar, less dramatic altogether although strong, sited just above the fiercely rugged shore where the Dunglass Burn reached the rock-torn sea at Bilsdean Creek. With no valid excuse for approaching the castle—for a less likely place for cattle rearing would be hard to imagine—they turned inland up the burnside to climb steeply up the dene and into the foothills of the Oldhamstocks area, where cattle did at least graze and there were farmeries and a village of sorts in a fold of the green hills. Here, in a wretched poverty-stricken hovel, they spent the night, the only available shelter; with David apologetic to be subjecting the renowned Sieur de la Bastie to such conditions. But the Frenchman made no complaints and proved entirely adaptable and philosophical. Unfortunately they learned little or nothing of any value on this occasion, save that no English forces had been operating in this area as yet, that Home of Dunglass, brother of the Lord Home, was away operating with other Home lairds in unspecified activities, and that times were hard, hard, and any buying of cattle would be welcomed.

Disappointed with Oldhamstocks and Dunglass, they moved on in the morning, ever southwards. They had two main quests now: to discover, if they could, whether the Homes had come to any arrangement with the invading English; and to consider the land, militarily, for purposes of defensive warfare in case Home and Douglas were not to be relied upon—this, of course, Antoine's remit.

In the days that followed they were able to accomplish a fairly useful survey for the second objective but nothing really conclusive about the first. The only possible indication gained, as it happened, was also their only brush with the English. This was at Ayton Castle, another Home strength, the vicinity of which they were approaching very cautiously, for it was a mere eight miles from Berwick-on-Tweed, when they were all but run down by a troop of English horse, about two score of rough-looking characters, some with women held before them on their saddle bows, most burdened with gear and booty and with a number of laden led-horses, obviously a raiding party. Fortunately these ignored the four travellers and clattered on up to Ayton Castle, no doubt tired after a long day's foraying.

David and Antoine had intended to spend that night at Ayton village but decided that this would be too risky in the circumstances, and so moved back three miles to Reston in the Eye valley. And there they learned that this group of Northumbrians from Alnwick, Percys, were indeed making Ayton Castle their base, and that Home of Ayton was still in residence there. Also that they were not raiding Home lands locally. Admittedly this did not necessarily mean that this Home was actually co-operating with the English—he could be under duress, and the locality being spared for some other reason—but it could be one more indication.

Too near Berwick and the border for comfort now, they turned inland into the Merse proper, that fair, blood-soaked land of low grassy hills, shallow valleys and far horizons, dotted with peel-towers, huddled farm-touns and small ancient churches. And here certain circumstances did not fail to impress them. There were ample signs of earlier raiding—burned homesteads and kirks, ravaged barns and deserted hamlets—but there was nothing recent in all this, the visitors not having to be very experienced to perceive that this was all the result of *last* year's invasions. Life was going on apparently fairly normally round about, with no new devastation nor smoking ruins. The travellers were eyed warily but no one panicked and they were not challenged. Nearly all this eastern Merse area was Home land or that of their allies, the great lairdships of Wedderburn, Bassendean, Blackadder, Manderston, Polwarth, Marchmont, Paxton, Hutton, Whiteriggs and many another. But as they proceeded westwards the picture began to change, with ever-growing signs of savage oppression and wanton destruction: men, women and children hanging from trees, mutilated—and some not many days there—wells choked with bodies, stock wantonly slaughtered, farmeries burned out, towers roofless and abandoned, most of it clearly recently done. They were running out of Home land, here, into the territories of Kerrs, Turnbulls, Scotts, Elliots, Pringles and the rest, and it was evident that these Border clans at least were not being spared. The conclusion seemed, on the face of it, fairly clear—the Homes *were* being protected, for one reason or another.

When in one forenoon they had to avoid English raiding bands twice, fortunate in one case in perceiving new smoke clouds rising ahead and so effecting a quick departure; and in the other in being able to hide in thick woodland; they decided that they had probably learned sufficient and should now return northwards.

That evening, in the Ersildoune area of Lauderdale, they were cheered by the news that at least the raiders were not having it *all* their own way. Apparently a large English band, from the Priory of Hexham no less, ravaging their way up Teviotdale after wrecking the village of Denholm-on-the-Green and on their way to do likewise by the town of Hawick, had camped for the night in the riverside haugh of Hornshole and, glutted with easy conquest, rape, food and liquor, had slept in drunken stupor, failing to set adequate guards. And the youths and boys of Hawick, their fathers and brothers never returned from Flodden, had sallied out with axes and knives and clubs, in their scores, and fallen upon the raiders in the darkness and slaughtered them as they lay, not an Englishman escaping, and had borne back the Hexham Priory banner, blue and gold, to Hawick in triumph.

It sounded a more inspiriting note on which to ride home.

They had been away from Garleton for almost two weeks, and were glad to be back. That night, in his own bed, David heard the door of Antoine's room, next to his own, open quietly and soft steps descend the turnpike stairway. They did not return until nearly dawn.

Next day, the Byres party came up to meet the Sieur de la Bastie and hear the news, a radiant Mirren acting hostess. David watched to see Kate's reaction to the Frenchman, and found himself much relieved when she appeared to be only moderately affected by his charm, good looks and gallantry. That he was becoming jealous of young Kate's favours struck him as rather ridiculous but hardly to be denied.

Lord Lindsay, like Sir David, was eager to hear their account of their travels, and what conclusions they had arrived at. Their inference that it seemed probable that there was indeed some agreement or alliance between the previously inimical houses of Douglas and Home, and that there was an understanding with the English not to attack their lands, left the two older men very thoughtful, and all asking what it might mean. The devastation in the western Merse and Roxburghshire troubled and alarmed. Was it only a question of time before the raiding reached East Lothian? Or would the Douglas influence here protect them? The very enunciation of that thought caused all to eye each other guiltily, suddenly aware of the dangers of more than ravishment. Antoine's military investigations were not reported on in any detail, naturally. But he did say that Dunbar Castle could still be one of the keys of the kingdom, and that it ought to be taken back into the keeping of the crown, particularly in present circumstances.

Out of some discussion, Lord Lindsay announced that when they returned to Stirling, he would accompany them. That would be in two days, they decided.

Mirren looked dashed, but Sir David otherwise.

David himself escorted their visitors back to the Byres that evening, unnecessary as this might be, and thereafter took an unconscionable time over his leave-taking of Kate. They would call for her father two days hence. Meantime, he would scratch out some small verse for her, in appreciation . . .

6

They arrived back at Stirling to some considerable stir, for the Queen-Mother had had her baby only the day before, another boy, who was to be named Alexander, Duke of Ross. Mother and child were well enough, although the infant was small and less than robust.

This development was important in more than any personal aspect, for of course it changed the succession situation, pushing back Albany to third place and Arran to fourth— which might affect the coming of the Regent-elect, to some extent. Also it strengthened Margaret Tudor's position, and therefore Douglas's—which worried the Chancellor and Privy Seal.

These two were still more worried when, closeted in William Elphinstone's bedchamber presently, they heard the findings of the investigative mission, and knew their fears confirmed. If both Angus and Home were in Henry's pay, as now looked probable, the situation was very serious, with these two comprising one third of the Regency Council and Arran not to be relied on. That left only the three churchmen as trustworthy, and Elphinstone, as he sadly asserted, a broken reed indeed. It also meant that no decisions of the regency, or of the Privy Council either, would long be secret from the English. Something would have to be done, and quickly.

Clearly, Albany's coming from France would have to be expedited, if at all possible. But how? They could send urgent envoys, but they had no means of bringing effective pressure to bear on anyone so well-established and authoritative in the French community, especially with the French king loth to let him go.

Antoine had a suggestion to make. The Chancellor's own nephew and former secretary, David Beaton, now studying at the University of Paris, was a great favourite with both old King Louis and Albany himself. Even more so with

Queen Anne of Brittany. And he was most persuasive as well as able. If anyone could convince the Duke to come and the ageing King to permit it, David Beaton could.

The Chancellor seemed scarcely to have realised that his nephew could be so valuable. But it was decided to send an emissary to France and to enlist Davie Beaton's aid. They would send the new under-tutor, John Bellenden, who like David Lindsay had been a fellow student with Beaton at St Andrews and knew him well.

The suggestion, from Tantallon, that Angus had ambitions actually to marry the Queen-Mother aroused much interest—although the two prelates dismissed the poison story as mere idle gossip. But their interest was not so much concern nor indignation as, in fact, satisfaction. For, as they pointed out, if Margaret was fool enough to agree to such marriage, this would play into their hands and give them complete control of the King. It was almost too much to hope for.

Telling of the Hawick youths' triumph over the English raiders in Teviotdale, led David to suggest that more of such spirit was called for, that too much was being accepted as inevitable. They should learn from these boys. Hit back. Surely they could carry the fight into the enemy's territory on occasion? Raid over the border into Northumberland. They had learned where at least two of the raiding parties had come from, Alnwick and Hexham. Scots raids into these parts would soon bring back those beauties, teach them a lesson. Antoine strongly supported this attitude. He, as a soldier, would gladly lead or take part in such a raid. This one-sided terror should not be allowed to continue, since Home, as chief Warden, did not appear to be checking the evil on Scots soil.

Their hearers agreed that this might well be worth a trial.

The two churchmen were glad of the arrival of Lord Lindsay. There would be plenty for him to do. They were dependent on too many clerics and too few seasoned warriors and trustworthy nobles.

Young Jamie's greeting for his returned friend was heartening, all but overwhelming, so rejoiced was he to have back the companion he appeared to believe he had lost for ever. Abbot John said that the child had been inconsolable, often refusing to eat and crying himself to sleep at night. David found it touching to be so favoured, but recognised how tying this could become for such as himself. He settled into the citadel routine again with mixed feelings, his taste of freedom having unsettled him.

So it was that, a week or two later, he was indignant when, Antoine, having been given permission to organise and lead a major foray into Northumberland, he himself was not permitted to go along. This on the grounds that he was too important for the King's well-being to be away again so soon, and on a dangerous employment. Besides, he was no soldier and probably would be of little value. This was not Antoine's decision but the Chancellor's.

That raid was a notable success—although almost certainly more bloody than David would have appreciated. The Scots had not ventured as far south as Hexham and Alnwick but they had brought devastation and alarm to a wide area around the valleys of Till, Glen and Heiton, paying particular attention to Ford—where the late monarch had reputedly discarded his famous chain—Etal, Crookham and the vicinity of Branxton and Flodden, to drive the message home. They had even approached Berwick-on-Tweed, from the south, as near as two miles; but of course were in insufficient strength to consider attacking that strongly fortified walled town. The Sieur de la Bastie and other leaders came back acknowledged heroes—and David muttered his exasperation. He even made a short poem out of it which he entitled *The Complaint of the Unwanted Warrior*.

Perhaps partly as a result of this expedition, King Henry sent a message to the Scots. He had to send one anyway, to congratulate his sister on her successful birth-giving. But he added to it with an angry denunciation of murderers, thieves and robbers daring to invade his territories, and ended up, in extraordinary fashion, by demanding that the Scots parliament should forthwith proclaim himself Lord Protector of Scotland.

Even Bishop Elphinstone, out of his vast experience of erratic human behaviour, conceded that the man must be slightly mad.

But further and still more alarming news from that direction arrived at Stirling shortly—that Henry and Louis of France had patched up a peace, that Henry was to get certain territorial concessions and in return was actually offering his younger sister, Mary, as wife for Louis when a divorce from Anne of Brittany should be effected. Not only did this mean that Henry would now be free to turn his military strength against Scotland, but an ominous clause of the peace treaty was quoted—that Louis had agreed to stop all Scots inroads over the border into England, on pain of major French displeasure. There was no corresponding mention of *English* inroads into Scotland.

This dire stab in the back delivered by their trusted partner in the Auld Alliance, on whose behalf their late King had invaded England at such cost, left the Scots outraged and fearful, its possible effect on Albany's coming clearly serious. A parliament was hastily convened by the Regency Council, once more ignoring the statutory forty days' notice. Representations and protests fell to be sent to King Louis, an answer given to King Henry over his absurd protectorship claim—now seen in a rather different light—and the nation's loins girded anew, however lacking in potency.

Unfortunately, and not for the first time, that parliament was more notable for internal division than united action. The urgent threat produced two violently opposing factions whose arguments went like this. Scotland, in her present state of weakness could not fight both England and France; therefore since England was the closer and greater threat, they must seek to appease France, however badly Louis had behaved. After all, the French had been fighting the English for centuries, and at heart hated them—and had been traditional friends of the Scots. It ought not to be too difficult to bring them back to their accustomed collaboration. The Earl of Arran led this faction. The other persuasion argued that with their young King James heir to Henry's throne, and the safeguard of Henry's sister here in Scotland, they would be wise to make peace with England and avoid further disaster. After all, it would cost nothing to let Henry use the title of Protector, if so he desired; it carried no constitutional authority. Peace with England, then, and an end to all this of fear and folly. Needless to say, Archibald, Earl of Angus was undisputed leader of this party. David, watching and listening, was highly interested to learn whether Alexander, Lord Home would publicly support this point of view; but he remained notably silent.

The Chancellor clearly disapproved of both these attitudes; but it was his duty to chair the proceedings, not to lead the discussion. The split Regency Council's opinions had to be put by the Primate, Archbishop Forman of St Andrews, for William Elphinstone, present but huddled in a furred bedrobe, was now too frail for his voice to be heard. With the Earls of Lennox, Bothwell and Glencairn siding with Arran, and those of Atholl, Huntly and Crawford taking their cue from Angus, and other lords forming up behind each, it was largely left to the clerics to lead the more spirited course. Fortunately the majority of the shires and burgh commissioners followed the churchmen's line and voted for more independent action. Nevertheless, it was a near thing. By skilfully manipulating the voting system so that the pro-French party had usually to support the clerics' motions against the English faction, the Chancellor could largely ensure that the worst follies were avoided. For instance, they got a reply to King Henry passed, stating that while the parliament appreciated his kind offer of protection, it believed that Scotland had the power and the will to protect *itself*, as it had always done in the past.

Other decisions reached included plans for a swift and major mustering of troops, lords' levies, clan forces, lairds' retainers, town train-bands and the like, chains of beacon fires to be lit on hilltops throughout the land as summons. It was agreed to send envoys to Denmark, with which country Scotland had a loose alliance, to request military aid in the present situation, Lord Lindsay to lead such embassy. And various measures were to be put in hand to ensure, as far as possible, the nation's readiness for full-scale war. It would have been as well, in the circumstances, if the Lord Home could have been replaced as chief Warden of the Marches, but none felt sufficiently strong as yet to challenge him, and no real proof of any treachery was available.

The Queen-Mother did not attend this parliament. And two days after it had ended, the word reached Stirling that the young Countess of Angus had died, at Tantallon.

That anxious summer of 1514 passed without the feared invasion, and by August Scotland was daring to breathe again. Surely if Henry had been going to attack he would have done so by then, with the campaigning season nearly over? He was, it was reported, personally busy at Tournai, in Hainault, consolidating his position in the Low Countries territory he had managed to wring from King Louis, although his main armies were not now involved. So the northern kingdom might be safe from assault for another six months or so. Then, on the sixth, the news broke; the Queen-Mother had married Angus, at a private ceremony conducted by a Douglas priest in her own quarters of the castle. It was only eleven months since the late King's death.

If the Chancellor and those close to him were privately elated, the nation at large was scandalised. That Margaret should have esteemed their beloved monarch so little as to marry again so soon was shame; and to one so doubtful in his allegiance added to the disgrace.

Archibald Douglas had been sufficiently arrogant before; now he became insufferable.

Archbishop Beaton was not long, of course, in informing Margaret officially that, under the terms of her late husband's testimony, endorsed by the Regency and Privy Councils, she could no longer retain the custody of the young King, which now fell to the Regency Council. Since that Council included the Earl of Angus, and likewise the Lord Home, the situation was less than clear-cut however, especially with Bishop Elphinstone so ill. It seemed probable that he would not live much longer—nor wanted to—in which event much would depend on the mercurial and unreliable Arran's vote in the then five-man Council. But any tentative suggestion that a new member might be added was countered by Arran himself, who perceived his strong position, and by Home, if not by Angus who suggested that his uncle, Gavin Douglas, would be the best choice. So there was stalemate.

The new situation did somewhat improve David Lindsay's position, however, for, trusted by the prelates, he was placed more firmly in charge of young James, indeed given the new title of the King's Master Usher. Abbot John, also, was made full tutor, Gavin Dunbar's position being left vague.

All this, to be sure, made little difference to the young men's life in Stirling citadel looking after their royal charge. Undoubtedly David felt the constrictions of it to be more grievous than did the Abbot, being of a more restless temperament and energetic nature. No amount of sliding down hillsides on cows' skulls—which had become Jamie's favourite pastime—acting horse, with the monarch on his shoulders as knight, playing bowls, quoits and the like, sufficiently used up that energy; and much as he approved of his small ward, he was constantly seeking opportunity for missions which would get him away from Stirling for brief spells at least. De la Bastie was his principal hope in this respect, but came up with nothing effectual meantime.

William Elphinstone died in October, praising God that he was on his way to better things at last, but bewailing the state in which he had to leave his native land and bequeathing heartfelt advice—never to trust any of the Tudors, and to try to reform Holy Church before it was too late. This last was the gist of his final bedside interview with David Lindsay, clutching his wrist with a claw-like hand, voice only a whisper but an urgent one. The Church had grown shamefully decadent and was destroying itself—yet it could and should be the strongest influence in the land. He, one of its shepherds, had failed it, God forgive him, too occupied with affairs of state, man's business instead of God's. But Davie—he had been given the gift of words. Use it. Words could change the world more surely than the sword, although they had the same letters. Use them to show Holy Church its follies. Folk would often heed a poet when they would not heed a preacher. Christ's Church must be saved . . .

David, no churchman, was troubled by this charge, not seeing what *he* could do about it. He discussed the matter with John Inglis, who himself was something of a symbol of the church's decadence, appointed Abbot by influence at an early age with no responsibilities other than to pay out of the abbey revenues a sub-prior to manage the monastic affairs for him. John thought that the recent battle for the archbishopric of St Andrews would make a dramatic piece—but might not gain the approval of the winner, Primate Forman. Perhaps something less controversial? What about the sale of pardons? A poem about a pardoner— scope for eloquence there, surely? Or one of multiple benefices? David acknowledged the possibilities but wondered as to both popularity and effectiveness. What would the Chancellor say, for instance? How many benefices did *he* hold?

Scotland mourned a great and good man whom it could ill afford to lose.

Lord Lindsay returned from Denmark, empty-handed.

What with one thing and another, that Yuletide was little more joyful than the last.

Nevertheless, in its aftermath it proved to have its compensations, even death revealing a brighter side. For on the last day of the year, another elderly actor on the scene made a final bow—Louis the Twelfth of France—to be succeeded by his nephew and son-in-law Francis the First, aged only twenty. And this young man made a very different monarch from his uncle, as was quickly proved. He sought to reverse the French policy of war with the Empire and the Vatican, which meant that Henry of England was not so important to him; and he saw the alliance with Scotland as worth maintaining. To this end he was prepared to allow his Lord High Admiral, Albany, to leave France at last.

So, when the winter's storms were past, the Regent-elect would sail.

There was other interesting news, belated in its arrival in Scotland, but perhaps with some significance. King Henry, at Tournai, was displeased over his sister's remarriage—mainly, it seemed, because she had not sought his permission, but also in that her new spouse was non-royal and a pensioner of his own.

It seemed that the tide of events could ebb as well as flow.

7

Tides do more than ebb and flow, however. They can storm
and flood and divide. The news that Albany would be there
to govern them before long had other effect on some than
hope and satisfaction. On James Hamilton, Earl of Arran,
in especial. It seemed that, by this time, the Lord Admiral
had convinced himself that his rival would in fact never
be allowed to leave France, and with the Queen-Mother's
marriage folly, the way was all but clear for his own
assumption of the regency. The death of Louis, and the new
French attitude, altered all; and Arran recognised that he
would have to act, and act fast, if he was to forestall Albany
and grasp the supreme power in Scotland. And act he did.

In a surprise attack, in conjunction with the Earls of
Lennox and Glencairn, he took the great castle fortress of
Dumbarton, which dominated Scotland's main west-coast
port and the Clyde estuary, ejecting the governor Lord
Erskine whom, as a Queen-Mother's man, he claimed was
not to be trusted. The remaining ships which Arran had
brought back from France were still anchored at Dumbarton;
and the great Hamilton territories, of course, lay not far to
the south.

On word of this extraordinary development reaching
Stirling, Angus took it as a declaration of war on himself—
which to some extent it undoubtedly was—and stormed off
westwards with such force as he could muster, including
much of the castle's garrison, calling for more Douglas
support to follow on. Suddenly it was civil war.

Chancellor Beaton and his associates were worried and
wrathful, but were scarcely in a position to take any very
effective action themselves. They could not put large bodies
of armed retainers in the field to bring these warring nobles
to heel, as they would have wished; and the fact that the
opponents were both on the Regency Council made it all
the more difficult. Another question was—what would

Lord Home, the third of the five, do now? If, as they feared, he joined Angus, then there would be only the two prelates left in the Council not involved—or, put another way, three fifths of the Council would be at war with each other. It was a dire situation. Whichever side might win in this struggle for supremacy, the lawful and constitutional authority, or what was left of it, was almost bound to suffer.

The Lords Lindsay, Fleming, young Borthwick, and others considered still loyal, were sent off urgently to raise such numbers of men as they could as a possible counter-balancing force.

It was three days after Angus had left that David, taking his charge, now nearly three years old, on his shoulders to the hurly-hackit, was halted by a considerable clamour, shouting and clatter of hooves from the direction of the castle gatehouse and outer bailey. Interested, he turned his steps towards the parapet-walk of the East Battery which overlooked the gateway, drawbridge and tourney ground.

There was plenty to see. The entire approach area was full of mounted men with banners and pennons, sun gleaming on the steel of armour and weaponry. Horsemen at the front of all this throng were streaming in over the drawbridge and under the portcullis, hooves drumming on the bridge tim-bers; but as fast as the numbers thinned at this end, they were made up for by new riders coming up out of the narrow streets of the climbing town. There were many hundreds involved, clearly.

Young James clapped his hands at all the colour and stir. David was eyeing the colours too, urgently, noting that there was no sign of the blue chief and red heart of Douglas, but plenty of the red and white of Hamilton on display. But almost more interesting was the scattering of the white lion on green of Home amongst them, along with Cunninghame of Glencairn and Lennox. It rather looked as though Lord Home had made a different choice from that anticipated.

David hurried down the twisting stairways to the inner bailey, now packed with the newcomers and their stamping, steaming horses, mud-spattered and foam-flecked. These beasts had been ridden far and fast. There were larger banners here, those of the lords themselves. David would have lowered the child from his shoulders but Jamie beat on his

Procurator's bare head to emphasise imperiously that he wanted to stay where he was, to see all from a height.

The leaders of this invasion were obviously inside the Chapel Royal, which opened off this inner bailey. David pushed his way through to the doorway, guarded as it was by sentries with drawn swords. He continued to advance, despite the glares and threatening gestures of the guards—after all, who had more right to enter the Chapel Royal than the child on his back?

"The King's Grace!" he said authoritatively, and they let him through, if doubtfully.

Inside, the scene was dramatic. Arran, Home, Lennox, Glencairn and other lords, in full or half armour, stood at the transept confronting two other and smaller groups. One consisted of the Queen-Mother, Gavin Douglas, the Lady Erskine and one or two others of the court; the second of the Chancellor, the Bishops of Galloway and Moray and a couple of secretaries.

Arran was speaking. ". . . and I tell you again, this misrule, indeed lack of rule, cannot go on. I will not permit it to go on. The land is without any true governance. It is time and past time that governance was restored. *I* shall restore it."

"The Duke of Albany should be here within weeks," Beaton said. "*He* is the choice of parliament . . ."

"We have been hearing that for a year and more! The nation cannot wait for Albany. We require governance now, not some day."

"Why wait until now to use force, my lord?" the Chancellor insisted. "Now, when Albany has been given permission to come, and but awaits weather and tide?"

"Because Scotland cannot wait on the whim of the King of France! Because I do not believe that Albany *wishes* to come! Because Angus has wed the King's mother and the realm is about to be grasped by Douglas! And worse—King Henry has ordered him to carry our young liege-lord, and his brother, over the Border into England, with their mother . . ."

"That is a lie, James Hamilton!" the Queen-Mother said.

"It is no lie. We have it on the best authority." Arran's glance flickered over to Home. "Your husband, Countess of Angus, has not attempted it yet only because, he writes, that it is too dangerous, lady."

"Address me as Your Grace, or not at all, my lord!"

"As to your style, lady—you should have considered that before you wed Angus!"

"Where *is* my lord of Angus?" Beaton demanded.

Arran whinnied a laugh. "Fleeing for his life—probably for the Border! We taught him and his precious Douglases a lesson! In the Pass of Aberfoyle, when he thought to approach Dumbarton. Save for this lady's feelings, I would say that he was fortunate to escape with his life, if undeserving!"

There were exclamations at that—in which Jamie Stewart took the opportunity to join in, with chuckling laughter; which, of course, had the effect of turning all heads towards where David stood with the child still on his shoulders.

For a moment or two there was an uncertain pause. Then Arran flourished a half-mocking bow, and the other lords followed suit. "Your Grace!" he said.

Embarrassed, David put the boy down—who immediately clamoured to be taken up again, where he could survey all so much better.

"I do not believe you, James Hamilton!" the Queen-Mother announced coldly, ignoring her son's presence. "Douglas is not so easily vanquished! You lie, in this, as in all! Now—I have suffered sufficient of your company," and she turned, for the vestry door.

"I fear that you must needs suffer more of it, Countess," he told her, smiling thinly. "You are coming with me to Edinburgh Castle. And His Grace and his brother also. His Grace will be more secure there. From . . . ill-wishers. Yourself, likewise. We ride within the hour. I pray you, go prepare yourself."

There was a stunned silence in the church.

It was Beaton who recovered his voice first. "My lord— you cannot mean this! It is not to be thought of!"

"We ride within the hour," Arran repeated. "And they ride with us. See to it."

"Are you crazed, man? You cannot do this. I will not permit it. As Chancellor of this kingdom. And senior on the Regency Council."

"You cannot stop me, clerk! My men control this Stirling. The Regency Council has outlived its authority."

"This is treason, against the King's Grace!"

"Not so. We but take His Grace to safety. Here, where Douglas comes and goes at will, is far from safe. Edinburgh *I* control."

"I will not go with you, fool!" Margaret exclaimed.

"You needs must, Countess. Come—or be taken! For nothing is more sure than that you go to Edinburgh this day."

"You, my lord of Home—*you* cannot consent to this, this outrage?" Beaton demanded.

"It is necessary. For the safety of the King and the realm," Home said shortly, his first contribution to the exchange.

"But you have no right . . ."

"One hour," Arran interrupted. "We have seven hundred men here. I do not wish to have to use them! This lady, His Grace and the infant—these only." The Earl came over to David. "Give me the King," he ordered.

David looked over at the Chancellor, who shrugged helplessly. "His Grace will be better with me, my lord . . .

"He will be very well *without* you, sirrah! Come to me, Sire."

James clung to David, and yelled.

"I assure you, my lord, that you will have a deal less trouble if you leave him in my care." David, surrounded by armed men, could by no means resist; but delay *might* achieve something.

Arran, with no desire to look foolish trying to pacify a screaming, frightened child, nodded. "Very well. Have him at the gatehouse, ready to ride, within the hour. Barncluith—go with him. See that all is in order." And he pointed to the door.

An esquire in full armour, dirk in hand, came over to grasp David's arm and propel him and his charge, back on his shoulder, towards the door, beckoning two men-at-arms to accompany them.

Thus escorted they went back to their own quarters, where an unbelieving Abbot John had to be convinced that it was not all some game. Then they gathered and packed a selection of the boy's clothing and gear. There did not seem to be anything else that they could do.

James scowled at the intruders and would not let go of David.

Presently a servitor came for Gavin Dunbar, as usual closeted in his own chamber, requiring him to attend on the Queen-Mother forthwith. It looked as though he it was who had been selected to accompany the royal family to Edinburgh.

When, in due course, they took James to the outer bailey and gatehouse, they found it as they had guessed; Dunbar was to go with the King, and they were to stay. Archbishop Beaton was there, and agreed that there was nothing that they could do meantime but accept the situation. He would never have thought that Arran was capable of this. He wondered whether Home had put him up to it? In which case, had Home's assumed alliance with Douglas collapsed? And did he remain, possibly, in Henry's pay? It was all complicated and confusing. Had all their suspicions been mistaken? Or was Home playing some very deep game indeed?

David ventured the opinion that Home had infinitely keener wits than either Arran or Angus, and therefore he was more likely to use them than they him.

Whatever the answer was, they certainly did not discover it that day, with Home keeping himself very much in the background and Arran very much in charge—and scarcely to be questioned. When the Queen-Mother delayed her arrival, there was an angry scene, with men sent to fetch her without further procrastination, in whatever state she was. Brought in furious protest, with the Lady Erskine carrying the new baby, also Gavin Dunbar looking more than usually unhappy, there was another trying interlude when his mother took James from David and handed him over to Dunbar, amidst shouts and pummellings. This undignified proceeding was clearly unsuitable; and Arran, already impatient, all but bellowed an order to mount and depart, without any further leave-taking. The King of Scots was carried off, in a flood of tears, before a nervous poet-tutor, his young brother happily sleeping through all. Margaret Tudor rode off, set-faced, between guards.

Those left behind eyed each other, at a loss.

Some sort of action fell to be taken, but what, that would be in any way effective, was less than clear. It could be assumed that Angus would quickly recover from this set-back and gather his fullest Douglas strength to hit back. Whether that strength would be sufficient to capture the great fortress of Edinburgh Castle, repossess his wife and the royal children, was another matter. Anyway large-scale civil war seemed now certain. And Henry Tudor's attitude had to be considered. If Arran had thought it necessary to act thus before Albany could arrive, might not Henry think the same, and decide to invade first?

The Scots realm was in utter disarray, and all too aware of it.

Archbishop Forman, who had not been at Stirling for this encounter, was hurriedly sent for, from St Andrews. Whether the archbishops, as representing the rump of the Regency Council, could command any worthwhile authority in the land remained to be seen—after all, Arran and Home together could make an equal claim, and had vast numbers of armed men to back it. Beaton was Chancellor and Forman Primate of Holy Church; but Arran was fourth in succession to the throne and Home was Chamberlain and Warden of the Marches.

David was summoned to the Chancellor's quarters the day after the Primate arrived. He found there the two archbishops and the Sieur de la Bastie.

"Lindsay—come, sit," Beaton said. "We have work for you. With the Seigneur, here. We have got to act swiftly, where we can. Not a great deal is open to us, as you know. But we could, perhaps, take and hold Dunbar Castle. And it is important, and vitally placed, as you also know."

Antoine gestured. "It is strong. But I believe that it could be taken."

David sat and said nothing.

"It is a royal castle, although Douglas-held meantime," the Chancellor went on. "We have reliable word that Angus is mustering all his power, and his allies' power, to defeat Arran. Mustering in Douglasdale, in Lanarkshire. Presumably to attack Arran's main seat and base of Hamilton, in Clydesdale. No doubt in order to draw Arran's strength away from Edinburgh, so that he, Angus, can make a swift dash eastwards and take Edinburgh Castle and so recapture the Queen-Mother and her children. So we assess the situation. Huntly and his Gordons and the Lord Drummond and his Strathearn hosts have already come out in his favour and are marching south. It will be surprising if Angus neglects fully to use his *own* people, such as those under his uncle at Dunbar Castle."

It was not for David, with de la Bastie present, to stress how strongly sited was Dunbar, even if its garrison should be reduced.

"Dunbar, in our hands, would serve two ends—even three—for it is indeed one of the keys of the kingdom, well-named. It would be a blow to Angus. It would be a threat to Home, on the very edge of his territories. And it could menace any English advance by the coastal route from Berwick—as it has done so often in the past. Dunbar should be ours."

"No doubt, my lord. But because it is so close to Home land, and none are more warlike than the Home moss-troopers, even if we can surprise and take it, many men will be required to *hold* it. Or it will again be surprised and taken from us."

"Think you that we do not know that, young man!" Archbishop Forman said. "Your Lindsay levies should be sufficient for that, surely."

"Yes—that is it," Beaton went on. "The Lord Lindsay is already sent to gather the Lindsay strength in Lothian. His is probably the most strong force that we can raise in those parts. So the Seigneur, here, and yourself, will go to the Byres, and use that force which he has gathered to assail, take and hold Dunbar Castle."

Antoine and David exchanged glances. "We can attempt it, to be sure," the former said.

"It is important. One of the most useful things that we could do, without any large army," Forman emphasised.

"It is perhaps the only move that we can make at this stage to warn and threaten Home," Beaton agreed. "And that is vital."

"Have you learned, or come to any understanding, my lords, as to what the Lord Home is at?" David wondered. "Why he seems to have turned against the alliance with Angus? And appears to be working against King Henry now, when before we thought otherwise?"

"It is hard to tell," the Chancellor admitted. "But we see the change as only happening since two matters have become known—Albany's coming and Henry's disapproval of his

104

sister's new marriage, and therefore his disapproval of Angus. If it was indeed these that changed Home, then it could mean that he was most probably working for Henry."

"But—this of taking the Queen-Mother and the King to Edinburgh? That does not look like aiding England!"

"Think you not? I reckon that it could be a deal easier to win the King and his mother out of Edinburgh Castle than out of Stirling here. Especially for the Homes. And the road mostly in Home country thereafter all the way to the Border!"

"You mean . . . ?"

"I mean that if I was James Hamilton, I would be watching my partner Alexander Home with an eagle's eye! Especially if Arran was to have to dash off to defend Hamilton, and left Home in charge at Edinburgh!"

"Lord . . . !"

"That is one reason why haste is advisable for this of Dunbar Castle. Dunbar is on that quickest and best route from Edinburgh to the Border. So—you will ride tomorrow, my friends. And we shall send urgent word to Albany to hasten his coming, by all means . . ."

Whether in fact all this speculation as to Lord Home's duplicity and intentions had any basis in fact, and urgency of the essence, it was good to get away from Stirling and to come to Garleton and the Byres again, Antoine almost as appreciative as was David—and even more effusively received. Unfortunately they were unable to spend as much time threat, with their respective female attractions, as they had anticipated and desired, for it turned out that the Lord Lindsay had found it more convenient to muster the Lindsay strength, such as it was after the losses of Flodden, at the much larger castle of Luffness on the shores of Aberlady Bay some three miles to the north. David was a little surprised at this, for the castle of Kilspindie, Greysteel's establishment, sat just on the other side of the great bay from Luffness, too near for comfort in the circumstances. But Kate declared that her father had ascertained that Greysteel himself and practically all his men from Kilspindie had gone to join the Earl of Angus's army in Douglasdale, so that there would be no threat from that quarter—which made a hopeful indication for Dunbar's present situation.

Kate indeed rode with them the next morning down to Luffness, to David's satisfaction. They found the place in a great stir, with some ninety men gathered there, in addition to its own garrison, more of a holiday atmosphere prevailing than anything more warlike since nobody knew quite for what they were assembling and it was all a welcome change from the monotony of the daily grind. Luffness Castle had been the first Lindsay property in Lothian, acquired by marriage with a Dunbar heiress in the late twelfth century, and formed a most impressive stronghold, with tall twenty-foot-high curtain walls, topped by parapet-walks forming a square with four-hundred-yard sides, protected by circular angle towers at each corner, all behind a deep water-filled moat. Great drum towers for the drawbridge and portcullis faced the bay, and a massive central keep rose in the midst. It had two castletons or retainers' hamlets, one to the south known as Luffnaraw and one to the east, on the bay shore, somewhat grandiloquently called the port of Luffness although in reality only a small fishing haven. It also had a Carmelite monastery and church to the south-west; and nearer Aberlady village, suitably separated from the monks' establishment, a nunnery. All in all, a fine place. Its superiority belonged to the Earls of Crawford, chiefs of all the Lindsays; but now these were grown so great, with properties all over Scotland, that they but seldom came to Luffness, which had long been left in the care of hereditary keepers called Bickerton but who themselves had fairly recently been superseded by a branch of the house of Hepburn.

They found Lord Lindsay with the present keeper, Sir Adam Hepburn, superintending the conversion of part of the castle's mill premises and brewhouse at Luffnaraw into extra barracks accommodation for the assembling man-power. The Lord Patrick was in two minds when he heard of the newcomers' mission: glad enough of some definite action to put the men to, who were getting somewhat out-of-hand in their mustered idleness; but at the same time concerned that they should be expected to tackle, all un-trained as they were, so ambitious a task as trying to take Dunbar Castle. If such concern likewise preoccupied de la Bastie, as seemed probable, he did not show it but main-tained a confident front. And, at least, with Greysteel's departure for Lanarkshire with his Kilspindie men to go by, it looked hopeful that his brother, Sir George Douglas, would have similarly weakened the Dunbar garrison.

Antoine emphasised the need for haste and asked how soon he could march, with the maximum numbers of men? Lord Patrick said that there was a sizeable contingent to come across from Lindsay lands in Fife, by boat, any day; but that, anyway, they could not all be armed and equipped for the march before three or four days more, at least. The Frenchman, a stranger on foreign soil as he was, demonstrated his authority of command, as well as that of the Chancellor's orders, by declaring courteously but firmly that that would not serve, that the situation would not allow them so much time. They must move the following night. Dunbar was only fifteen miles away. They could do it in a night march and be in a position to attack at first-light in the morning, with maximum surprise. Lindsay looked doubtful but did not assert that it was impossible.

In the meantime, Antoine went on, David should make openly, alone, for Dunbar. He could go again as cattle dealer and fish buyer. He was known as such there. Learn all he could, spy out the situation at the castle. Then meet the attackers outside the town just before dawn with his information. This could be of great value.

It at least was refreshing to have someone in charge who so knew his own mind.

So David took Kate home, bade goodbye and was instructed on how to take care of himself. Then he changed his clothing, to fit his new merchantly role, and set out for Dunbar.

He met with no problems en route and arrived at the town in the late afternoon, making his way to the same harbourside hostelry which they had used before. He was accepted there without question, remembered by some of the habitués.

It did not demand a great deal of contrivance to bring the talk round to the purchase of fish and the suggestion that in fact the castle garrison might be in a position to sell quantities more cheaply than the fishermen themselves, on account of their levy on catches. This brought forth the anticipated flood of protests and objections. And when he innocently proposed a visit to the castle to check on present terms, he was more blithely told that there was little point in that, for scarcely anybody was left in the place, and nobody of any authority. All were gone on some Douglas ploy in the west, some muster—no doubt to the sorrow of honest folk. There would be nobody to talk to about fish prices.

David did not indicate how glad he was to have this information. But he did ask if the fish levy was being maintained in these circumstances? To be answered bitterly that it was, that the extortioners were still insisting on the castle's full quantity, otherwise they would not lift the boom to allow the fishing boats into the harbour—although what the handful of men did with all the fish only the Devil knew, who looked after them!

This general animosity towards the garrison sparked off an idea in David's mind. When did the boats tend to come in from their fishing, he wondered? Was there a normal time of day for the coming and going? He was told that, at this time of year, there were two favoured times, some fishermen preferring to go out at dawn and return at midday, others to sail at midday and come back at nightfall. The castle people were not prepared to raise and lower their boom across the harbour mouth just whenever it suited the fishermen.

So that meant that a number of craft could be coming in, with their catches, and others going out, empty, at about the same time, at midday? And where were the main fishing grounds? That depended on the weather and the season, he was informed; but at present the herring, the favoured crop, were most readily caught about three miles out, on a stretch running east of the Craig of Bass where the deep water suddenly shallowed to the coastal shelf.

Mulling over all this with his ale, David perceived opportunity. A change of plan was called for. So presently, making excuse that he could use the evening to visit a nearby farmer on a cattle buying project, he went out into the breezy dark, saddled his horse again and rode out of town—not to any local farmery but back north-westwards as he had come. He aimed to intercept Antoine and the Lindsay strength earlier than arranged.

The darkness posed something of a problem, of course, even though he knew the roads hereabouts very well. The difficulty was that he did not know which route his friends would choose to take from Luffness, for marching men. There were three or four possibles. However, all must converge at one point, where the outflow of the River Tyne could be forded by men on foot, at the head of Belhaven Bay. This was some four miles west of Dunbar. He would wait for them there—and pray that they would not be overlong delayed.

It was strange to sit there alone in the chilly, windy darkness, listening to the steady boom of the breakers on the distant sand-bar of the bay, the splash and tinkle of nearer water, the creak and sigh of the trees, the calling of the night birds and the soft horse noises, hour after hour. He got cold, of course, and every now and again had to exercise himself to regain warmth. The quiet peace of it all was in such notable contrast with what was intended.

Eventually, despite the chill, he fell asleep—to waken with a start, cramped and stiff, to the stir, a vibration on the night air rather than any actual sound. He had never experienced this before but recognised nevertheless that it was the quiet approach of a large body of men deliberately being as silent as they could, under strict control. He rose and waded the ford to meet them.

Antoine and the Lord Patrick marched at the head of a fair-sized column, with a local man to act as guide. They were surprised that he had come thus far to meet them.

"I have come because we should change our plans," he announced. "I believe that we can do better than any surprise assault."

Whilst the men were fording the Tyne, in some disarray, he told the leaders what he had learned. "This of the fishing boats," he elaborated. "If we could put men on three or four boats, and looking like fishermen, when they come to hand over their levy of fish to the castle, they could seek to win inside with the fish. There are not many men left in the place. And most would not be manning this boom, surely . . ."

"But how to get our men into the boats? And the fish?" the Lord Patrick demanded. "Talk sense, Davie!"

"See you—this is Belhaven Bay. There is a small fishing village at Belhaven itself. We go there, take over a few of *their* boats. They will not be setting off to fish until dawn, no doubt. We could sail out to the fishing grounds east of the Craig of Bass. The Dunbar boats will be there, soon after sun-up. The Dunbar men hate the castle and the fish levy.

We can use that hate. Get them to work with us. Sail back
with them and their catch."

"*Parbleu*—he has it!" Antoine exclaimed. "This could
serve us well. How many men could we use in it?"

"Not many. But then, we would not require many, I
think. It will depend on the boats. How many there are at
Belhaven. And how many Dunbar craft fishing off the
Bass. There are five or six fishers to each boat, I learned. We
could perhaps put four of our men into each Dunbar boat, at
sea, dressed as fishers . . ."

"So we cannot expect to use more than a score of men?"

"They say that there are no more than a handful in the
castle, now. I could not ask for numbers."

"I say that it is too risky," the Lord Patrick said. "If it
fails, as it well may, then the garrison is warned."

"Then we are no worse off. It would mean a delay in any
land assault, yes, if that was to be essayed at first light.
Unless it could be done at the same time? But that would be
difficult to ensure, almost impossible . . ."

"No—we shall try this of the boats," de la Bastie decided.
"But we have one hundred and twenty men here. What to
do with the others meantime?"

"There is much woodland behind Dunbar. At Eweford
and Lochend. You know it, my lord? Barely a mile from the
town. Sufficient to hide our people during the day. If this of
the boats fails, then we can rejoin the others at Eweford and
put in the dawn assault next morning."

"My friend—you have used your head well!" Antoine
commended. "It is worth the trial. How far to this
Belhaven?"

"Three miles—less. An hour's march."

Round the head of the shallow sandy bay they went, to
ford the Beil Water at West Barns of Beil and come to the
village of Belhaven half a mile further. It still lacked a couple
of hours to dawn and the place slept peacefully. It was no
part of their intention to create an outcry, and they marched
their men, still silently, straight to the little harbour. There
they counted seven fishing craft as well as a number of
smaller boats.

There were perhaps a score of cothouses lining a single
narrow street; but there was also a group of hovels close
to the harbour itself, with drying nets draped from poles

outside. Whichever the others were, these seemed certain to be fishermen's houses. David, with Antoine and Lord Patrick, went to knock on doors.

The first produced an alarmed-looking, elderly man, naked from his bed. Seeking to sound both soothing and authoritative at once, David announced that this was the Lord Lindsay of the Byres and that they came in the name of the King and the Regency Council. They required his help.

Struck dumb, the man stared.

"You are a fisherman? We require fishing boats. We shall pay well for their use. To take some of our men out to the fishing grounds. You have a boat?"

"Yes, Yes, lord. But . . ."

"Who else have boats? Which houses?"

"Many, lord. But . . ."

"Put on some clothes. Quickly. We have need of haste. Show us these other houses."

"Do not gawp there, man!" Lord Patrick barked. "We have not got all night!"

It took longer than they would have wished, but presently they had the owners of five of the fishing craft assembled, and approximately clad, however bewildered, along with sundry other men, and explained to them what was required. If there was no enthusiasm, there was no actual opposition either. Clearly what was wished of them would pay a deal better than any day's fishing.

It was agreed that five of the Lindsay men should sail in each of five boats, with the owner and one other oarsman. They would borrow fisherman's clothing and be taken out to the Bass area, and hope there to be transhipped to Dunbar boats. If by any chance this last was not possible, then they would themselves sail for Dunbar at midday and hope that the castle garrison would be as eager for their fish as that of the local craft.

The Belhaven folk had no love for the Douglases and were prepared to co-operate, for suitable reward.

By the time that all this was arranged, it was time to sail. Antoine elected to go with the boat party and the Lord Patrick was left in charge of the main body, to proceed to Eweford. In a scarlet and gold sunrise they pulled out of Belhaven harbour, David and Antoine advisedly in the same boat.

111

They had to go north by west for some five miles to reach the fishing grounds, and with a quite stiff westerly breeze and choppy sea the square brown sail was of little use to them. So it was a question of rowing nearly all the way. The passengers took their turn at the oars, if not all expertly, the five boats keeping fairly close together.

They made slow progress and, save for the rowers, it was very cold out there on the water. Presently other boats appeared. Although they all seemed alike to David, the fishermen knew where each came from, Dunbar, North Berwick, Skateraw, Canty Bay or Peffermouth. They kept close to those from Dunbar, of which there appeared to be seven.

When it came to the fishing the local boats acted as one unit, trawling the nets between them for the herring shoals. Long lines, with hooks baited with mussels, were also put out, the boats kept moving slowly with just a couple of oars.

David was impatient to approach the Dunbar men, but Antoine said to wait for a while. They must have fish caught, that was essential. So they fished and drifted and rowed, as the sun rose higher in the sky. Indeed, the passengers were apt to sleep, after their busy night.

After the first up-drawing of the nets, and quite a fair haul of herring, before continuing they rowed over to the nearest group of Dunbar boats, hailing them. David was a little concerned that he might be recognised as the erstwhile cattle dealer; but he saw none that he knew amongst the Dunbar fishermen.

Within easy shouting distance, he explained that he was speaking for the Lord Lindsay and the Regency Council. They intended to take Dunbar Castle back from the Douglases and into the King's hands, as was right and proper. They sought the fisherfolk's help, as leal subjects. And they could promise that when the castle was in leal hands again, there would be no more levies on the Dunbar fishermen.

As expected, this produced wary but no very positive reaction, although the last part had some effect.

David went on to explain what was required. The interest quickened. And when the matter of generous payment was added, he had their attention.

But what if the assault failed, lord, he was asked? What would happen to *them*, the Dunbar men who had helped in it?

Why should it fail, with so few in the castle? But if by mischance it did, they could always say that they had been forced to it at swordpoint.

That was accepted. David asked these men to pass on the word to the other Dunbar craft, taking their agreement as established.

So, after another hour or so's trawling with the nets, the assault party transferred, not without some near-mishaps, to the seven Dunbar boats, after suitable rewards to their Belhaven friends. Then, with a reasonable catch, and the good wishes of the beneficiaries, they set off for Dunbar.

Now the breeze was astern and they could dispense with the oars—which was welcome, with the boats overloaded. After all the waiting and inaction the party evinced a tension now. David's worry was that the extra men in each boat might arouse suspicions in the garrison.

It took barely an hour to run back to Dunbar. And there, keyed-up as they were, they had to linger, under the very castle walls, until the people therein deigned to notice them and lift the massive boom of timbers and chains which barred the entrance. Fretting, they sat in the swaying craft, waiting.

However, the delay at least revealed, presently, that only three men appeared to be on duty to deal with the fish levy, two to crank the great handle of the pulley device which creakingly raised the heavy boom, the other to lower a couple of rope-ladders from the castle walling down to water level. Three only—never had David hoped for anything so fortunate as this.

They let the first boat pull in without making any untoward move. The system appeared to be for some of the fishermen to climb up one ladder with a sample of their catch, in wickerwork baskets, for the garrison to pick their choice. Then they returned down the second ladder whilst others were climbing the first.

Exchanging glances, David and Antoine signed for their own craft to move in to the ladder as the first boat was edging away. Grabbing one of the baskets, David made a somewhat unhandy job of clambering up the swinging

113

contrivance with it. Antoine waited until he was almost up before following.

On the masonry platform David put down his load, wordless, in front of the three men-at-arms. As these stooped, to select the best fish, he looked around him, scarcely able to believe that he could have gained entry to this almost impregnable stronghold so easily. He took in the layout of this part of the strung-out castle. Nobody else was to be seen save these three on fish duty—until Antoine appeared with his basket.

Almost simultaneously one of their men came up the second ladder, quickly followed by another. Antoine threw his basket down beside David's and, catching the other's eye, gave a quick nod.

Reaching inside their borrowed fishermen's smocks, they gripped their dirk-hilts, to wait until all three of the garrison men were stooped over the catches; then, whipping out their weapons, they leapt, to bend and press cold steel to the backs of two red necks.

Startled, the trio straightened up, gasping. The third man reached for his own dagger, but before he could draw it, one of the Lindsay party from the second ladder hurled himself upon him, pinioning his arms. David and Antoine transferred their dirk-points to the front of their victims' throats, and their fourth man disarmed all three.

They stared at each other, almost laughing. In less time than it takes to tell they had achieved an entry, with only four men and not a drop of blood shed.

Signalling for the others to come up, they had to decide how to proceed from here. From their previous visit they had a fair idea as to the plan of the castle, with its various towers and bartizans based on rock stacks and linked by covered bridges and corridors. But they could not know where the rest of the garrison was likely to be found.

De la Bastie had no scruples about methods of finding out. Sizing up the three captives, he chose the weakest looking and flourished his dirktip under the man's chin, pricking it slightly to draw blood.

"Where are the others of your people?" he demanded. "Tell us, if you value your wretched life!"

The other goggled, spluttering, but said nothing.

A second and deeper prick loosened his tongue. He

pointed and gabbled, but so incoherently that the Frenchman was mystified. David suggested that the man should lead them, instead of directing, and Antoine agreed. The other two were tied up and left in the care of some of the fishermen. Others of the boats' crews elected to come on with the two dozen attackers. Pushing their unhappy guide before them, the quite large party set out, dirks, daggers and a variety of improvised weapons in hand.

They went through two tower basements and along two corridors before the prisoner halted and pointed dumbly to a closed door before them. Clearly he did not want to be first through that doorway. Nodding, Antoine gestured the man back, then he and David moved forward quietly. They could hear the murmur of voices from beyond the door.

Waiting until his party were massed close behind him, Antoine raised his hand, flung wide the door, and led the way in at a bound.

The chamber was a vaulted dining hall and about a dozen men lounged about a long table littered with platters and beakers, in every attitude of relaxation, some head on arms, apparently asleep.

They had no chance, of course, outnumbered, in the face of armed and determined intruders. Some attempted resistance but most were simply overwhelmed where they sat. It was all over in moments.

Obviously this was the main residential garrison; but there would almost certainly be a guard on the main gate and drawbridge. So, taking half their strength, Antoine and David made their way in that direction, this part of the castle being familiar to them. They found three men in the gatehouse, very much at ease, the drawbridge up and no access from the land possible. These were so surprised to be assailed from within that they put up no show of opposition.

Dunbar Castle was in the hands of the realm's lawful representatives again, in a coup which could have had few parallels for speed and lack of fighting. David's praises resounded.

Soon they had the drawbridge lowered and David was on his way, on foot necessarily, to Eweford and Lochend, to inform the main body that they could come out of hiding and ride openly and freely to their objective. Perhaps he crowed a little.

8

They sent couriers post-haste to Stirling to inform of the situation. But after two or three days it was decided that David himself should go there, to find out the Chancellor's plans and to learn what went on on the wider scene. The Lord Patrick would accompany him as far as the Byres.

So they rode westwards, released. To David, for one, any fortress was just as tedious as another to be shut up in.

That evening, David lingered long at the Byres, being made a hero of, his protests weakening as time went on. It was late before he knocked up the gatehouse keeper at Garleton. At least there were no problems with Mirren, who was already in bed with his father.

In a long day's riding he made it to Stirling by next evening—and with the news he brought, was well received, his story having to be repeated again and again and, as happens, losing nothing in the telling. Inevitably it was suggested that he should make a poem out of it all.

He discovered that there had been no reports as yet of any major clash between the Douglases and the Hamiltons; but it was only a question of time. However, there was news from France. A courier had come with a letter for his uncle from David Beaton, to say that Albany was about to sail with a large following which would include Davie Beaton himself. Albany would bring back with him the remainder of the Scots fleet left in French ports by Arran, and ought to be arriving at Dumbarton in perhaps two weeks' time after receipt of this letter.

This development, it was confidently hoped, would change the entire situation. Another two weeks . . .

David was not to be subjected to any lengthy incarceration in the fortress on this occasion, for he was commanded to return whence he had come, to tell de la Bastie to remain at and hold Dunbar Castle with whatever garrison was necessary, but to send all the men that he could spare to the Lord

Lindsay, who was then to bring on his main strength west-wards. They were going to assemble as large a force as possible at Dumbarton to welcome Albany, since it was by no means certain that his coming would be unopposed. Lennox was holding Dumbarton Castle for Arran and might make matters difficult; and Angus could conceivably put in an attack likewise, although this was less likely in that area.

The new Regent was certainly not coming to any bed of roses.

Back the sixty-five miles to Dunbar, then, David rode, via the Byres—where he learned that the Lord Patrick was again at Luffness with his levies. So once more, with Kate, he proceeded thither—and lingered rather on the way. His relationship with Kate was progressing satisfactorily in one respect, less so in another. She was obviously fond of him and liked to be in his company; but there were inhibitions, mainly on his part. With any other young woman he would not have hesitated. He would have pressed his suit, made his intentions all too clear. But Kate he had looked on over the years as all but a little sister. She was still only sixteen and although she looked a woman now and sounded like a woman, he could not get over the feeling that she was really still only a child, not to be misused, endangered. So he was pulled this way and that, ever seeking her company, hard put to it to keep his hands off her, but always having to restrain himself, a man torn. Perhaps the tearing process did not leave the girl entirely unscathed either.

At Luffness they found that Lindsay had fully one hundred men gathered, some having come back from Dunbar where they were not required for garrison duty.

David proceeded south-eastwards, alone, for Dunbar. There the atmosphere, in town as in castle, was vastly different from heretofore, de la Bastie having already established good relations with the townsfolk. The drawbridge was down and David rode in to the salutations of the guards.

Antoine, surprised to see him back so soon, agreed that probably his garrison could be further pruned without danger. He seemed to be well settled in already, very much in command as captain of a fortress. He was glad to hear that Albany was on his way, although regretting that he himself was not to be at Dumbarton to greet him. There had been no troubles at Dunbar and no signs of any Douglas nor Home counter-measures.

So next day David marched slowly back westwards, at the head of thirty men-at-arms, the fifteen miles to Luffness. Lord Patrick had now managed to muster a total of one hundred and twenty, so that in fact one hundred and fifty set out on the long march across the waist of Scotland, not far off one hundred miles, to Dumbarton.

Going by Leith, Linlithgow, Falkirk, Denny and so into the Stirlingshire hills of Touch, Gargunnock, Kilsyth and Campsie, they crossed the watershed of the land, deliberately going by these unfrequented ways to avoid possible clashes with either Arran's or Angus's supporters. In five days of steady tramping, and in fortunately good weather conditions, they began to slant down towards the Western Sea, in all that time meeting with no opposition—one hundred and fifty men, of course, are not lightly to be opposed. But they saw no sign of hostilities nor destruction either; indeed it would have been easy to conclude that all talk of internecine strife and civil war was mere hysterical exaggeration. But admittedly this area was meantime not the location for any trial of strength.

Marching down into the Vale of Leven they began to meet with other bodies of armed men, large and small, all heading south to the Clyde. All were somewhat wary of each other—Colquhouns, Buchanans, MacGregors, Grahams, Drummonds—as well they might be, since most would be unsure as to which side in this present complicated conflict their various lords and chiefs would be on. This was the area known as the Lennox, and the Earl of Lennox it was who had assailed and taken over Dumbarton Castle from the Lord Erskine, Queen Margaret's friend. And Lennox was for Arran and the Hamiltons.

So the Lindsays followed the River Leven, flowing out of Loch Lomond, as wary as any, down towards Dumbarton itself.

But at the town and port, which huddled below the great conical castle rock, they found vast crowds and an almost holiday atmosphere. The Chancellor and Primate were already there, with a great concourse of nobles, churchmen and their retinues. Lennox had thought it judicious, in the circumstances, to issue forth from the castle in peace and at least seem to take part in the welcoming proceedings, although how he would behave when Albany arrived remained to be seen.

All in all it was a peculiar situation with, on the surface, everybody in convivial mood, waiting for the long looked for coming of the Regent who was to restore and reunite the young King's realm; whilst underneath all was tension, concern with what was likely to follow, wondering who was for whom, assessing of likely strength, debating as to who could be trusted and for how long. Even speculation as to what the Duke of Albany would be like. It was said that he was richer than any King of Scots, rode abroad with a court of two hundred, and could speak only French. How could such a man cope with Scotland and the Scots, in present circumstances?

For the look of things, the Earl of Lennox could scarcely deny the Chancellor of the realm, not to mention the Primate, quarters in Dumbarton Castle, which was of course a royal fortress, like Stirling, Edinburgh and Dunbar; so David Lindsay and his lordly kinsman found themselves in the odd position of being able to ride up to this powerful, enemy-held stronghold and gain admittance without question. Not their men, however; these were told in no uncertain terms that there was no room for men-at-arms. The town being full to overflowing, they had to quarter their people in nearby villages, as did others.

Fortunately, in view of the crowding and the underlying stresses, they did not have long to wait, for favourable winds and fine weather brought the French flotilla in unusually short time; and only two days after David's arrival, fishing boats brought the news that eight large vessels were beating up the Firth of Clyde past the Cloch Point and should make Dumbarton in a couple of hours. The excitement mounted.

When the white sails at length appeared, the castle cannon boomed out in salute and a host of small craft put out to escort the convoy into port. Folk thronged down to the harbour area.

The main jetty had been cleared for the principal ships, but it was not large enough to take them all. Two only came slowly in, furling sails, the rest lying off and dropping anchors. The crowds waited, expectant. There were no cheers. The Chancellor and the welcoming party stood at the pier head, dressed in their best.

However, their best was hardly good enough, when presently the \newcomers disembarked in a riot of colour, finery, even perfume wafted before them on the breeze. The first off the gangway, after the sailors had rigged it, was a brilliant figure, superbly handsome and dressed at the height of French fashion, a young man with a small pointed beard and curled hair.

"That is not Albany," the Chancellor said. "Albany is older."

"A papingo, whoever he is!" Archbishop Forman snorted. "These French—vanity of vanities!"

But when this vision came near to them, he hailed them in a good Scots voice. "Ha, Uncle! How good to see you! It is a long time."

"Lord—Davie!" the Chancellor exclaimed. "It's yourself! Sakes—I'd never ha' known you! By the Mass, you've changed!"

"Not for the worse, I hope? The years take their toll, they say—even of you, my lord!"

"H'r'mmm. You have brought Albany, then . . . ?"

"Why, yes. And a wheen more! For your delectation. My lords—your servant!" David Beaton flourished a bow.

Others were descending from the first ship, a chattering, laughing throng surrounding a stately individual of early middle years with a look of assured but somewhat depressed authority; a tall, elegant man with a slight stoop. He seemed to be eyeing all before him with resignation, if not disfavour.

David Beaton turned to wave this group onwards with a large gesture, smiling widely, clearly a man who got much enjoyment out of life. He sang out a flood of fluent French, *Monsieur le Duc* recurring frequently.

Albany came stalking up at the head of an ever-growing retinue of loquacious and overdressed courtiers, who made so much noise that young Beaton had to shout to effect the introduction to the Chancellor, Primate and sundry lords and bishops. Albany acknowledged their greetings gravely, with nods of the head but no words, David Beaton translating the welcoming phrases. It seemed to be a fact that the new Regent spoke no English, much less Scots, and the Chancellor's nephew was there in the role of interpreter.

120

David Lindsay marvelled that one whose father had been of pure Scots blood, indeed a son of the King of Scots, and who himself bore a notable Scots title and the surname of Stewart, should never have troubled to learn a little of the language—when, for instance, de la Bastie, pure French, had mastered it almost like a native. Most of the Scots nobility knew a little French fortunately, although generally more able to write it than to speak it, like David himself. But communication was clearly going to be difficult.

That language was not going to be the only difficulty was quickly apparent. The Frenchmen, now being reinforced by still larger numbers from the second ship, were not used to walking, it seemed, nor prepared to make a start otherwise on this occasion; and since the castle lay over half a mile from the harbour, and once reached, offered a steep climb up to the residential quarters, horses were now demanded, and were not immediately available. There were plenty of mounts in and around the town, of course, all the lords and lairds and their escorts having come on them, but these were stabled and tethered far and wide, and finding sufficient for a couple of hundred Frenchmen would take time. So an uneasy hiatus developed there at the pier head, with more and more French coming ashore in boats from the other ships, and conversation at a painful minimum. Davie Beaton appeared to find it all an excellent joke, but few others did. It made hardly an auspicious start.

David Lindsay was one of those sent off to find horses, and was glad to escape.

In the end, sufficient mounts were found to carry Albany and his more immediate entourage to the castle, with the Scots, including the two archbishops, walking alongside. Since there was neither room nor welcome for most of the newcomers in the fortress, the rest fell to be quartered in the town, overcrowded already as it was, so that much reallocation of accommodation was required, to the offence of the dispossessed, and less than appreciated by the visitors, who obviously thought it all much beneath them. David found himself involved in this invidious task also, and did not enjoy it.

Later, in the castle after the banquet for the guests, he was approached by David Beaton.

"Do I not remember you, from St Andrews?" he asked,

pleasantly. "Are you not Davie Lindsay? *You* have not changed so very much."

"No. But you have! Become the great man. Confidant of princes!"

"Scarce that. But one lives and learns, especially in France! You are at court, here?"

"I am, and I am not. I am the King's Procurator and Usher. But since the King is taken out of my care, by the Earl of Arran and the Lord Home, I am at something of a loose end. So my Lord Chancellor employs me on this and that."

"Oh, we will get young James back into your good keeping, never fear," Beaton declared with easy confidence. "This nonsense of Arran must be halted, and quickly. He is a weakling and only needs a firm hand. Home I do not know—but he sounds different."

"He *is* different, yes—a strange man. Devious. But clever, I think."

"Perhaps the wits behind Arran?"

"Perhaps. But I fear there is more to it than that. What he intends we know not. But he is a man to watch."

"There are too many of those in Scotland! We shall do more than watch them!"

At his so assured tone, David shook his head. "It will be none so easy. Dealing with the Earl of Angus, in especial. The Douglases are not so readily put down. We have made a start with Dunbar, but . . ."

"We shall divide the Black Douglases from the Red and so halve their power. De la Bastie—you have seen him?"

"Very much so. We have worked together. A fine man."

"He is. And an able soldier. I urged the Duke to send him. He could be very useful."

"Already he has been so. He now holds Dunbar Castle for the King."

"Dunbar, eh? Taken from the Douglases? Useful against the Homes. Aye, and against Tantallon itself. What of Fast? Fast and Colbrandspath Tower, both. Are they taken also?"

"No-o-o." David recognised that he must adjust his opinion of this confident character who clearly knew what he was talking about, and even after years in France remembered the lie of the land and its strategic importance.

"Tell me more of Home, and what he is at. This man to watch."

David informed the other of all he knew and what was suspected and conjectured about the Lord Home and the involved game he seemed to be playing, Beaton making shrewd comments. This developed into something of an inquisition on others of the players on the national stage. To even things up somewhat, David asked about Albany himself. What sort of man was he? This of speaking only French—did it imply lack of interest in Scotland? How strong a man was he? So much was expected of him; would he be able to achieve?

"He is a man it takes time to know. But able, strong of will but not of himself so strong. And with the hottest temper of any I know!"

"Lord! And this is the man who is to save Scotland?"

"He could do well enough, with the right folk to guide him!"

"Such as yourself?"

"Why, yes. And perhaps you?"

"I am hardly so ambitious."

"Nonsense, man! You, the King's guardian! When we get James back to your care, who more to effect? He who holds the King . . . !" He smiled. "What of James? Is he an interesting child? Sound in his wits and person? I have brought him a gift. A parrot."

"You have? A papingo? Apt!"

"How mean you—apt?"

"It was something that the Primate said. About Frenchmen and papingoes."

"Ah, I see. Popinjays! Perhaps Forman is right. But never forget that even parrots have strong beaks and can bite! So—we must get our young monarch back, and present him with the papingo."

"And how do you propose to do that?"

"By using the wits the good God has given us—how else?"

It did not take long for David to discover how justified young Beaton was in his authoritative assurance. With everything having to be translated between the Scots leadership and Albany, and the Chancellor his own uncle, Beaton was in a position to do a lot more than interpret—to adapt, suggest, advise and make his own contribution. And with wits sufficiently sharp, and obvious drive and ambition, he could not only influence but all but direct events.

One very prompt example of his abilities was in the matter of the Earl of Lennox. In a fashion, Lennox was their host here; but of course the fortress was in his hands unlawfully, his position equivocal to say the least. Using this situation in masterly fashion, David Beaton went about the business of transferring Lennox's allegiance from Arran to Albany, by seeming to assume that this was already the case and manoeuvring Lennox into the situation that it was accepted by all—and so, more or less, by Lennox himself. All said in the name of Albany, of course. He confided to David Lindsay that he thought it important not only to detach Lennox but to use him to bring over Arran himself. His cause had been much weakened by Albany's arrival undoubtedly, and being a weak man, he should be the more easily disheartened by desertion. Encourage a Douglas assault on him and his Hamiltons, therefore, by all means possible, and he would come over to Albany, nothing more sure. Then Home could be isolated, and they could deal with Douglas.

David marvelled, but was impressed. Beaton seemed to have formed a liking for him; and quite clearly his was the hand which was going to guide Albany—so that he was worth staying close to.

There was no point in remaining at Dumbarton. So in a couple of days, largely taken up with scouring the country-side for horses, a vast cavalcade set off eastwards for Edinburgh, to be followed, on foot, by what amounted to an army of marching men. Some small evidence of David Beaton's power was demonstrated here, in that David Lindsay, detailed by his kinsman to stay with and lead the Lindsay contingent, on foot, found this arrangement countermanded by higher authority and himself instructed to ride with Albany's group—which suited him very well. In fact, he found himself trotting beside Beaton most of the time. Not far behind rode a French servitor with a green parrot in a cage.

Before setting out, the Chancellor issued a summons to a parliament at Edinburgh, again the forty days' notice having to be dispensed with.

It took the cavalcade three days to reach Edinburgh, having halted at Kilsyth and Linlithgow, their company being joined, en route, by many lords and lairds from the surrounding areas, so that they made an impressive array indeed as they approached. There was some debate as to whether to halt and wait a few miles off for the marching host behind before making an entry, in case of armed opposition, the Chancellor so advising. But his nephew said otherwise. They had heard that Home, as well as holding the castle there and the royal family, had managed to have himself appointed Provost of the city; so, it being a walled town, its defences much improved since Flodden, if Home wanted to oppose, he could easily have all the gates closed against them. They should go forward confidently then, seeming to assume him loyal and welcoming,. They made a large enough party not to be readily attacked within the walls.

Albany accepted this counsel.

They advanced, amidst some tension, but saw no signs of opposition, although their approach must have been visible from the castle for many miles. At the West Port they found the gates open—and not only that but Home of Wedderburn, high in the Home hierarchy, waiting to receive them in the name of his chief with a number of the city magistrates and the new Dean of Guild. The Lord Home greeted the Duke of Albany, the Chancellor and the Primate, he announced, and wished them well. Wedderburn's words were suitably civil, but his looks and attitude were less so.

Filing in a long procession through the narrow streets, across the Grassmarket below the castle rock, and up the West Bow beyond, it became obvious that they were not being conducted to the fortress itself. Albany and the French not having been here before did not perceive this; but the Chancellor asked where they were going, and Wedderburn curtly informed that they were bound for the Abbey of the Holy Rood, the castle being much too overcrowded already.

Digesting this and its implications, they rode on through the crowded streets, the Edinburgh folk eyeing them warily, wisely reserving judgment until certain important matters were clarified, such as relative strengths and attitudes.

Down the Canongate, at Holyrood, the Abbot necessarily accepted the invasion with as good grace as possible, with two archbishops involved; but of course there was accommodation therein for only a very small proportion of the great company, and David once again found himself detailed, with sundry others, to find billets and stabling for large numbers of disgruntled visitors, nearly all of them offended at the quality of lodging eventually provided in the town.

This thankless task performed, he felt distinctly guilty when he discovered that he himself was to share notably superior quarters, next to Albany's own, with young Beaton, who cheerfully took charge of all; even Lord Lindsay had poorer lodging.

That evening, David had his first close demonstration of Albany's quality. He and Beaton were having a quiet beaker of wine together after a somewhat scratch banquet provided hastily by the Abbot, when the Duke himself came storming in from his adjoining chamber flourishing a piece of paper amidst a flood of French. Beaton listened respectfully, his glance on the letter the while.

David knew enough French to get the gist of Albany's complaint. He had sent a herald up to the castle, a mile away, requesting its governor to deliver up the keys to himself, as Regent, whereafter he would come and pay his due respects to the young King of Scots, as was suitable. And now the herald was back with this damnable letter and a garbled report that the Lord Home said that he, Albany, was not Regent yet until parliament confirmed him in that position, and therefore had no authority to demand the keys of Edinburgh or any other royal castle. He could come and pay his loyal duty to King James, but only as a subject and kinsman, and he should come alone and without armed escort.

Beaton nodded, not apparently appalled, and when he could interrupt the flow read aloud the letter's contents which contained approximately the same message and were signed, 'Home, High Chamberlain'.

The Duke scarcely heard him out. Furiously he snatched back the paper, crumpled it up and flung it at the fireplace. Not content with that, he pulled off the handsome velvet and jewelled cap he wore and hurled it after the letter, sweating comprehensively the while. A small fire burned in the grate and the hat, better aimed than the paper, was almost into the flames. Beaton stepped over and rescued it, returning it to its owner with a bow and a smile. Albany grabbed it, glared, and marched back to his own room without another word.

As David stared, the other grinned. "I have rescued that cap, and others, before!" he observed. "I told you that John Stewart had a hot temper."

"Sakes! Scarcely auspicious in a ruler!"

"Oh, we can put up with that. So long as he listens to reason when the temper cools. But—this of Home is interesting. He appears to be playing for time. Putting off any conclusions until after the parliament. Why, I wonder? What will that gain him?"

"Waiting to see how the cats will jump?"

"Perhaps. But from what you tell me, he is a jumper, not a waiter! No—there is more to it than that. There are only three ways for cats to jump, anyway—Albany, Arran and Angus. Home entered this present enterprise of abducting the King and bringing him here with Arran—although previously, you say, he had been in league with Angus. But Arran is the weakest of the three now that Albany is here. So Home has to choose between Angus, who is tied to England, and Albany and France. He keeps Albany at arm's length meantime—so it must be the Douglas. Home, I think, prepares to desert Arran and rejoin Angus!"

"It could be. He and Arran made strange bedfellows from the first."

"So—we must change his mind for him! Douglas! We must whittle away at Douglas. In the interests of Home's future!"

"I would have thought that Douglas, Angus himself, was the greater menace, the most powerful."

"Powerful, perhaps—but a deal less clever. Home I see as the cleverest noble in Scotland today. And wits can usually improve on power."

Some results of Davie Beaton's deliberations on the theme of Douglas were fairly quickly apparent—even though the action seemed to come from others, principally, at this stage, from his uncle. The old Bishop of Dunkeld had died and Gavin Douglas, Provost of the High Kirk of St Giles in Edinburgh, Angus's uncle, was astonishingly offered the bishopric by the Primate, at the Chancellor's bidding. More than that, to ensure a prompt acceptance, the elder Beaton proposed to instal and consecrate the new Bishop, at his own costs, in the Cathedral of St Mungo in Glasgow—it all having to be done forthwith in view of the Chancellor's other pressing commitments. This was too great a temptation for Master Gavin, who had always pined for the episcopate, and he succumbed with the required speed—the first defection in the Douglas camp.

Then the Chancellor acted again. He contrived the arrest of the Lord Drummond, Angus's maternal grandfather and chief of the Douglas's main supporting clan in the Highland area, and confined him in the royal prison castle of Blackness-on-Forth. The charge was that Drummond had insulted and assaulted the Lord Lyon King of Arms, the chief herald of the realm, who ranked as the King's personal representative and whom to strike could be construed as treason. It had all happened some time ago but nothing had been done about it. The pretext served.

It was hoped that Douglas, and likewise Home, would read the signs aright.

Whilst this was going on and the armed strength of the Albany camp was massing in the area just west of Edinburgh as all awaited the opening date of the parliament, David Lindsay was given his own orders. If they came via young Beaton and sounded like suggestions arising out of mutual discussion he had no doubts as to the authority behind them. He was to go to Dunbar and urge de la Bastie to assail and take the small Home strength of Colbrandspath Tower, near Dunglass—Dunglass itself might be too strong. This would serve further advice on Home. And thereafter David was to bring back de la Bastie to Edinburgh. The Lord Lindsay would go with him to take over the captaincy of Dunbar meantime.

David was well enough pleased to get away, as ever—especially as it meant that he could see Kate, coming and going. She was much in his thoughts these days.

A pleasant evening at the Byres and, with a brief call at Garleton in the by-going, they rode on next morning to Dunbar. Antoine was glad to see them, he tending to weary of castle keeping, eager for news of Albany and especially of Beaton, in whom he seemed to have much interest, and delighted to hear of the orders to assail Colbrandspath, to enliven the monotony of garrison duty.

So he and David rode south-eastwards next morning with a small escort to spy out the land. Their objective lay ten miles away on the main route to Berwick and the south at a hazard thereon known as Pease Dean—indeed this was the reason for the existence of the tower, for the precipitous sides of the Pease Burn here forced travellers into a position where they must pass close under the walls of the hold, to which they must pay toll if they were to proceed. Such robber-barons' keeps were all too common; but though impregnable to ordinary travellers and even men-at-arms, they were not usually proof against artillery. Unfortunately the much stronger Home castle of Dunglass lay not much more than two miles to the west, and any approach with cannon must be observed and no doubt contested.

So they took a roundabout route, inland, by Innerwick and Oldhamstocks, and so down the rapidly falling Pease Burn from the Lammermuir foothills. From a vantage point directly above the gut of the steep ravine, they could look down from scrub woodland on the fortalice, and consider.

It was a simple square tower of four main storeys and a garret, set within a small irregular courtyard, all cut out of the hillside in such a way that it dominated the roadway, leaving no other access. It would be a hard place to take defended, all but unapproachable from below and although overlooked by the higher ground this was only at some distance off and the necessary descent would invalidate any possible advantage.

"Cannon," Antoine said. "Only cannon will take that hold without a lengthy siege and starving them out. Cannon, up here."

David nodded. "So say I. But—could cannons' muzzles be depressed sufficiently to fire down there? For the balls not to go high above the tower? At Flodden, they say, all the fine cannon were useless because they could not fire down the hill at the English."

"Downward-sloping pits dug," the Frenchman said. "I have seen it done. It should be possible."

"And the noise? Cannon fire will bring out the Home strength from Dunglass and elsewhere."

Antoine nodded. "Then we must counter that. We need few to fire the cannon. Our main strength must mass to seem to besiege *Dunglass*. Keep them held there."

129

"But—how to get the cannon up here? Up this steep rough hillside . . . ?"

"Dismount them. The smaller guns, falcons, serpentines and the like from Dunbar. On horses. It can be done."

David was doubtful as they rode back.

But Antoine knew his own mind. He had inherited almost a dozen assorted cannon when he took Dunbar, mostly small pieces and fairly old; by detaching three of these from their wooden carriages and then loading barrels, carriages, and ball and shot and powder on a string of pack-horses, he solved the problem of mobility. But for his demonstration against Dunglass—for it was to be only that—he required many men. He had a garrison of only around fifty and some must be left to guard Dunbar Castle whilst some were needed to assault Colbrandspath. So, to make an impressive-looking force to threaten Dunglass, he sought volunteers amongst the townsfolk and fishermen of Dunbar. He had, of set purpose, made himself popular in the town, with the raising of the fish levy giving him a good start; and by offering to pay a suitable wage, he obtained an excellent response, indeed more than he could equip and seem to arm from the castle stores. But fifty he could use, and with a score of his own garrison that ought to make a sufficiently formidable force, at a distance, to keep the Dunglass folk from issuing forth. There was a danger in this device, of course, in that someone in the town, disaffected or merely loud of mouth, might talk sufficiently for word of it all to get to Dunglass and Colbrandspath. Delay, therefore, was to be avoided.

So, with only one day for preparation, they set off before dawn, a somewhat unruly and untidy company, the Colbrandspath assault party with about a dozen local men leading the pack-horses, and, behind, the strung-out seventy or so for Dunglass under Lord Lindsay.

They parted company at the fishing hamlet of Skateraw just as the sun was rising out over the Norse Sea, the attack party to take the more difficult and hidden inland route, the others to march direct for Dunglass on the coast.

It made a slow and taxing journey, with the heavily laden pack-animals having to be led and coaxed over much rough and trackless country, the last miles the worst, down through steep and broken scrub woodland with many fallen trees and the horses slipping and slithering. But at length they won into a position similar to that they had been in two days previously, directly above Colbrandspath Tower, perhaps one hundred and fifty feet higher and giving a range of not much more than two hundred yards for the cannon.

Prospecting the site, Antoine chose a position where they could find sufficient depth of soil, of a sort, to dig his downwards facing pits for the guns at a sufficient angle for the muzzles to bear on the buildings beneath. This entailed much labour and required the erection of a small barrier of stones immediately below each cannon in order that on the discharge and recoil the carriages would not hurtle forward and down the slope.

There was no indication that their activities had been noticed from the fortalice below.

"We shall now waken these sleepers!" Antoine declared. "They have lain long enough . . ." and he stooped to apply the burning fuse to the touch hole of the first cannon, a falcon. The explosion drowned his words.

They could hardly miss altogether at that range but that first ball struck the keep walling about halfway down, creating a shower of dust but doing little damage to the thick masonry. The next shot hit lower still. This would not do. The higher on the walling the thinner was the masonry, always; and the ideal place to bombard was of course the roof and parapet-walk, thinnest of all.

As they raised the gun muzzles a little men appeared on the said parapet-walk shouting and gesticulating. The third cannon's ball went over their heads but sent them scurrying below.

Reloading, they tried another realignment. And although this time two of the shots went high the third did smash into the stone slates of the roofing, tearing a great hole therein and no doubt wrecking the garret chamber beneath. As the echoes died away they could hear screams.

Thereafter, by trial and error, they pounded that hapless tower and its lean-to courtyard buildings with repeated salvoes. And quite quickly what had to serve as white flags appeared at two of the small windows to flap urgently.

"They have had enough," David said. "Nor do I blame them, unable to hit back . . ."

"Listen!" Antoine said.

131

Clearly, from the north-westwards, came the booming of cannon.

"Dunglass! That must be the Homes, firing on our people. They must have cannon there."

"No doubt. They will have heard *our* guns. Perhaps they think that it is general war!" De la Bastie shrugged and pointed downwards. "These, at least, make conveniently swift submission. Will you go down, my dear David, and accept their surrender? And if, by chance, they play any tricks or make difficulty blow this horn and I will open fire again immediately."

"But—if *our* cannon can thus easily win us this hold, could not the cannon, brought from Dunglass, just as easily win it back?"

"That is true. Therefore, I fear that we cannot hold it. It will be necessary for us to destroy it. With the remainder of our gunpowder. Better so than wasting our strength trying to hold a useless tower."

That made sense. David moved off downhill with most of their party and approached the fortalice, all ready for trickery. But there was none. Eight shaken men, unarmed, and two women emerged, assisting two other men, blood-covered and evidently wounded in the bombardment, one of whom it transpired was Home of Colbrandspath himself. They assured that there was nobody else in the place—only the barking dogs and stamping horses in the courtyard stabling. David was embarrassed by what he had to do and say—he had never thought that there would be women in the hold—but steeled himself to the task. He told them that they were free to remove anything that they especially valued from the tower, which was to be destroyed in the name of the King and his Regent, and that they could go down meantime to the fishing hamlet at the shore below—or elsewhere as they desired, although he did not recommend Dunglass. He enquired for the wounded but although the laird himself seemed to have a broken shoulder and sundry lacerations there appeared to be nothing dangerous, the other man bleeding from a scalp wound, painful but superficial.

David checked indoors to ensure that there were no undisclosed problems and then sent a man up to Antoine to inform that all was well and that he could bring down the powder for the demolition.

So, presently, with the sad tower party sent off to Pease Bay with their wounded, their horses laden with household goods and their snarling dogs but with no actual apologies—although David for one felt like making them—they prepared to blow up the fortalice. The lower six foot thick walling, of course, would defy any powder they had available so they confined themselves to the upper storeys which, wrecked, should serve to make the place uninhabitable for some time. In the end they achieved a great bang and showered stones and fragments and a vast cloud of dust and smoke. Thereafter they set off north-westwards along the coast road, satisfied that Colbrandspath Tower would be no menace to honest travellers nor to the Regent's causes for a while to come.

They picked up their main force sitting well out of range of Dunglass Castle's guns and all marched back to Dunbar, duty done.

Two days later David and Antoine rode for Edinburgh, via the Byres and Garleton and some welcome feminine company for each, leaving Lord Lindsay in charge of Dunbar and its castle.

They were just in time for the parliament, which opened in the large church of the Abbey of the Holy Rood. There was a surprisingly good turnout, considering the short notice and the unsettled, dangerous times, and undoubtedly most present would be supporters of the new Regent. It had been hoped that the young King might have been there for the opening, even under strong Home guard, to lend significance to the occasion; but no response had been received to the invitation sent up to the castle. As a precaution, a large contingent of the force camped outside the city had been brought in to secure the entire Canongate–Holyrood area in case of interference by whomsoever.

Albany not being officially Regent yet, and no high commissioner having been appointed under the seal of the monarch, the Chancellor had to open the proceedings himself, after a fanfare by the herald-trumpeters and an introduction by the Lord Lyon King of Arms. Albany sat to one side with Davie Beaton standing close-by to interpret. Every corner of the great church was filled with spectators, even up in the clerestory galleries, the French contingent making itself notably conspicuous. David Lindsay and de la Bastie perched in a window embrasure of the crossing.

The Chancellor, after prayer, declared, in welcoming all, that this assembly was necessarily a convention at this stage, not a parliament, since a parliament required the King's summons or that of his Regent, and present circumstances precluded either. But since the previous parliament, in the King's presence, had nominated John, Duke of Albany, to be Regent, it but required this assembly to make formal confirmation of the Duke, here present, in that office, for him to *become* Regent in fact and fullest authority. He could then declare the assembly to be a parliament, competent to take all due measures required for the realm's well-being. Was this understood by all?

There were general cries of assent.

He put it to the gathering, then—did the lords spiritual and temporal and the commissioners of the shires confirm the Duke of Albany in the Regency? It did not require to be put in the form of a motion, with proposer and seconder, since it was already a due decision of another parliament. Only any rejection would require to be proposed and seconded.

There was a great shout of acceptance from all parts of the church and continued cheering. There may have been some voices raised in dissent but if so they were completely lost in the din.

The Chancellor took it as sufficient confirmation and did not ask if there was any counter-motion. Instead he turned, in the hubbub of acclaim, with something between a bow and a flourish, towards Albany.

"My lord Duke," he said strongly, "this convention of the Three Estates has duly confirmed you in the office of Regent of this realm during the minority of James, by God's grace King of Scots, with all the authority of that office. Do you now, as is your undoubted right, authorise me to declare this a due and lawful parliament?"

His nephew murmured a translation in the ducal ear and Albany nodded. "*Oui!*" he said briefly.

"Then I do so declare. And, in the name of this parliament of the realm, I request you, my lord Regent, to move to and take the throne here as is your right."

So, amidst further cheering, Albany rose and stalked over

to the high chair set in the midst of the chancel but facing the nave and company, actually the Abbot's seat, and sat. After a moment or two, young Beaton slipped discreetly over to stand behind. He stooped and handed the Duke a paper.

Still sitting—for when the crown stood everybody must stand—Albany read aloud. It was a short speech in English of acknowledgment and thanks—which he mangled sadly —ending with what was presumably a promise to fulfil his duties and honour the confidence all had placed in him to the best of his abilities. This over, he dropped the paper and launched into a flood of French so fast that few in that church who were not his countrymen could have made anything of it. This went on for some time, and ended with a large gesture.

The French spectators applauded enthusiastically— although their part called only for respectful silence—and Antoine smiled.

"If he is as strong as his words, Scotland is safe!" he murmured.

The Chancellor turned. "My lord Regent—if my nephew may repeat in our tongue for those who did not catch every word . . .?"

Davie Beaton offered his own version—and de la Bastie's raised eyebrows once or twice seemed to indicate some slight emendation. He declared that the Regent was determined to restore the royal authority, to ensure close relations with his master in France and peace in the land, to put down all warring factions with a strong hand. First he would require King James to be delivered into his hands, with his royal brother; all royal castles to be yielded up to his keeping; all minions of the King of England, high and low, to be banished the realm; all pensions, subventions and doles paid by the King of England to be stopped and made unlawful, under pain of treason; all justiciarships and sheriffdoms to be resigned into his hands for reallotment, likewise wardenships of the marches; all heads of houses, families and clans to be held responsible for the good and leal behaviour of their people.

All this took a little digesting and there was a deal of talk, exclamation and muttered comment. But on the whole the reaction was favourable—of course Angus, Arran and Home were noticeable by their absence, although some of their supporters were present, for instances the Homes of Wedderburn and Blackadder, as representing the shire of the Merse.

The Chancellor allowed the gathering its head for a little, then rapped on his table for silence. He asked if any wished to question or remark on the Regent's intentions, any or all?

The Earl Marischal rose. "How does the Regent propose to gain the custody of the King's Grace and his infant brother?" he asked. "Is it likely that the Queen-Mother, Countess of Angus, would yield up her sons when she holds them secure in this city's fortress? And is known to have sworn to deliver them to none. Especially as she named the Duke of Albany!"

The Chancellor elected to answer that key question. "The former Queen's attitude and prejudices are well known," he agreed. "Particularly towards my lord Regent. But she cannot deny the expressed demands of parliament, save by putting herself outwith the law. So it is suggested that this parliament names eight lords, of whom four will be chosen by lot, these to represent the parliament, who will go up to the castle and require the lady to hand over the King and his brother. This to *parliament*, not to the Regent. Thereafter, it is hoped that parliament will decide to entrust the royal children into the Regent's good keeping. Is this procedure agreed?"

There was some debate about this, but most acceded that it was clever and should provide a face-saving device for Margaret Tudor, if she could be persuaded that she had little chance of retaining possession of the King.

The Chancellor nodded. "We believe that such persuasion can be effected," he assured. "We have proof that the King of England is still insisting that King James, as his heir-apparent, be brought into his own keeping in England. And has recently sent monies by the Lord Dacre, chief English Warden of the Marches, to Dr West, the English ambassador here, secretly to effect this end, the Queen-Mother agreeing. It must be clear, therefore, to all, to this parliament and to the nation itself, that the Countess of Angus is no fit person to retain the keeping of the King of Scots."

This revelation had the desired effect and the members promptly expressed their approval of the proposed procedure. Eight lords' names were quickly forthcoming and lots drawn produced the Earls Marischal and of Lennox and the Lords Borthwick and Lindsay. The last not being immediately available, the Lord Fleming's name was substituted. David Lindsay was interested that Lennox allowed his name to go forward, putting him more firmly in the Regent's camp.

Since the possession of the King was the key to all, it was decided to adjourn the sitting meantime for resumption when the royal situation was more clear, the rest of the Regent's declared programme being accepted—if it could be implemented. The four chosen lords would repair to the castle forthwith—and most of the parliament with them, obviously.

David, Antoine and young Beaton walked up the Canongate, High Street and Lawnmarket together amongst the crowd of parliamentarians and others. Albany and the Chancellor did not go, recognising that it would look better without them. Most of the French stayed behind also when they discovered that walking was involved.

Up at the final approach to the fortress, where the Lawnmarket opened on to the tilting ground on a sort of shelf of the castle rock, the Lyon King of Arms, who had led the procession, went ahead with his trumpeters to announce the parliamentary delegation. The remainder all held back meantime.

They heard the trumpets sounding and presently the clash and clang of the drawbridge coming down and the portcullis going up at the gatehouse towers. There was a pause, and then Lyon turned to wave the main party up.

There a notable sight met them. Flanked by armed guards, Margaret Tudor stood just within the gateway, fairly obviously pregnant again. She held by the hand King James on her right, and on her left stood Archibald Douglas, Earl of Angus, whom all thought to be besieging Arran at Hamilton. Looking distinctly awkward about it, he held the infant Duke of Ross in his arms. Young James seemed somewhat wan and distinctly sulky.

At sight of the King, of course, everybody had to doff bonnets and bow low. There was some embarrassment, since it meant that in the sovereign's presence all announcements must seem to be addressed to him.

Lyon, with practised eloquence, declared that parliament in its wisdom had decided that, with His Grace's permission, of eight lords nominated four chosen by lot should come to interview the Queen-Mother, Countess of Angus. William Keith, Earl Marischal, a bull-like man of middle years, was clearly somewhat offput at having to address the lady through the child monarch. He cleared his throat.

"Sire—your parliament has decided that, for your realm's weal, Your Grace should be taken into the keeping of the said parliament. For your safety. It has accordingly chosen four lords, of whom I am one and the others are my lords of Lennox, Borthwick and Fleming, here present, of which Your Grace's lady-mother should select three. To whom to deliver Your Grace and your royal brother, forthwith. This is the will of parliament." He ended that abruptly and coughed again.

Margaret Tudor eyed them all coldly. "Your parliament is no parliament—since the King had not called it," she said briefly.

The Earl Marischal frowned. "Ah, but it is, Madam. Since the Regent has named it so."

"I recognise no Regent for my son, other than myself."

"But the parliament of this realm does! The previous parliament nominated my lord Duke of Albany Regent. This parliament has now confirmed that nomination."

"How can it, my lord? Since it is no parliament, only a convention. A convention cannot make or confirm a Regent for the King's Grace. Only a true parliament might do that—which this was not when it sought to confirm Albany."

"But, Madam . . ."

This argument, which looked as though it might proceed indefinitely, was cut short unexpectedly and by the monarch himself. Eyeing all the new faces before him, James suddenly caught sight of David standing there and let out a whoop of joy.

"Da Linny!" he shouted. "Da! Da Linny!" And snatching his hand out of his mother's, he launched himself forward.

But Margaret Tudor reacted swiftly and grabbed the boy's doublet at the neck to jerk him back sharply, and when he yelled, to shake him in markedly unregal fashion, amidst howls of fury.

There followed some considerable upset, with shouted protests, fists shaken, the castle guard closing up and Angus addressing his wife urgently. David Lindsay, at his young charge's salutation, had involuntarily stepped forward also, arms extended, and now found himself in front of all, uncertain whether to go on to James's side or to move back into suitable anonymity.

The Queen-Mother solved that problem for him at least. Turning, she flicked an imperious finger at the captain of the guard and pointed upwards. That man shouted an order, and promptly, with a rattle of chains, the heavy portcullis of iron bars interlocked in a great grid came crashing down to slam into place at the bridgehead, cutting off one party from the other.

Staring through the iron network, both sides considered, whilst their liege-lord bawled and struggled.

The Queen-Mother retained the initiative. "Go back to your convention and your so-called Regent, my lords," she called, above the noise, "and tell them, and him, that I accept neither the one nor the other. Think you that I would give my children into the keeping of a Frenchman who has only these two infants between him and the throne he covets? I hold this castle by the gift of my late husband, your sovereign-lord, who also entrusted me with the keeping and government of my children. Nor shall I yield them to any person whatsoever." She paused. "In respect of this so-called parliament, I require a respite of six days to consider their mandate. You may now leave the royal presence."

In the circumstances that seemed to be that. However, this peculiar confrontation was not quite over yet, for one of the principals, who had hitherto remained practically silent, now chose to speak up, and to odd effect.

"*I* do not deny this parliament and its rights," Angus said abruptly. "And I urge my wife to accept its requirements, as is lawful."

All stared, scarcely believing their ears. All except Margaret Tudor, that is. If she was shocked, she showed no signs of it. She did not even glance at her husband.

"Go back whence you have come, my lords," she repeated. "Tell the Frenchman what I have said. Come back in six days and you shall have fullest response to your unacceptable claims." She turned, dragging James with her, to stalk back through the gatehouse pend, a determined, graceless figure.

For a few moments Archibald Douglas hesitated, still with the apparently sleeping infant duke in his arms. Then he shouted through the iron bars. "I, Angus, call on all to note that I do not dispute the parliament's will and commands and would have consented to surrender these children." He swung round and hurried after his wife.

Into the astonished silence, Davie Beaton's voice sounded clearly. "Now that is the most interesting word spoken this day!"

None there denied it.

On their way back down through the city streets, David asked Beaton what he made of it all. Had they been too clever? Or had the Queen-Mother been cleverer? And this of Angus—what did it mean?

His namesake seemed not at all put out. "One cannot but admire the woman," he said. "She has courage, spirit and wits—a King's daughter indeed. But she cannot win—and knows it. This of six days' interval—she leaves herself a postern for escape. She cannot for long defy the expressed will of parliament. This convention talk is but a device. Angus knows it and so has sought to cover himself. *He* will not have his wide lands forfeited by the same parliament for treason!"

"You think that was it? A strange thing, as against his wife."

"That first, yes. But there may have been more to it. I have heard whispers that there has been trouble between them, despite her being with child by him. This might be important. If we can detach Douglas . . ."

"I think that you go too fast, Beaton," de la Bastie put in. "Why did Angus come here? And secretly. From Lanarkshire. Not to attend the parliament, it seems. He would guess that Albany would demand the King. He is not a fool. Nor craven."

"Yet he covers himself, with this parliament. And opposes his wife before all. I say that is good news."

"Did you not expect, then, to have James delivered to us?" David asked.

"No," the other said simply.

That gave them pause for a while.

"I was much interested to see the young King. And to observe how greatly he seems to love you, friend,"

Beaton went on. "This could be of the greatest import, hereafter."

"I am fond of the child," David said stiffly. "Liege-lord as he is." He changed the subject. "What I would wish to know is where was the Lord Home this day?"

"*Moi aussi*," Antoine agreed.

"No doubt he prefers to keep out of sight leaving others to make the moves he devises," Beaton suggested.

"Nor is he the only one, at that!" the Frenchman answered, smiling.

The other bowed, and shrugged.

Back at Holyrood David was not present to hear Albany's reaction to all this, but he was a witness of the remarkable scene the following day in the abbey church when, at the resumed sitting of the parliament, a messenger came hotfoot in to hurry to the Chancellor's table, there to stoop and whisper. The Archbishop stared, frowned, and started to his feet. Ignoring the Lord Gray, who was holding forth on the need for an increase in the number of sheriffdoms, he went over to the Regent's throne and spoke urgently, his nephew translating, eyebrows raised.

Albany did more than raise his brows. He jumped up, glaring around him, snatched off his velvet cap and, since there was no available fire to hurl it at, flung it to the floor and stamped upon it again and again. Then, amidst a cataract of French eloquence, he left them all standing to storm to the vestry door and out.

The sitting undoubtedly was suspended.

Out of the uproar, the Chancellor eventually gained a reduction of noise. "My lords and commissioners," he exclaimed. "We have just heard that last night, under cover of darkness, the Queen-Mother, with her husband Angus, secretly left the castle, taking the King and his brother, and rode, it is thought, for the north!"

The din resumed. Young Beaton had to shout. "Where is the Lord Home?" he demanded.

It was the messenger who answered. "He remains, it is believed, in the castle."

"This parliament stands adjourned," the Archbishop declared.

9

It was marching again, the thirty-five miles from Edinburgh to Stirling, three days' tramp, the slower in that they had cannon lumbering along—and not just any cannon, minor pieces, but the huge Mons Meg itself, Scotland's mightiest, which even the late King had not aspired to take to Flodden, but which Albany—or more likely, Davie Beaton—had decided was worth the labour of trundling all the way from Edinburgh Castle behind no less than a score of plodding oxen. The army might have made slightly better time than the oxen, all eight thousand of them; but even so, it was slow progress. In the absence of the Lord Patrick, still at Dunbar, David found himself in command of the Lindsay contingent and chose to march with them as often as he rode his horse, in the interests of morale.

Albany had moved with speed and decision. Word had reached him that although Angus had gone on north-eastwards for the Douglas lands in Angus and the Mearns, presumably to raise more men, Margaret Tudor and her children had been dropped off at Stirling. Admittedly that fortress was the strongest in Scotland and presumably she felt that she would be safest there—hence Mons Meg being brought, for if anything could batter Stirling into submission it would be that monster. The attendant army was to ensure that Angus did not return to effect a rescue. So the force which had welcomed Albany at his arrival at Dumbarton and marched with him eastwards to encamp outside Edinburgh all this time, was to see some active service at last, with additional numbers recruited by various lords.

There was urgency about it all for a courier had been intercepted from the Queen-Mother to Lord Dacre with a letter, obviously an answer to one from King Henry, in which she agreed that a sufficiently large English force should be sent to Scotland to achieve her rescue at Stirling where she was now immured and thereafter the delivery of

herself and children into Henry's care in England, where
James would formally be declared heir-apparent to the
English throne, requiring his future domicile in England.
The letter added that if she was besieged by the usurping
Albany and the parliamentary rebels, she would cause young
James to stand in a prominent place on the castle walling,
wearing his crown, so that Albany's supporters would see
that they were guilty of highest treason in taking up arms
against their liege-lord. This courier had been captured, but
another might have got through. So Albany tended to
glance behind him as it were, as he marched, back towards
the Borderland. Home was now believed to be in his own
territories there, and Arran was goodness knew where, his
present attitude uncertain to say the least.

They reached Stirling on 4th August. Marshalling the
mass of troops wherever they would seem to present the
greatest threat to the castle—although of course they represented little or no threat in fact—Albany had Mons Meg
dragged up to a position on highish ground where it could
be seen, and out of range of the citadel's own cannon but
well within its own greater range. Then the Lord Lyon was
sent forward to repeat his message of two weeks before at
Edinburgh Castle, demanding that the keys of this fortress
be handed over to the Regent and the King's royal person
delivered into the custody of the lords of parliament
appointed.

When there was no least reply from the gatehouse towers,
Lyon went on to inform the castle's captain, if he had not
already perceived it, that the great cannon known as Mons
Meg had been brought from Edinburgh and was in a position
to hammer this fortress into compliance—if so he and the
Queen-Mother chose. But if this had to be done then he, the
captain, supposing that he survived the bombardment,
would be held responsible for the damage done to a royal
castle and would have to pay the price. When still there was
no response, Lyon and his trumpeters returned to the
Regent's party around the artillery.

The young Lord Borthwick, as Hereditary Master Gunner
in succession to his father who had not survived Flodden,
thereupon lined up his Mons Meg to try to hit a small flanking tower of the castle which would be well out of the way
of any part where the royal family might be lodged—for

of course any possible danger to the King and his brother was unthinkable, and much complicated potential gunnery. They had not forgotten Margaret Tudor's expressed intention of putting James in a prominent position to inhibit any assault. Borthwick had never fired this monster previously, with its enormous charge of powder and huge ball, and was distinctly nervous, fearing a misfire or a flashback such as had killed James the Second fifty-six years before. David and all the rest stood well back, leaving the Master Gunner to his privileges.

Despite all the precautions, none were prepared for the tremendous blast of the explosion which seemed to pulverise the senses for a few moments. Mons or Mollance Meg had been founded in the middle of the previous century by a noted blacksmith named Kim of Mollance in Galloway for his Maclellan chief—just why was insufficiently explained—but it had proved so efficacious at James the Second's siege of the hitherto impregnable Douglas castle of Threave that the King had thereupon appropriated it, and it had become the showpiece of the royal artillery, show rather than effect, for it had scarcely been used in other than salute since.

The first shot was sufficiently effective for the most demanding, even though its aim was less than accurate. Pieces were seen to fly off a building well to the left of the tower target, and a barracks behind seemed totally to disintegrate with further unidentifiable damage beyond, so overwhelming was the force of the projectile. All stared as the smoke cloud blew away on the breeze, daunted despite themselves.

Not Davie Beaton however, who cheered loudly, urging Lord Borthwick to try again, bearing a little to the right; the elevation was fair enough. Albany stroked his pointed beard.

It took some time to recharge and reload—and everybody stood still further back, covering their ears, as the fuse was applied for the second time. This shot missed the flanking tower also, but demolished in a cloud of dust a considerable length of perimeter walling and parapet-walk, as well as taking the roofs off some outbuildings further on, part of the menagerie. Beaton applauded again and turned to David to ask, as one well acquainted with the layout of the fortress, where would be the best place to aim a third shot, to have maximum effect on the defenders? Clearly with this brute of a cannon they could pound the place to pieces almost at will.

David was less happy. "I mislike this," he said, inadequately. "It is . . . too much. James will be terrified. Endangered. We do not know where he may be. We dare not fire into the main parts of the castle . . ." He was thinking also of the Abbot John, still presumably therein.

He was interrupted by the boom of lesser cannon and smoke blossomed out from one of the citadel's batteries. Everybody flung themselves down, except Borthwick, who shouted that they need not fear, that they were well out of range here. Sure enough, a fountain of earth and stones erupted fully three hundred yards short of their position. And another shot from a second cannon did little better.

"Where will the young King certainly *not* be?" Beaton demanded. "They have not learned their lesson yet!"

"Who knows, for sure? But—the Well Tower, probably. It is above the old kitchens and brewhouse. They would never be there, surely. That is it, to the right of the Chapel Royal—you can see the chapel gables with their crosses. But, for God's sake, keep well to the right! They might have taken refuge in the chapel . . ."

"You hear, my lord?"

"Have a care, of a mercy . . .!"

Borthwick relaid his piece with suitable solicitude but increased confidence and called on one of his assistant gunners to check the alignment. This time he achieved success, with a direct hit which blew the Well Tower into fragments and went on to shatter further quarters behind.

There was rather more general cheering now; but even so, David Lindsay did not join in—until de la Bastie gripped his arm and pointed. There, from one of the gatehouse towers, a white sheet was being hung out over the walling. David was now prepared to cheer with the rest.

Lyon went forward again, and presently waved all others to approach. As he did so the drawbridge began to descend and the portcullis to rise. By the time that the Regent's group reached the gateway, a small party was waiting for them at the bridgehead. It was uncannily like a repeat of the scene at Edinburgh Castle two weeks earlier. Standing there was Margaret Tudor, holding by the arm King James; and beside her was a man with the infant Duke of Ross in his arms—only this time it was not Angus but the Lord Erskine. There was one other difference—the boy monarch held a great iron key in his hand. No word was spoken on either side. Only the baby whimpered.

The Queen-Mother gave her son a push forward, as once again all bowed in varying degrees. James, scowling uncertainly, moved a few steps out on to the bridge timbers and stopped, in the face of that phalanx of armoured men. He looked as though he might turn and run back, when Beaton nudged David Lindsay.

"Sire! Jamie!" the latter called. "All is well. It is Da. Da Linny." And he pushed his way to the front.

"Da!" the child cried. "Da—oh, Da!" And came running.

David strode out on to the bridge before all to meet him, and caught the boy up into his arms, key and all, to hug him and be hugged.

A great clamour of exclamation and relief arose. The Regent moved forward.

Not so Margaret Tudor. Frowning coldly she turned, and with a swish of skirts stalked back into the castle, still without speech. Lord Erskine, hereditary keeper of this citadel, was left looking uncertain, with the other child sobbing against his shoulder.

Led by Albany, the newcomers surged forward over the drawbridge and in through the gatehouse pend, the King up on David's shoulder now—although he was getting too big for this, at nearly four—somewhere in the midst, still clutching the symbolic key of the fortress, which nobody appeared to want.

Abbot John, pushing against the tide, hurried to greet them.

Joyful was the reunion for those three, whatever the atmosphere of constraint and hostility in the rest of the castle.

In due course they learned what was to happen, from Davie Beaton. During the two days' interval Beaton spent much time with David and the Abbot, and therefore with James, who was now not to be parted from them; he clearly found Lindsay's company to his taste—and no doubt perceived advantage in becoming known and accepted by the child monarch. He revealed that Albany was going to take

146

the Queen-Mother back to Edinburgh and keep her in the castle there, more or less a prisoner and a hostage for the good behaviour of her husband Angus. The King, however, with his brother, would remain here at Stirling, for security, in the care of David and Abbot John, the Earl Marischal being left in command of the citadel. It was not thought to be in any real danger now, from Angus or other, for there was no other cannon like Mons Meg in the kingdom, and that monster was being taken back to Edinburgh also. Arran's attitude, like his whereabouts, was unknown; but in the circumstances he was not the man to besiege Stirling to grasp at the King. And Home was now isolated in his Border area and scarcely in a position to mount any major thrust meantime. In fact, the Regent's situation was now reasonably well-established, his strategy working out well—and young Beaton, without any unseemly flaunting, did not pretend that the strategy was not his own, the success thanks to himself.

So, after two days, Albany and his entourage departed, taking Margaret Tudor with them, the army and Mons Meg following on. If the Queen-Mother was desolated at leaving her children she revealed no signs of it, coldly self-contained throughout; and James, for his part, was not moved to tears. The baby duke was left in the keeping of Lady Erskine, who would remain at Stirling, although her husband would go with the Queen-Mother to Edinburgh.

David, holding the King's hand, watched them go, from a gatehouse tower parapet, with mixed feelings. He had young James and Abbot John again—but he was going to miss Antoine de la Bastie and, yes, Davie Beaton also. And he was back to confinement in a fortress once more, his period of freedom apparently over.

A week after this departure a small group of the royal guard arrived from Edinburgh with a green parrot in a wickerwork cage, as gift for the King's Grace from a devoted subject.

10

In the months that followed, David Lindsay came to the conclusion that he was something of a misfit. He had been greatly pleased and indeed flattered those four years earlier when the late King had appointed him Procurator and companion for his infant son. And still he esteemed that position and would have been much offended had he been displaced by someone else. He was genuinely fond of young James, and more than appreciative of the fact that the boy so evidently approved of himself. Nevertheless, he found the life he had to live both trying and tying, to a degree. It was mainly this of being cooped up in a fortress, to be sure; but it was more than that. He just did not have enough to do. He was a restless, energetic man, and although interested in music and poetry and the like he required physical as well as mental activity. It might have been different had the times been otherwise and peace in the land. Then he and his charge would not have been so confined, and life had been vastly more free, with visiting, riding abroad, even hunting and hawking available for the young monarch and his attendants. Nothing of the sort was possible under present circumstances. He almost envied John Inglis who seemed to suffer from no such cravings for involvement and activity; he probably would have made a good monk, a real monk, not a sham abbot.

There was also the matter of Kate. Being fifty-odd miles from her was damnable. Who knew what might be happening at the Byres? Attractive as she had now become, men would be swarming round her like flies.

The Earl Marischal, in command at Stirling, was not the sort of man who would see any need to cater for a younger man's moods and fancies.

News of the world outside the fortress was but scanty. It had been different before, when the Chancellor was based there, and couriers and letters were arriving constantly to keep him informed. Now the Archbishop remained with the Regent, at Holyrood, and it seemed to be nobody's business to inform the King's guardians at Stirling. Only once, in mid-September, did any near involvement in current events reach them. A hard-riding troop of the Regent's men came pounding up to the castle from Edinburgh, demanding to know whether the Queen-Mother had arrived? When, astonished, the Earl Marischal told them no, and how could she, their spokesman said that if she did appear, she was to be admitted but then held secure until the Regent sent for her. He went on to declare that the lady had told Albany that Edinburgh Castle and its grim towers and cells was no place for a princess to be delivered of her child, and since she was now nearing her time she demanded that she be taken to her own house of Linlithgow for the birth. In a weak moment the Regent had acceded and under guard she had been allowed to go. But before they reached Linlithgow, Lord Home with a much stronger party had ambushed them and had taken the Queen-Mother. Clearly it was all plotted beforehand. Nobody knew where she had gone—the assumption was that she might have come here to Stirling to try to pick up the royal children . . .

This news at least gave them something to talk about in the fortress with much speculation as to where Margaret Tudor might be now and whether she was likely to appear at Stirling, demanding her sons, backed by the power of Home and possibly Angus also. But it did nothing to lessen David's feelings of constriction; indeed the reverse, for the Earl Marischal insisted on tightened security so that even brief visits down into the town by members of the garrison were stopped.

It was some ten days later that there were developments—the arrival, not of Margaret Tudor but of Davie Beaton. He rode up, with only two of his uncle's men-at-arms as escort, but in his usual assured good spirits, paid civil respects to the Earl Marischal, made a fuss of young James and his papingo—which he rejoiced to hear was proving a great success—but made it entirely clear that it was David Lindsay that he had come for and that they had work to do.

David did not think to take amiss such cool authority from this young man, little older than himself and with less official status, being a mere student at the Sorbonne, although apparently lay Rector of Campsie in his uncle's archdiocese to provide him with an income. Seemingly they were for the road, bound for the north, on the realm's business.

Why David should be involved became clearer later. It seemed that still nobody knew where the Queen-Mother was, but it was suspected that she would probably make for her husband who was believed to be still recruiting in Angus, the Mearns and Aberdeenshire. It was important, needless to say, that no large-scale threat should be allowed to develop in that area, especially as the Earl of Huntly and his Gordons were allies of Douglas and the Queen-Mother. It so happened that the alternative powers up there, insofar as the shires of Angus and the Mearns were concerned, were the Earl of Crawford, chief of all the Lindsays, and his son-in-law, the Lord Ogilvy of Airlie. Crawford, an elderly man, had been lying distinctly low during all the national upheavals—he had succeeded to the earldom when his nephew was killed at Flodden. But he was nevertheless one of the most powerful lords in the land—and that same nephew had been married to the Lord Home's sister. It was advisable, then, that Crawford should be convinced that his interests lay with the Regent, and David could see some point in himself being enrolled in the business of trying to influence his chief. But why Davie Beaton should take on the task, personally, was not so clear.

They rode off next morning north-eastwards, across Forth, by Strathallan and Strathearn to Perth, and then onwards through Gowrie into the vast valley of Strathmore, the mightiest vale in all Scotland, fifty miles long by eight to ten wide, of fertile, tilled land and fair pasture, between the green Sidlaw Hills and the majestic blue ramparts of the Highland Line known as the Braes of Angus. Young men, they rode hard, and there was little opportunity for elaboration or discussion—David not complaining, so gratified was he to be out of Stirling and more or less free again. Perth was the same distance from Stirling, in the other direction, as was Edinburgh: thirty-five miles, and they made it in four hours. Then, after resting their beasts, on for another three hours to Meigle, on the Isla, in Strathmore. And there, with the sun sinking and their mounts weary indeed,

David was somewhat surprised when his companion turned northwards, up Isla-side, not onwards for Forfar and Brechin, between which lay Finavon Castle, the main seat of the Earl of Crawford.

"We shall go see my Lord of Airlie first," Beaton explained briefly.

They had another six miles to go, with the scene changing now notably and rapidly, wooded foothills and green cattle-dotted ridges, the river winding in shadowy valleys and always the great purple mountains rearing ahead. David had never been in Angus, and was not unaffected by the mighty barrier of soaring peaks, of rock and heather and high wilderness, which he understood went on from here into infinity, the dread and storied Highlands, which all his life he had been taught to shun and fear.

With the Isla becoming ever more of a torrent, peat-brown, and its valley course narrowing and steepening in the September evening gloom, they came at length to a thrusting headland, almost a vast wedge of cliff, where another lesser but still savagely foaming stream came in a deep ravine to join Isla—the Melgam Water, Beaton mentioned. And up there, at the clifftop, where there was the glow of the last of the sunset, lights glimmered from windows. He set his faltering horse to a daunting zigzag track which worked its difficult way up the flank of this proud prow of land. Clearly he had been here before.

At the top they came out on to a small apron of grass, above which high walling, topped by a parapet, rose beyond a dry ditch cut deep into the living rock, dizzy towers soaring behind. The dark gap of an arched gateway was there and a narrow drawbridge was down, to span the ditch. A group of kilted men, broadswords drawn, stood at the bridgehead, waiting, silent. David did not like the look of them, Highland caterans. Presumably their approach had been observed, despite the evening shadows.

Beaton rode on easily to the bridge, raising a hand high. "We come to see the Lord James. And the Lady Marion," he called. "Friends."

At first there was no response. Then one of the men said, in a softly sibilant Highland voice so much at odds with his wild appearance, "The Lord Seamus is from home, sir. Yourself, who are you?"

151

"I am Beaton. David Beaton. From France. Is the Lady Marion here, then?"

"I will be after asking if she will see you, sir." Despite the speaker's civil words, when he turned to disappear into the gateway arch the others looked none the more welcoming, closing up to bar the way threateningly.

The visitors sat in their saddles. Beaton said something affable but the guards made no answer. Possibly they spoke only the Gaelic.

They had quite a wait there, in the gloaming, in silence save for the horses' champing and the owls beginning to hoot. Then the original challenger returned, and with him a woman—or, more accurately, a girl, for she appeared to be little older than Kate—a long-legged, slender creature with a cascade of golden hair loosely looped back from winsome features, but with a proud, not to say haughty carriage nevertheless. She was dressed in practical but attractive fashion, in a dark-green gown of woven stuff, shorter than was the Lowland style, over a white short-sleeved bodice which detracted nothing from a shapely figure. She stared out at them, a strange apparition to come across at that harsh fortalice on top of the beetling cliff.

"Marion! It is David—Davie Beaton. Come, come visiting! It is Davie, my dear."

They heard her quickly indrawn breath. But that was all. David was surprised. He had assumed that the Lady Marion named would be the Lord Ogilvy's wife, daughter of the Earl of Crawford. Although this could be *her* daughter . . .

Beaton jumped down and all but ran forward, hand out, eagerness in every line of him. "Lassie—Marion! It is I—Davie. From France. Had you not heard . . . ?"

This was a different man from the one David knew, urgent, no longer assured, acting no part. Clearly this young woman meant much to him.

She scarcely seemed to reciprocate his urgency. "You!" she got out. "Here? I believed you still gone. In France, Davie Beaton. I . . ." She shook her fair head.

The guard drew aside to let him past, arms still outstretched. She made no move forward to him, however.

He faltered, hands dropping to his sides. "I came with the Regent, with Albany. I . . . had to come to see you, Marion."

They looked at each other, in strange, searching fashion for moments.

Then Beaton remembered David and his manners. "Here is David Lindsay of the Mount, the young King's Procurator and guardian."

"Lindsay? My mother was a Lindsay," the girl said, looking up. She sounded almost relieved at the intermission.

David bowed and dismounted.

"You have travelled far, sir?"

"From Stirling, lady."

"Stirling? That is far indeed. Sixty miles and more. Long riding. You will be weary, hungry." She appeared to be a deal more at ease in addressing David. "Come." She turned to lead the way within. "My father is not here meantime, but you are welcome to his house."

Airlie Castle was irregularly shaped, of necessity to conform to its highly defensive but awkward site, larger than Garleton but smaller than the Byres, and much more stark and strong than either. But internally it proved to be more comfortable than might have seemed likely. The girl conducted them through a vaulted great hall and upstairs to a pleasant lamplit chamber where a birch log fire burned cheerfully and aromatically and deer and wolf skin rugs littered the floor. Here she provided a flagon of wine and beakers for their immediate refreshment, whilst she left them to go down to the kitchens to arrange more substantial fare.

The two young men eyed each other. "So this is why we came to Airlie Castle first!" David observed. He almost added, and the reason why you chose to make this northern journey personally, likewise.

The other shrugged. "I wished to see Marion, yes. We are . . . friendly. I have not been here for two years and more. She is important to me. And her father is important to the realm, in this pass."

"To be sure . . ."

Presently they were sat down to an excellent repast of cold meats, with their hostess attentively presiding. She seemed to be a quietly competent woman, as well as attractive—but her hospitable attentions were rather noticeably devoted more to David Lindsay than to David Beaton, with whom there was an obvious sense of strain. She and Lindsay

153

decided that they were cousins, seven times removed. She revealed that her father was at present visiting her grandfather at Finavon Castle. When Beaton asked her if this was by any chance to do with the affairs of the Earl of Angus, she was non-committal, indicating that the Lord Ogilvy did not find it necessary to discuss all his business with her. It was amusing to see her questioner chastened in a way nobody else appeared to be able to achieve.

Interesting as this encounter might be to watch, fairly soon after the meal was over David excused himself to seek his couch, pleading fatigue after too much of being confined within fortress walls. Beaton confessed to no such weariness and did not offer to accompany them when Marion Ogilvy said that she would show the guest his chamber.

At a high tower room, feeling a certain sympathy for his travelling companion, David paused in the doorway. "David Beaton is working hard and doing much good for the realm's cause," he mentioned. "He is able, and wields much power. It could almost be said that he is the power behind the Regent, who speaks only French and depends heavily on Davie for guidance. He relies on him."

"Indeed. Then Master Davie will be well content. Since power is what he seeks, has long sought."

The way she said that gave David pause. "And you feel differently?" he asked.

"My feelings in this matter are neither here nor there, Master Lindsay. Who am I to concern myself with the affairs of the realm? Or of David Beaton!"

"H'mm. Yet—he came all this way, from Edinburgh, to see *you*, I think. Leaving the Regent. And his uncle, the Chancellor. At a time of stress." That was the best that he could do for one whom he was beginning to think of as his friend.

"Then perhaps his judgment is less reliable than the Duke of Albany believes! A good night to you, sir."

Perhaps he had not improved matters for his companion? Anyway, who was he to think to seek to meddle in matters of the heart—he who was scarcely achieving great things with Kate Lindsay?

In the morning, with Beaton taking a delayed and reluctant farewell of Airlie Castle, David forbore to ask, as they rode off down Isla-side again, how his companion had got on the previous night. But, after a while, the other did volunteer some comment. He said that Marion was a notably fine young woman and that he was devoted to her. But that she was somewhat out of sympathy with what he was doing, with the life that he had chosen to live. She did not understand the need for such as himself, with the gifts the good God had bestowed on him in wits and circumstances and family connections, to use them to best effect in the service of Scotland in its hour of need. She would have preferred him, it seemed, to be a stay-at-home, a rustic, a mere farmer perhaps—in which case what chance would he have to aspire to the hand of a great lord's daughter, he the seventh son of an impoverished Fife laird?

David murmured something about France being a long way from the Braes of Angus and scarcely conducive to successful courtship.

France was necessary for him, Beaton insisted. He had gone there of a set purpose, as the swiftest road to influence. He was proficient at languages and France was the key to the struggle between the Empire and the Vatican, and England too. Much that would affect Scotland was to be decided in France—as indeed he had proved. It had been only for a year or two and Marion was young. But she had been against it.

David observed sagely that women had their own peculiar viewpoints, and they left it at that.

It was a mere twenty or so miles' ride to Finavon, out of the valley of the Isla and over the moors of Kinnordy and Kirriemuir to that of the South Esk, which seemed to indicate that it was important and prolonged business which occupied the Lord Ogilvy there, since he could have ridden that distance and back in one day easily enough.

Finavon Castle was a big place and very fine, but not particularly strongly sited nor strategically placed to be the principal seat of one of the greatest nobles in the realm. Indeed it was strange that the Earls of Crawford should have chosen to live here in Angus at all, considering the vast estates and properties they owned all over the kingdom, particularly in Clydesdale—from which they took their title—Lothian and Fife. But nearby Glen Esk was one of the best hunting forests in the land and moreover, apt to be comfortably out of the way of most of the upheavals which so frequently disturbed Scotland.

The Earl proved to be a burly individual in his mid-sixties, heavy and slow of speech but amiable enough—although clearly a little disconcerted by this unexpected visit of the two young men on the Regent's behalf. He had assembled at Finavon, as well as Marion's father—a pleasantly genial and handsome man—a number of other Ogilvy and Lindsay barons and lairds from the area, and fairly obviously this was no mere hunting party or social gathering.

David found himself in the odd position of being accorded more respect than was his companion, partly no doubt because he was the King's Procurator but more likely because he was a Lindsay, son of the quite renowned Sir David of Garleton and a kinsman of the Lord Patrick, second in the Lindsay hierarchies. However, Beaton, his assurance most patently fully recovered, quickly came to the point of the visit and proceeded, whilst being suitably courteous to the Earl and the other seniors, to take charge of the situation.

At table in the huge hall Beaton declared that he had come directly from and on behalf of the Duke of Albany, to whom he was acting as secretary and assistant. The Regent was concerned about rumours that the Earl of Angus was drumming up support in this north-east of Scotland for a treasonable attempt on the person of the King, contrary to the expressed will of parliament. The Duke, well aware of the undoubted loyalty of the Earl of Crawford, the Lord Ogilvy and others here, believed that they were the obvious magnates to counter any such shameful preparations and hereby called upon them to take every possible step to maintain the authority of the King, the Regent, and parliament in these parts.

This announcement produced a certain uneasy stir amongst his hearers, and the young man proceeded to make it more uneasy still by asserting that the Regent and Chancellor expected the present reliably trustworthy company to keep them well informed as to the whereabouts, movements and probable intentions of the said Earl of Angus and his Douglas associates and allies in treason. Indeed, they had heard just a hint that Angus himself might conceivably be considering a visit in person to those very parts in the immediate future to try to enlist aid for his wicked cause; and part of his, and David Lindsay's, mission was to warn them of this dire possibility.

David swallowed, this being the first that he had heard of it; but he perceived that Beaton had guessed that this gathering might well in fact have been convened for the very purpose of meeting Angus—as had occurred to himself—and was taking a chance.

No one actually said anything although many glances were exchanged.

With seemingly complete innocence of any disquiet caused, the other went on to declare that the Regent had some eight thousand men assembled and ready to embark on shipping at Leith to sail up to this Angus coast and be here in a couple of days if need be, for the reinforcement and support of the loyal forces in the putting down of treasonable activities and the punishment of all evil-doers. Their lord-ships had only to call for help . . .

Their lordships duly considered that information, how-ever imaginative in its content, features thoughtful.

By the time that Davie Beaton was finished, nobody there was in any doubt that support for the Earl of Angus would be a highly inadvisable policy, that the Regent was already very well-informed, and that treason, a word which had cropped up half a dozen times, with all its dire impli-cations as to capital punishment, would be the charge levelled against all so involved. Oddly, it was only as it were by chance and at the end that a vital fact slipped out from the other side, when David Ogilvy of Inverquharity observed that if the Queen-Mother already had the young King in her keeping and was conveying him to England, as was reported, how could a charge of high treason against the monarch be sustained against supporters of the Queen-Mother's husband?

Swiftly Beaton rounded on the speaker. Who so reported? The King was secure in the Regent's keeping in the castle of Stirling—they had left him there but the day before. Treason was deliberate action against the King in parliament, the supreme authority in this realm. And what was this talk of England? Was Margaret Tudor not here with her husband, in the north-east?

If this tacit admission on Beaton's part that he was not quite so well-informed as he pretended registered with his hearers, it was not sufficient to affect their greater concern that young James was not in fact in his mother's hands, as clearly they had assumed to be the case and as presumably Angus was putting out. Crawford made one of his few contributions, asserting that their information was that the Queen-Mother was in the Borders with the Lord Home, indeed at Home of Blackadder's house, if she had not already crossed into England—as they believed, with the King's Grace.

Beaton recovered his composure admirably, declaring that all this was but a typical example of Angus's lies and duplicity. The King was safe, and if Margaret Tudor was not with her husband but in England so much the better for Scotland, and so much the weaker Angus's treasonable cause, as all must perceive.

David was surprised thereafter to hear his friend announce that they must be on their way back to Stirling and Edinburgh forthwith, that the Duke of Albany could only spare his own humble services for the four days required to come up here and warn and reassure their lordships and loyal subjects of His Grace. Also Lindsay of the Mount had to get back to His Grace's side, as his Procurator.

If this sudden departure seemed at all strange to the company assembled, relief at so expeditiously getting rid of awkward guests overbore it quite. No impediments were put in their way.

As they rode away from Finavon in mid-afternoon, however, David thought that he was entitled to an explanation. Surprised, the other said that it should be obvious. They did not want to be caught at Finavon if Angus arrived—and it looked, to say the least, probable that he was expected at any time. And also it was vital that he got this information about Margaret Tudor back to Edinburgh just as quickly as possible. It could be very important. If instead of being up here, as had been supposed, the woman was in the Borders with Home and Home was in collusion with Dacre the English Warden, and if it was all carefully planned and timed, as seemed likely, then they might well have an invasion on their hands at any moment, King Henry's strategy working out. In that case there could be thrusts on two fronts, Home and the English from the south and Angus from the north—and possibly even the mercurial Arran from the west. The sooner he was at Holyrood Abbey the better as far as Davie Beaton was concerned.

His companion thought that all this was a lot to build up out of what they had learned but did not labour the point with this so assured character.

Beaton was certainly in earnest about the need for haste, and they reached St John's Town of Perth before halting for the night. And, keeping up the pace next day, David decided to display a little initiative and self-assertion on his own part. With the ramparts of Stirling Castle rearing before them as they cantered down into the Forth valley, he informed his companion that he would accompany him on to Edinburgh and then proceed to Garleton. After all, nobody at Stirling would expect them back so soon, after a journey to the north-east. It was an opportunity to pay a much called for visit to his home. Beaton, with no reason to object, said that he would be glad of the continued company. So they rode on past Stirling, David feeling both guilty and elated.

They spent the second night at Linlithgow and by midday following reached Edinburgh, horses sorely tired. David would have headed on at once for East Lothian, but Beaton urged that it would be sensible to visit Holyrood first for news.

At the abbey they learned that word of the Queen-Mother's whereabouts had already reached Albany, from Border sources, that she had indeed been taken to Blackadder in the Merse by Home, but was now understood to be at Dacre's castle of Harbottle in Northumberland awaiting the birth of her child by Angus. Where Home himself was now, unfortunately, was not clear. That he had taken Margaret Tudor to Dacre's house was highly significant, of course. He perhaps remained there, plotting with Dacre; or he might have returned to Scotland. There was a suggestion that Angus was expected at Harbottle for his wife's lying-in, presumably coming by sea from north-east Scotland, but this might be no more than guesswork and rumour. At any rate, the Regent had taken certain precautions. He had signed an edict removing Home from the office of Chief Warden of the Marches and appointed the Sieur de la Bastie in his place, sending him back to Dunbar Castle and from there ordering him to mount a concerted assault on the Home strengths in the Merse, one after another, in a determined campaign to dispose of this menace once and for all.

De la Bastie could call on most of Albany's forces based in the Edinburgh area if need be.

Neither David nor Beaton was happy about this appointment of Antoine, much as they both admired him—not as Warden of the Marches, that is. A Frenchman as good as governor of the entire Border region would not be popular—even though he was probably the best military commander available. However, it was too late to change it now, although the appointment would have to be confirmed by the next parliament.

The suggestion that Angus might join his wife for her confinement was interesting, in present circumstances. If so it would mean that any trial of strength was likely to be postponed until after the birth—which would provide a welcome breathing space. But would he do it, a man not notable for thoughtfulness? Leave his mustered forces in the north-east to make the sea journey, and for an indefinite period, childbirth being notoriously unpredictable? He might, in order to concert plans personally with Home and Dacre. And, after all, the infant to be produced would be his first-born, and, if a boy, heir to all the Douglases, Master of Angus and third in line to the throne of England.

With these thoughts preoccupying his mind, David resumed his journey to East Lothian. They did not predominate for long however—not with Kate Lindsay ahead.

He rode straight to the Byres. His father and Mirren, at Garleton, could wait. David Beaton's involvement with Marion Ogilvy at Airlie and what seemed to him like the mishandling and non-success of that affair, had had quite a major effect on him, teaching him a lesson—or so he conceived. Clearly the diffident, tentative approach was not the right one for spirited young women—and Kate was sufficiently spirited he had no doubts. The firm and decisive attitude, not exactly masterful but as of a man knowing his own mind—as became, for instance, the King's Procurator—was called for, he felt.

At the Byres he could scarcely complain of his welcome, with the Lady Isabella greeting him warmly, the Lord Patrick, new back from Dunbar where he had been replaced by de la Bastie, genially avuncular, and the heir to the house, John, Master of Lindsay, on one of his infrequent visits from Pitcruivie in Fife, in back-slapping high spirits, his wife Eliza effusive. But it did mean that in front of all this amiably exclamatory company his meeting with Kate had to be much more casual and restrained than he had visualised, a quick embrace and chaste kiss being as much as the situation permitted. That she was looking lovelier than ever, and seemingly serenely self-possessed, did not help.

Thereafter frustration grew as, try as he would, he failed to arrange that they could be alone together. Always somebody was present, usually two or three, with endless talk about King Jamie, the Regent, Angus, the present ominous state of affairs, the situation in the north-east, the folly of de la Bastie's appointment as Warden of the Marches, and so on. Kate, in fact, seemed to be the least interested in all this, and so absented herself frequently from the discussion, to David's distraction. Unfortunately, it was a miserably chill day of early October with a thin drizzle of rain drifting in off the Norse Sea, precluding any suggestion of a companionable walk or ride together.

David found himself wondering, sourly, how Beaton would have coped with this? He decided, however, that Kate was not only more beautiful than Marion Ogilvy but even more satisfactorily rounded in places where it mattered, and with a readier smile.

It was not until early evening, the meal over at last, and David getting desperate, that Lady Isabella, informed by one of the maid-servants that a further supply of fish would be required for the morrow's breakfast was instructing her where to find the icehouse key and what fish to abstract when Kate volunteered to go instead, knowing better what was required. David all but knocked over his chair in his haste to offer escort for her to the icehouse—which he knew was dug into a grassy bank of the outer walled garden—to the grins of the company.

"I thought . . . that we were never . . . going to be able . . . to be alone!" he gasped, as he closed the door behind them.

"Alone?" she echoed innocently. "You want us to be alone for some reason, Davie?"

"Lord—of course I do! I have been trying to get you to myself ever since I came, Kate. For a little. But always others were there . . ."

161

"Why? Have you something to tell me? Show me? A new poem, perhaps? To recite . . . ?"

"No. Or, well, I *am* writing some verses about the King's papingo—a parrot which David Beaton brought him from France. But . . ."

"A parrot? Have you nothing better to write about than that?"

"No. Yes. That is not what I want to talk about, Kate. It is important. I . . . where are you going now?"

"To get the icehouse key. My mother keeps it with her other keys in this aumbry. We keep the icehouse locked, otherwise much meat and fish might be stolen. Do you not, at Garleton?"

"I daresay. But—we must talk. I have so much to tell you, my dear . . ."

"Good. And so you shall." She detached a quite large iron key from a sort of hoop linked to a chatelaine's leather girdle on which were many other keys, and handed it to David. "You take this. I will get a basket for the fish. And perhaps a platter too, for we could do with some more venison whilst we are there . . ."

So presently he found himself burdened with a wicker basket and a large and heavy earthenware platter as well as the key. "Where are you going now?" he demanded, almost plaintively.

"To get a cloak, stupid! It is raining."

Out into the damp evening they went then, and any idea of a romantic arm in arm or even waist-encircling progress was inhibited by the man's laden state and a flapping cloak. She led the way through the pleasance and the orchard, under dripping trees, to the outer herb, fruit and vegetable garden within its high walls, in a corner of which was a grassy mound, part of the natural lift of the land towards the Garleton Hill, which had been excavated to form an underground icehouse. On top was a rustic bower, or arbour, roofed and seated. It had been that bower which had been at the back of the man's mind all along.

Taking the key, Kate opened the heavy, creaking door. Chilly as the evening already was, the shock of cold air met them immediately. It was dark in there, as well as cold, as the girl moved inside, but she obviously knew just where everything was and called in David with the platter and basket after her.

The place was like a long cavern, quite extensive, lined with stone and vaulted as to roof, stacked waist-high on each side with boxes filled with ice, this renewed each winter from the shallow curling ponds and which, hidden in the earth here from sun and summer warmth, retained the required chill throughout most years. On top of the iceboxes were laid trays of meats and fish, sides of beef and mutton and venison, hams, poultry and wildfowl.

The idea of being holed up there in the dark close to Kate had been alluring—but the breath-catching cold and the smells were sufficient to counteract any such effects. Giving three stiff salmon for his basket and taking a solid haunch of roe-venison for herself, Kate pushed past him and out without any lingering.

When she had locked the door again, clutching his fish, David looked upwards. "We could talk in that bower," he suggested. And at the diffident note he himself could hear all too plainly in that, recollected his decision regarding firmness, and added much more strongly, more so perhaps than he realised, "Come—I have much to say to you."

She looked at him curiously. "It is not very warm for sitting outside," she said.

"Never heed. You will be well enough. Give me that meat."

'You are wonderfully fierce of a sudden, Davie! Is this how you treat your fine court ladies! That Mirren, and her like?"

"A plague on Mirren!" he declared, and began to climb up to the arbour. The wet grass proved slippery and weighed down as he was he all but fell twice, cursing under his breath. Even so he heard what in anybody else he would have described as a giggle, coming up behind.

In the wooden open-fronted arbour he dumped his fish and meat on the bench and turned, arms wide, to enfold the girl vehemently as she entered. The damp and voluminous cloak got rather in the way and, not anticipating this move and panting a little from the climb, she all but choked in his arms. Nevertheless her heaving, curvaceous and somewhat unsteady person was eminently claspable, even though the kiss he planted missed its exact target.

163

"Mary Mother!" she gasped. "What's to do, Davie Lindsay?"

"I . . . ah, sit down," he commanded.

She had to move the venison and salmon, and he had to do so again to make room beside her.

"I am very fond of you, Kate," he announced, strongly.

"Oh? Yes, I know," she agreed. "We have always been friends, have we not?"

"This is different. Kate—you understand? Different."

She stared at him. "What is different, Davie?"

"You. Myself. That was good enough, before. But now—you are not a child any more. A woman now. And I am a man. Wanting you!"

"Wanting . . . ?" Her voice faltered a little at that. Especially as he put his arm round her, or tried to do so, the heavy cloak no help.

"I mean *needing* you. Not just wanting. *You*. You only. As a woman—*my* woman. You and me, Kate!"

"Mercy!" She drew away somewhat, but not very far, for what with the viands and their containers there was not much spare room on that bench. "What has come over you, Davie?"

"Nothing. Or . . . perhaps everything! Do you not understand, girl? I *love* you! Love you, I tell you!"

"Oh—is that all!" Her relief was evident. In fact, she edged back closer. "That is nice, Davie."

It was his turn to stare, all but confounded. "Nice . . . ?" he got out thickly.

"Yes. Very nice. I have always wanted you to love me. You have taken a long time to say so! Why? Were you not sure, before?"

Quite put off his stride, as it were, he shook his head. "You . . . you mean this? You want it? Me? You love me, too?"

"To be sure. I have always loved you, Davie. Ever since I was little. You know that."

"But . . ." He could not, somehow, accept this as it sounded. "I mean *love*, Kate—real love. Not just affection, fondness. Love, the love of a man for a woman."

"Yes, oh yes. That is my sort of love, also. I am glad that you have come round to it, at last, Davie."

Still he found her attitude beyond him, his fine authority

and initiative eroded. "I am not sure . . . that you understand me, lass," he said, as though choosing his words with care. "This love, it is not just something which has grown out of childhood fondness, see you. It is deep, strong, from the heart, for all time, man and woman choosing each other . . ."

"And talking a great deal?" she interrupted, with a little laugh. "I did not think that there would be so many words about it all!" And she snuggled up closer.

He swallowed. "Kate! Kate!" was all that he could find to reply.

She unfastened her cloak at the neck and threw it back at his side. "See you, it is cold in here, Davie. This cloak is quite large. Room for us both in it. We will be warmer this way." And she tucked part of the velvet-lined cloak about him, her arm remaining thereafter round his waist.

The initiative might not be his, after all, but he was not the man to neglect such opportunity. He drew her to him and found her lips without any trouble, parting them after a moment or two.

They dispensed with words for a while, sighs and little moans serving very well.

When, presently, they paused for breath, he was not to be silenced, however. "My dear, my very dear!" he panted. "This is joy, beyond all belief! You are delicious, adorable, and I want you, need you, ache for you. But, but . . ."

"But what, Davie? Do I fail you in some way? Are your court ladies more, more adept? Or . . . ?"

"Lord, Kate—do not say such a thing! You are worth all of them together, and more. You are all delight, all loveliness. It is but that I am . . . afraid. Afraid that you may mistake. May not see this love as I do. You are young, you see . . ."

"I am seventeen. You just said, back there, that I was a woman now. And I am, never fear!" And reaching down for his arm, around her, she took his hand and raised it to cover, or almost, her full and rounded breast. "Is it not so?"

He could not speak for a little, so moved was he. And when he did find words, it was not to argue the matter.

"My love! My heart! My precious! Oh Kate!" he got out.

"That is better," she nodded. "As to age, you know, I

think that I am older than you are. Not in years but other-wise. I think that all women are."

"Indeed!" But he was not going to argue that one either, not with his hand where it still was, her nipple prominent between his finger and thumb. "Will . . . will you wed me, Kate?" he asked abruptly.

"To be sure. I wondered when you would bring yourself to ask!"

Again she had him silenced. Anyway, words seemed distinctly superfluous in this encounter. They came together again by mutual consent in vehement and comprehensive embrace—so comprehensive that somehow David's other hand found itself inside the girl's bodice and most happy to be there, as well it might be, and apparently welcome.

So they sat within that cloak, whilst the rain pattered on the roof and dripped around them, cold like time forgotten. Such speech as intervened was inconsequential.

That is, until Kate suddenly sat up. "When, Davie?" she demanded.

"When . . . ?"

"Yes, when? When shall we be wed?"

"Oh. Well—we shall have to think on that. I do not rightly know. I have not considered that . . ."

"Not considered! You say that!"

"My dear—how could I tell? I could not be sure . . . you might not . . ."

"How soon, then?"

He shook his head. "I do not know. Much will have to be considered. The times are difficult. The King's service . . ."

"Davie—you are not going to make excuses?"

"No, no. But placed as I am, I am scarcely my own master. And we may be into war, at any time. Would you wish us to start our married life shut up in Stirling Castle?"

"Why not? So long as we are together. As well there as any."

"Well . . . sakes, lassie—do not think that I would delay a day longer than need be! Lord—I want you, Kate, want you *now*! Not, not just some day . . ." This assertion promptly led to further urgent embracing and the postponement of less immediate considerations meantime.

After some indefinite lapse of time, Kate recollected that her family might have been expecting them back somewhat before this. They started up, almost guiltily on David's part—although guilt was not something with which Kate was much concerned—and were half down the slope before they remembered the salmon and venison and key, and had to go back. The man retained sufficient of his wits to reflect that it was probably seldom that comestibles played so prominent a part in the manifestation of true love.

Back in the castle, Kate forestalled any criticism or sly comment by announcing outright even as they handed over the viands, that she and Davie were now betrothed to wed, and was it not splendid? David, embarrassed anyway, was a little perturbed, believing it customary for the man to have to seek the father's permission before any such declaration was made. However, none of the company appeared to find anything unsuitable or even surprising about the announcement, taking it almost as though it had been inevitable—which set David wondering, as he responded suitably to the congratulations.

Leaving Kate that night was a protracted and grievous business, and it was late indeed before he got up to Garleton Castle, to an uproar of barking dogs, a sleepily protesting gatehouse porter, and his father and Mirren, wakened from the same bed but quite unembarrassed about it now, accusing him of thoughtlessness. It was much later still before he slept, his mind busy with so much. Only very minor amongst the recurring thoughts was the question of how effective had been his firm and decisive stance in the matter of dealing with women? Whether in fact the decisions had been all, or mainly, on his part? How much, indeed, had he improved on Davie Beaton's performance.

More vital considerations had no difficulty in imposing themselves.

11

Although the wedding was seldom far from David's mind in the weeks and months that followed, events succeeded each other so consistently, often impinged on each other, and even if they did not always actually involve himself were so apt to involve those with whom he was connected, that marriage seemed out of the question meantime. Indeed, once he had returned to Stirling, two days after that especial October night, he did not see Kate again for a considerable time.

First, there was the news that after a distressing and prolonged labour Magaret Tudor had had her child, a daughter; and that Angus had indeed been present and was said to be grievously disappointed that it was not a son and heir. This in itself was not very important as far as Scotland was concerned, but its repercussions were. King Henry made a great show of congratulating his sister, sending her gifts by the hand of a special ambassador, and took the opportunity to announce that this child, his niece, born on English soil, was henceforth under his personal royal protection and must not be removed out of his domains. Clearly she was to be used as a hostage, both for her mother's co-operation and for Angus's obedience and support. Angus, however, whether in defiance, pique or just his disappointment, abandoned his wife and child promptly and returned to Scotland. Reliable reports had it that he had not gone back to his assembled forces in the north-east but, of all things, had headed westwards to join Arran at Hamilton.

This greatly alarmed the Regent and the Chancellor for their greatest fear was always of a concerted attack by the hosts of the three former members of the Regency Council, Angus, Arran and Home. Hitherto there had never seemed much likelihood of Angus and Arran collaborating, the Douglases and the Hamiltons ever being at daggers drawn.

But this new move of Angus, if accurate, was ominous, especially as Home was known to be assembling his strength in the Borders.

Albany decided to counter this threat by direct action, and ordered his Warden of the Marches to proceed to the immediate arrest of the Lord Home, as warning to the other two. Since de la Bastie would require considerably greater strength than he had based on Dunbar Castle for this formidable task, part of the force kept permanently assembled at Edinburgh was detached; and since this included the Lindsay contingent, David was sent for from Stirling to take charge of this, no doubt at Davie Beaton's suggestion. Unfortunately, speed and secrecy for the operation being essential and David having to come from Stirling, the Edinburgh force was well on its way to Dunbar by the time that he reached Holyrood, and he had to go riding hard after it, without any opportunity to call in at the Byres.

It was good, at least, to be on active service again, and a pleasure to see Antoine once more. There was little time for companionable association however. Nothing was surer than that Home would hear of this armed force coming to Dunbar, well-informed as he must be in this area. So actual surprise would be well-nigh impossible. It behoved them, therefore, to gain surprise by contriving something which Home would not expect. De la Bastie saw it thus. Such a large force coming to Dunbar would be almost certainly aimed at the Homes, since Tantallon was all but impregnable and anyway the Douglas presence hereabouts was much muted these days. So what would Home anticipate? An attack on himself, at Home Castle, which would demand many men and considerable artillery since it was a strong place and surrounded by lesser Home strengths? This was the last thing that Antoine wanted to tackle. But suppose instead they made a gesture of assaulting Dunglass—as they had done before? It would be logical, the nearest Home stronghold to Dunbar—and they had already put nearby Colbrandspath out of action. What would Home do, known to be mustering his Merse forces? He would have to do something, or lose all credit with his own people. Almost certainly he would come to the relief of Dunglass. The problem was, would he come in person, or send others? They wanted the man himself, not some lieutenant—and if

169

possible, without a battle. Antoine believed that if he, de la Bastie, made himself prominent in the Dunglass attack, and made at the same time loud claims that he, as new Warden of the Marches, was going to demonstrate how feeble and ineffective was the previous Warden, Home would be almost bound to respond personally. So—an ambush on the way! When the man was protected by no castle walls.

David agreed that this was sound reasoning. But how could an ambush be successful if Home came with a large force, as surely he would?

Antoine had an answer for that, too; a two-fold answer. The narrow passes and constrictions of Pease Dean, as they had seen, ensured that any company proceeding towards Dunglass from the south must inevitably be stretched out into little more than double-file for almost a couple of miles—that was why Colbrandspath Tower was sited there. The Homes would send scouts ahead to ensure a clear passage undoubtedly; but if the ambushing force was well hidden in the high woodland above, leaving the track free, with timber felled and ready to roll down on the vital part of the elongated column in front and rear, cutting off the leadership group from the rest, then the thing might be achieved at comparatively little cost. Especially if prior to that another contingent was to work its way secretly down through these Lammermuir hills, to come into the Merse from the north-west and appear to be menacing Home Castle. This ought to have the affect of causing Home, assuming that he was indeed with the Dunglass relief force, to send back some part of his strength to the aid of his main seat, so weakening and confusing his strategy.

David was lost in admiration for this elaborate planning but saw not a few points where it could go wrong—and said so. Antoine admitted that this, of course, was so; but basically it was a sound projection, he thought, and militarily valid—for even if it failed in any or all of its aspects, nothing should prove disastrous for their own forces. And David was not forgetting that de la Bastie was one of the most experienced military figures in Christendom.

Without delay, then, the plans were put into operation. The available manpower, including many of the Dunbar townsfolk and fishermen who had co-operated in the previous Dunglass gesture, was divided into three units: one for the distant Home Castle, in the Merse; one for Dunglass itself; and the vital ambushing party for Pease Dean—the two latter to keep together meantime. The Merse contingent, under Sir Adam Hepburn from Luffness, was sent off as soon as it could be got ready that very night, to proceed as far as they could under cover of darkness on their roundabout, thirty-mile journey through the hills. A proportion of the rest were allowed to go roystering in the town, making no secret of the fact that they were bound for Dunglass in the morning—in the confident hope that Home would be apprised of it all almost by the time that they got there.

Not too early next day, and in no great hurry, with sundry cannon to trundle along behind, the quite large force made its way along the coast road south-eastwards the eight miles to Dunglass. As anticipated, when they arrived at the castle it was to find the Home garrison ready and waiting for them, battlements manned, drawbridge up and cannon mounted—indeed a couple of shots were fired at them as warning to keep their distance. Which was all as planned.

Antoine brought up their own artillery to give an answering salvo. But since the cannon on both sides had approximately the same calibre and range, and casualties were not the objective, all remained sensibly at arm's length, content to sound belligerent. Whilst this was going on and the besieging troops were satisfactorily positioned, Antoine and David rode quietly off alone for Pease Dean with prospecting to do, which it was important should not be obvious.

It all reminded them of the previous occasion. But this time they had a different problem. They sought what might not be easy to find, a place well above one of the narrowest sections of the track through the dean, sufficiently wellwooded to both hide a large number of men and to provide tree-trunks to fell and roll down, yet with the slope below steep and clear enough of trees not to impede the downward course of the rolled logs. In well over a mile of the twisting ravine, with the track traversing both flanks, there ought to be some such place?

It took them a good couple of hours to find, at the far south-eastern end of the pass, which was not ideal; and even here some clearing of the slope would be necessary—and such clearance would have to remain imperceptible. On the other hand there was the benefit that here were quite a number of large boulders and rock fragments scattered about which would serve as additional missiles if dug out.

They returned to Dunglass, from which the occasional boom of cannon had been resounding, to wait until dusk. Darkness would certainly not facilitate their task, but it was vitally important that no hint of their activities in the dene should be disclosed. How much time they had was a matter of guesswork—but then, to some extent, the entire exercise was that anyway. They reckoned that to give time for the news to reach Home Castle for a relieving force to be readied—a muster was already reported—and for this to make its way up this far would take most of two days. That is, from the previous night. The Mersemen, like all Borderers, were great horsemen, mosstroopers, and once mounted would cover the ground quickly.

With campfires being lit and the shadows of evening cloaking the withdrawal of the ambush party, they set out, armed with axes, mattocks and ropes as well as their weapons, all on foot. They could follow the road for a mile or so but after that must take to the higher rough ground, to avoid being observed by cottagers, and this made for very difficult progress in the darkness, amongst trees and broken terrain, with muffled cursing as accompaniment. There was no great hurry, however.

It was even difficult to find their chosen spot at night although they had marked it carefully earlier. But eventually Antoine and David were satisfied, and they could get to work. Tree fellers went to chop and lop and trim, well behind the terrace area selected for the launching of the attack, and teams of men dragged the trunks down to position them on the very lip of the steep, held in place by wedges of small stones. Others dug up and rolled rocks and boulders and poised these similarly—this activity at two points about one hundred yards apart, leaving a gap. At least there was plenty of manpower for the labour.

The two leaders were particularly careful about the next phase of the work, superintending all of it personally. The steep bank below their terrace had to be cleared of anything large enough to obstruct the hurtling logs and missiles; but such clearance must not be visible from the track in daylight. There were two or three major trees which could not be disposed of without leaving an obvious scar, and these would have to be left, hopefully; but it was mostly small scrub hawthorn and bushes which could be cut away and the branches and leafage then arranged, to look natural. Fortunately, being October, the foliage was sear and brown anyway.

This all took a deal longer, in the darkness, than might have been expected, and there was more noise than desirable—although nobody was likely to be lurking about Pease Dean during the night. It was almost dawn before de la Bastie was satisfied and the men could take some rest, sleep if they could.

With daylight there was more to be done, chilled as they were, and it all had to be effected most discreetly and silently in case of there being anybody abroad to observe. Assault positions had to be allocated, mostly high above the track but some below it, well out of sight, should there be any breakaway in that direction. Also some men down on the road itself but westwards a little way, towards Dunglass. Then there were lookouts to post, up on the high flank of Eweside Hill, where they could see for miles down the Eye Water valley, the almost certain approach route for any fast-moving company from the Merse.

All this done, they settled down to wait, with strictest orders to all groups to remain hidden from the road and make no noise. Now was the time to catch up on the night's missing sleep. Antoine and David remained with the main high-placed party, about one hundred and fifty strong.

All day they waited, and as the hours passed began to fret. By the time that the autumnal sun was sinking behind the Lammermuir heights to their west, they were worried. Had they miscalculated? Had the required information not reached Home Castle? Or was Lord Home away? Or could he possibly be taking a different route to Dunglass? Through the hills, as they had sent Hepburn, much slower as this would be? Or was he not coming at all, leaving Dunglass to its fate?

By late afternoon Antoine was sufficiently concerned to send a runner up to the lookout position on Eweside Hill, to ensure that the men there had not all fallen asleep or otherwise failed in their duty; but he came back presently to declare that there was no failure up there and that despite the far-flung and all-round prospect, the watchers had seen nothing to report all day.

They were reconciling themselves to the spending of another uncomfortable, hungry and probably wasted night in their hiding places when, with dusk falling fast, a panting, breathless man came bounding and slithering down through the woodland from Eweside. They were coming, he gasped, nearly there indeed. Not coming up the Eye Water as expected, but from the higher ground of Coldingham Muir, due eastwards. A large mounted company, perhaps three hundred or more. Only come into sight of Eweside as they topped the rise by Auldcambus, not much more than a mile away.

Antoine did not wait to hear more, leaping up to shout orders, alerting all and sending messengers racing to warn the outlying units. If the Homes were only a mile away when this man left Eweside Hill, they were less than half that now.

The runners were hardly away and the others hurrying to their action position when David held up a hand. Clearly to be heard was the drumming of distant hooves.

"On us already!" he exclaimed.

Antoine shook his head. "Not many," he jerked. "No large number of horses, there. And going fast. Scouts."

"Aye—that will be it. Home will well know the dangers of this pass, and will be sending scouts through first, to ensure that all is clear. Sakes—I hope . . . !"

The Frenchman nodded grimly. "That none of our people down there attack such scouts! Then all would be lost. They have their orders, but . . ."

There was no time to do anything more about it. Round a bend in the track below came a tight group of about a dozen horsemen, two-abreast, cantering. It was fairly deep shadow down there now, but it was possible to see that they were in half armour, with typical Borderers' helmets and lances.

"No—pray that none challenge them!" David muttered.

But quickly the riders were past the area directly below where the lowermost ambush party were hidden, ensconced behind the trees and cover that was not only to protect them from view but from any boulders and logs which might overshoot their target. Pounding round the next bend in the track, they were no longer visible.

"We shall soon hear if the far party halt them!" Antoine said.

They heard only the hoof beats drumming on, the sound gradually fading. The listeners heaved sighs of relief.

"Home is no fool," David declared. "He came by a roundabout route we did not think on. And he prospects this Pease Dean before entering. But—coming at this hour? You think that he did this of a purpose? To arrive at Dunglass with the dark? To surprise us? Assault by night?"

"It looks so. Some hundreds of cavalry riding down a resting camp in the darkness could make much havoc, cause panic. It could be. Clearly we must not underestimate my lord of Home!"

In a few minutes they heard hoofbeats again, but this time in still lesser volume. Then two horsemen appeared from the west, below, at the gallop now, obviously the scouting party's messengers sent back to advise Home that the pass was clear.

Now—an end to this long waiting.

They stood poised. They heard hooves once more, but different now, many, many, but not drumming, pounding, the jingling of harness and the clank of mail, even the murmur of voices. Antoine had his horn at the ready.

The problem now was the lack of light; the track was deeper than ever in shadow. And it was vital to identify the leadership group as the company filed through—or all their effort could be for naught.

In the event, there was no real difficulty for, after a short column of perhaps a score of mosstroopers had trotted past, a smaller party rounded that bend—and these rode under banners, one large and three less so. None in that cohort was likely to display a great banner save the Lord Home himself. Admittedly the devices on the flags could not be distinguished; but the chances of them being anything but the white ramping lion on green of Home were remote indeed.

"Ha! Pride of birth can prove a weakness," de la Bastie commented. "Now—another few lengths, and then . . . !" With the banner group directly below Antoine blew a single long blast on his horn.

Immediately all was changed, dramatically, violently. Men leapt up to knock away the wedges holding the piled tree-trunks and boulders and to push them over the lip of

175

the slope, to go hurtling down the steep and to keep up the process from the stacks collected—this at the two ends of the hundred-yard gap. Down and down the great logs and rocks plunged and bounded, and on the track alarmed horsemen, staring upwards, reacted urgently, wildly and differently, some rearing their mounts to a curveting halt, some spurring ahead, some reining round and back and even down the farther slope, in utter chaos.

On and on the bombardment of deadly missiles continued, to crash down on the road and beyond, carrying away horses and riders in flailing, yelling disaster at both ends of the gap, but mainly at the southern end where by far the largest concentration of logs had been stacked, stretching towards that bend round which new files of horsemen were appearing to tangle with their fellows who had turned back in dire disorder. And in the middle, isolated in the gap, the banner party circled and huddled and struggled with their terrified horses, cut off front and rear by the smashing cataracts of wood and stone and soil.

Judging his moment, Antoine blew another two quick blasts—this for a few selected trees and boulders to be sent down, spaced in the hundred-yard gap itself, since he did not want the leaders there to reckon themselves to be safe and so have time to recover initiative and seek control of the situation. Nor, however, did he want them, Home himself in especial, to be killed or maimed, so these missiles went off singly and intermittently, allowing time for some avoiding action on the track below.

The Home banner party broke up necessarily and satis-factorily, some hastily dismounting to take refuge down the farther bank and behind trees.

Again assessing the timing heedfully, the Frenchman blew his third signal, three long blasts. And all his people, save for small groups at the two extreme ends who still continued with the bombardment, flung themselves down the slope, swords and dirks drawn, in a tide of yelling humanity, leaping and sliding, David and Antoine with them. At the same time the men from below the road showed themselves and came clambering up to play their part.

It was, at this stage, almost inevitable success, there being no escape for the leaders who were outnumbered ten to one. Most were now on foot amongst the milling horses, and although some put up a token resistance, it was only that. The Lord Home, stocky, grizzled, impassive-seeming, stood, arms folded, in a dignified silence.

Whilst all but a few of the attackers swung left and right to man the barriers of wood and debris which had piled up on and about the shelf which carried the road, to prevent any rallying of the mosstroopers to their lord's aid, Antoine came and bowed courteously, if somewhat breathlessly, to Home.

"I trust that you suffered no hurt, my lord, in this unseemly ambuscade?" he enquired. "It has been lacking in finesse, shall we say? But it is the fortunes of war—since war you appear to have chosen!"

"I would not call this war, Frenchman!" the older man said. "What now?"

"If you will remount, my lord, we shall seek quiet and our evening meal. At Dunglass. No doubt you have ridden far and will be anhungered?" As an afterthought, he added, "My lord Duke, the Regent, would like a word with you."

They found that they had captured the lairds of Wedderburn, Blackadder and Paxton also, these taking their fate less calmly than did their lord.

They collected sufficient horses to mount these four prisoners, David Lindsay and a small escort, and these would make their way downhill through the woodland to a small lower and winding path which led to a narrow ford beneath a waterfall of the Pease Burn and thence up to the main track again, further west by almost a mile. Thereafter it should be a clear ride to Dunglass. Antoine, like any good commander, would remain, to fight off any counter-attack by the mosstroopers which might develop—although such would be difficult to mount successfully in the circumstances—and then to extricate his force, up again through the higher woodlands as they had come, terrain where they ought to be safe from mounted harassment in the almost dark.

So David found himself acting captor to the former Lord High Chamberlain, chief Warden of the Marches and member of the Regency Council, and was less than comfortable in the role. But having gone to so much trouble to take their prisoners he was not going to risk losing them now, and maintained strictest control, with each of the four Homes' horses tied to one of their escort's. In fact, he experienced no trouble, and rode into the campfire-lit siege camp presently, at Dunglass, in some triumph, with the great banner of Home held upside-down.

It was almost two hours before de la Bastie arrived with his force, all in high spirits over their all but bloodless victory, having had little difficulty in persuading the leaderless and bemused mosstroopers that there was nothing to be gained by seeking to attack so potent a force of unknown numbers in the darkness and sloping woodland. These might come on in daylight, although this seemed not very likely.

At any rate, Antoine gave orders to pack up, to harness the cannon, break camp and march, there being nothing for them at Dunglass now. Leaving the fires blazing there, amidst a certain amount of confusion but in cheerful mood, the reunited host turned for its night march back along the coast road for Dunbar.

Next day, at the head of his Lindsay contingent again, David escorted his illustrious prisoners to Edinburgh, passing no nearer to Garleton and the Byres than the town of Haddington, to his much regret.

At Holyrood, handing over the Homes to Albany, he drew considerable praise from both the Regent and the Chancellor—and grins from Davie Beaton—despite his disclaimers that all the credit must go to de la Bastie. The older men appeared to imagine that he was proving to be some sort of military expert—of which, to be sure, Scotland was in all too great need—and would no doubt be useful again hereafter. A little worried about such false pretences, he rode on to Stirling the next day, escape to action over again for the meantime.

Eager as he was for movement, action, enlargement from the confines of Stirling Castle, David could hardly have been more surprised to receive a bare two weeks later a summons back to Edinburgh—or, at least, if not a summons a special courier from Davie Beaton requesting him to come forthwith on the realm's business, which in the circumstances amounted to the same thing. His surprise was the greater when, no details being vouchsafed, all he could elicit from the courier was that he imagined that it would be concerned with the matter of the disappearance of the Lord Home.

Leaving a tearful King James once more in the care of Abbot John, and to the Earl Marischal's disapproval, he set off, wondering.

Edinburgh he found more like an armed camp than ever, more men-at-arms everywhere. At Holyrood he was the recipient of an extraordinary story. Beaton, not in the least chagrined as might have been expected, indeed seeming almost amused at the sequence of events, mischances and apparent misjudgments, recounted it all. The Regent, thankful to have Home safely accounted for and advised that clemency would probably serve better than the mailed fist, at this stage, at least as far as the unpredictable and weak Arran was concerned, decided to try to detach the Hamilton from his new-found ally Angus and so isolate the latter and at least neutralise the second of the troublesome triumvirate. To this end he had prevailed on the Edinburgh city magistrates to dismiss the captive Home as their Lord Provost, an office he had held amongst so many others—the capital found it convenient to have great Lords as their chief magistrates in troubled times—and in his place to appoint the said Earl of Arran, Lord High Admiral. Sending Arran word of this, at Hamilton, with a gracious letter, Albany said that this was an excellent opportunity to settle their differences in a chivalrous fashion and let bygones be bygones, assuring him of safe conduct to Edinburgh and all good treatment thereafter. In token of which, and to demonstrate his good faith, he would then hand over to Arran the erring Lord Home, as a sort of hostage, to his safe keeping. And Arran had come, forthwith, had been installed as Lord Provost, and after an amicable meeting with the Regent had taken Home into his custody. And the very next day they both had left the city, secretly, and ridden post-haste for Hamilton, there to rejoin Angus. The Earls of Lennox and Glencairn had adhered to them there, and all five great lords had signed a band, or contract, to unite all their power to bring down the Regent. So now Albany was assembling the greatest army seen in Scotland since Flodden, to march on Hamilton.

David, needless to say, was appalled at this catalogue of folly and seeming incompetence, with all the good work at Pease Dean undone, wasted, the situation worse than before indeed, the three traitorous lords united and joined by two more. Was the Regent mad? For the first time, David questioned, although not in words, Beaton's shrewdness, since surely Albany would not have done all this contrary to his interpreter's and adviser's counsel?

But the other seemed nowise upset. The situation was now excellent, he asserted—all for the best. Albany was essentially a lazy man, he pointed out, despite his hot temper, much too prone to put off, to leave comparatively well alone. He had to be spurred into drastic action against these lords, military action on a major scale. It had to come to that in the end—to demonstrate who was strongest. Having Home taken prisoner was a useful move, a moral victory which must much decrease that proud noble's reputation in the Borders and amongst his own people. And by exercising clemency towards Arran, the Regent would gain a valuable card to play with parliament and the nation. But hitherto Arran had committed no real offence, nothing with which he could be charged or proceeded against lawfully. Now he had. He had set at large a prisoner of the crown and thus had laid himself open to an accusation of treason. He could, and must, be proceeded against. Moreover, all three highly placed rogues were now conveniently shepherded into a corner together, at Hamilton, and two others of doubtful loyalty now confirmed as traitors. The situation was simplified, the decks cleared.

David had his doubts about all this, but kept them to himself.

The army being assembled again on the Burgh Muir of Edinburgh—to march against the city's Lord Provost—was certainly large enough, Davie Beaton calculating that it would number between thirty and forty thousand all told. But how reliable it might be was another question and, to be sure, it was completely inexperienced as to warfare and less than unified, with constant bickering already breaking out and even bloodshed between the units of the various lords. David was interested to discover that the Lindsay force had been reinforced by almost three hundred and fifty from the Earl of Crawford, and two hundred others had come from the Lord Ogilvy of Airlie; so the visit to the north-east had not been fruitless.

The Lord Patrick arrived from the Byres to take charge of this contingent, with David as second-in-command—which in effect meant that whilst Kate's father rode comfortably with the Regent and other lords, her betrothed had to march on foot with the men. Not that David complained; it was all better than the constrictions of Stirling.

The foot set out on 25th October in crisp autumn weather, good for marching, with almost forty miles to go and three days to do it, to Hamilton in Clydesdale, a straggling, untidy column itself three miles long, this not counting the artillery which came along behind—and which, by the very nature of things was bound to be well known about at Hamilton long before it could get there; but this could not be helped. After a disorganised and delayed start they got only as far as Calder Muir, a mere dozen miles, the first day, all those men scarcely commending themselves to the countryside which they traversed, nor the areas in which they camped, a plague of scorpions sent to scourge them as the Prior of St Cuthbert of Calder picturesquely complained, involuntary host to many. The second day they did better, reaching Allanton on the South Calder Water, this on account of the thin drizzle of chill rain which discouraged delay and foraging; and there, at darkening, they were joined by the Regent and his entourage of nobles and knights, including of course Davie Beaton. Hamilton was only nine miles further, in the wide vale where the Clyde and Avon joined.

A somewhat noisy council of war was held, with too many advisers with scant experience of warfare taking part. David, to his embarrassment, found himself being appealed to for opinions, with his new-minted reputation as a military man, but contributed little other than to declare that while a show of strength with all this host encircling Hamilton town and Cadzow Castle was necessary and valuable, it would be folly to launch any sort of assault as was being suggested until the artillery came up. This was coming along at its usual oxen-paced trundle far behind, the mighty Mons Meg included; and although Cadzow might not be a great fortress to compare with Stirling, Dumbarton and Edinburgh, it could cost dear to take without cannon. This sensible advice did not commend itself to the firebrands loud in favour of martial flourish and knightly derring-do. Some there were unkind enough to suggest that the King's Procurator should stick to tutoring bairns, or even poetry.

However, Davie Beaton, always careful not to seem publicly to overstep his role as interpreter and secretary to the Regent, winked over at his friend in token that he at least got the point.

In the event his counsel turned out to be unnecessary and indeed the entire proceedings a distinct anticlimax for the vast majority, although Albany was probably pleased enough when in early afternoon the forerunners of the great host arrived at the Netherton of Hamilton and began to semi-encircle the town and its adjacent large castle of Cadzow—the presence of the River Clyde, broad and deep, immediately to the north making unnecessary any massing on that flank. While this was proceeding a large white flag was seen to be hoisted from the castle battlements, the drawbridge rattled down and a party rode out under a lesser white flag and a banner bearing gules, three cinquefoils ermine, for Hamilton. As this group neared the Regent's company, it could be seen to include a horse litter under a handsome heraldic canopy, the heraldry impaling the royal arms of Scotland with those of Hamilton.

All stared at this in some doubt.

Surprise was increased when, on closer view, the litter could be seen to contain the tiny figure of a very old woman, shrunken within a voluminous fur cloak yet sitting up straight with confidence and dignity. As this strange equipage came up, one of the attendant riders actually raised a trumpet and blew a resounding flourish, as though calling all to suitable and respectful attention.

The summons over, a voice, remarkably strong and authoritative to issue from such an ancient and withered female, said, "Which of you is John Stewart? Or Johan, as I understand he calls himself! Ah, you is it? So we meet, Nephew, at last."

Albany had understood enough of this to urge his horse forward to near the litter, and after a slight hesitation, to remove his velvet cap and to bow over the claw-like hand outstretched to him. "*Madame ma tante!*" he said. "*Je vous salue . . .*"

"Eh? Speak up, man! And speak so that I can understand you. Or, guidsakes—is it true that you can only speak the French? Alec's son!"

Discreetly Davie Beaton moved up and translated that.

"Who are you, young man?"

"The Chancellor's nephew, Countess. David Beaton, secretary."

"Ha! One of that penniless brood, frae Fife! At least you look as though you might hae mair wits than that turkey-cock of an uncle of yours. Or this Frenchified nephew of mine! And call me Highness, boy!"

"Certainly, Highness."

And Highness she undoubtedly was, as well as sounding it, the Princess Mary, daughter of James the Second, mother of Arran, through whom indeed James Hamilton had gained that title and earldom held by Thomas Boyd her first husband. Now in her eighties, she had been the sister of both James the Third and Alexander, Albany's father—and clearly none were to forget it.

The Regent was at something of a loss as to how to deal with his autocratic ancient relative, but the lady suffered no such problems.

"You, Davie Beaton—come nearer. I refuse to shout to you! Tell this silly son of my pig-headed brother that he must cease all this stupid bickering and marching about the country forthwith. He and my equally stupid son, both! There's been ower much of it and it's to stop! I have told James and now I tell this John. They are cousins and they will behave like cousins, for the realm's weal. Tell him so."

Beaton, bowing, conveyed an edited version of that to the Regent, who looked blank.

"Aye. Now, boy, tell him that I have a paper for him, back there. He will get it when he comes to eat his food. I got my fool James to sign it before I sent him off out of harm's way—no' that far, mind. He can be back in an hour or two—ooh, aye. He has signed that he'll be done with this nonsense, that he'll acknowledge this cousin of his as Regent, that he'll send a' those men of his back where they belong and keep the peace hereafter—a' that, so long as John Stewart does the same, takes a' this unseemly host out of my sight and signs a decent bond o' cousinly love and affection. Tell him."

Even Beaton swallowed at that, and was perhaps less diplomatic about his translation than usual. But Albany got the gist, blinked rapidly, and licked thin lips. He murmured something incoherent in French.

"What does he say, you Davie? Has he no' got even a decent *French* tongue in his heid?"

Actually the Regent had said nothing to the point but Beaton said it for him. "My lord Duke is . . . gratified, Highness. At your wisdom and good offices. But he would wish to know what may be the situation with regard to the Earl of Angus and the Lord Home? With whom, we understand, my lord of Arran has contracted a band against the Regent. And the Earls of Lennox and Glencairn, likewise?"

A pair of washed out blue but still keen old eyes considered him shrewdly. "Those limmers!" she said. "Och, I sent them off three days back. That Douglas is a trouble-maker, if ever I saw one! But then the Douglases aye were that, mind. Alecky Home is different—a fox! You'll have to watch that one—or this Johan will! But Archie Douglas will never come to much."

"Yes, Highness—no doubt." David Lindsay, listening nearby, noted that Beaton did not even trouble to translate all that. "But—where are they? Are they with my lord of Arran? Nearby?"

"Na, na—what do you take me for? I tell you, I sent them off. I'll have nae Douglases in *my* house! Nor Border thieves like the Homes, either. Angus has gone to Douglasdale. Whether Home is still with him, guid kens—but I jalouse he will be gone back to work on his ain Merse reivers, who will not have sae high an opinion of him, I'm thinking. After yon stramash when he was taken like a bairn on a chamber-pot in some dene or other! Lennox has returned to his Heilants—and guid riddance! And Glencairn to wherever he comes frae—Cunninghame, belike."

"So-o-o!" Belatedly, the younger man gave a summary of this to Albany, who clearly could scarcely believe his ears. He launched into a flood of dramatic-sounding verbiage, in which waving hands at least were eloquent.

"My lord Duke says that he appreciates your good efforts, Highness," Beaton told her, carefully selective. "He rejoices in your tidings. But can scarcely believe that this threat to the realm's peace could be so readily disposed of."

"Is that so? But then, he doesna ken his aunt! Mind—it isna right disposed of yet. He has to do *his* share, tell him. To sign a paper for James, *my* James, assuring him of all amity and guidwill. And James is to remain Admiral, see you—that is part of it. They will need to shake hands on it, the two o' them, before all is in order."

"And you, Madame, can ensure that my lord of Arran, the Lord High Admiral, can be here presently for this shaking of hands?"

"Och yes, laddie. I ken where he's at. He'll come—if I tell him. Now—tell my owerdressed nephew that there is meat and wine for him and his, ready in my hall. No' for ower many, mind—two hundred, at the maist." And without further ado, with a gesture to her trumpeter who blew a single sustained note, she ordered her litter and escort to be turned round and to head back for Cadzow Castle, without so much as looking to see who followed.

In some little confusion the Regent and his entourage conferred and, since there seemed to be nothing else for it, to do as they were told. They rode on after the old lady, leaving orders for the vast host, with contingents still arriving and the artillery of course still far behind, just to camp where it was, as best it could. Beaton went to the trouble of urging David Lindsay, once he had seen to his men, to join him in the castle—and adding that, by what they had just heard and seen, it looked as though Scotland's troubles might be over and done with if only this old woman had been the Regent!

Cadzow was a fine and extensive castle, although no fortress citadel, and later, David sat down in a comparatively modest place in its huge hall, to an excellent repast, in cheerful, almost boisterous company, much tickled that where they had expected battle they found feasting instead. Nobody appeared to be worrying about the possibility of a surprise attack by Douglas forces.

The meal was almost over and the company getting ever noisier as the drink had its effect, when there was a diversion up at the dais end of the hall. The Earl of Arran himself came clanking in, dressed in spectacular black and gold inlaid half armour, an esquire carrying a crested and plumed helmet, attended by a group of Hamilton knights in heraldic surcoats over steel—all highly impressive. The noise in the hall died away.

Arran bowed to his mother and looked doubtfully at Albany sitting beside her. He said nothing.

The Regent was less than voluble, likewise. He rose to his

feet, but that was as far as his reaction went. Since he represented the crown, most others felt that they ought to rise also. An uneasy pause ensued.

Their hostess, remaining seated, suffered no such restraints. "So there you are, James," she said. "Well—speak up, man. He has seen your paper—this cousin of yours. And is prepared to sign the like, for you. But—you had best speak the French if you want an answer! How any man seeks to rule this unruly realm and yet canna speak the language, guid kens!"

Her son cleared his throat. He had, of course, spent a considerable time in France and had a fair command of French. "I greet you, Cousin," he said, in that tongue, but lacking conviction. "I . . . wish you well. I accept you as Regent for our liege-lord James. I desire peace. I renounce my band with the lords of Angus and Home. I request full acknowledgment of my position as Lord Admiral of this realm. And of fourth person in this kingdom." That all came out like a lesson well learned, levelly but without emphasis.

After a pause, Albany shrugged expressive shoulders. "I accept and agree," he said briefly. "I shall so sign."

Again silence, this time broken by a bark of a laugh from one of the earl's little group of supporters, a markedly handsome young man in a strongly virile, almost animal way, powerfully built and with a glittering eye.

"Lord God—here's a bonny sight!" this individual exclaimed. "A nation's fate decided so. By two such . . . paladins!"

There were gasped breaths throughout the hall—for although these words themselves were innocuous enough, there was no hiding the scorn with which they were enunciated.

"Hold your tongue, sirrah!" the old lady observed, but almost equably. "Or I will have it held for you!"

"Madame!" the speaker said, making a flourish of a bow, difficult in armour.

"The Bastard," the man next to Lindsay murmured. "Sir James Hamilton of Finnart, the Bastard of Arran."

David was as interested as anyone there. Few had not heard of the Bastard of Arran, young as he was, the style by which he was generally known. Arran, although twice married, was a widower, with no lawful son, his daughter married to the Lord Drummond. But he had at least two illegitimate sons, this, and the other Sir John Hamilton of Clydesdale, a man of similar moral fibre to his father. But this Bastard was different, a roystering, quarrelsome, unscrupulous character, but a fighter, brave as a lion and one of the best jousters, sworders and tournament knights in Christendom, in this last respect on a par with Antoine de la Bastie. Most had believed him to be still in France, left behind when his father returned to Scotland.

The Regent was looking at this character, and clearly not liking what he saw. David wondered whether they were going to be treated to a display of the famous Albany temper and cap-hurling—and Davie Beaton, in this instance, not in a position to do anything about it. But the Princess Mary, very much mistress in her son's house, took firm control.

"Shake hands, James," she commanded imperiously. "Do not just stand there. Where is that laddie Beaton, with the paper?"

Thus summoned, Beaton was able to come forward to the Duke's side, producing a document from his doublet and the ink-horn and pen which always hung at his side.

The Regent accepted Arran's reluctantly outstretched hand in no very amiable fashion, quickly dropped it and took the pen and paper from Davie, to lean over the table and dash off a spluttering signature. Then he promptly resumed his seat, duty done. It was left to Arran to pick up the signed agreement, and Davie his pen.

The Bastard hooted another laugh. "God save the King's Grace!" he shouted. Nobody quite knew what to make of that in the circumstances, whether to cheer in the traditional fashion, to ignore it, or just to look embarrassed, sensing that it was perhaps not complimentary to these two close supporters of the crown. Their hostess, however, retained her grip on the proceedings and, rapping on the table, ordered the troupe of musicians waiting in a deep window embrasure to strike up. To the scraping of fiddles and the clang of cymbals, then, Arran stood clutching his paper, looking distinctly at a loss despite all his armoured finery. It was the Bastard who led the way over to a side table, across the dais, where they sat down to eat.

Crisis was over, in the short term—and possibly in the longer term also.

In the chamber which Lindsay shared with Davie Beaton that night, the latter was in cheerful mood—not that that was unusual. Who could have prophesied, he demanded, that it all would go so well, so easily? The dangerous triumvirate was broken. Arran would be no more trouble, he swore, so long as that old woman lived. Home's credit was diminished for the second time, with this contract or band rejected. And Angus was now out on his own. They would march for Douglasdale in the morning, a mere score of miles or so—but he very much doubted if Angus would wait for them there. He wondered whether Albany realised how fortunate he was?

David did not know, but doubted whether the prospects were quite so rosy as all that. Arran was a weathercock and his mother could not, in the nature of things, hold him for long.

Perhaps not, the other acceded. But more pressure could be brought to bear. And there was now a new jouster in the lists—the Bastard. Properly used, that one might serve them very well—and not only with Arran. He had known him in France and had recognised his quality.

A quality for ill, for strife and havoc, David suggested, but Beaton waved that aside. Strife and havoc had their value in troubled times, if suitably harnessed and controlled—and he thought that he could control the Bastard of Arran sufficiently to be of use.

As ever, David wondered at the extraordinary self-confidence of this peculiar friend of his.

They sent word next day for the artillery, wherever it might be, to turn around and go back whence it had come. Then, ordering three-quarters of their vast army to start on its own return journey, and judging that even the remaining ten thousand was over-many to march through the Lanarkshire hills to Douglasdale, the Regent and the mounted portion of his host, to the number of about fifteen hundred, set off south-eastwards up Clyde, leaving the rest to come along at a marching pace. David had little difficulty in contriving that he rode now, rather than marched, with Albany's party. Arran, less than enthusiastic, came along too, and the Bastard with him, much more willingly—and it was to be noted on their journey that Davie Beaton found his way not infrequently to the latter's side.

At Dalserf they turned southwards out of the Clyde and into the Avon valley, but soon left this again to follow up a tributary, the Nethan, to Lesmahagow, all territory belonging to Arran. Thereafter they began to climb through bleak lifting moorland, with the hills drawing ever closer, until they reached the watershed of Broken Cross and the land began to drop again towards the vale of the Douglas Water. Then, in late afternoon, with Douglas Castle itself only four miles away, a scouting party was detailed to ride ahead to discover if possible what was the situation there. Surprisingly the Bastard volunteered to lead this, as a seasoned campaigner, and pointing out that this was his own stamping ground and that he knew every yard of the way, Craignethan on this river being his seat. No one liked to display the suspicion which most felt about this offer, but Davie Beaton typically solved the problem by suggesting that David Lindsay, their own expert on such affairs, should go along too, the Regent relieved to agree and Hamilton showing no resentment.

So Lindsay and the Bastard of Arran set off at the head of a score of horsemen to make a discreet and roundabout approach to Douglas Castle, the den amongst the upper Clydesdale hills which had given birth and name to the great and warlike house which had grown to cut so wide a swathe in Scotland. David found the other a cheerful if daunting companion, full of stories and accounts of exploits which in another would have sounded like idle boasting but in this man somehow rang true. He also commended himself by his evident admiration for Antoine de la Bastie.

Amidst lengthening shadows they reined up on a shoulder of Poneil Hill and looked down the vale to its castle, set strongly between two lochans and marshy areas representing a widening of the Douglas Water, difficult to approach save by the one easily defended causeway, but no very large or impressive place to have been the cradle of so powerful a line, indeed not a great deal larger than Garleton. But it was not so much the size that concerned the observers as the fact that it seemed so entirely peaceful in the fading light, no armed camp around it, no campfires, no bustle of men, indeed little sign of any activity at all.

"I think that our hawk has flown, as I judged he might," Hamilton commented. "But I will ride down openly, to find out. I am known here. They will speak with me at the castle."

"And I will come with you. Look like your esquire," David said firmly. "None would expect to see such as yourself alone, anyway."

The Bastard grinned, unoffended by his companion's obvious doubts, and with a single man-at-arms they spurred down into the valley.

They met with no challenge approaching along the causeway. At the castle they found the drawbridge up and the portcullis down and men watching them from the gatehouse parapet.

The Bastard hailed them. He had a strong and carrying voice. "I am Hamilton of Finnart," he called, in case they did not recognise his heraldic surcoat. "Come seeking my lord Earl of Angus."

"He is not here. He is gone," came back to them. "All are gone."

"Gone where, man? Where?"

"Gone to Cavers in Teviotdale, sir."

"Cavers? Teviotdale? Why there? Has he gone there with the Lord Home? On the way to the Merse?"

"No, sir. The Lord Home did not come here. He went off to the Merse earlier. I believe that my lord of Angus goes to Cavers on his way to England. To Morpeth, in Northumberland, to see Her Highness, his lady wife."

"Ha! England again?" Hamilton glanced at David. "Are you sure of this?"

"So he intended, sir. Do you wish to come inside, Sir James? There is none here but myself, as captain. But you are welcome . . ."

"No—it was the Earl I looked for. But, I thank you. I must return . . ." Waving a dismissive hand, the Bastard reined his horse round.

"That did not take long!" David said.

"It would have taken you a deal longer to learn it, without me!" the other pointed out.

"I recognise that. Was it here at Douglas that you were, with my lord of Arran, when his lady mother sent for him? No, no—it could not be. Too far. You could not have come in the time . . ."

"We were only at Barncluith, a few miles from Cadzow. We watched your host arriving, indeed, from there."

"Yet Angus and Home must have learned of what was done. Swiftly. This breaking of the band. How?"

"That was all done three days past. At Cadzow. When we heard that Albany's great army was on its way. My most formidable grandmother did it all. With a little help from your humble servant! Convinced my poor sire that he was riding the wrong horse. Told Angus that he was a fool and could not win in this struggle. And commanded Home to get out of her house. All done, the band torn up, and Albany's paper signed, three days ago. A pretty scene, I tell you!"

David stared. "Then . . . then we need never have marched at all! Forty thousand men!"

"No harm in a little marching! And it brought about this pleasing association, did it not?" Hamilton laughed mockingly.

They picked up their men on the ridge to return to Broken Cross Muir with their information.

The satisfaction at the Regent's camp could scarcely have been greater at hearing the news. The situation as it had developed had not looked so bright since Albany's arrival in Scotland. Arran had changed sides and ought to be kept so without too much difficulty; Home was isolated and discredited; and Angus sufficiently discouraged to be returning to England and his abandoned wife. Scotland should have a breathing space at least, if not something rather better than that.

Orders were issued for all the various units of the army to head for their home territories and the main body for Edinburgh.

David Lindsay thought that he might at last be able to contemplate matrimony. He might, indeed, be able to arrange a visit to the Byres before his return to Stirling, to discuss times and seasons and other relevant matters.

Alas for such hopes. The Regent's party had only reached the Calder area, in Lothian, when it was met by an urgent courier from the Earl Marischal at Stirling Castle with the tidings that the infant Duke of Ross, the King's brother, had died. The child had never been robust, but there had been no indication that his life was endangered. He had, apparently, suddenly sickened and collapsed, with little warning.

This intelligence had a much greater impact on Albany and his entourage than the natural regret at the cutting off of a young royal life. Inevitably it meant trouble. There would be bound to be accusations of neglect from Margaret Tudor, if not worse. And since the child duke had been second heir to Henry of England's throne also, that awkward monarch would be certain to have something to say about it—and it would put the new daughter of Angus and Margaret into a still more significant situation as far as the English crown was concerned. Still more important, perhaps, it made Albany himself heir-presumptive to the *Scottish* throne, something which could markedly affect events and attitudes.

It affected David Lindsay, at any rate, and right away. For it was decided that he should return forthwith to Stirling Castle, Davie Beaton with him, to discover the full details of the prince's death, for official announcement, and to ensure that all was well with King James. So there would be no visit to Kate Lindsay yet awhile. Disappointing as this was, David was by no means mollified by Beaton's announcement, as the two young men rode away northwards, that after he had investigated matters at Stirling, he thought that he would take the opportunity to go a little further, to Strathmore, and visit Airlie Castle—all, of course, in the interest of ensuring that Angus's potential threat in the north-east could now be discounted, at least for the time-being.

12

It was mid-January before David saw Kate Lindsay again,.
for after the upheavals of November it was unthinkable that
he should leave the young monarch's side during the festi-
vities of Yuletide, which that year were especially prolonged,
at Stirling Castle, to try to make James forget the loss of his
brother. In January, however, a parliament was called in
Edinburgh, despite the bad time of year for travel, for good
and sufficient reasons, and it was decided that David Lindsay
should be in attendance for possible consultation, along
with the Sieur de la Bastie. So the day before, he was able to
pay his long-delayed visit to the Byres.

Whilst reproachful that he had not contrived a return
before this, and accusing him of lack of enthusiasm, Kate
presently displayed sufficient of that quality herself to make
the visit memorable. Despite the occasional flurry of snow,
she insisted that they go riding and led him down to the
coast two miles distant, where on the hard sands of Aberlady
Bay, the tide being out, they could gallop wild and free.
Kate was an excellent horsewoman and on the two miles
long sand-bar to the bay she had ample opportunity to
challenge David, putting up groups of wild geese in honking
protest in the process. The challenge, and sheer physical
excitement of it all, in streaming wind, drumming hooves
and splattering surface water, also had the effect of arousing
their appetite for each other's persons—if such arousal was
necessary—so that, coming off the bay with the fading
light, without actually having to discuss the matter, they
found themselves conveniently in the vicinity of the monks'
hay barn of the Luffness Monastery, just to the west of the
castle, near the monastic fish ponds, a most suitable and
sequestered place to allow their steaming mounts to cool off
and eat some hay. The hay was apt for more than feeding
horses, to be sure, and at this time of day the barn the last
place the good Carmelites would be likely to frequent,

outlying as it was. From tethering their beasts outside, to each other's arms inside, was but a logical step, and to sitting down on the hay a natural sequence. Thereafter nature almost but not quite prevailed, the forthcoming marriage not so much discussed as all but anticipated. They had, after all, already put in overmuch waiting. Perhaps it was the monastic ambience which helped them impose the final restraint.

The return to the Byres was at the comfortably sedate pace necessary for holding hands when on horseback.

Before he left next morning with the Lord Patrick for the parliament, David agreed that the wedding should be, God and the Regent—or Davie Beaton—willing, on St Katherine's Day, 30th April, a propitious date surely, as Kate's saint's-day; and at the monastic chapel of Luffness, not only a mere couple of hundred yards from their hay barn but in which featured the fine recumbent effigy of the illustrious ancestor of them both, Sir David de Lindsay, Baron of Luffness, Regent of Scotland for Alexander the Third, who had died on the St Louis Crusade around 1268 and his body been brought back here by one of the dispossessed Scots monks from Mount Carmel—the reason for the monastery being there in the first place. All most auspicious.

The parliament was again held in the great chapel of Holyrood Abbey, and this time, because of snow-bound hill passes and short notice, there was to be no very large attendance. David found Antoine de la Bastie with Davie Beaton, and the latter explained the urgency for this meeting. Henry the Eighth, no doubt in collusion with his sister, was accusing the Duke of Albany of poisoning his nephew in order to become second person in Scotland, and declaring that clearly the life of the young King James was now at risk. In the circumstances he claimed that it was now vitally necessary to get rid of Albany before he did more and irreversible damage. As Lord Protector of Scotland therefore, he called directly upon the Scots parliament to unseat and banish the Regent and to appoint the Queen-Mother, his royal sister, in his place.

This arrogant formal demand had been delivered by the English ambassador, along with a private warning to Chancellor Beaton that King Henry had now some four hundred prominent Scots in receipt of his pensions, many of them lords, bishops and commissioners to parliament, and these could be relied upon to vote against the Regent. This, Davie Beaton averred, was undoubtedly a gross exaggeration; but even if it was only one-quarter true it could be a serious threat. So it had been felt advisable to call the parliament, necessary to return a suitable reply to Henry, as swiftly as possible to prevent any rallying of pro-English support, which in the nature of things might be expected to be strongest in the distant parts of the realm where the central and loyalist influences would be weakest.

There was another reason for an early parliament. There had been a great battle at Marignano, near Milan in Northern Italy, between the French and the armies of the Emperor Maximilian and the Pope, at which the French had gained a notable victory. This enabled King Francis to grab the major prize of Milan, aim at Venice, and so upset the entire balance of power in Europe, a situation which could affect Scotland. Those in the know—including, it appeared, Davie Beaton—believed that this would make France much too strong for Henry Tudor's liking, and that he would break his truce with Francis, and indeed was being urged to do so by the Pope and Emperor, and being offered Milan itself as reward if France could be defeated, Cardinal Wolsey, Henry's Chancellor and adviser, supporting this course. And if France again became involved in a war on two or more fronts, under the terms of the Auld Alliance Scotland would almost certainly be requested to join in. Also, it must not be forgotten that Albany was still Lord High Admiral of France.

Lastly, the Lord Home had fled to England again and sought the protection of Henry against the Regent. Something drastic would have to be done about Home.

As parliaments went, the one of 1516 was brief to the point of being little more than a formality, all over in an hour or two and with sundry outstanding issues remitted to the Privy Council. The main business, answering King Henry's insolent demands, was swiftly dealt with. If there were any of his bought men or pensioners present, they did not reveal the fact, prudently no doubt in view of the outburst of fury on the part of the great majority when they heard the details. It was indeed some time before the

Chancellor could regain order. There was no dubiety about the reply to Henry, only the ability to make it sufficiently civil in tone for an official document. It was in the end left to the Chancellor to draft a letter, to express the undeniable and unshakeable independent sovereignty of the King of Scots in parliament, that parliament's complete satisfaction with the present Regent which itself had lawfully appointed, its rejection of any theme of protectorship or any need therefor, and its reminder that any claim by the former Queen-Mother for supervision of the young monarch, much less to be Head of State as her brother had suggested, had been invalidated by the said lady's remarriage to the Earl of Angus.

To cool down tempers, the Chancellor brought this item to a somewhat abrupt close, and introduced that of the European situation and the sudden advancement in power of France, with its probable effect on England and therefore on Scotland. This being all less comprehensible to most of those present, and on the face of it less immediately urgent, it would probably have been remitted to the Privy Council to keep an eye on. But at this point in the proceedings the Regent made one of his infrequent interventions. A sudden flood of French and some arm-waving left the majority none the wiser but the Chancellor looking uneasy and even his nephew less sure of himself than usual. Davie's translation, whatever gloss he might seek to put on the matter, could not disguise the core of it—namely that the Duke of Albany desired parliament to grant him leave of absence to return to France.

There was consternation in the chapel, shared most evidently by the Chancellor—which indicated no prior consultation. A score of voices were upraised in protest. The Regent looked surprised but scarcely perturbed.

As the din continued, the Archbishop had a quick word with his nephew, who went back to the Regent and spoke urgently and most evidently persuasively. After some exchange, Davie returned to the Chancellor, who rapped for quiet.

"My lord Regent desires it to be known," the young man declared, "that the absence which he seeks is only for a short period, a matter of a few months. It is vitally necessary for his private affairs that he should return to France for such time. He has not seen his Duchess for long. Properties and estates require his attention. And he reminds all that he is Admiral of France and a French citizen. In the present situation, with warfare in the Middle Sea area, he must be available for consultation by the King of France. His duty."

There were cries about prior duty to the kingdom of which he was the Regent and as to the perilous state of Scotland, particularly with this threat of Henry's spleen— which Davie translated.

"My lord Duke says that there need be no fears. That with my lord Earl of Arran, here present, adhering firmly to the King's cause, the Earl of Angus outwith the country and presently in some disarray, and the Lord Home, of whom more hereafter, no longer a danger, the immediate situation is better than at any time for long. Forby, my lord Regent will be able to concert plans with the King of France, should it come to war, to circumvent any threat to Scotland by the King of England and to arrange for mutual support."

Shouts filled the church to the effect that all knew what had happened when last France had required Scotland's support against Henry. Also that Angus could be back at any time and his manpower still undefeated. And that Home would be a menace so long as he lived.

The Chancellor, and no doubt his nephew likewise, saw that on this issue the parliament was not going to be prevailed upon. He declared that the matter would require further information and debate and, bowing towards the Regent on his throne, proposed that they move on to the next item, the subject of the Lord Home, former Lord High Chamberlain.

This was much more to the assembly's taste, for Home was less than popular, both too arrogant and too clever for most. So the Archbishop had no problem. He declared that Home was now in England, in the care of King Henry, of whom it was believed that he had long been a substantial pensioner, and had appealed to the English monarch against his own liege-lord's Regent and government. This was highest treason. If there were any doubts, it could now be revealed that he had been receiving more than a pension from King Henry. Some time ago, the Sieur de la Bastie, now chief Warden of the Marches, had been commissioned to proceed through the Merse and eastern Borders to enquire into the situation prevailing there and the depredations of

English raiding parties after the disaster of Flodden field. And there he discovered that although the raiding was indeed savage and destructive of life and property far and wide, none of the Home lands were being ravaged. Most evidently there was an arrangement between the Homes and the Lord Dacre, the English Warden—and this at a time when the Lord Home was himself chief Scots Warden. The Sieur de la Bastie was here present this day and would substantiate this.

Antoine called down from the clerestory gallery where, with David Lindsay, he was watching the proceedings. "I so substantiate and declare, my lord Chancellor."

"And David Lindsay of the Mount, His Grace's Procurator and Chief Usher, acting with the Sieur de la Bastie, will so confirm."

"I so confirm," David agreed briefly.

"Does anyone wish to question these most reliable and distinguished witnesses?" the Archbishop asked, as though this was indeed a trial in a court of law.

One man there at least found all this unsatisfactory, the young Earl of Moray. "What need is there for all this?" he cried, jumping up. "This is but beating the air! We all know that Alexander Home had committed the highest treason of all, the murder of his sovereign-lord—my own father! Let him pay the price, I say. Indeed I, Moray, demand it."

There was a tense silence, part embarrassment. Few present had not heard something of the story which this young man had assiduously spread abroad ever since Flodden—and no doubt believed—that in the late stages of that disastrous conflict, the Lord Home had returned to the scene of carnage after chasing the English right wing cavalry deep into the Cheviots, and when the battling and wounded monarch saw him, and upbraided him for riding off and leaving the Scots left flank unprotected, Home in a fury had raised his sword and slain King James. Where the young man had got this story was not clear, for he had not himself been at Flodden; but he propagated it assiduously. This was the first time, however, that it had been raised as it were officially. No one, even Home's most bitter enemies, would have paid much attention had not the Earl James been the late King's illegitimate son by Flaming Janet Kennedy and so a half-brother of their present sovereign-lord.

The Chancellor coughed. "We, ah, note your claim and accusation my lord Earl. But such charge would require strong substantiation. Sound witnesses. If you can produce such witnesses, or other corroboration, an indictment of regicide could be added to the other citations for high treason. But lacking this, I fear, no."

"How can I produce witnesses to that fell deed?" the other cried. "All others around the King my father died with him. Only this, this abject dastard, rode free from that field, to continue with his villainies!"

"Yes. Or, no doubt. Perhaps you will seek or continue to seek, for due corroboration, my lord, so that such possible charge can be made? As, indeed, shall we all. Now—my lord Regent, we pass to a related matter. It is inconceivable that the high office of Lord Chamberlain of this realm should remain in the keeping of so undoubted a traitor as the present Lord Home. Accordingly, it is proposed that the chamberlainship should be removed herewith from the said Alexander Home and bestowed upon the Lord Fleming of Cumbernauld. Is such removal and new appointment approved by this parliament? Or is other nomination to be put forward?"

Acclaim for Fleming, a sound man, was forthcoming and no alternative was put forward. On this convenient note the session closed, leaving the Regent's return to France as it were in the air.

David returned to Stirling with Albany's authority, via Davie Beaton, to inform the Earl Marischal that he should have leave of absence from King Jamie's service for two weeks flanking St Katherine's Day next, 30th April—a mere thirteen weeks to wait.

Well before that time, David was surprised to have a visit from young Beaton, who called in at Stirling Castle on his way back from another assault on Marion Ogilvy at Airlie in the Braes of Angus, using as his excuse his desire to pay his loyal duty to his liege-lord and to see how the papingo was thriving—Beaton, of course, recognising the value of maintaining close links with even an infant monarch, at this stage, to ensure advantage in years to come. He was in especially good spirits on this occasion, for it transpired that he had achieved success with the fair Marion in a sufficient degree to obtain a promise of marriage from her at some unspecified date. They would be wed, he asserted, when he got back from France.

David congratulated him, interested that his peculiar friend should be so obviously set on marriage when he seemed the sort of young man to whom conjugal bliss would be less than a priority. Clearly he was deeply in love—and this side of his vivid character the more commended itself to Lindsay. But what was this of France, he wondered? Was the Regent indeed going, and he with him?

Beaton shook his head, promptly reverting to his more usual image of intrigue and manipulation. No, Albany was sending *him* back to France, to seek to facilitate the ducal return, as a personal ambassador to King Francis. The project was that he should try to convince Francis actually to recall the Duke officially for consultation and advice—which as Admiral and a French citizen the Regent could not refuse; but to sweeten this call, for the Scots parliament, by offering certain advantages to Scotland, a firm treaty, improved trade terms and arms and men. Beaton grinned over this— for, he explained confidentially, he was also going to France as an ambassador for his uncle, the Chancellor, with exactly the opposite secret objective. He was to seek to delay the Regent's departure for as long as possible!

All but incredulous, David shook his head. How was this possible? And to what end? Such deceit and ill-faith. What did it, what could it, mean?

The other objected strongly, if amusedly, to these terms. It was not deceit nor ill-faith but statecraft, diplomacy, for the best advantage of all, he claimed. How did Lindsay think dealings between princes and realms were conducted? By straightforward exchange and handshakes, like buying and selling cattle? Seldom that, but by more devious means. Power had its own requirements and niceties, and could not be manipulated as by a bull charging at a gate! As witness the latest move to bridle Angus. It was expensive and difficult to maintain in arms and idle a great host, as at present, just in case Angus decided to set in motion his undoubtedly massive Douglas might. And it was important that he and Home should not ever again act in concert. They were both presently in England. So a messenger had been sent to Angus indicating that the Regent desired only amity and goodwill between them, unlike Home whom parliament had branded traitor and forfeited from all rights and privileges. The Regent urged Angus therefore to return to Scotland, to aid in the governance of the realm, the more so as he himself was intending a visit to France and would expect Angus to take his due place on the Council of Regency during the French interlude. Albany had further assured that there would be no reprisals or other moves against Angus if he so returned.

David reacted predictably. What was the point in this? Undoing all that had been gained at Hamilton. Asking for further trouble. Putting Angus back into a position to have his way with Scotland.

The other was only too happy to explain—for fairly evidently the strategy was his own. Who were the enemies of the Regent and therefore of the Scots realm, in order of menace? Henry of England, the Queen-Mother, Angus, Home and Arran—others did not matter. Angus and Home, in England, were available to be used by Henry against Scotland, as was his sister. In that five, Angus was the weak spot, for he might be enticed home by offers of clemency and a seat on the forthcoming Regency Council, thus getting him out of Henry's grasp. Margaret his wife was unlikely to return with him, with their baby daughter. And Home dared not return, to face parliament and trial for treason. Angus and his wife were scarcely a happy couple and this would further come between them. Margaret without Angus would have little influence in Scotland. So Henry would be left with Home, whose teeth were largely drawn. It but remained to ensure that the remaining opponent, Arran, now largely tamed, did not come together again with Angus. This could probably be assured through envy and jealousy, for they had never loved each other. They would both be on any Regency Council inevitably, but the other members could be carefully selected to support Arran rather than Angus. And there would be one in particular— the Bastard of Arran! He was twice the man that his father was, ambitious and able however unscrupulous, and he, Beaton, was cultivating him. Given this sudden promotion to a position of power, and recognising whence it came, the Bastard could be relied upon to sway his father and others and keep Angus very much isolated. So, if Albany must eventually return to France for a time, all would be held nicely in balance until his return—God willing!

Left more or less speechless by this intricate web of manoeuvre and interaction, David did not essay argument or even further question. But he did marvel at the character and attitudes of this man, the same who was so sure of his abilities to move great folk and their affairs of state like chessmen on a board, and at the same time to be wholly and humbly devoted to an Angus lord's daughter and grateful that she had consented at last to marry him.

David said goodbye to his friend and wished him God-speed on his visit to France—although wondering how much God would be involved in it all. He himself reverted to more vital contemplations, his own forthcoming marriage.

13

David and Antoine de la Bastie rode downhill towards the sparkling expanse of Aberlady Bay flanked by its twin headlands of Kilspindie and Gullane Points, with the burgeoning young green of the Luffness woodlands filling the foreground, and far beyond the blue sweep of the Firth of Forth, all the long varied coastline of Fife rising to the shapely twin breasts of the Lomond Hills—as fair a prospect under the sailing cloud galleons as any man could look for in all southern Scotland, that breezy, bright last day of April 1516. The two horsemen were scarcely concerned with the view, however, even though probably all the far-flung loveliness of sun and shadow and glitter was not without its subconscious effect on the younger man at least on this long-awaited day. Scotland's fickle weather could have been so much less co-operative, and a repetition of the driving rain of yesterday would have presented a depressing problem and handicap—and even more so for the bride, in the circumstances.

There had been strong objections to having the nuptial ceremony at the little monastic chapel of Luffness, especially from the Lady Lindsay and other females of the two families, even from Mirren Livingstone who now was more or less accepted as a sort of proxy-wife for David's father and who took an almost proprietorial interest in the entire affair as self-appointed adviser and consultant. The obvious place to hold a notable wedding, they all said, was the great church of St Mary, Haddington, a splendid building, all but a cathedral, where there was room for hundreds—not a poky little monastery chapel, however pretty its setting, which would hold no more than a score or two. Even the local parish churches of Athelstaneford or Aberlady would have been better, they averred, with more accommodation, suitable for showing off the ladies' finery—and the bride's also, to be sure. But Kate had been decided—it would be at Luffness Chapel and nowhere else. She did not, of course, detail reasons for this odd choice; that hay barn, visible from the chapel door, certainly never would have occurred to anyone as having any relevance. David himself was entirely happy with the venue. The fewer the folk present the better, as far as he was concerned, his priority to get the business over and done with as quickly as possible with the minimum of fuss.

"What do you intend, David, hereafter?" Antoine wondered. "Where will your Kate live? At her old home, here? At Garleton, with your father and our generous Mirren? Your own property of The Mount, in Fife? That is far away—although not quite so far from Stirling, perhaps. You will not leave the King's service, I think, so you must remain for most of the time at Stirling Castle. But a close-guarded fortress is no place in which to immure a young bride."

"Yet she says that she wishes to stay with me at Stirling. That she does not mind about being enclosed—as long as she is with me." David coughed a little at the sound of that.

"She may think otherwise, after a little."

"I recognise that. But I would not wish her to continue to bide at the Byres—my wife." Again the little cough. "Nor in my father's house at Garleton, with Mirren. And The Mount has been empty and shut up for long. I could not put her there, alone . . ."

"You have a problem. Perhaps if she becomes désenchantée with Stirling Castle in time, you could find lodgings for her in the town below. Where she would feel less shut-in—as you yourself do, I know."

"That is possible. But I do not think that the Earl Marischal would permit me to leave the King's side, of a night, to be with her in the town. I sleep in an anteroom of his bed-chamber . . ."

"You can scarcely instal Kate there!"

"No. But we can find a room somewhere nearby. Happily Kate is fond of James. When I brought him to Garleton they got on very well. He still talks of her. That should help."

"I wish you well in it, David." That was accompanied by a typically Gallic shrug.

"It should not be so very difficult? You would not have me to give up my position as Procurator and Usher to the King? I would not wish to do that . . ."

Leaving their horses at the castle stables, they walked the few hundred yards to the monastery, where they had a word with the Prior, John Bickerton, who would officiate, assisted by the Athelstaneford parish priest. David would have liked Abbot John Inglis to have at least taken some part in the ceremony—although somehow he would scarcely have felt properly married if John had actually been the celebrant—but the Earl Marischal would not hear of both of them leaving the young King at the same time. Antoine was going to act groomsman, a great honour David acknowledged, and had come from Dunbar for the occasion.

They made their way to the chapel, which stood some distance apart from the other monastic buildings in woodland perched on the lip of a sort of winding water-filled ravine, which was in fact the flooded original quarry out of which the sandstone for the building of both the castle and the monastery had been hewn, over two centuries before. It was no large edifice, normally only required for the worship of about a score of monks; but it had three parts, the raised chancel to the east, the monks' nave in the centre, with its own door, and a slightly larger westerly portion not normally in use—for the castle had its own inbuilt chapel—save as a storage space. This had been cleared for today, and would hold some thirty extra persons standing, although some might not be able to see through the screens all that went on up before the altar in the chancel. Already a number of guests had installed themselves there, in the most advantageous positions, and clearly were not going to allow themselves to be pushed to the sides or otherwise displaced by late arrivals. The monks' nave was reserved for the two families and principal guests. Quite a crowd had assembled outside, monks, men-at-arms from the castle, fishers from Luffness Haven and villagers from Aberlady.

David and his groomsman, having arrived in good time, were uncertain whether to wait inside the chapel or out. They decided that it would be less embarrassing outside. There, a little apart from the rest, they stood, David distinctly ill at ease. Normally he was on the best of terms with the local folk, but today he felt separated from all and uncomfortable—after all, he had never before been one of the principals at a wedding. De la Bastie, however, seemed entirely his urbane self, smiling to all.

They waited.

The hour of three after noon struck on the monastery bell, which thereafter continued to toll, presumably in nuptial joy although it sounded the same as for a funeral. Promptly, through the clangour, the sound of chanting could be heard, getting louder, as down the path from the monastic complex paced a choir of singing boys leading Prior Bickerton, in full canonicals, with two monkish acolytes and the Athelstaneford priest following. Some more monks came along behind in the ordinary off-white habits of the Carmelites.

The Prior sketched a casual blessing over the assembled crowd, the choir continuing to sing and the bell to toll. Bickerton bowed formally to David and gestured for him to follow into the chapel.

Therein, at the chancel step, they were signed to wait whilst the Prior and his assistants went up to their places before the altar. The choristers came in behind, chanting still. David muttered to his friend that there was not going to be much room for the bride and her party with all this lot. And where was she? All was supposed to start at three.

Antoine made soothing noises.

The choir kept up their somewhat monotonous chanting, the Prior seemed lost in contemplation of eternity, the parish priest fretted and the congregation now packing the western extension shuffled and pushed and tried to shoo away new arrivals, their hitherto muted chatter soon all but drowning the singing.

Presently the bell stopped ringing and soon thereafter the choir too fell silent, presumably having exhausted its repertoire or perhaps its lung power. An uneasy hush descended upon those at the back of the chapel, with only whispers and stirrings, although the crowd outside seemed unaffected.

David all but groaned aloud. Who had invented this torture for bridegrooms? It was to have been a quiet, simple wedding. Antoine, spreading French hands, observed philosophically that women were ever thus.

How did *he* know, since he had never been married, the sufferer demanded?

After a further seemingly endless hiatus, it occurred to David, staring at the recumbent effigy of his great ancestor and namesake, carved in full knightly Crusader armour there under his canopy at the left of the chancel, that Sir David de Lindsay, Regent of Scotland two and a half centuries ago, would never have stood for this. And why should *he*? After all, he was the King's Procurator and the principle mover in this distressing affair—at least, if he was not, who was? Moreover his groomsman was Scotland's Chief Warden of the Marches, Governor of Dunbar Castle, and one of the foremost knights of Christendom. Well, then.

Abruptly he turned, glared at the choristers and raised a hand to point. "Sing!" he commanded. Anything would be better than this uneasy hush. Up at the altar the Prior came out of his trance to wave a confirmatory hand. David strode to the arched doorway, to stare out.

The crowd outside gave him a welcoming cheer and the choir inside started up their chant again, if somewhat raggedly. David came back to his friend's side, who smiled, and patted the gold-slashed sleeve of his fine wine-coloured velvet doublet. There were some giggles from behind.

Waiting resumed, and somewhere an argument broke out about positioning.

How much longer the bridegroom could have stood it was uncertain, when a second outburst of cheering outside seemed to indicate developments at least. Even so there was no improvement in the situation for an unconscionable time, until David's brother Alexander came stalking in, dressed more splendidly than the bridegroom, and proceeded to take charge, officiously pushing back people here and there, ordering the choir into a tighter huddle, gesturing towards the Prior and otherwise making himself objectionable. David scowled at him.

Then a new sort of silence fell upon all save the singing boys, and even they distinctly faltered. Kate, on her father's good arm, appeared in the doorway. David's scowl dissolved, to be replaced by an aspect of sheerest wonder and bliss.

Radiant, flushed, eyes shining, dressed all in white satin and silver, he had never seen her more lovely, a vision of lively, challenging beauty and delight.

The singers, recovering, changed their somewhat mournful chant into something more rousing, and to this father and daughter moved forward into the chapel, to be followed by Lady Lindsay and Sir David and the other family and principal guests, two by two. With the place already all but full, very quickly something of a pile-up developed, with Alexander Lindsay unsuccessfully seeking to marshal all and making confusion worse. Protests developed, too.

David found Kate at his side, at last. He took her arm. "Where have you been?" he demanded—but a deal less reproachfully than would have seemed possible a minute or two before.

"Where . . .?" Innocently she gazed at him. "Why, just coming."

Gulping, he nodded, as though entirely satisfied with that explanation.

"Oh, David—at last!" she breathed.

"At last!" he echoed, heartfelt.

It was almost as though Prior Bickerton said Amen to that as he turned to take charge, in sanctimonious but authoritative tones. All was now in hand, even though it was not every day that a monastic leader was called upon to marry anyone, save perhaps to Holy Church. He advanced upon the happy couple, totally ignoring the parish priest, and launched in Latin into what was presumably the marriage rite. David recognised a word or two here and there, but did not greatly exercise himself to construe and try to follow, quite content to eye Kate and let this business get itself over as quickly as possible. It was necessary, he recognised—but as far as he was concerned, their real coming together as man and wife had taken place in that hay barn some time ago.

Surprisingly soon, the ring exchange was indicated, and rather fumbled through, responses muttered, and Antoine and Lord Lindsay stood back to allow the bridal pair to be pronounced duly wed in the sight of God and all present— the only occasion when the Prior reduced his rate of outflow from what had been almost a gabble. Then peremptorily he signed for them to kneel, enunciated a sonorous blessing, and stood back.

Apparently it was all over, and, taken a little by surprise, David was about to raise Kate to her feet when the Athelstaneford incumbent, entirely disregarded hitherto, evidently decided that if he was going to have any part in the proceedings it must be now, and came forward hurriedly to pronounce his own and much more detailed benediction.

The Prior countered by signing to the choir to start up again.

So bride and groom rose and embraced—and promptly were all but submerged in a tide of other embracings, in that very confined space. Chaos prevailed. Outside, presently, David looked longingly beyond the thronging well-wishers to that red-tiled hay barn across the pasture.

Congratulations, salutations and humoursome advice over, they rode in large company back to the Byres, David insisting that his new wife sat before him on his own horse, somewhat uncomfortable for both of them as this was, so that at least he could have his arms around her under the cloak which she donned over her satin and silver. Jogging up and down at a trot, this certainly engendered a distinct emphasis on her femininity, much appreciated by the man. That cloak was a blessing, too.

The feasting and jollifications thereafter seemed interminable, at least to David Lindsay, who was clearly not good at weddings. Speeches and toasts by the Lord Patrick, Sir David and Antoine were all very well, being reasonably brief; but others joined in and were less so, the parish priest for instance who, on the strength of having baptised them both—only yesterday, it seemed to him—and now was a little tiddly, decided to make up for his virtual exclusion from the nuptial ceremony by going on at great length now. When Alexander, David's younger brother, rose to add his witticisms about the married state, conjugal rights and the problems of first nights, the bridegroom had had enough and sought to make it plain by his glowering. He leant over to whisper in Kate's ear—who had hitherto been accepting all this a deal more patiently than had her new spouse.

"Make excuse to your father to leave, for a space," he directed. "Slip away."

"Why?" she asked, surprised.

"Best that way. Do it now, while Alex still havers on."

"How can I? What excuse . . . ?"

"Anything. Say that nature demands it! Go, lass—and wait for me out there. I will join you after a minute or so."

And when she still displayed reluctance, he added, "My first husbandly command, Kate!"

Shrugging, she murmured to Lord Patrick on her other side and rising, made for the dais door behind their top table, all eyes upon her.

Alexander in full flood, did not pause. And after a little more of it, David got to his feet, observed to his host and hostess that he would go see that Kate was all right, and headed for the door also.

He found his wife just outside and looking somewhat bewildered. "Come," he said, taking her arm.

"Where? Why? What has come over you, Davie?" she demanded.

"We go to Garleton. Forthwith."

"No? But why . . . ?"

"Lest worse befall us than listening to endless speeches! A bedding is planned."

"Oh! Oh, no!"

"Yes. Antoine overheard my precious brother discussing it with another. We can do without that, I say!"

"Yes. Yes . . ." She was no longer reluctant or doubtful.

He led her to the courtyard door and the stables.

The age-old custom of bedding the bride was still carried out, on occasion, however unpopular with newly-weds. The tradition was that the happy couple could be escorted to their bridal chamber, the bride by the male guests, the groom by the female, and there ceremonially undressed, to be deposited naked on the marriage bed, the interested and considerate escorts not departing until they were satisfied that the marriage was being consummated in due and effective fashion—frequently, to the consequent ineffectiveness of the new husband, and the then obvious need for instruction and aid. It could all provide a unique opportunity for those involved, of course—except perhaps for the newly-weds themselves.

Not even delaying to collect Kate's cloak, they unhitched David's horse and rode uphill for Garleton, having instructed the stableboy to inform Lord Lindsay in due course where they had gone.

It was an early hour to seek their couch, but neither found this in any way regrettable. Even the fact that the couch itself was on the small side, being in fact David's own agamist bed, in his topmost tower room, that wherein poetry once had been composed. Now a new idyll and rhapsody was to be essayed—and the door locked.

Kate suddenly was shy, unwontedly silent. David could have done with something of the atmosphere and tempo of that day in the hay barn. But he recognised that his own eagerness was likely to be best served by patience and understanding at this stage. He declared that a beaker of wine was called for on this occasion, and, unlocking the door, left her, to go fetch it.

When, after suitable delay, he returned, it was to find Kate in bed, back turned to the door. He went to her, and sat, to stroke her hair.

"My dear, my dear!" he said.

She kept her head down, face covered.

"It will be . . . very good. You are very lovely. A delight," he went on, stroking, soothing. "So very fair, so darling a creature."

Muffled amongst the bedclothes her voice came. "Oh, Davie—why? Why? When before, I, I . . . !"

"It is but this day's doing, my sweet. All the bustle and the waiting and the many folk, to talk to, all the staring. That time, we were alone, just you and I. But now —now we are alone again. Ourselves. It will be as before. But . . . better."

"Yes. Yes, that is it. I know. I am sorry, Davie . . ."

"Hush you. Fret nothing. Just wait, lass." He slid a hand under the blankets to her bare shoulder, gently to caress it. Gradually that hand moved down, to the swell of her breasts, strangely cooler than the rest, to cup the fullness of one. He felt her quiver and kept his hand still for a while, nor knew any complaint in that. Then slowly he began to stroke the nipple and quite quickly felt it rise and stiffen to his touch. And as it stiffened, so the stiffness and tension began to go out of the rest of her, and her breathing slowed but deepened.

Presently he moved his hand over to the other breast and she stirred a little to receive it, sighing. This nipple required little attention, but got it nevertheless. Her breathing changed again, still deep but faster.

Suddenly she exclaimed and sat up, turning to him, eager now. "Davie! Davie! Davie!" she whispered, and her arms

211

went round his neck, her lips seeking his. "Oh, thank you! Thank you!"

Words superfluous, they clung together. Then, even whilst her breasts pressed and rubbed against him, "Quick!" she breathed. "These clothes . . . !"

"Then let me go for a moment, foolish one!" he chided, smiling. "Loose me—or how may I? A moment—but one moment . . ."

"I will help you . . ."

"Faster without you, lass! See . . ."

Swiftly he flung off shirt and breeches, kicking off shoes, leaving his hose meantime. Impatient, unashamed now, she threw back the bedclothes, waiting in all her urgent loveliness to receive him, a vision of the Creator's most demanding, attractive and essential creation, nubile and vital young womanhood. Groaning his pent-up, hoarded need of her, he stumbled to take what she so unstintingly offered. Their coming together was the most natural and fulfilling thing in the world.

Some unspecified time later there was a knock on the bedchamber door and David's father wondered, mildly for that man, if they were there and in good order? He was lucky to get even a grunt in reply.

Next morning, however sleepy, they were off with de la Bastie eastwards. Oddly, it was the Frenchman who had conceived the notion that they should spend their first days and nights of wedded bliss at Fast Castle on the Merse coast, the most remote of the Home strongholds which Antoine had captured. He asserted that it was the most extraordinary place he had ever seen, away from all the haunts of men, and he could think of nowhere more desirable for a pair of newly-weds requiring only each other's company. David had had no better idea and Kate was happy so long as they should be on their own. Their parents and friends had suggested all sorts of alternatives, indeed scoffed at the thought of going to some barbarous thieves' hold in the Borderland—but then, as Antoine pointed out, none of them had ever been at Fast Castle.

So they rode companionably with de la Bastie and his escort, by Athelstaneford and Markle and Preston-on-Tyne to Dunbar, where Antoine dispensed with all but two of his men-at-arms and picked up instead a middle-aged couple who would act as servitor and housekeeper at Fast, along with a pair of pannier ponies laden with provisions. Thus equipped, they proceeded on in the afternoon, south by east, past Dunglass and Colbrandspath Tower, both now garrisoned by the Warden's men, and up on to the windy heights of Coldingham Muir, with the Norse Sea stretching to infinity on their left and the heathland merging with the Lammermuir Hills on the right, a suddenly all but unpopulated land under great skies, with only a few small farmeries and shepherds' cothouses, where the curlews and the peewits called endlessly and the wild geese flighted.

Across this strange plateau land, odd to be so close to the sea, they rode for a full hour at the sedate pace of the pannier ponies until, with the sun beginning to sink behind them, they came to the most isolated farmery of them all, a place of baaing lambs and lowing calves, called it seemed Dowlaw, the demesne farm of Fast Castle. Beyond it a little way, the moorland appeared to stop abruptly for the sea to take over, although on a very different level.

After a word or two with the farmer, on towards this lip of the world foreground they trotted—to the visitors' mystification, for as far as eye could see there was nothing thrusting higher than a whin-bush or an outcropping rock. Then suddenly they were at the edge, and smiling, the Frenchman drew rein. He did not have to say anything.

Kate gripped David's arm, lips parted but speechless. Sheerly the land dropped away to nothingness, dizzily, a steep apron of heather and cranberries and deer-hair grass for perhaps fifty feet and then vertical, precipitous cliff dropping many hundreds of feet to the wrinkled surging waves of that fierce white-fanged seaboard. In a savage but majestic sweep the land reached away north and south to the extent of vision, the entire vista breathtaking in its immensity.

Antoine pointed, half-right and downwards. There, quarter of a mile away and halfway down the beetling cliff, a tall, slender stack of bare rock thrust up out of the boiling tide close against the main headland. And perched on top of this tapering pinnacle of stone was a similarly slender castle, reddish-brown towers and turrets around which the seabirds wheeled and screamed in white clouds.

"Fast!" de la Bastie said, relishing their reactions. "Or Faux, I understand it was in origin, from our French for treachery!"

"Lord!" David exclaimed. "So *that* is Fast Castle! I . . . I can believe that treachery was hatched there!"

"And you brought us here for our, our . . . ?" Kate left the rest unsaid.

Antoine beamed. "Were *I* new-wed, I could esteem few places more to my taste! No?"

The honeymooners eyed each other and David grinned. "I see what you mean!" he conceded.

The girl made a face, glanced flushing at the Frenchman and then laughed, reining her horse's head round, south-wards.

They rode along a dizzy clifftop track for a little way until abruptly they had to urge their reluctant mounts down an ever steepening slope, part heather, part naked stone and scree, with the foaming white breakers smashing far below. Round the lip of a sheer rock chimney they circled gingerly, the horses ever more uneasy. Reining up, where the track was just a little wider, Kate dismounted, preferring to lead her beast and trust her own feet. The others pretended to humour her by following suit, the servitor and wife heaving sighs of relief. Soon the horses were all but squatting on their haunches so steep became the descent, the pannier ponies in fact proving the most sure-footed. In the dark, or in wet weather, that descent would be barely possible.

Perhaps halfway down that towering headland their precarious approach reached a yawning gap between the cliff-face and the insular stack. And across this narrow chasm a slender filament spanned, a meagre gangway, evidently a drawbridge of sorts. The motherly soul who was to act housekeeper, already in a state bordering on terror, let out a wail at the sight.

There appeared to be no place for horses across that alarming access, but a ledge of the main cliff-face had obviously been further excavated and enlarged nearby, with iron rings set in the rock, clearly for tethering beasts. Tying their reins, the visitors stared from this sea-eagle's eyrie of a place to Antoine de la Bastie and back again.

"Will you not do very well here, my friends?" the Frenchman asked. "Sufficiently private, is it not?"

Four figures had come to man the battlements above the gatehouse opposite, waving, grinning. Antoine stepped carefully down to the drawbridge head—for even this approach was no more than naked rock—reaching out a hand to assist Kate. The servitor required David's assistance to get his gasping, protesting spouse even that far.

There was a rope stretched above the gangway on one side, to act as handrail—a help in windy weather, the Frenchman explained unnecessarily, striding across—and gripping this tightly, the newcomers edged after him, forbearing to look downwards.

The stronghold was little less unusual within than without, all floors being on different levels, thanks to the contours of the rock top, vaulted ceilings sloping and often angled and rooms oddly shaped and generally small. But there was a fair-sized hall, strewn with sheep and deer skins, where two great fires of driftwood blazed and sparked and hissed, and a vaulted kitchen down a steep stair cut in the naked rock below, from which arose an appetising aroma of cooking meats.

Whilst the housekeeping pair and the escort were taken down there by one of the four-man garrison, Antoine led the bridal couple up a tightly winding turnpike stair to a little gannet's-nest of a bedchamber skied in the very topmost tower of the place, its windows, when unshuttered, opening on to the most stupendous vistas of ocean and cliff and circling seabirds. But even here a fire burned brightly in a tiny fireplace, and while Kate exclaimed at the view, David asked how on earth they got the fuel for these fires in such a situation—for they had seen no woodland within miles, on Coldingham and Lumsdaine Muirs.

"There is a shaft cut in the rock, part natural crevasse, crevice, is it? This opens to a great cavern in the foot of this pinnacle. There is much driftwood washed up on these so savage shores, and it can be hoisted through the cavern roof and up this shaft. Also stores, fish, gear, for there is a little landing stage for boats down there—but only to be reached in calm weather. Fresh water likewise, led from a well to a rock cistern. Oh, the Home who built this hold knew what he was at!"

"I swear that he must have been a man with an uneasy mind, nevertheless!"

215

"Perhaps. I doubt whether he built it to bring a bride to, certainly!"

"But you saw it as meet for such purpose!" Kate said. "Why, I wonder?"

"Say that had I been in David's place there is nowhere in this land where I would have preferred to bring you, my dear," de la Bastie told her, deep-voiced. "I thought about it, you see. Yes. I envy this friend of mine—I confess it, frankly!"

Meeting his gaze, the girl flushed and looked away towards the far horizons.

Downstairs, they all partook of a hearty if rough and ready repast prepared by the garrison, the main ingredients being roast lamb, bread, honey and ale. Then Antoine, leaving the two escorts as guardians, took the other four men-at-arms and his departure, kissing Kate and clasping David around the shoulders, his message unspoken but clear.

The new incumbents were left to make what they would, and could, of Fast Castle.

That night, in the lofty roost, to the recurrent thunder of the breakers and the weird chorus of the night birds, they made love with a new passion and abandon, to a repeated satisfaction hitherto undreamed of. Kate proved to be a natural lover, and what was not instinctive, she learned fast.

They wakened early but lay late, encouraged thereto by the elements. For overnight an easterly gale had sprung up, and that precarious steeple-top hold shook and trembled alarmingly to the batter of it, the pounding of the wind, the crash of the waves and what they thought was driving rain against their window until they realised that it was spray from the mighty seas which were exploding in crazy violence on the jagged rocks far below. In the circumstances, bed and mutual comfort were the obvious antidotes.

Later, fed and every corner of that breakneck castle explored—which did not take long for it could not be large by the nature of its position—and the weather contraindicating any outdoors activity, they decided to investigate the rock shaft, which Antoine had mentioned, to the cavern beneath. This proved to be reached from a trapdoor in the floor of a storeroom off the kitchen premises which, when raised, revealed a distinctly frightening black hole in the naked rock, clearly an enlarged natural fissure, down which a rope-ladder disappeared and up which came both a hollow booming sound and a strong smell of decaying seaweed. Despite this daunting approach however, Kate asserted that she wished to discover more, quite prepared to face the swaying ladder—provided that David went first.

So, provided each also with flickering lanterns, they took deep breaths, and the husband, with every appearance of nonchalance, put foot on the first rungs and commenced the formidable descent, his lantern less than helpful. A score or so of rungs down, he called up that it was none so bad so long as care was taken, a fondly foolish injunction. He felt her weight affecting the hang of the ladder thereafter and heard an occasional exclamation.

Such exclamation was as nothing to the one he himself emitted when, presently, with the noise of surging waters suddenly louder, he felt the ladder swing much more freely and, as he realised that he was now entering the cavern proper, he was engulfed in a sort of black snowstorm, all but smothered in a softly buffeting cloud which enveloped him and his lamp. In the consequent darkness it took moments for him to understand that this was in fact a great host of bats, in fluttering panic; and his own sudden panic subsided even as they beat musky-smelling tiny wings about his face. He called up a warning to Kate, assuring, out of swift masculine recovery, that there was nothing to be afraid of.

Swaying to and fro like any pendulum now, he descended further and as the bat cloud thinned his light reasserted itself—but insufficiently to reveal any bounds to this cavern, around or below—although the boom and swish of the waves sounded now very close. Evidently it was a very high and extensive place. Increased outcry from above indicated that Kate had entered the bat-level.

Then, amidst the rush and surge of the tide in that dark, hollow enormity another strange noise became apparent— a whining and groaning, less than reassuring, punctuated by a kind of barked grunting. It took some while, with a subsequent plopping and slapping noise, for him to realise that this must be seals protesting and taking to the water—which presupposed ledges around the cave base. Unfortunately his lantern shed little light downwards. He shouted up this latest information.

When he became aware that the ladder was swaying progressively less wildly, he recognised that it must be anchored somewhere and therefore he must be nearing the bottom. Soon his feet touched solid if weed-hung rock, and lowering the lantern he saw that he stood on quite a wide ledge a few feet above the black swirling water; also that the round eyes of numerous grey seals were regarding him glassily, some in the water, some still on ledges, like old moustachioed men, peering.

Kate arrived breathless beside him, as wide-eyed as the seals, and together they gazed around. The lamps were unfortunately insufficient to do much more than reveal that the cave was huge, only the wet walling immediately nearby being visible. Also to be seen beside them was a rough timber jetty or landing stage, with a quite large coble-type boat tied thereto, high prowed of vaguely Viking ship build, which rose and fell regularly on the tidal surge. What the lanterns did not reveal was any opening for the cavern; and no hint of daylight glimmered anywhere.

What *was* fairly clear was from which direction the booming noise was coming. But since no light showed thereabouts, there must be a major bend in the cave or more than one, before the entrance, making it a secret place indeed.

There were oars in the boat, but they reckoned that with a storm blowing outside, any exploration afloat could wait. They did move around gingerly on foot, the seaweed slippery, where the ledges allowed, disturbing more seals, also birds of some sort which made off unseen but with a great squawking. They established the fact that there were at least one or two branches to the cavern, the floor of one sloping upwards to well above high-watermark, and here they found quite a large store of driftwood stacked; likewise fishing nets and lobster pots.

When they could go no further, in this state of the tide, they returned to the ladder foot, to climb back whence they had come. Going up seemed much less alarming than coming down into the unknown. David, counting steps, came to the conclusion that the cave roof must be over one hundred feet in height, and the fissure shaft at least another hundred feet above.

Safely back within the castle walls, they agreed that their

218

awareness of what lay beneath them much added to their conception and understanding of the entire Fast establishment, as well as increasing their wonder over the designs and concerns of its builders.

The gale raged for two days and nights of blustering fury, a continuous assault which the castle almost seemed to defy with more than assurance, with sheer malevolence. As Kate imaginatively put it, Fast appeared to cling to its rocky perch with one fist whilst shaking the other in the face of the storm. The honeymooners made no complaint, with other preoccupations to the fore. Indeed the elemental battle outside seemed to enhance the fairly elementary proceedings within.

The third morning, however, dawned calm and bright, with only mild zephyrs of air caressing the cliffs, the sky blue and the sea a gleaming dazzling infinity, innocent of all malice, with only a slow, majestic heavy swell to hint of past confrontation. In these circumstances active young people felt called upon to stretch their legs, and ventured out of their eyrie to make their careful way up the precipitous track to the farmery of Dowlaw, where Antoine had taken their horses to be stabled. Thereafter they went riding far and wide over the folded green and brown plateau land of Lumsdaine and Coldingham Muirs, where the scattered small black cattle grazed amongst gold-blazing whins and wind-twisted hawthorns, arousing waterfowl from the many pools and lochans and setting the blue hares loping off in all directions. Every now and again, in their lively cantering hither and thither, they came back to the clifftop track, with its breath-catching, plunging vistas and the glittering plain of the sea. And each time their eyes were apt to be drawn further south-eastwards still, towards where, a few miles on, a mighty headland reared itself high above the rest of that lofty seaboard, imperious, tremendous.

"That can only be St Ebba's Head," David decided. "The highest ness, they say, in all east Scotland south of the Orkneys. Shall we go?"

Her answer was to spur ahead.

Following, heedfully now, that dizzy track, up and down, round plunging chasms and gaping chimneys, passing many ancient earthworks and Pictish fortlets, after almost three miles they began to climb consistently towards that thrusting promontory of soaring rock which, as they drew near, could be seen to have a permanent halo of thousands of circling seabirds.

The headland surmounted, they were more than rewarded for their trouble, for the place was almost beyond description in its awesome grandeur, character and dimensions. It comprised, in effect, three abrupt hills strung together by green saddles, their seaward faces cut sheer and undercut by the ocean into a succession of fierce crags, stupendous and dropping straight into the seething deeps of the tide from cornice edges, the escarpment honeycombed with utterly inaccessible caves and clefts and guarded by innumerable sentinel stacks and pillars. But breathtaking as all this was, it was the birds which made the greatest impact, tens of thousands, myriads, of fowl not only circling and diving but festooning every ledge and shelf and cranny of cliffs and stacks, clinging crazily almost atop each other, from sea-level to cape-top—gulls of every description, fulmars, kittiwakes, puffins, cormorants, shags, guillemots, divers and a host of others, in their screeching, quarrelling, mating multitudes. Seals dived and bobbed below.

Long the couple stood, dismounted, and stared, Kate clinging to David's arm, not too close to the edge despite his bravado for, calm as the day was, this place appeared to generate its own winds, up and down draughts of sudden vigour which could send them staggering. The horses did not like it at all, and kept pressing backwards, ears flattened.

At length they dragged themselves away, and were re-mounting when they perceived an elderly man coming along the track towards them, leading a stocky garron laden with timber—the first human being they had seen since leaving Dowlaw. Surprised at such meeting up here, they paused to greet him.

"For why do you bring wood to such a place as this?" David enquired. "Do not say that anyone would build up here?"

"Och, it is for the beacon, just." The man pointed to the very topmost pinnacle of the highest hill. "Yonder, Maister. I have to keep the beacon fed. Keep plenties o' wood up there, so it can be lit of a stormy night. Aye, and these last nights it burned a deal, I tell you, wi' yon gale. I'll need twa-three mair loads than this, aye."

"A beacon? Up here? For why?"

"For the shipping, Maister—the shipping, what else? To warn ship-maisters o' this right wanchancy coast, in hard weather. To keep their distance."

"So! Then it is a noble task you perform, friend. Of your own goodwill?"

"Na, na—the nuns o' Coldingham Priory pay me. No' that much, mind—but, och, they're just weemen and dinna ken what it's like here o' a wild night, feeding the fire. Saving your presence, lady!"

"And are there many ships lost on this terrible coast?" Kate asked.

"Ooh, aye—plenties. Plenties. A wheen mair than there need be, forby."

"Why? What do you mean?"

"The wreckers, just, Satan burn them!"

"Wreckers . . . ?"

"Aye, wreckers. Och, they're aye at it."

"What do you mean, at it? At what?" David demanded.

"D'you no' ken, sir? It's a right trade, here—and an ill trade, guid kens! Mind, no' sae much o' it since yon Home o' Fast and his rogues were outed."

"Home? Of Fast?"

"Aye, him. The laird. He was aye the worst—him and them that went before him. Right devils they were."

"You mean that Home deliberately sought to wreck ships? But how?"

"Easy. Douse my beacon and march a tight party o' his men carrying blazing torches along this bit path, northwards, towards Fast. The shipmen reckon it's St Ebba's Head light and ken where they are. In the dark o' a gale, mind, they'll no' ken the light's moving. So it lures them on. The ships may keep their distance off shore, or so they jalouse—but this side o' Fast, and the other side too, there's reefs stretching oot, the Branders, the Souters and the Rooks, and wi' the bend o' the coast the chances are the ships will strike one or the other. Hech, man—that's why Fast was built where it is!"

"In God's good name—can this be true?"

"True, aye—why should I lie? A'body kens it, hereaboots. It's aye been the way, at Fast. Many's the time I've had to run for my life, frae yon beacon, because o' Home's men.

221

Others too, mind. Ooh, aye—fine pickings they've had frae the wrecked ships, ower the years. And drooned men tell nae tales!"

David and Kate eyed each other, appalled. "So that was it!" he breathed.

"Oh, Davie . . . !"

Taking their leave of the old man, they rode back to Fast, in a very different mood from previously.

Somehow, after that, Fast Castle's remote and extra-ordinary situation did not appeal so much, especially to Kate. Even of a night the seabirds' wailings were apt to change into the cries of drowning men and women. The castle might, in fact, have been built there for completely other reasons—although they were at a loss to think of any. But the beacon-man's tale rang horribly true.

In a couple of more days they decided that they had had sufficient of Fast, and packed up, to head for home. Their attendants could not have been more thankful. They stayed three further days with Antoine at Dunbar, who proved entirely understanding over their feelings—he had not heard about the wrecking links with Fast—before they returned to Garleton, honeymoon over.

14

David brought his bride to Stirling at the beginning of May, to warm greetings from Abbot John and great rejoicing on the part of King James, both at seeing his friend back at last and at the presence of Kate, with whom he had always got on well. Now five years old, he was a pleasant child, somewhat precocious with being solely in the company of adults, normally good-tempered and fun-loving although capable of tantrums. The Earl Marischal and the Lord Erskine, the castle's hereditary keeper, were glad enough to welcome the Lord Lindsay's daughter also, even though they both clearly considered that her husband had always required keeping in his place. Lady Erskine was less enchanted. Hitherto the only woman of quality resident in the fortress, autocratic and of middle years, the arrival of a young, lively and attractive creature like Kate, higher born than herself—she was a daughter of Sir George Campbell of Loudoun—scarcely appealed.

The accommodation problem was satisfactorily solved by John Inglis vacating the room he had shared with David, an anteroom of the royal bedchamber, for a smaller apartment nearby, leaving the other to the newly-weds—for James would not hear of his beloved Davie sleeping anywhere else but in the next and intercommunicating apartment to his own, but was quite prepared to accept Kate there too. This did mean that the Lindsays' privacy was liable to be invaded frequently by the young monarch; but fortunately he tended to sleep long and soundly of a night—although there were occasions when, after some childish upset or frightening dream, he rushed in to share their bed with them.

The other problem, of Kate possibly feeling that she was too much immured in a fortress, proved to be less trying than David had feared. She did not seem to be so oppressed as was he by the stern enclosing walls and battlements.

Moreover, the land being as nearly at peace at the moment as ever it was, the Earl Marischal—who took his duties seriously—was prepared to let the young couple ride abroad frequently, and even to take the monarch with them on occasion, with suitable escort of course, hunting in the Stirling mosses of the meandering Forth, hawking and visiting. It turned out to be a good summer, and Stirling, on the verge of the Highlands, had some wonderful country on its doorstep, and all new to Kate.

All was not quite peace and harmony in Scotland that summer, of course—it never was—even though David was not personally involved and Stirling only remotely concerned. After some months of welcome quiet for Regent and country, there was an outbreak of trouble in the Borderland, the usual raiding and rapine, at first sporadic then gradually showing a pattern. Lord Dacre's name was much bandied about but the identity cropping up most frequently was Sir Andrew Kerr of Ferniehirst, chief of one of the two branches of that unruly clan; and the raiding and bloodshed was confined to the West Merse, Teviotdale and lower Tweeddale, carefully avoiding the Home country; indeed the Homes of Wedderburn, Polwarth and Cowdenknowes were reliably reported to be taking part. The victims tended to be Turnbulls, Elliots, Pringles, Scotts—and these were all Home foes and rivals rather than Kerr's. It looked somehow significant.

It was de la Bastie's duty, as Warden of the Marches, to deal with all this, but he had insufficient forces at his disposal to tackle the combined strength of the Kerr and Home clans, plus Dacre's Northumbrians. So, whilst appealing to Albany for more men, he sought to demonstrate the crown's authority in the area by making sundry minor but strategic gestures of his own, where he believed that the impact might best tell. And in one of these, a call in force one evening at Home Castle itself, he made infinitely more impact than he could have hoped—for he found the Lord Home himself therein, with his brother Sir William and the wanted Kerr of Ferniehirst, in secret conclave, with only a moderate number of mosstroopers to protect them. After a brief but bloody affray, the Warden's men triumphed, and he took all three notables prisoner, to bear them to Edinburgh next day.

This wholly unexpected development created a great stir. It had not been realised that Home himself had returned to Scotland, from King Henry's care, nor that he had been involved in the present Border turmoils at any more than the longest range. Why he had been rash enough to venture back at this stage was not to be known—although no doubt he had some nefarious end in view. His capture, at any rate, changed the entire situation, with Arran more or less tamed and Angus meantime marking time and watching his step heedfully as he did so. Scotland's major trio of dissidents, for once, were all under control.

This time there was to be no undue clemency or delayed action. Home was promptly immured in Edinburgh's Tolbooth, like any common felon, to be brought to trial for high treason at the earliest possible moment, and his brother and Kerr with him. It was already September and the hearing was set for the beginning of October.

It was at this stage that David Lindsay became involved, if in a minor way. De la Bastie was to be one of the principal witnesses, of course, and he asked for David to substantiate his testimony in respect of some of the earlier charges of treasonable activity. So David went to Edinburgh for the trial, and took Kate home for a visit to the Byres at the same time.

The trial, under the Lord Justice General, the Earl of Argyll, was of course a foregone conclusion, little more than a formality—at least as far as Lord Home was concerned. It was inconceivable otherwise, for his guilt had been so blatant and long-continued that there could be no real defence. Indeed he did not deign to put any forward, treating judges, prosecutor and witnesses with a lofty disdain. His brother and Kerr did however fight their cases, but to no advantage. David's testimony was less than necessary. All three were found guilty of highest treason and condemned to death—although Albany, never a harsh man despite his hot temper, and with a view to Border pacification, remitted Kerr's sentence so long as he kept the peace. But for the Homes there could be no such mercy.

Alexander, third Lord Home, met his end, with dignity, on the scaffold outside the Tolbooth the very next day, 8th October, and Sir William the day following. Their heads were thereafter exhibited on spikes above the said Tolbooth, as warning to others. Neither left any male issue.

Much of Scotland breathed a sigh of relief.

Albany and the Warden thereafter lost no time in leading an expedition in major force—the army which had been assembled in answer to de la Bastie's appeal—to parade through the Borderland, with Sir Andrew Kerr in chains, making an especial demonstration at Jedburgh, the Kerrs' main town, before freeing Ferniehirst to return to his own castle. Dacre and his Northumbrians kept discreetly to their own side of the borderline.

It looked as though the realm might have a reasonably trouble-free winter.

Perhaps that was too much to hope for. The very next month two new and unexpected challenges arose for the Regent and government, both with a personal flavour. The first was odd indeed. The previous Duke, Albany's father, second son of James the Second, had had two wives, the first a daughter of the Earl of Orkney, by whom he had produced a son, Alexander. But this marriage had been set aside by Holy Church as within the prohibited relationship, and thereafter it was pronounced by the Scots parliament of the day invalid. The Duke then married his French countess, and the present Albany was born, and accepted by all as heir. The earlier half-brother had grown up quietly, no trouble to anyone, in his native Orkney. Now this Alexander Stewart, in middle years, unaccountably elected to make formal claim that he was in fact legitimately born, the elder son, the former marriage having ended in divorce, not annulment, and that therefore he should himself be Duke of Albany, second person in the kingdom and Regent, the papal injunction false and the subsequent parliamentary veto nullified. Why, at this late stage, he should have brought forward this extraordinary plea was a mystery—although most assumed Henry Tudor to be behind it, for no one else would seem likely to gain anything by it, and Henry was a born fisher in troubled waters. Albany was flabbergasted. He had never so much as met this curious half-brother, and few in the realm had even heard of him—although he was, to be sure, a grandson of James the Second and a cousin of the late monarch.

The second blow fell within days—the arrival of a new

ambassador from France, one Francis de Bordeaux, with a request, indeed a command from the King of France for the prompt return of his Admiral, the Duke of Albany, and a threat, however diplomatically put, not to renew the Franco-Scottish alliance. The same ship brought a private letter to his uncle from Davie Beaton, informing that King Francis was in fact in process of realigning his policies, and was getting no help from the Emperor and Spain in his efforts to retain his prize of Milan and his other North Italy conquests and so was using possible alliance with Henry of England as threat—hence this gesture towards cancelling the Auld Alliance with Scotland. He, Davie, was doing his best in a difficult situation, but bigger guns than himself were called for. He urged Albany's speedy appearance in France.

In some perturbation, the Regent called an urgent special meeting of parliament.

David Lindsay heard about this from Antoine de la Bastie, who attended the parliament as Chief Warden, and thereafter paid a visit to Stirling to see his friends before returning to his duties at Dunbar. According to him the Alexander Stewart business had been more or less laughed out of court, the assembly refusing to take the Orkney claim seriously; but on Albany's urging, eventually passing a formal renewal of the parliamentary ban on any assertion of lawful status by Stewart, with warning of stern crown action if such claims were persisted in. All saw King Henry's busy hand behind this bizarre incident, but hoped that this reaction would see an end to it.

The French problem was not so readily disposed of. Antoine himself, who knew King Francis personally as something of a weathercock, thought that probably masterly inaction was the wisest course, that Francis and Henry would never be other than essential foes, and that all this would blow over of itself sooner or later. But Albany was worried, declaring that the Franco-Scottish alliance was absolutely essential for the realm's well-being and must be rescued at all costs, and quickly. He reiterated his urgent demand for leave of absence, as Regent, to return to France. Parliament had been loth to agree again, at this juncture, considering possible Orkney developments; and the fact that the Queen-Mother, now back at her brother's court, was demanding the right to return to Scotland to visit her son—and with Henry ever declaring that she ought to be Regent for his nephew, Albany's absence would be as good as an invitation. A compromise had been reached, that the Duke should have parliament's agreement to travel to France on a brief visit, but only when the realm's affairs made this reasonably convenient—an equivocal decision on which both sides put their own interpretation. As postscript to all, the assembly emphasised its acceptance of Albany as second person of the kingdom.

As parliaments went, it was scarcely memorable or decisive. But at least it had produced no rumblings from either Arran nor Angus nor their factions. The former, of course, was upset by the Orkney claim, which if it could be successfully pursued, would reduce him to fourth person instead of third. He had not actually taken part in any of the debates, but his son, Sir James Hamilton of Finnart, the Bastard of Arran, had been very prominent, forceful and effective—a man to watch, clearly. As for Angus, he had in fact spoken against his wife being allowed to return to Scotland, his personal relationship with that awkward princess seeming to preoccupy him more than somewhat.

The parliament over, Yuletide was soon upon them, its preparations and the twelve days of Christmas and New Year celebrations a welcome period of relief for all from problems of rule and governance amongst the nations of Christendom—holy days indeed, however less than holy some of the ongoings. At Stirling, Kate and David enjoyed their first Yule as man and wife, with young James almost like their own son, entering into it all with marked enthusiasm. David wrote a poem to celebrate the occasion, short enough for the King to memorise and declaim it, word-perfect—and to go on declaiming it until they could bear it no longer.

It was in fact June before Albany finally got away to France, with even then the Scots very reluctant to let him go. And before that, much had transpired. The new Regency Council had to be set up, for one thing; and proved difficult indeed, with much rivalry, faction-fighting, lobbying, offence given and taken. Eventually it was composed of the Archbishops of St Andrews and Glasgow and the Earls of Arran, Angus,

Argyll and Huntly—much too large, but each required as check and counter-balance against others. Beaton, as Chancellor, would preside. A majority of this group decided that the young monarch, in the interim, would be safer in Edinburgh Castle than in Stirling, as more effectively under their eyes; and although others doubted, the royal entourage was brought to the capital in May—to David's and Kate's satisfaction at least, so much nearer home and at the centre of things.

Then, as it were, to prepare the way for, it was hoped, successful negotiations with King Francis, Albany sent the French ambassador on ahead with the suggestion that Scotland was prepared to have its young King betrothed to Francis's daughter Louise or her sister Madeleine, a shrewd move advised by Davie Beaton, which would give France pause.

Finally, just before he left, the Duke created a further upset of his own, by announcing, without consultation with others, that he was leaving the Sieur de la Bastie as Lieutenant-Governor of the kingdom during his absence—just like that.

There was, of course, a general outcry and protest, Antoine himself pleading to be excused. He was popular enough, admittedly, but the appointment of a foreigner to such a position was hardly acceptable and the position itself of questionable validity and scope—for where did it place its incumbent in relation to the Regency Council? Which was the supreme authority? No one knew, least of all de la Bastie himself. But Albany was adamant. He wanted someone he could trust absolutely at the helm, he informed privately. And a soldier, not a cleric, he insisted. There might well be the need for swift, drastic and military action, and he certainly could not depend on the squabbling ragbag of councillors to provide it effectively. When Antoine pointed out that any such armed action would be apt to be in the Borders area anyway where he was already Warden of the Marches and had full authority to act, the Duke countered by reminding that, as Warden, he had no power to order a mobilisation of the nation's manpower, nor even any major army, and this certainly might be necessary at shortest notice—and God help the realm if it depended on the Council, all pulling against each other!

This, then, was the Regent's last official act before setting sail for his native land.

So David Lindsay found himself in a rather extraordinary situation for a young man of no especially lofty birth and position, close and most favoured companion of the monarch and intimate friend of the new Lieutenant-Governor. Moreover, being now resident at Edinburgh, he saw much of de la Bastie, who inevitably had to spend a greater proportion of his time in the capital than at Dunbar.

It was not long before there was occasion for Antoine to act. As Warden of the Marches he employed spies along the Northumbrian borderlands to give him prior warning of invading bands; and only a week or two after Albany's departure, one of these sent reliable information that Margaret Tudor was on her way northwards with a large train, clearly heading for Scotland. Obviously she—or Henry—had only waited for the Regent to be out of the country before making her move.

Antoine had to think fast—but he was good at that. The Borders were still in an unsettled state. The Homes had lost their chief and his brother and a third brother, Sir George, was now fourth Lord Home, but a man of retiring disposition. Despite this the clan were seething with resentment and on the look out for vengeance. The Kerrs were certainly not to be relied upon, and the other Border clans were scarcely more so, for in the nature of things these, or their leaders, were the most open to King Henry's briberies and blandishments. Moreover, if Margaret had only been waiting for this opportunity, what of her husband Angus? Although lying low meantime, and seeming not to desire his wife's company, he might also have been waiting—and the Douglases were notably strong on the Middle and West Marches. The Tudor approach *could* be the signal for a major uprising in these parts; and if that happened, what might it spark off elsewhere?

In this first test of his position and authority, the Lieutenant-Governor had to act with decision and tact as well as speed. He had to inform the Regency Council, of course; but fortunately or otherwise its members were apt to be scattered about the face of the land unless specifically called together—and there was no time for that. Getting the Chancellor's agreement without difficulty, Antoine

230

mustered as many men as he could in the Edinburgh area, at short notice, and considered how, as it were, to carry the councillors with him in this matter. Beaton himself was getting too old and corpulent for this sort of foray; Arran was away at Hamilton, and Argyll in the West Highlands. But Angus was only at his castle of Tantallon, and it would be wise to have him under supervision anyhow. So he should be asked to ride to meet his wife, as representative of the Regency but at the Lieutenant-Governor's side. And, as counter-balance, in case of Douglas trouble developing, the young Earl of Morton, head of the Black Douglases, who lived at Dalkeith only six miles south of Edinburgh, should come along too—for the Black Douglases were ever suspicious of the Red, or Angus, line, who had been instrumental in pulling them down in James the Second's reign and rising to power in their stead. The Teviotdale Douglases were Black. In addition, Antoine took David Lindsay along, ostensibly to give the Queen-Mother first-hand information about her son—for nothing was more certain than that she could not be allowed any direct contact with the King.

So, some fifteen hundred strong, they marched eastwards, picking up Lord Lindsay and some of his people at the Byres. At Tantallon, Angus had been sent warning of their arrival but with insufficient time for him to assemble any sizeable force. He came along, distinctly doubtful, with a mere hundred or so of a following.

On southwards through the Home country they headed, their numbers precluding any possible attack by that troublesome lot. Halfway down the Eye Water's valley, one of Antoine's scouts brought him word that the English company, some three hundred in number, had crossed Tweed at Berwick and were apparently coming on. De la Bastie promptly sent Lord Lindsay and David spurring ahead to inform Margaret Tudor that she and her party must not enter Scots territory until given due authority to do so.

With a small escort the two Lindsays rode on at speed, wondering what their reception might be from the autocratic Queen-Mother. Down past Ayton and Burnmouth they cantered, and on beyond, between Lamberton Muir and the cliff-girt coast, with Berwick Bounds now only three miles ahead. But, well before they could reach that so-debatable borderline, itself three miles north of the town, they spied the large company in front of them, near Lamberton Kirk, already a good two miles into Scotland. And, to add to the offence, at the cavalcade's head flew the large red and gold standard of the royal Lion-Rampant of Scotland.

The Lord Patrick swore comprehensively.

He swore again presently even more fluently when, near enough to perceive features, he recognised, riding in front beside Margaret Tudor, none other than the Lord Dacre himself, the English Warden, handsome and arrogant. And on the lady's other side, the grim-visaged Home of Wedderburn.

At the approach of the Lindsays, the oncoming column drew rein. The Lord Patrick was not going to doff his bonnet, in the circumstances, but compromised by raising a hand high in some sort of salute to the King's mother. Before he could say a word she spoke, haughtily, in her clipped southern voice.

"The Lord Lindsay, I see. You are something late to greet me, my lord, are you not?"

Lord Patrick gasped and swallowed. "I . . . I . . . Madam, that is not my concern, nor my function. I am here at the command of the Lieutenant-Governor of this realm, and the Regency Council, to remind you that you, and this company, should not have crossed into Scottish territory lacking permission and safe-conduct. You must turn back . . ."

"God's death—how dare you, sirrah! How dare you speak me so? *Me*, lately Queen of this realm and mother of the King of Scots! Have you lost your wits, man?"

"No, Madam, I have not. I but obey the express commands of the Governor and Regency. None from another realm may lawfully set foot on Scots soil without the prior permission of the King's representatives, duly appointed. This has not been obtained . . ."

"Who are you, or any, to speak to me of the King's representatives? The King is my son and I journey to see him. I warn you to watch your words, Lindsay, or you will rue the day!"

The Lord Patrick jutted his chin. "The words are not mine but those who sent me. And you, lady, know well their truth and worth. As does the man who has the effrontery to ride here at your side!"

Dacre grinned but said nothing.

"Who may these be who have sent you? This so-called Governor and Regency," Margaret demanded.

"The Sieur de la Bastie, First Knight of Christendom, whom my lord Duke of Albany appointed Lieutenant-Governor during his absence. And the Earl of Angus, your present husband, representing the Regency Council."

That gave even Margaret Tudor pause. She frowned.

Following up his advantage, Lindsay went on. "The Governor, my lord of Angus, and their host, are on their way to meet you. No great distance off. I require that you return to Berwick Bounds and there await them."

The hoot of laughter from Dacre was eloquent.

"Now we *know* that you are out of your mind, sirrah! You expect me, the Queen, to turn back?"

"You are no longer Queen, Madam, but Countess of Angus. And the Earl of Angus will meet you at Berwick Bounds."

"Is he, then, as besotted as yourself? I shall do no such thing, Lindsay."

They glared at each other, clearly impasse reached.

David coughed. So far he had not spoken, but some moderating intervention appeared to be called for. "My lord—Lamberton Kirk, here?" He gestured towards the small isolated parish church which stood a few hundred yards back from the roadway. "Perhaps the princess could wait there? In the shelter of Holy Church! Medial ground? Since she will not go back."

"M'mm." His father-in-law looked uncertain.

"Not that I would think that even such sanctuary would ensure the Lord Dacre's safety from the Governor's wrath, were he to find *him* there!" That significant addition might serve two ends, he hoped.

Lord Patrick shrugged. "That could serve, perhaps. Madam—you may wait in the kirk, here. For myself, I would hope that this Englishman at your side will wait there with you—that he may receive his desserts so richly earned by his savageries against this realm! I would think that he would hang, here and forthwith!" That enabled him to end on a suitably strong note.

It was Margaret Tudor's turn to look a little uncertain. She turned to confer with Dacre and Wedderburn, who both looked preoccupied. Presently she nodded. "Very well," she said briefly, and reined round her horse's head in the direction of the church.

Dacre spoke. "Then, having seen Your Grace safely to your welcome, in the name of your most royal brother, I shall return to my own place." That was dignity itself.

"And I shall escort my Lord Dacre back to Berwick Bounds and English soil," Wedderburn added, as carefully.

Lord Lindsay smiled broadly.

There was some confusion and toing and froing amongst the company as to whom went where. Presently it became evident that, in fact, the majority behind the Queen-Mother were either Dacre's or Wedderburn's men, and would return with their leaders, leaving only a comparatively small group to go to the church. The Lord Patrick sent David back to inform de la Bastie as to the situation.

He did not have to ride more than four or five miles to encounter the main body. Antoine smiled at his report; Angus frowned.

When they reached Lamberton Kirk it was to find Margaret Tudor within and Lindsay pacing outside on guard, whilst the escorting parties glared at each other like chained dogs. The fifteen hundred marshalled themselves around the place, as though for a siege.

De la Bastie led the way in, Angus with no evident anxiety to greet his wife. That lady was sitting alone up in the little chancel, beside the altar, looking grim. With the newcomers, the church was crowded.

Antoine bowed with Gallic flourish. "Madam, I greet you. I am de la Bastie, the Regent's Lieutenant. You have come further north than we had anticipated."

She ignored him entirely, looking beyond to her husband. "You, Anguish, are in bad company, I see." She had always called him Anguish, but what had started as something of an endearment had for a year or two now held a different significance.

"Lady!" he jerked, and apparently found nothing else to say.

"I have been insulted by this man, Lindsay," she went on.

"Most unkindly handled—I, the King's mother. I look for apologies and better treatment. See to it."

Angus shrugged.

Antoine tried again. "Princess—the Lord Lindsay, I am sure, only carried out his orders. Had you sought safe-conduct and awaited it at Berwick, there would have been no . . . *contretemps*! I should have greeted you there in person."

"Frenchman—*I* do not require the permission of any foreigner, or any other, to enter my son's kingdom. I shall visit James when and how I please. Remember it, in future."

"Madam—it grieves me ever to contradict a lady, in especial a royal one. But you mistake, I fear. When you remarried, according to your late royal husband's express command, you forfeited all rights of guardianship and authority over the young King's Grace, such authority to be vested instead in the regency and parliament of the realm. These, since you left this realm for that of your royal brother, have adjudged you to be, shall we say, an unsettling influence with King James. This you know well, for it is no new development. Therefore you cannot be allowed to visit His Grace. I am sorry, but that is the position."

"How dare you! You would part a mother and her child?"

"*You* did that, Princess. You chose to remarry, knowing well the terms of the late King's edict."

"A dead man's grudging hand!" She turned. "You, Anguish, my husband—you stand there and listen to this, this upjumped Frenchman, miscall and assail me! Are you a man or a louse?"

"Watch your words, lady!" the Red Douglas snapped, stung. "You should not be here. You should not have come, lacking *my* agreement. It is as the Frenchman says. The regency declares that you cannot see the King. You should return whence you came."

"Lord God—this from *you*! You, whom I wed, at such cost! This is not to be borne!"

"You should not have come," the Earl repeated flatly.

"I *have* come. And *will* see my son. None can debar me from entering Scotland—its former Queen."

"Your husband can, Madam," Antoine said.

"He would not dare! I warn him, and you sir, that my royal brother Henry has a long arm and an iron fist! He thinks little enough of you, Anguish, as it is. Turn me back now and I swear that he will make you rue it!"

Angus coughed—for of all Scots he did not have to be told the weight and virulence of Henry Tudor's wrath. "For myself, lady, I do not forbid that you enter this realm. I but repeat that the regency refuses that you see the King." And he looked at de la Bastie.

"It is as my lord says," Antoine nodded. "We do not forbid your visit to Scotland. But you may not see His Grace, Princess."

"We shall see about that!" She rose. "Enough of this talk. I will be on my way."

"And we shall escort you, Madam. Your royal son's Procurator and Usher, David Lindsay of the Mount here, will inform you as to His Grace's well-being and progress. For a mother's comfort." De la Bastie bowed again, and turned to lead the way out.

So, to his alarm, David found himself having to ride at Margaret Tudor's side. Stiffly, jerkily, he forced himself to recount something of James's state and condition, with long silences—the longer in that she showed little sign of interest. However, when after a while she unbent enough to ask a question or two, he warmed a little to his task, unable to keep his affection for the boy wholly hidden. It was scarcely a successful conversation, but by the time that they reached Dunbar, to spend that night before proceeding to Edinburgh, he felt that as well as having done his duty he perhaps had discovered just a little more humanity and feeling in this strange woman than he had believed was there.

He was thankful, nevertheless, when he could leave her, at Dunbar.

15

Margaret Tudor, back in Scotland, was an embarrassment for most who had anything to do with government and the monarchy. And being the woman she was, she did not seek to temper the wind towards any. On her marriage to James the Fourth, Linlithgow Palace had formed part of the marriage settlement, and presumably it was still hers, since no steps had so far been taken to deprive her of it legally. At any rate, it was standing empty, and Margaret promptly headed therefor and took up residence.

Quickly she made her presence felt, with orders to the Regency Council that her son should be brought there to lodge with her. When this was as promptly refused, she demanded that she should be admitted to Edinburgh Castle to visit him, and arrived in the capital in some style, to press her claim. This proving equally unsuccessful, she remained in the city, pursuing an alternative project—none other than seeking to reclaim, at law, the sum of four thousand merks, being rents of her dowry properties in the Forest of Ettrick, uplifted and appropriated by her husband in her absence—embarrassing in a more personal way for that member of the Regency Council. Angus had to defend himself in court, with the plea that a wife's property became legally her husband's on marriage—which the judges chose to uphold. In cold fury the lady then declared that the dastardly Douglas would not find himself in a position to steal any more of her revenues hereafter, since she would be no longer his wife. She would sue for divorce, on the grounds that he was living in sin with Janet Stewart, daughter of the Laird of Traquair. This public washing of soiled linen—which was no news to most in Edinburgh and the Borderland—improved neither her nor her husband's position, especially when it transpired that Home of Wedderburn had married Angus's sister, an injudicious liaison, to say the least. The Red Douglas star was scarcely in the ascendant.

There was worse to come, much worse—and the impact of it was to grieve David and Kate Lindsay sorely. Edinburgh had hastily emptied itself of almost all who could afford to move out temporarily, on account of a visitation of the plague; and the young King and his entourage, for safety, were installed in the castle of Craigmillar, on higher ground some three miles to the south-east of the city, a strong place of the Preston family but pleasantly situated and much less daunting to live in than the grim fortress citadel. It was there that the dire news reached them. Antoine de la Bastie was dead, murdered.

The details were sufficiently clear, indeed flauntingly so, for the Homes were boasting of it. They had hated de la Bastie from the day he had opposed the Lord Home and moved against Dunglass, Colbrandspath Tower and Fast Castle. His appointment as Warden of the Marches had further infuriated them, for they looked on that position as more or less hereditary in their family. Execution of their chief and his brother they blamed largely on the testimony of the Frenchman at the trial. And the confrontation at Lamberton Kirk, in their own Merse, appeared to have been the last straw. They, and Home of Wedderburn in particular, had decided to settle scores.

They had gone about it with some cunning. No large-scale battle was sought, in which the Warden's forces would likely win. The Frenchman had the reputation of seeking to settle problems in his bailiwick in person, where possible. So the Homes had staged a small mock outbreak of lawlessness at Langton, in the Merse, not far from Wedderburn itself, where they had one of the Wedderburn brothers make a minor assault on Langton Tower, a Cockburn place, and create something of a botch of it. No doubt Cockburn was in the plot, for he was married to a Home. Anyway there was much sound and fury, if little else, the word was duly brought to Dunbar Castle, and as expected, the Warden set out, with only a small company, to investigate.

Reaching Langton, some twenty-five miles from Dunbar, without interference, he had apparently found the trouble over and peace returned. But whilst making his enquiries he and his people had perceived that they, and Langton Tower, were surrounded. Large numbers of mosstroopers had hidden themselves in the surrounding scrub-woodland—for like so much of the Merse, the area was boggy and un-drained, more or less impassable wilderness, a source of much of the Homes' immunity from the processes of law. Recognising that the encirclers meant business and that he was hopelessly outnumbered, with what looked like the entire strength of the Homes mustered, de la Bastie had sought to form up his modest party into the classical cavalry wedge-formation, to try to drive their way through the encircling host at any weak spot, and then head for home and reinforcements. But his followers, unfortunately, saw this as a forlorn hope, and scattered in panic.

Left with only two or three close companions, Antoine had dashed off, more or less on his own, heading eastwards, as he had come, following roughly the line of the Langton Water by the Nisbet area and Mungo's Walls. On a splendid mount, he forged ahead. But this was the very heart of the Home country and his enemies knew it like the backs of their hands, whereas the Warden did not. Shrewdly, deliberately, they used their knowledge and superior strength to drive and manoeuvre their quarry into ever more swampy ground. Worse and worse became the going and presently the Warden's fine horse was floundering up to its hocks in mire. Alone now, Antoine turned to face his assailants. He had no least chance, of course. Attacked, on foot, by a score of Home sworders, he fought to the last, the death-strokes actually being administered by Wedderburn's two younger brothers, John and Patrick Home. Wedderburn's own part in the proceedings was to come up then, dagger drawn, and raising the Frenchman's handsome head by its long, carefully braided hair, to hack and saw at the neck above the half armour gorget until he had bloodily decapitated the fallen body. Then, swinging the head by its tresses, he ploutered his way back to his horse, mounted and with the grisly trophy at his saddle bow, led his triumphant following back westwards, not to Wedderburn but all the way to Duns town, almost the Home capital. There, he hung the head on the market cross, announcing to all and sundry that this was suitable reward for any who thought to interfere with the Homes in their own Merse. Let all take note. He rode off, leaving his trophy there.

Appalled, the Lindsays mourned a friend, and feared for a land where such a deed could be perpetrated.

There were repercussions, of course, public condemnations and outrage, assertions as to condign punishment and so on; but a marked slowness to take any appropriate action. To be sure, the death of the nation's Lieutenant-Governor and Warden left a power vacuum, and there was much dubiety about who was to fill it. This was for the Regency Council to decide, lacking Albany's instructions, and there was no unanimity there. It was no situation for elderly clerics, and there was no obvious strong man of note outside the said council to bring in. So the choice fell between the four earls thereon, really between Arran and Angus, although Argyll and Huntly were each suggested as possible compromise candidates in place of the two real rivals. But both were, as it happened, Highland clan chiefs, of the Campbells and the Gordons, and the predominant Lowland interests would take ill out of such seeming to hold sway over them. So it came down to the Hamilton and the Douglas, as from the first had seemed almost inevitable.

Arran, of course, as third person in the realm, could claim superiority; and Angus's standing at the moment was not at its highest. But Arran was notoriously weak, a weather-cock, and middle aged now; whereas Angus was younger, a fighter if not always a successful one, and head of the most powerful house in the kingdom. The scales were fairly evenly balanced. Meanwhile, nothing effective was done about the Homes.

Then Arran played a strong card—or, at least, his son, the Bastard did. He claimed that Angus had been privy to the entire de la Bastie incident—after all, Wedderburn was his brother-in law—and it was asserted that his brother, Sir George Douglas of Pittendreich, had been visiting Wedderburn the day before. What truth there might be in all this was anybody's guess, but it was sufficient, in the climate prevailing, to swing the vote in Arran's favour.

That ineffectual individual was duly sworn in as not only Lieutenant-Governor of the realm but as Chief Warden of the Marches also. David Lindsay was not alone in fearing the worst.

In this, however, David was mistaken, reckoning without Sir James Hamilton of Finnart, the Bastard. For that young man was the reverse of ineffectual, and suddenly he was powerful indeed. By a strange turn of the wheel of fortune, in fact, from being almost unknown by most he quickly proved to be the real ruler of the realm, *pro tempore*, his father only nominally so. Strong, decisive, ruthless and unscrupulous, he was the sort of character that Scotland was apt to throw up in an emergency—and possibly the sort that awkward nation needed from time to time.

His first move, in Arran's name, was to order the arrest of Sir George Douglas and Kerr of Ferniehirst, as allegedly part and art in the murder of de la Bastie—as warning to Angus. Then he commanded Wedderburn and the other Homes to present themselves for trial. Needless to say they did not do so—nor were expected to. But the trial was held, nevertheless, the Homes *in absentia*, Douglas and Kerr protesting their innocence, Angus lying notably low. The two captives were awarded what amounted to a not proven verdict and dismissed with a warning that any further association with the Homes would seal their fate. Wedderburn and his brothers were found guilty and condemned to death, and the entire clan of Home given notice of dire retribution if there should be any further defiance of the lawful authority.

Then a large force was assembled to march south to the Merse.

David Lindsay found himself sent for, by the Bastard, to accompany this expedition, as a former colleague of de la Bastie and as one who knew the Merse and the Homes passing well, also now with some small reputation on tactics, little earned as this might be. Hamilton had not forgotten their association on the ride to Douglas Castle, it seemed. Always well pleased to escape from the constrictions of fortress life, he went gladly. Since presumably they would be picking up the usual Lindsay contingent en route, he took Kate along, to deposit at the Byres once more, the only woman with the host.

Arran himself was present on this occasion, but very evidently his son was in charge of all, the Earl a mere figurehead. The Bastard welcomed David, not warmly for he was not a warm man, but cheerfully, and was gallant, in a fleering, heavy-handed way, towards Kate. He made no attempt to hide the fact that this was *his* expedition and that all would be done his way. A dashing figure in black, gold-inlaid half armour and plumed helmet, he outlined the projected programme as they rode side by side—without, of course, actually seeking David's advice. The object was not any major confrontation, despite their numbers, he informed—the Borderers were difficult enough folk to conduct without unnecessarily arousing their hostility at the start to the new Warden of their Marches. It must always be remembered that the real menace was Angus and the Douglases, these Homes and Kerrs and the like mere pin-prickers. These must be kept in their place, of course, and shown who wielded the King's authority; but full-scale hostilities were to be avoided. This demonstration in force was more to give warning to the Douglases than to savage the Homes. They would make no uncertain gesture towards the Homes and let the Merse see the power of the Governor and Warden; but thereafter they would proceed through the Douglas lands of Teviotdale and Tweeddale, to leave Angus in no doubt as to the realities of the situation. This was explained as they marched from Edinburgh down the Lothian coast, by Musselburgh and Salt Preston, in order to, as it were, show the flag to the Red Douglas lairdships of Longniddry, Kilspindie, Stoneypath and Whittinghame, and of course, Tantallon itself.

David was less than enthusiastic over all this. To him it sounded more like a development of the Hamilton–Douglas feud than a punitive measure against the murderers of Antoine de la Bastie. He said as much.

Hamilton pooh-poohed that but pointed out that it was essential to recognise that the Douglases and the Homes must not be allowed to become allies, as might well happen; and of course the Douglases were much the more powerful and dangerous, nationwide, not only in the Borders. It was necessary that judgment on the Homes over the murder should be seen to be carried out; but the security of the realm itself was vastly more important, and this expedition was concerned with that also.

So the host of some four thousand men moved in almost leisurely fashion down the coast, impressive as to size and appearance, all banners and armour and even some of the late King's cannon, although not the heavier pieces which would have slowed down progress even further, something like a holiday atmosphere prevailing. No great mileage per day was possible in these circumstances, and not much more than a dozen miles was achieved before the first evening—but that conveniently brought them to the area of Longniddry, Aberlady and Kilspindie, all Douglas territory, where the army could satisfactorily encamp and demand food, forage and shelter—a most suitable method of demonstrating the facts of life to the Douglas lairds, including Angus's own uncle at Kilspindie, without actually having to take overt hostile action. Leaving Arran and the Bastard at Luffness Castle, David was able to take Kate three miles inland to the Byres and Garleton.

Next day the army also came that way, leaving the coast where there were no more Douglas properties meantime, to pick up the Lindsay contingent and proceed south-eastwards over the Garleton Hills and across the Vale of Tyne, skirting Haddington, heading for the Lammermuir foothill lands of Whittinghame and Stoneypath, Douglas places also, where a similar procedure was enacted. The descent of over four thousand men on a property for even one night, requiring their keep and accommodation, was a salutary experience and expense for any laird, and all done in apparent good will and in the name of loyal duty.

They had heard that Angus had left Tantallon and was thought to be at his lesser property of Tyninghame, nearer Dunbar, and this being a mere six miles or so from Whittinghame, the host marched that way the following morning, as it were in the by-going. If Angus was indeed at Tyninghame he did not reveal himself, and the Governor's leadership party made no attempt to call, deeming their close passage sufficiently significant. On past Dunbar they went, where Arran, as new Warden, made a brief token appearance for the benefit of the garrison, and appointed a new keeper. Then on to Dunglass for the night, forfeited Home property, still in crown hands.

Now in almost wholly Home territory, they made their leisurely way next day, by Colbrandspath and through the hills southwards for Duns, the Merse capital. As far as David Lindsay was concerned, there was an air of unreality about the entire proceedings, no least haste, little sign of military aggressiveness nor even preparedness for attack. Nothing was more certain than that their unhurried progress would be well-known to all the Home country. Yet the Bastard was clearly unapprehensive—and David knew him to be a realist. He began to suspect that all had been, somehow, arranged beforehand.

At Duns, after the longest day's march, the army happily quartered itself on the burgh, to the lesser delight of the townsfolk, its respectable women in particular. In the morning, after a late start, they moved on a few miles to Wedderburn and Langton.

Here, nothing could have been more agreeable, and generally welcoming. Both strongholds were thrown open to the visitors. The Homes of Cowdenknowes, Ayton and Polwarth were there to greet the Warden and Governor in most civil fashion, all hospitality offered. Unfortunately Wedderburn himself and his brothers were from home meantime, actually visiting friends over on the English side of the borderline; but they would undoubtedly wish all goodwill to be shown to the new Warden. Their houses were at the Warden's disposal.

Since all the condemned Homes' property was already specifically forfeited to the crown, this might seem an unnecessary gesture.

Nevertheless, Arran accepted all graciously, his son for the most part keeping in the background for the moment. A certain merest token harrying of the properties took place, more or less ignored by the leaders on both sides. And after something like a banquet, Cowdenknowes announced that the new Lord Home himself was awaiting them at the burgh of Lauder, to hand over the keys of Home Castle to the Governor. Lauder was not in the Merse at all, but some twenty miles to the west, in Lauderdale, and almost equally far from Home Castle.

David was more than ever surprised when he heard Arran declare his satisfaction with this change of programme, but to wonder about suitable accommodation en route across the high moorland of Polwarth, Wedderlie and Spottiswoode Mosses? The Bastard put a word in here, to inform that the Douglas tower of Evelaw stood approximately halfway, in the Wedderlie area, and would provide a suitable halting place for the night. Cowdenknowes added that it would be his pleasure to escort them in person.

So this very unusual disciplinary expedition set off due westwards next morning, receiving hospitality in passing at Redbraes Castle, the seat of Home of Polwarth, and proceeded on across the high, barren moors, not really part of the Merse so much as the southern foothills of the Lammermuir range. They came to the remote Douglas hold of Evelaw in the evening—and it was noticeable how much less agreeable was both their reception and their attitude here. Douglas of Evelaw had few cattle or sheep left to him when the host moved on in the morning.

It was only some ten miles, through low green hills and mosses, by Westruther and Spottiswoode, to Lauder town, where they duly found the inoffensive George, fourth Lord Home awaiting them with the keys of Home Castle. This last had been forfeited at the time of his brothers' executions and indeed garrisoned by crown representatives since, so this key presentation was something of an empty gesture. But Arran seemed well enough pleased, and his son was only in a hurry now to get on. When it transpired that the getting on involved, not going back eastwards to the Merse to deal with more Homes, but due southwards to Tweeddale and Teviotdale to further demonstrate against the great Douglas lands therein, the Lord Lindsay, for one, called a halt. He had come, and brought his men, he pointed out, to seek out and punish Homes, not to harry and threaten Black Douglases, with whom he was on friendly terms. Anyway, most clearly his contingent was not required, with hostilities apparently the last thing contemplated. He would return to the Byres.

Arran did not seek to detain him, and the Bastard only smiled. David elected to accompany his father-in-law, having had enough of this odd perambulation. At the head of their Lindsays, therefore, they left and rode off northwards for Lothian again, chewing over the problems of a kingdom with a child as monarch, the struggles for power, and how poor a second justice was apt to come to personal and family ambition. They agreed that Hamilton of Finnart was a man to watch, in more ways than one; and that there was a real danger of civil war again breaking out on a major scale between Hamilton and Douglas, with the nation's weal foundering between them. The sooner Albany came back the better, for Arran obviously was useless, a mere cipher.

Their opinion of the new Governor was by no means revised when, a couple of weeks later, after returning from

245

showing the Hamilton flag rather than the Lion-Rampant through the Borderland, Arran announced that in the interests of peace and the realm's well-being, he was graciously pleased, in the name of the King's Grace, to pardon Home of Wedderburn, his brothers and accomplices, and to remit the forfeiture of their properties, on the understanding that hereafter they remained staunch supporters of the said King and his peace.

Antoine de la Bastie was to remain unavenged.

Chancellor Beaton sent an urgent message to the Duke of Albany, to cut short his visit to France and to return to Scotland before the Regency Council fell apart and the realm with it.

16

It was not Albany who arrived, a couple of months later, in answer to the Chancellor's appeal, but Davie Beaton his own nephew. And very soon after his landing, that authoritative young man arrived at the gates of Edinburgh Castle—to which the young King returned, the plague in the city having died away with the colder weather of autumn. Ostensibly Beaton came without delay, officially to convey the greetings of the King of France, and likewise of the Regent Albany, to the child monarch; but in reality he came to see David Lindsay. He was delighted to find him wed, and declared that, God and a certain young woman willing, he intended to follow him into the estate of matrimony at the earliest possible opportunity.

But much as he made of Kate, and the benefits of marriage, that was not what he had come so promptly to discuss. He proclaimed himself much concerned over conditions prevailing in Scotland since he left, and recognised the need for urgent improvement of the situation. But that would not be so easy now, he pointed out.

"Was such ever easy, in this awkward realm?" David asked. "We are, of all peoples, the most difficult to lead and to manage, I do believe! All pull in different directions, preferring to fight each other rather than the common foe . . ."

"Yes, yes—we all know that," Beaton interrupted impatiently—which was not like him. "But this is different. The present situation. The kingdom is now on a steep slope, with little or nothing to prevent it plunging on downwards to disaster, civil war the least of it. Henry of England, we know, is just awaiting his chance. He intends to take over this realm. And what has happened and is now happening, is just what he requires. He intends invasion—when Douglas and Hamilton are fully at each other's throats and most of the kingdom backing one or the other. Then, fullest invasion, with all his might—and the ground, to be sure,

247

well prepared before him. He intends, this time, to be ruler of Scotland."

"But—has he not always sought that? This is not new . . ."

"It is new—his present opportunity, and new moves. Do you not see it? Never before has all been so greatly in his favour. And he is already moving. Already he has set afoot his first endeavours. He will start the trouble at our back door—the Highlands. He is in touch with Alexander, Lord of the Isles, and other great chiefs, Maclean of Duart, Macleod of Dunvegan and others, to lead a great Highland revolt and assault on the Lowlands, with promises to aid them establish an independent sovereignty—this whenever the Hamiltons and Douglases come to actual warfare. This news the French king has, on best authority—and approves, since it all will keep Henry busy and the *French* back door safe. So that Francis can turn his whole strength against North Italy, without looking over his shoulder across the Channel!" Beaton shook his head, unusually perturbed, exasperated, for that normally so confident young man. "The fools here, Angus and Arran, and this Finnart all speak of—they cannot see it! Or will not. And I, *I* can do little about it, as matters are . . ."

David swallowed at what was implied in that, the assumption that his visitor took it for granted that he *ought* to be able to affect and guide the affairs of nations in some degree, the sublime arrogance of it.

"What can any of us do?" he mumbled, embarrassed for his friend.

"I could have done much. With Albany here. He needs me, as interpreter. And heeds me. So I can effect much. But with him in France, here I have not that power. I am but a Fife laird's youngest son!"

"And the Chancellor's nephew," David reminded.

"That, yes. But you will not have failed to note that my uncle is not the man that he was. He grows old and heavy, heavy in mind as well as in person. He is now something of a broken reed, I fear, as Chancellor—tired. Yet he is all that I have, to help steer this yawing ship of state! So I must needs use him."

Again the other marvelled at the attitude behind that.

"See you," Beaton went on, "Forman, Archbishop of St Andrews and Primate of the Church in Scotland, is worse than my uncle, older, frailer, useless. So the Church, which should be the greatest power in the land next to the throne, is feeble, all but leaderless, its bishops and abbots and priors divided, corrupt and largely ignorant, respected by none. Holy Church therefore counts for little or nothing. This could, and should, be changed."

With that, at least, Lindsay could be in full agreement. "The Church is in sorry state, yes. A shame on the nation. Sunk in sloth. But—what can be done about it? Save perhaps by the Pope in Rome? Who, I fear, cares little."

"Aye—and Henry, who is shrewd, mind you, is using this likewise. His Chancellor, Wolsey the Cardinal, is feeding the Vatican with carefully chosen tidings about the Church in Scotland. We hear much, in France, of both the Papal and English courts. Francis is well served with spies. Wolsey would have the Pope to declare the Scottish Church decadent and in default—and it has not paid its dues to Rome for long! So, its hierarchy could be declared incompetent and removed from office, for the time-being. And, to be sure, the nearest metropolitan set in charge over it, to put matters to rights—the Archbishop of York! That age-old story of the English kings—spiritual hegemony over Scotland, as a first step towards complete dominance, via the archdiocese of York. Believe me, Henry Tudor will stop at nothing."

"But—but surely this is impossible? To put the Scots Church under the English! It is centuries since that folly was brought low, that pretence."

"Not so long. Our Church has always claimed independence, but it was only in the reign of James the Third that we attained metropolitan status and our own archbishops. A mere fifty years—and what is that in the life of Holy Church? Right up till then, the ridiculous claims of York maintained. And what one Pope could ordain, another could cancel. It is a real danger. And how Henry would chuckle! The Pope needs help to save all North Italy from the French, with the Emperor so weak. He might well strike a bargain with Henry."

"This is beyond all. Can your uncle do nothing?"

"He might do much—if he would. If only old Elphinstone had been alive! So I must play on my Uncle James. Play strongly."

"You mean . . . ?"

"My eminent relative has other weaknesses besides corpulence, a fondness for young women and consequent sloth in matters religious! He has ambitions also. He would dearly like to be Archbishop of St Andrews, Primate of Scotland, and a cardinal if possible. For these baubles he would do much, exert himself somewhat, I believe."

"So? And how would the realm benefit, in its present straits?"

"So long as he is still Chancellor, and presides over the Regency Council, in name at least, he could use the revived power of Holy Church to large effect. If he would. Monies, my dear David. The Church is rich indeed—if the siller can be wrung out of it. Bribes—Henry Tudor is not the only one who could bribe adherence. We Scots have a sad weakness for siller! And excommunication—a notable power and threat, feared by most men, even the highest, and fiercest. The Primate can excommunicate!"

David blinked. "You, you think to use this, these powers of the Church, in matters of state? Use Holy Church as a weapon to gain your way?"

"To gain the *realm's* way. The realm's safety. Why not? Other kingdoms do, as I know well—France, Spain, the Empire, Henry himself. Why not Scotland?"

"You will never convince the archbishops and bishops to this, Davie. Even you!"

"Not the others, perhaps. But I think that I need only persuade my uncle, see you. With me behind him, as Chancellor *and* Primate, the others will not matter much. Not *that* much!" And he snapped his fingers.

Helplessly, Lindsay wagged his head. "Even you . . ." he repeated. And then, "But would all this be necessary, anyway? It would take time, after all—much time, surely? And the Regent will be back long before that. Albany— with your help, no doubt!—Albany will come and take charge soon."

"That is where you are wrong, my friend. Albany will not come soon. Albany stays in France."

"But—he was given only four months' leave of absence— and that is now past . . ."

"Think you he takes that seriously? He loves France, his home, a deal more than he loves Scotland, I assure

250

you—and I scarce blame him! He has an excellent life there, all to his every taste—here nothing but troubles. Besides, the King of France will not let him go. Especially now, after de la Bastie. Nothing more sure. Not for a long time, I swear."

"You say so? This is . . . bad. Grievous news. If others knew . . . !"

"Others must not know. Keep it to yourself, David."

"I will, I will. But—your uncle? How will he see all this? Can you bring him to it? If he is so weary?"

"I think that I can. That possible cardinal's hat I shall wave, will beckon him! To be Primate as well as Chancellor—that is something few could hope for. If I can give him that hope, I believe I have him. Ambition he does not lack, only vigour. And that, surely, *I* can supply!"

"But how? I think that you have a sufficiency of ambition yourself, yes. But you are only a nephew . . ."

"I aim to be rather more, my friend. See you, if I was constantly at his shoulder, pushing him, making decisions for him, his left hand if not his right—then it all might be achieved. It would take time, to be sure. The French archbishops have secretaries. I propose to make myself my good uncle's secretary. To his marked advantage—and pray God, the realm's!"

David stared. "You could do this? Have yourself accepted, appointed, to such position? Sufficient to precede others? The Chancellor must have many secretaries and assistants already . . ."

"To be sure but none so close as I shall be. I shall be his *personal* secretary, something he has not got, either as Chancellor or as Archbishop of Glasgow. Oh, it will be a Church appointment, never fear. The archdiocese of Glasgow has lay benefices and offices amany, some with most adequate siller attached! I shall draw one of these out of him, and become lay rector of this or lay capitular of that—and so provide myself with suitable wherewithal to support my new state at the same time! I, after all, require the necessary means to keep a wife hereafter!"

"So-o-o! You have it all thought through."

"Most of it, man—most of it. There are one or two details to decide, still! But none beyond me, or the situation, I think. David—with you ever close to the King, and myself

251

guiding the Chancellor and effective ruler of Holy Church, what may we not achieve?"

"I have no say in matters of rule and policy . . ."

"You are *there*, with much influence over our young monarch. You have more power than you think, David Lindsay of the Mount! You could rise high."

"I have no wish to rise high. I see what happened to one who rose all too high, Antoine de la Bastie! I suggest that *you* should take warning from that—for such could happen to you also, in this sad realm!"

"That would be in God's good hands. I am a great believer in God, David—although not always in His earthly servants, self-appointed as most are! But—this of de la Bastie, yes. A shameful affair, shameful for Scotland—and grievously harmful, forby."

"More grievous for Antoine! He was my friend."

"Mine, likewise. You do not forget that it was I who brought him to Scotland? But, more important for this realm, he was the friend of the King of France and of Albany also. Both are affected, in their different ways. Francis is furious—one of his most favoured subjects savagely murdered, and his assassins pardoned. He sees it all as a blow at France, an insult to himself—and Scotland will be the loser. Partly why he approves this of the Lord of the Isles' revolt. Albany will have to work the harder to win the renewal of any treaty and the proposed betrothal of young James to a French princess. As for Albany himself, he will be the more loth to return to Scotland, I fear."

"Yet he is the more needed!"

"True—but we will have to survive lacking him, nevertheless—of that I am sure. Hence my plans to stir up Holy Church. Who knows—we may yet bring those Homes to justice, and avenge our Antoine."

"I pray so. Indeed, I do."

"Yes. Now, this of Hamilton of Finnart, who appears to be cutting so wide a swathe here today—tell me of him. I knew him in France awhile, but never closely . . ."

Oddly enough, David Lindsay was the means of bringing together, in some measure, these two so very different yet able and effective young men who each thought to play a major role on the Scottish stage. Beaton, learning that

252

David was not exactly friendly but on fairly familiar terms with the Bastard, sought an arranged private meeting, clearly purposing to make use of Hamilton's qualities of drive and energy, if possible, rather than to see him as a prospective foe. Possibly the other thought along similar lines—although David had little doubt in his own mind as to which would be likely to triumph in any duel of wits. Anyway, he saw no harm in bringing them together, in his own quarters in Edinburgh Castle—for both had occasion to visit the fortress frequently on the business of the Governor or the Chancellor. They made an interesting and dangerous pair, and Lindsay was duly wary of both, but recognised that each had qualities which Scotland required, and might counter-balance the one the other.

They appeared to get on reasonably well together, although David had no doubts but that there would be no hesitation on either's part of promptly discarding the other should they discover any influence to be in the way of their own intentions. On one matter, they were in entire agreement, meantime at any rate—that Angus must be kept very much in his place; likewise his wife.

They were aided in this by that ill-matched pair themselves. Margaret, from Linlithgow, announced that, since her husband now had Janet Stewart of Traquair living in open sin with him at Douglas Castle in Douglasdale, divorce was inevitable and urgent. She therefore made application, through Archbishop Forman, for Papal decree. Angus, for his part, at first made no response to this, no doubt concerned about Henry Tudor's reaction. However, if so, he need not have worried, for that autocrat, well informed by his spies, promptly made declaration that his sister must withdraw her suit forthwith, that divorce was morally wrong and repugnant in the sight of God, especially in a member of his own family. She must be reconciled to her husband. Presumably Henry assessed the Douglas power as too potentially useful to be lost over a mere female whim. Emboldened by this, Angus proclaimed to all and sundry that *he* was in fact the injured party in that his wife was flagrantly consorting at Linlithgow with a very young man, oddly enough a Stewart also, Henry Stewart, son of Lord Avondale. King Henry then made it known that he was sending another Henry, one Chadworth, an Observantine friar, to Scotland to effect a reconciliation between the erring couple, in accordance with the Almighty's holy will and precepts.

This comedy was still not yet fully developed, for of all things, Margaret now appealed to Albany in France, writing in most friendly terms, urging him to use his new influence with the Pope—for his wife's sister had recently married the Pope's nephew, Lorenzo de Medici, Duke of Urbino—and assuring him of her support and goodwill in all matters.

Whilst Scotland buzzed with all this, at least it helped to keep more active hostilities from breaking out that winter and spring, both between the Douglases and the Hamiltons and over the Border from England—and scandal was infinitely to be preferred to civil or national war.

In this pleasing lull, Davie Beaton—source of much of the information—came one day in late April to Edinburgh Castle, to announce to David Lindsay two items. One that he was now official personal secretary to the Archbishop of Glasgow, and lay Rector of Killearn, in the sheriffdom of Stirling; and two, that he was to be married to Marion Ogilvy shortly and desired his friend's company and support on that occasion, and Kate's too if she would come.

So two weeks later it was back to the Braes of Angus, at Airlie, to that frowning castle in the jaws of its glen where, if Marion Ogilvy welcomed them with a quiet warmth, her father did less. Lord Ogilvy clearly considered that his youngest daughter was marrying beneath her, and Marion had no doubt had a hard task in getting him to permit her union with the penniless seventh son of a Fife laird, however notable his uncle. Undoubtedly this indicated some lack of perception in her father; but the Angus glens were far from the hub of power, and Ogilvy was presumably unversed in the realities of the situation.

Marion and Kate got on well from the start, very different personalities as they were: the one calm, restrained, assured; the other lively, demonstrative, eager. Apart from the Lindsays, none others on Beaton's side were present, none of his family—which probably added to Lord Ogilvy's doubts about the match.

The night before the nuptials, David again saw a very different side of his friend's character. The castle was full to overflowing, with much of the nobility of Angus, the

Mearns and Aberdeenshire, and the bridegroom was allotted no very splendid accommodation. In his small tower room, David found him pacing the floor in some agitation, in the May twilight.

"David," he said, "this of marriage. It is . . . difficult. A man requires . . . guidance. So much to put to the test, lacking experience in the matter. Marion is so fine, so gentle. I love her dearly, dote on her—but in some ways I scarcely know her! We have been but little together, see you. I fear to disappoint her, hurt her, offend. *You* are married now, and happy, I swear. Can you help me . . . ?"

David swallowed a grin. "This is not like you, friend! Do not tell me that you are so inexperienced? French women, they say, are none so backward . . . !"

"No, no—but that is different, quite. Not to be considered where Marion is concerned. Handling such women demands but little nicety. But this, the marriage bed, with one gently reared and so delicate of her nature . . ."

"I think that she is probably less delicate than you deem her! What I have learned of women is that they are made of stouter stuff than we are apt to think. In some ways, stouter than are we! I counsel you not to fear for her . . ."

"But—tomorrow. Tomorrow night! The bedding—the marriage bed. That first night together. How do you advise? Leave her, leave her . . . not alone, but, but unassailed? At first? Give her time? Did you . . . ?"

"I did not. Lord, Davie—she is wedding a man, not a eunuch! Even if you are now Rector of Killearn or whatever it is! She will expect a man's attentions, I swear! I say be gentle at first, yes—but not over-gentle! Play the eager husband, or she may doubt your need. Or your . . . capabilities!"

"You think so? Your Kate . . . ?"

"My Kate is all woman—and so is your Marion, or I am much mistaken." David felt that it was time to lead to a change of subject. "I would not have thought you the man to doubt yourself—you, who seek to move men and realms to your devisings! Even your own uncle. Is he falling in with your wishes? Now that he has you as secretary?"

Beaton changed back to normal almost in a breath. "He commences to do so, yes. He makes the first moves to unseat Andrew Forman—although God may do that for him, for the man is sick and failing. I have told him that Angus seeks to gain the Primacy for his own poet-uncle, Gavin Douglas, now Bishop of Dunkeld, perceiving much advantage for his cause in that. This has much spurred on my good relative! It is true, forby—although less urgently so than I have suggested. He, my uncle, has already appointed a new Bishop for Caithness, which was vacant—a brother to the Earl of Atholl, and so it will aid in bringing that useful earldom to our side. And I am seeking to have him translate Abbot David Arnot of Cambuskenneth to the bishopric of Galloway—on condition that Arnot then allots the revenues of the Abbey of Tongland therein directly to the Archbishop at Glasgow! It is a surprisingly rich foundation, I discovered. Other moves I have in mind for the reform of Holy Church!"

"Reform? Scarcely the word, I think?"

"Reform, yes—in a manner of speaking. Making the Church a more effective force in the realm. And I have written to Albany seeking his good offices with the Pope, like Margaret Tudor, to have my uncle's promotion to St Andrews expedited, with the possible cardinal's hat, and to forestall any move by Henry of England and Angus to put Gavin Douglas therein. I have not been wholly idle, you see."

David wagged his head. "I wonder if Marion Ogilvy knows what she is marrying!" he exclaimed. "Have you told her what you are? What you seek to do? The life she is like to lead?"

The other looked away. "I have not troubled her with such matters. Should I have done? That is not a woman's part."

"Nevertheless, if she is going to live with *you*, she will have to live with all that, your life. After Glen Isla and the Braes of Angus, it will be no little change! And, Davie—where are you going to put her? To dwell? Living as you do, ever on the move. At this Killearn?"

"No, no—that would never serve. There is a rectory there, yes—but no place for my wife. I will take a lodging in Edinburgh, near to the Abbey of the Holy Rood, where now I dwell in my uncle's quarters, when in the capital. So she will be near you and your Kate in the castle, also. When I am away she will have your company . . ."

Next day the wedding was celebrated in the castle chapel by the parish priest, reminiscent of David's and Kate's own in that the place was too small for all of the company to crowd in, it all making for a simple ceremony, with the emphasis on the feasting afterwards. The bridal pair gladly took David's advice to avoid any possible bedding spectacle by contriving to slip away before the banquet ended. They arranged to meet the following afternoon at St Mary's Abbey of Coupar-Angus.

David Lindsay's parting with the Lord Ogilvy was little less frosty than his welcome had been although he did bring himself to say that he felt sure that Marion would prove to have wed one of the most important men in the kingdom—a prophecy which was received with blank incomprehension. Kate, as Lord Lindsay's daughter, and attractive, obtained a slightly more genial leave-taking.

They found the bridal couple awaiting them at Coupar-Angus, not in the travellers' hospice but at the abbey itself, where the Archbishop's and Chancellor's secretary had prevailed upon the Abbot to provide them with suitable accommodation for the night, unusual for a monastic establishment as this might be, in principle if not in practice. David forebore to ask the new husband how he had fared, but Beaton was in high spirits and Marion gently glowing, so presumably all was well.

They rode on westwards together, the best of company, heading for Perth, to cross Tay, where they were allotted fine quarters in the famous Blackfriars Monastery—and where Beaton regaled them with the story of the murder of James the First within these same walls less than a century before. The day following they reached Cambuskenneth Abbey, near the Forth crossing at Stirling, and again were received with respect and given excellent hospitality—and free. The others were learning some of the advantages of travelling in the company of one influential in Holy Church.

It was when passing through Stirling in the morning that they found the town buzzing with news. A great Highland revolt had broken out. Donald Galda MacDonald, Lord of the Isles, with Maclean of Duart and Macleod of Dunvegan and many other chiefs, had risen in arms and were marching southwards. Already they were said to have overrun much of Lochaber and were heading towards Atholl, declaring that the Highlands and Isles were about to become an independent realm.

It appeared that Scotland's peaceful lull was over and the Beaton marriage celebrated just in time, the Lord of the Isles presumably having proved too impatient to await Henry Tudor's co-ordinated assault—unless this was already under way. Beaton now was suddenly all the man of action, bridegroomship temporarily forgotten, or at least in abeyance. He must get back to his uncle's side at the earliest possible moment. David Lindsay should bring on the young women to Edinburgh without delay, but he himself would dash on ahead, killing horseflesh if need be. In vain the girls, both excellent horsewomen, protested that they could keep up with him. Davie Beaton left them there on the outskirts of Stirling, spurs digging cruelly. Marion Ogilvy was thus quickly to learn the kind of man she had married.

17

Thanks to the two young men, Beaton and Hamilton, rather than to their elders, the Chancellor and Governor nominally in command, prompt action allowed the kingdom a breathing space. On the recognition that the two important men most immediately threatened by the Lord of the Isles' advance were the Earls of Argyll and Atholl, whose territories lay in the way of the Highland horde and who would therefore be apt to fight most strenuously anyway, these two were given fullest powers and commissioned to go and halt the Islesmen at all costs, with the Gordon chief, the Earl of Huntly, to co-operate on the eastern flank, and the bishops of all the contiguous sees instructed to assist with men and arms, but above all, money, to hire more fighting men, Atholl's brother thus swiftly having to earn his new elevation to the diocese of Caithness. Argyll, the Campbell chief, as Lord Justice General and with most to lose, was put in overall command, appointed Lieutenant-Governor of the Isles, and promised vast grants of MacDonald and other lands if he prevailed.

There was no sign of any increased activity from the English side of the Border, so it appeared that Donald Galda had indeed miscalculated and acted before Henry was ready.

In the event, it was almost wholly a clan battle which took place, with great ferocity, in Ardnamurchan, actually over into Argyll—to the satisfaction of most Lowlanders, who much approved of Highlanders destroying each other, whatever the cause. The conflict was indecisive in that there was no obvious victor; but since the Isles host withdrew back into Lochaber and Morar thereafter, with Donald Galda himself wounded, the winner could be claimed to be Argyll. The Bastard of Arran, who went along in an advisory capacity, as representing his father, certainly so claimed. And when, shortly afterwards the Lord of the Isles died, presumably from his wounds, leaving no near heir, the rising petered out and the island clans returned to their own fastnesses, the thing was accepted as full victory. Whether Argyll could gain possession of the promised territories was another question.

The Hamiltons were cock-a-hoop and somehow appeared to claim most of the credit—to Douglas fury. Davie Beaton made no such boasts, but was quietly satisfied.

However, although the Highland trouble had gone off, as it were, at half-cock and was now disposed of, it had its side-effects in seeming to start off a series of minor outbreaks between Hamilton and Douglas supporters in the Lowlands, as a climate of mounting violence prevailed. None of these could be likened to civil war, for Angus himself lay remark-ably low, whether at Henry's behest, who was not yet ready, or in order to provide his wife with no further ammunition in her campaign against him, or even perhaps in preoccupation with his new mistress, was not to be known. The violence, although widespread and worrying, remained small-scale, in the Borders, Ayrshire, Lanarkshire, Dumfriesshire and Galloway—until the April of 1520, when the dreaded major hostilities erupted at last, and in the streets of the capital itself, of all places.

It was sparked off by a conjunction of two official events, called for consecutive days, a session of the parliament to consider what was to be done in view of the Regent's con-tinued absence, and a meeting of the town council and guilds of Edinburgh to elect a new Provost for the city, the day before. The Earl of Arran had been Provost, amongst his other appointments, for a succession of terms—it was a point of pride for the capital city to have one of the leading men of the kingdom as a civic head, even though most of the duties were performed by deputies inevitably, not always a satis-factory arrangement. On this occasion a move was afoot amongst the magistrates and guild brethren to appoint a more practical if less decorative head, and one Robert Logan, of the Restalrig family, a prosperous merchant, was being put forward. This was considered to be an insult, not only by Arran who was seeking re-election but by the nobility and aristocracy generally, and the usual pressures were being brought to bear—and with the town filling up with lords and lairds and their trains for the parliament next day, the said pressures could be powerful, the more so when the Earl of Angus arrived from his western fastnesses, for the parliament, with a tail of no fewer than five hundred fighting men.

Arran and his entourage happened to be at Dalkeith, six miles to the south favouring the Earl of Morton there with his company—it was part of his policy to keep the Black and Red Douglases at loggerheads by all means possible—when he heard, not only that Angus had arrived in Edinburgh after lying low for so long, but that he was making a bid for the provostship, not for himself but for his nominee, his own uncle, Sir Archibald Douglas of Kilspindie, the grim Greysteel. In high dudgeon the Hamiltons set out for the city to put a stop to this.

But on arrival at the Greyfriars Port, the southern gate in the tall Flodden Walls, he and his party found the gates shut and barred against them—an unheard of situation. It was midday, and Arran as well as being Lieutenant-Governor of the kingdom was still Provost of the city until either re-elected or replaced. Outraged, he and his shouted their fury and threats. But demands for the gates to be opened immediately were met with assertions that the closure was on the orders of the magistracy, so that no further lords and their armed men should be allowed in to threaten the town council until the election of the new Provost was duly and satisfactorily effected. No amount of protest and hectoring had any effect—and those massive gates and high walls, so hastily erected and strengthened after the Flodden disaster, were stout and strong. Although the Bastard and others set their men to attempting to break in, without battering rams, cannon and scaling ladders they could do little. So the Governor and Provost had to wait outside in impotent rage until the magistrates eventually gave the order to reopen. And then it was to learn that Sir Archibald Douglas of Kilspindie was indeed effectively, if not perhaps duly, elected Provost of the capital.

Arran, on entry, making his way through the crowded streets seemingly largely filled with hooting and jeering Red Douglas men-at-arms, decided that probably the castle would provide safer lodging, in the circumstances than his usual quarters in Holyrood Abbey, and rode thither in major wrath—and it was only then that David and Kate heard of it all from the Bastard, so isolated was the royal citadel from much that went on in the city below. The Chancellor was sent for from Blackfriars—and needless to say Davie Beaton came with him.

A council of war followed—or better, a council of non-war, for obviously it would take very little now to set off a dire confrontation and slaughter in the streets. Although nominally the conference was between the Governor, the Chancellor and Huntly, as members of the Regency Council—Archbishop Forman was now too frail to leave St Andrews and Argyll was still in the Hebrides trying to subdue the island clans—the Earl Marischal was brought in as responsible for the monarch's security and Lord Erskine as Keeper of the fortress. But probably most were well aware that the real decisions were apt to be made by the two young men there only as advisers, Davie Beaton and Sir James Hamilton of Finnart, and that in the circumstances prevailing these two might well clash since the Hamilton interests were not necessarily best for the realm. The Lord Lindsay was sent for, but until he arrived, Beaton suggested that David Lindsay should sit in, in his place.

After an angry and somewhat incoherent harangue from Arran, embarrassing to all, the Earl Marischal, with sufficient seniority to interrupt, announced that he was much concerned for the safety and position of the King's Grace in this situation—which should be the concern of them all. With the Hamilton faction now more or less occupying the castle—for all Arran's entourage had followed him up into the citadel—the Douglases might well come storming up demanding their ejection. And if this was refused, they could possibly mount an armed attack—which would have to be repulsed. This would have the effect of seeming to put the young King entirely on the Hamilton side, which would be injurious to the royal position and the realm's well-being. The crown must be seen and known to be above all faction fighting. Lord Erskine backed this stance, declaring that if the Douglases did attack the castle, the only effective way of keeping them out was the use of cannon fire. And that would indeed set the city and nation ablaze, initiating civil war, the very thing that they were seeking to avoid.

Arran all but choked in his offence and reproach over this suggestion. Was he not Lieutenant-Governor of the realm? And second person after its monarch whilst Albany was absent? Who had more right to seek the shelter of the capital's castle from the shameful assaults of the blackguardly Douglases?

Huntly supported Arran.

Davie Beaton murmured in his uncle's ear.

It was at this early stage in the proceedings that the captain of the guard came in, to whisper to the Keeper. Frowning, Erskine announced that a large party of Homes had ridden up to the Greyfriars Port from the south, and had been refused admittance by the town guard there, on the orders of Sir John Hamilton of Clydesdale, the other of Arran's illegitimate sons. But they might well get in at other gates.

Arran half rose from his chair in his agitation. "Those scoundrels! Border thieves and murderers! They must not enter. To join with the Douglases! All the gates to be shut and barred. Immediately." He pointed a trembling finger at the guard captain. "You—see to it. Forthwith. All city gates barred."

Davie Beaton spoke up, not having time on this occasion to use his uncle's lips. "But, my lord—is this wise? The Homes, little as we may love them, have every right to be here, to attend tomorrow's parliament. After all, your lordship yourself granted them free and full pardon for de la Bastie's murder! Lord Home is a lord of parliament. And Wedderburn and Cowdenknowes are commissioners for the Merse and Lauderdale." He said that reasonably and respectfully.

The Governor glared at him. "You, sirrah—keep your tongue between your teeth! The gates will be closed. When I require your advice I will ask for it!"

"And I shall be honoured, my lord." That was silky. "But may I remind your lordship that by closing all the ports you will be cooping all the Douglases and their friends within the city streets. An explosive situation! All but seeking for worse troubles. There could be fighting with the town guard."

The Bastard nodded briefly towards Beaton and gripped his sire's arm—but the Earl shook him off.

"All gates will be closed," Arran repeated. "That is my command. As Governor. And I am still Provost of this city, since the appointment of this rascally Douglas is clearly by force, and unlawful."

The captain of the guard departed and there was an uncomfortable silence around that conference table.

The Chancellor broke it, less than confidently. "My

lords—this of the provostship. It could be dangerous, very. Cause an uprising of the citizens. I agree that Douglas of Kilspindie's appointment is wrongous and should not stand. But the magistrates and guilds do seek a change, as is their right. If you, my lord Governor, were to insist on being Provost again, there could be serious disturbances. You could force the citizenry to side with the Douglases. That must be avoided at all costs. It would, I say, be wise to declare that neither a Douglas nor a Hamilton should be Provost, at this juncture. But one of their own choosing. This man Logan was to be their choice as chief magistrate. Let him be installed, then, and the Douglas ousted. Then the citizenry would be your better support, my lord."

Arran began to splutter but his son spoke first. "My lord Governor does not require the provostship of this, or any other town, to support his dignity," the Bastard said strongly. "He has a sufficiency of duties, lacking this! He but recognises that this city, containing as it does this great castle and the King's Grace, must remain in leal hands. As Provost, he can seek to ensure that. But if this Logan, or other, can fill the Provost's chair effectively, and keep the Douglases out, then I am sure that my lord would not object."

This time it was Davie Beaton's turn to nod in the other's direction.

Arran looked at his son doubtfully, cleared his throat but did not speak.

"How can this be achieved, and Kilspindie unseated?" Huntly demanded. "The Douglases will resist it."

"If the Regency Council issued a decree that neither a Hamilton nor a Douglas should be Provost in this pass, parliament tomorrow would endorse it and it would have the force of law," the Chancellor declared. "I so propose."

It was not a meeting of the Regency Council as such, but three of its members were present, and the absent Argyll could be relied upon to support the Governor. A nodding of heads seemed to clinch the matter, and Arran did not raise his voice.

Then the Earl Marischal returned to his earlier contention. "I still am concerned for the King's Grace," he said doggedly. "Erskine, and you Lindsay, agree? This royal citadel must not appear to be a refuge of the Hamiltons in this pass. The Governor himself may have good right to be here, but not his people. My duty is to our Prince, in this matter."

"I say the same," Erskine added.

"This is not to be borne!" That was Sir Patrick Hamilton, not entitled actually to take part in the conference but sitting behind his brother, Arran. "Are we to be thrust out, to our deaths? For the sake of some notion of these lords! I am kin to the King's Grace—as are others here. We are entitled to the shelter of this castle until such time as this Douglas menace and riot is lifted."

"To be sure," the Governor agreed. "My people stay."

"My lord Governor—surely you see the danger?" the Marischal insisted. "You give the Douglases a rod to beat you with! They could claim that the Hamilton faction is using the King to shelter behind. That you drag the crown into your feuding. I am the *King*'s governor, appointed by the Regent Albany."

"And I am the Keeper of this fortress—as of that of Stirling," Erskine said. "Also appointed by the Regent. I say that you must leave."

"You will seek to put us out then, my lords?" the Bastard demanded, grinning. "I think that you will have . . . difficulty! We have over five score men with us. How many have you?"

There was a momentary silence as men eyed each other, masks dropped. Into it David Lindsay spoke, scarcely confidently but earnestly. He looked at the Bastard, not at Arran or his brother.

"Have you, Sir James, perhaps overlooked a small matter? This citadel can protect you meantime, yes. But it can also imprison you. You could all be held here . . ."

"*That* none would dare, I vow! Not even the Marischal or Erskine!" the Bastard broke in. "Have you lost your wits, man?"

"Not so—that is not my meaning. It is the Douglases who could imprison you herein. Coop you up like poultry. Merely by encamping on the tourney ground beyond the gatehouse and drawbridge. There is but the one door to this hold. If they sat there, in strength, you could not win out into the city. They could keep you, my lord, from attending the parliament tomorrow!"

265

He had made his point. The Hamiltons looked at each other.

"The parliament—I *must* be there!" Arran exclaimed. "Forby, it would be no parliament without me, the Governor."

"I think that you mistake, my lord," the Earl Marischal said grimly. "If the King's Grace is there, and the Chancellor, it is a due and proper parliament."

"The child? James . . . !"

"Aye. He is now eight years old and a fine lad, and wise enough for his years. It is time that he is more shown to his people, their sovereign-lord. We say that he should now attend the parliaments, at least the openings. And it would serve to improve it, the proceedings, the royal presence."

The Chancellor nodded. "That is true. The King there, bickering and railing should be less, the Douglases be something restrained. Others likewise."

All saw that, even Arran.

"But this of the castle," he went on. "If we are not to bide here—where? Holyrood is wide open to assault. No defences and a score of entrances, to abbey and church. No safety there. And if we leave the city, go to Craigmillar or Dalkeith, we might not gain entry again, without bloodshed. Angus will stop at nothing . . . !"

Davie Beaton spoke briefly to his uncle and then raised his voice. "My lord Governor—the Archbishop's lodging. The Blackfriars' Monastery—it is the most secure house in Edinburgh. Why my lord Chancellor chooses to bide there perhaps!" And he smiled. "It has high walls and gates easily guarded but opening on to the Cowgate as well as the Blackfriars and Niddrie's Wynds. A large courtyard and sufficient space for your people. And it is Holy Church premises. You would be safe at the Blackfriars, my lord."

The Earl looked at his son, who inclined his dark head. "And getting there?" he asked. "Without attack."

"It is evening now and near dark. Soon the streets will be empty, the Douglas men-at-arms all in the dens and stews and alehouses."

So it was agreed, just as the Lord Lindsay arrived, with a substantial following and the word that they had come in by the East Port and found it broken down and smashed, with bodies lying around, apparently having been attacked and stormed by a party of Homes under Wedderburn, who had been denied entry. While the Governor was exclaiming at this, Lindsay interrupted to say that there was worse news than that. Before leaving the Byres, he had learned that Wedderburn and the Homes had assaulted the Priory of Coldinghame, slain the Hepburn Prior and six of his family and installed as Prior none other than William Douglas, brother of Angus.

It was in a state bordering on consternation that the meeting broke up, therefore, and the Hamilton leaders were escorted by the Lindsays down to the Blackfriars' Monastery, fortunately without incident, their own retainers instructed to find their way discreetly in small groups thither—for it was vital that, if possible, there should be no further and large-scale battling and riot before the parliament, which might make its sitting impossible, in the disorder.

Next forenoon, with the city tense but no rioting having taken place, David and Abbot John prepared their royal charge for his important appearance. James, at eight, had grown into a lively, well-built and good-looking boy; but although normally cheerful and biddable was liable to moods and sulks and flashes of violent temper. On such occasions Gavin Dunbar, now awarded the archdeaconry of St Andrews and the deanery of Moray, but still nominally the royal tutor, could do nothing with him, and even John Inglis had difficulty in coping; only David Lindsay had the boy's unfailing devotion and usually could soothe his tantrums and even prescribe punishments and achieve contrition.

But this April day there were no problems, with James looking forward to his outing although a little nervous— probably less nervous than his elders, at that.

Dressed in his best—and that was less than grand—the monarch, mounted on a quiet horse, rode in procession from the castle down the Lawnmarket, the High Street and the Canongate to Holyrood, through watching but mainly silent crowds. There were a few wavering cheers when some perceived, by the royal standard, that the little boy was their liege-lord, but these came to little in the prevailing perturbation. The citizens feared the worst. James, who seldom indeed emerged from the castle, chatted happily to

David and the Abbot and scowled at the Earl Marischal whom he had never liked, honest and reliable as that man was.

Outside the abbey there was already trouble, clashes between the retinues of lords allied to one side or the other, and the Chancellor and his nephew were thankful for the early arrival of the King, whose presence it was hoped would restrain the trouble-makers.

Within the great church the atmosphere was little less tense, although neither Arran nor Angus had so far put in an appearance. In the chapter-house, James was installed to await his official entry.

From there, presently, a great commotion developed outside, of shouting and clatter, and in a minute or two the Lord Lyon King of Arms, in charge of ceremonial, came hurrying in to urge that the monarch should make his formal entrance immediately, as a calming influence. Angus and the Governor had now both arrived, with their companies, and were facing each other like angry dogs, hurling insults and threats, church or no church.

So the trumpeters and heralds were lined up, a stirring fanfare blown and, led by Lyon, young James made his entry behind the Earl Marischal bearing the sword of state and the youthful Earl of Erroll, the High Constable, carrying the crown on a cushion, David and John Inglis in close attendance, the Chancellor and his secretary and clerks bringing up the rear. The boy was led to the Abbot's chair in the chancel, acting as throne, where he sat, the officers of state flanking him and the two young men directly behind. The Chancellor, at his table near the chancel steps, bowed, sought permission to commence the proceedings, and taking it as granted, called on the Abbot of the Holy Rood to commend their affairs in prayer to the All Highest. It so happened that the said Abbot was none other than Master William Douglas, brother of Angus, who had so recently had himself invested as Prior of the wealthy priory of Coldinghame, in the Merse, also, over the murdered body of the previous Prior. Presumably he had come north therefrom with the Homes. His prayer was sonorous but brief.

Quickly Archbishop Beaton went ahead with the agenda, before any disturbance could develop. "The principal reason for calling this assembly, Your Grace," he read out, "is the difficulties caused by the continued absence of Your Grace's Regent, the Duke of Albany, and what steps can be taken both to expedite his return from France and to ensure good government and Your Grace's peace meantime. To that end, it must be recognised by all, the establishment of a just and peaceful solution to the problems besetting this capital city of Edinburgh is vital. Therefore, with Your Grace's permission, I propose to deal with this matter first. The Regency Council recommends that, in the interests of amity and the realm's weal, the provostship of this city meantime should not be held by either a Hamilton or a Douglas. Robert Logan of Restalrig has been nominated by the magistrates and guild-brethren. It is proposed therefore that the said Robert Logan should be confirmed as Provost of the city by this parliament, all other contenders to stand down."

"Seconded!" the Marischal jerked, almost before the other stopped speaking.

"I protest!" That was Angus, loudly, from the front row of the nave where he was surrounded by his Douglas lords and lairds, prominent amongst whom was his uncle Sir Archibald Douglas of Kilspindie wearing the Provost's chain of office. "I am a member of the Regency Council—and this is the first that I have heard of such proposal. I do protest."

"My lord of Angus, although sought for, was not found," the Chancellor declared speciously. "But of the five other members of the said Council, a majority were in favour of the proposal. Therefore your protest fails, my lord."

"Then I move here and now that this preposterous proposal be rejected."

"And I second!" That was a chorus, from a sufficiency of Douglases.

"Then there must be a vote, since the motion is proposed and seconded, as is the counter-motion. But I would remind all that this decision could seriously affect the peace of this realm. Either a Douglas or a Hamilton as Provost of Edinburgh, in this pass, could well lead to grievous hostilities. As already has been shown. So, think well! I will take the negative first. Those in favour of rejection of the motion, show."

David had been counting heads, as far as he was able in the crowded nave, and concluded that it would be a close thing. The Douglases could rely on the Homes and the votes of most of the representatives of the East and Middle Marches of the Borderland, as well as support from Angus itself, the Mearns and much of Fife. Arran could count on the West March, Galloway, Ayrshire, Lanark, the Chancellor's Glasgow area, and Stirlingshire. And there were the Edinburgh city representatives. Much, he decided, would hang on the attitude of the *Black* Douglases.

A score of Douglas hands were raised immediately, but elsewhere there was distinct hesitation, as men looked around them, calculating, debating, or fearful of the Red Douglas glares. Gradually a few more arms rose. The Earl of Morton, head of the Black Douglases, who had been Arran's host at Dalkeith, ostentatiously stood with arms folded across his chest—which chest was noticeably well-protected by handsome inlaid half armour. David heaved a sigh of relief at the sight.

"Thirty-three!" Davie Beaton sang out. "Thirty-three against the proposal."

"Those in favour, show," his uncle directed, his voice uneven.

Fewer hands went up than David had anticipated—until he noticed that Morton still had his arms folded. He was abstaining; and no other Black Douglases voted either, nor some others who were their friends.

"Thirty-six, thirty-seven, thirty-eight!" Beaton counted, throatily. "No—thirty-nine for the motion, my lord Chancellor."

"Then I declare the motion duly carried," his uncle got out. "Neither Douglas nor Hamilton shall be Provost of Edinburgh meantime, this parliament has declared. Sir Archibald Douglas of Kilspindie will therefore vacate in favour of Robert Logan of Restalrig."

There was pandemonium in the church, voices upraised, fists shaken, hands on dirk-hilts—swords being forbidden at a parliament. Quickly the noise increased. King James, who had sat quietly until this, began to looked alarmed, and turned round to David. The Chancellor beat and beat on his table with his gavel for order, and was ignored.

Not only was no heed paid, but here and there in that nave men actually came to blows, the Homes not backward. As the din grew louder and an ornate lectern crashed over,

James jumped down from his throne and ran behind to clutch David's hand.

David spoke urgently to the Earl Marischal, who nodded and turned to the Lord Lyon, gesturing. That perturbed individual was only too glad to oblige, and ordered his trumpeters to sound. A distinctly uneven flourish followed, and to its ragged blare the royal party marched out, in less than perfect order, to the chapter-house, the session thus abruptly adjourned, leaving chaos behind.

With the noise from the church ever heightening, the Marischal decided that the sooner King James was back in the castle's safety the better, David and all agreeing. Concerned about the Chancellor and Davie, however, the latter suggested that half of the royal guard should wait behind to provide security for the Beatons, and the Earl acceded. So, a reduced company, guard close about them, they emerged into the abbey precinct, clove their way under the unfurled Lion-Rampant banner through the milling crowd of men-at-arms there, mainly Douglases by their colours, to the horses and mounting, set off up the Canongate at a much more spanking pace than they had come down, young James frequently looking apprehensively behind him. The crowds had disappeared from the streets now, doubtless not expecting the parliament to be over so soon, and they clattered the mile of cobblestones up to the castle in short time, thankful when their beasts were drumming hooves on the drawbridge timbers.

David Lindsay, however, felt unhappy thereafter about his role in the situation, recognising that he might seem to have left the Archbishop and Davie rather in the lurch, to scuttle for safety. But his first duty undoubtedly was to the King, whose safety and well-being was paramount—and the position had been threatening, to say the least. What had been developing within the church was bad enough, in all conscience; but what might have happened outside amongst all those unruly retainers, mosstroopers and men-at-arms when word of trouble inside reached them, had been much more dangerous. And the boy had been frightened. He could only hope that the section of the royal guard left behind and his father-in-law's Lindsays would provide sufficient escort for the Beatons. Arran and his Hamiltons and allies could look after themselves.

271

How the Hamiltons sought to do just that became all too evident presently. The first news of it was brought by Davie Beaton himself arriving up at the castle with the detachment of the guard a couple of hours later. For that so positive character he was in some agitation. He told David that only his uncle's holding up of a crucifix and threat of excommunication had prevented a violent assault on the persons of Arran and other Hamiltons by the Homes and some Douglases at Holyrood—although Angus himself had sought to restrain his followers and had in fact succeeded in keeping most of them in the church, giving opportunity for the Governor and his people to get out and force their way through the thronging, struggling retainers outside to their horses, and so had managed to dash up to the Blackfriars' Monastery's security without major conflict. The Chancellor and Davie had followed with the royal guard. And there they had found the Hamiltons in furious conclave, the Bastard now very much in command. Quickly it became apparent that it was to be open war. The Governor's life had been threatened and the full weight of his authority must be mobilised to punish the offenders. But that would take time. Meantime the Douglases and their savage friends must be shown that they should not meddle with the Hamiltons. Every available man in the city capable of bearing arms was to be mustered forthwith, in the King's name; also the levies of every friendly baron, for the protection of the Governor. Angus was to be summoned to attend an urgent meeting of the Regency Council, there at the Blackfriars. If he came, he was to be held prisoner; and if not, as was likely, a specially selected party of the toughest men-at-arms, under the Bastard himself, would go out and snatch him. With Angus held hostage for their better behaviour, the Douglases would be brought to heel.

Davie said that he and his uncle had protested that this was madness and would only lead to worse violence, outright war in the city, and that the King's name should on no account be brought into it. But they were shouted down, the Bastard refusing to listen to reason. So he, Beaton, had come up to the castle with the borrowed guard seeking aid to try to put a stop to this folly. If the Marischal, the Constable and the King of Arms were to come down to Blackfriars and in the King's name forbid any such use of the royal authority, and seek to dissuade Arran from permitting such madness, then the worst might yet be averted.

David was doubtful, but took the other to see the Earl Marischal.

That sober individual would have none of it. His duty, he declared, was to the King, not to Arran, whom he despised. Let him and Angus fight it out between them—and if they slew each other in the process, so much the better for the realm! The royal guard was certainly not to be involved in such feuding. At Beaton's urging, however, he agreed that he could not stop the High Constable and the Lord Lyon from going to Blackfriars if so they wished—but no royal guard.

Young Erroll and Sir Thomas Pettigrew of Magdalensyde, the Lyon, were more receptive, and agreed to do what they could. David Lindsay, still feeling guilty about abandoning the others at Holyrood, said that he would also accompany them; and with Lyon's trumpeters as escort, the tight little company rode down through the town to Blackfriars. The streets were full of men-at-arms looking for trouble.

Admitted to the heavily guarded monastery, they found the Hamiltons preparing for war, and Archbishop Beaton depressed and more or less resigned to whatever transpired. But he went with the newcomers to reason again with Arran and his son.

The Constable and Lyon made no more impression on the Bastard than did David Lindsay and the Beatons; and his father appeared to be wholly under his influence. Arran's brother, Sir Patrick Hamilton, seemed prepared to listen, but the others ignored him. Speaking for the Earl Marischal, Lyon, supported by David, made it very clear that the King's name must not be used in any mobilisation of manpower. This was feuding between Hamilton and Douglas, that only. It was difficult to demand that the Governor should keep the King's peace, since he it was, in the absence of the Regent, who had the authority to enforce it.

In the midst of this argument it was announced that two representatives of the Earl of Angus were at the gate, requesting interview with the Governor. They were alone, so no trickery seemed probable; and one was clad in a Bishop's habit. Arran was for refusing them a hearing but the Chancellor persuaded him that there could be no harm in learning what they had to say, the Bastard shrugging acquiescence.

The visitors proved to be the brothers, Gavin Douglas, Bishop of Dunkeld, and Greysteel, Sir Archibald of Kilspindie, uncles of Angus. The latter was outspoken, grim and did not beat about the bush. Angus had heard, he said, on reliable authority, that Arran was seeking to raise the city in outright attack on Douglas and was even purposing to capture the Earl himself, by deceit. Any such dastardly attempts would be brought to naught, needless to say, and avenged. But his nephew, desiring the minimum of bloodshed and loss in this personal controversy, proposed that instead of full-scale battle in the city streets, with many innocent lives endangered, they should settle their differences in more knightly fashion by making something of a tourney of it—as had been done a century before at the North Inch of Perth. He, Angus, was prepared to meet the Earl of Arran in single combat at, say, the Netherbow Port. But since Arran was nearly thirty years the elder and might consider the contest unfair, he would be willing to fight any suitable representative—but no bastards or low-born ruffians! If this appeared to hazard too much on a single individual, then they might field perhaps a score on each side, as champions for the rest, the losers to abide by the result. Was this not better than outright war?

While the astonished and uncertain Hamiltons went into conclave over what to do about this, Bishop Gavin drew aside to where the Chancellor, his nephew and David Lindsay stood listening.

"My lord Archbishop," he said, low-voiced but earnest, "as men of peace, surely we can do something to prevent this armed strife and bloodshed? I appeal to you, who consecrated me Bishop, to use your high authority in Holy Church to halt this evil before men die. In the name of God!"

The Chancellor shrugged heavy shoulders. "What can I do? What heed will they pay to me? You, my lord—is it not *you* who should be addressing yourself to your nephew Angus? He it is who is issuing this challenge to arms, is it not? *He* is the aggressor in this sorry conflict."

"He seeks now to limit it, at the least! It is Arran and this Bastard who seek to ensnare and it may be slay Angus. This plot we are told of, to trap him, by calling him to a false Regency Council—you, on that Council, and Chancellor, my lord, cannot surely be party to such shameful villainy?"

"No, no. This is wild talk. Not to be credited. Who, who told you this, man?"

"It matters not—but one sufficiently knowledgeable. You as Chancellor it is who calls the Council meetings, no? You cannot but know of these hostile intentions, I think! When you, as priest, should rather mediate for peace, surely?"

Unhappily the Archbishop wagged his grey head. "Not so, not so!" he exclaimed. "I tell you, I swear that I have no hostile intentions towards Angus. And if others have, I am not party to it. I swear it on my conscience!" In his discomfort and confusion, Beaton smote beringed hand on chest to emphasise his innocence—and unfortunately, the blow clanged hollowly. Presumably he had taken the opportunity, while his nephew was up at the castle, to go and don a shirt of mail below his linen rochet for safety's sake, with trouble looming.

"Alas, my lord, methinks your conscience clatters, and tells another tale," Bishop Gavin said drily, as Davie Beaton grinned widely and nudged Lindsay in the ribs.

Distinctly put out, the Archbishop sought refuge in belated dignity and the claims of seniority. "My lord Bishop—I would remind you to whom you speak! Of your position in my archdiocese! I . . . I . . ."

He was saved further embarrassment by Sir Patrick Hamilton coming over to them from the other group to announce that they had indeed agreed to fall in with Angus's suggestion and meet the Douglases in combat, a score to each side. They would insist, however, on having umpires appointed to ensure fair play and had told Greysteel so.

David Lindsay, for one, did not wonder that the Hamiltons had so decided, since, of their own people, they were probably outnumbered by the Douglases three to one at least. To raise and arm the townsfolk, or some of them, would take time, and probably would arouse but little enthusiasm in the circumstances anyway. The offer seemed much to their advantage.

To restore his credit, if possible, the Chancellor raised his voice to declare that if the Earls of Arran and Angus could agree on such substitute for all-out conflict, why could they not meet together privately and come to some understanding, man to man, as honest Christians should, without the sacrifice of other men's blood? Surely this would be to the credit of both?

The Bastard snorted his reaction to that, and the support of Davie Beaton and Lyon, as well as Bishop Gavin, for the Chancellor only made him the more harshly adamant. With Arran himself leaving all to his son, and Sir Archibald Douglas declaring strongly against any such feeble parleying as the Archbishop proposed, the thing was decided. The Hamiltons would meet the Douglases, a score a side, at the Nether Bow in an hour's time. There was still time to settle this business before the light failed.

So the Douglas envoys departed, and the Bastard at once got down to the task of selecting the twenty toughest warriors to uphold their cause, mainly Hamiltons of course but including some notable champions amongst their available allies. The Master of Eglinton, heir to the Earl thereof and a famous tourney fighter, came into this category, with one or two others. There was no lack of volunteers, and a great sharpening of swords, dirks and spear heads followed. The Lyon and the Constable took their leave, desiring no part in it all.

When all was ready, the Governor's contingent formed up to make a move from Blackfriars, first Arran and his lords and lairds, then the chosen score of stalwarts, then the mass of the Hamilton retainers and their friends, and finally the Beatons, David Lindsay and others, in the part of somewhat apprehensive onlookers. It was Davie Beaton's highly appropriate suggestion to have the entire procession preceded by the monastery choir chanting sacred songs.

Thus they left their secure haven, on foot, for the steeply climbing Blackfriars Wynd and the crowded High Street, the choir a help in gaining them passage. Well before they reached the Netherbow Port, they could see the Canongate beyond wholly blocked by masses of ranked men—the Douglases, most evidently. They noted something else also; all the openings off the High Street, the wynds, alleys and side streets, had been blocked by up-ended carts, barrels and other barriers, an ominous sign.

The Hamilton leadership halted about one hundred yards from the solid front festooned with the red heart under blue of the Douglas banners, the choir stopped singing and discreetly retired, and the chosen twenty moved forward in tight formation. The two sides glared at each other, and there was considerable shouting, jeers and challenges. The citizenry gave all a notably wide berth but folk hung out of the windows of the tall tenements on either side, to watch.

Angus, Sir Archibald and some others came forward a little way, beckoning, but Arran and his people stayed where they were. Laughing, the Douglases came on, to comfortable speaking distance.

"Greetings, Hamiltons!" Angus called, mockingly. "You have come, at last, for our sport! I feared that you had no heart for it. Have you managed to find a score of heroes to face Douglas? Or perhaps do you need *two* score, to our one?"

When he got no answer to that but snarls, he went on. "My lord of Arran, I hope that you will honour us by your presence in the forefront? But if, as I fear, your advancing years and well-kent delicacy restrain you, I trust that your paladins will be led by one worthy of our Douglas steel and no bastard felons! We have our own delicacies, see you!"

The Hamilton growls grew the louder, and sundry insults were thrown back. Arran maintained a dignified silence.

Seeing that he was going to get no satisfaction in this exchange, Angus changed his tone. "This of umpires or arbiters, which you require. They must be men of birth and respect. I suggest two from each side. I have my kind uncles here, Greysteel and the good Abbot William of the Holy Rood. They will serve very well. And you?"

"I will so act," Sir Patrick Hamilton shouted.

"And I," Sir Robert Hamilton of Preston volunteered.

There was some confusion over this, as the Douglases returned to their own stance, for it had been assumed that Sir Patrick would in fact be one of the leaders of the Hamilton twenty, he being a noted tournament performer and having, many years before, defeated the supreme Continental champion, the Netherlands Chevalier Cokbewis, in a renowned fight before James the Fourth. In this misunderstanding, the Master of Eglinton was the obvious substitute but of course he was not a Hamilton and most there felt that one of their own should lead. The Bastard, to be sure, would have led, but Angus's remarks had cut him to the quick, and clearly ruled him out.

In his resentment that fierce young man turned on his uncle, with whom he had never been on good terms. "You—why *you* as umpire?" he demanded hotly. "Is it more to your taste than fighting? You, the celebrated jouster! In your old age, have you grown soft? Fear to put your steel to the test?"

"Damn you—watch your words, sirrah!" the other cried. "I will accept such talk from none, in especial from such as you!"

"Go then, Uncle, and watch bolder men than yourself fight and die!"

"God's curse on you, bastard smaik! I *shall* fight this day where you dare not!" Sir Patrick yelled, raising his fist. But instead of striking his nephew, he snatched out his sword and held it high. "Through them! Through!" he cried, the Hamilton slogan. "At them—the Douglas dogs!" And without waiting to see who followed, or any more formal start to the contest, ran forward towards the Douglas front, half armour clanking.

Friend and foe alike were taken by surprise. Montgomerie of Eglinton recovered first and went racing after the older man; and in something of a straggle the rest of the chosen twenty came on behind, lacking all formation.

The Douglases had little more time to react. Angus drew his sword and waved it right and left, to bring his twenty into the favoured wedge formation with himself at the apex. They were barely in position when with Sir Patrick almost upon them, the Earl leapt to meet him, shouting, "A Douglas! A Douglas!"

The two leaders met in a clash of steel and flurry of strokes. But from the first it was an utterly unequal contest. Hamilton was twice Angus's age, and more experienced or not, had run the intervening distance in heavy armour, was breathless and his sword-work unco-ordinated, his outburst of anger still affecting him. Unsteady on his feet, he stumbled in avoiding only the third major thrust, and in seeking to recover his stance, jerked his head to one side, baring his throat above the steel gorget. Angus saw his opportunity and did not hesitate to take it. He slashed sideways, and his sword half severed the other's neck, the blood gushing forth in a scarlet fountain. Sir Patrick fell to the cobblestones before ever even Montgomerie came up with him.

After that unnerving start it was in fact a massacre rather than any true contest-of-arms. The Douglases were in formation, protecting each other and sure of themselves, whereas the Hamiltons arrived in a straggle, panting, disorganised and already disheartened by the falling of their leaders—for the Master of Eglinton, assailed by two others as well as Angus, went down under a hail of blows. In yelling, screaming, bloody horror the twenty fought and reeled and died, in almost less time than it takes to tell.

Well before the last of them fell, the Bastard's fury and hate triumphed over his judgment, and he launched himself forward from his father's side, sword waving, shouting for all Hamiltons to come and avenge their fellows on the dastardly Douglases. Most followed him, however unwisely.

If it had been a massacre before, it was little better than wholesale carnage now, for with the entire mass of the Douglases and Homes engaged, the attackers were outnumbered at least three to one, and with almost every aspect of the encounter against them, arriving piecemeal against a solid phalanx, lacking any coherent strategy, desperate from the start. The Hamiltons fell in their swathes and few Douglases and Homes fell with them.

The Bastard himself seemed to bear a charmed life. He was an excellent sworder admittedly, and undoubtedly benefited from the fact that neither Angus nor most of his kind deigned to cross steel with one born out of wedlock, even though a knight. He fought on savagely, but presently, standing on a mound of slain, he found himself almost alone, with such Hamiltons as had survived tending to disengage and hurry off up the High Street, even he saw that the cause was lost meantime. Hotly he swung round and hurled his dripping sword at Angus, who stood grinning, and cursing brokenly, turned his back on the shambles, slipping and slithering on the causeway that ran with blood. But he himself refused to run, limping with a kind of dignity, wounded but unbowed, back to where his father, no warrior despite being Governor, Warden of the Marches and Lord High Admiral, waited in misery, wringing gauntleted hands.

"Run, Bastard—run!" Angus called after him, but restrained any from attacking that proud back. "To your sorry sire! Begone, so that Douglas can cleanse this causeway of you and your like! Run, Bastard!"

He still did not run, but reaching his father, who seemed rooted to the spot in his consternation, grasped his arm and all but dragged him off up the street, pursued only by the hoots and jeers of the triumphant Douglases.

The two Davids, Lindsay and Beaton, still watched from a pend mouth, appalled at the slaughter—the Archbishop had already fled. Recognising that in their slaughter-lust euphoria the Douglas men-at-arms might well make little distinction between Hamiltons and mere bystanders in this blood-soaked street, they too made a hurried departure. The last they saw of the Lieutenant-Governor of the realm and his son was the Bastard, perceiving a townsman with a mean horse standing beside one of the up-ended carts, going up and taking over the nag and when the man objected, knocking him down with a mailed fist and then clambering on to the beast's back to pull up the Earl behind him and clatter off up the High Street, a strange sight to see.

When the two Davids reached Blackfriars Wynd, they found it choked full of excited folk and could by no means make their way down to the monastery. Fairly obviously the Bastard and his father could not have got down there either. So they turned back and slipped down Niddrie's Wynd, parallel, and so into the Cowgate, thus managing to reach the monastery from the other side. They found the gate wide and unguarded and sundry drunken characters in possession. A hand-wringing monk told them that all was lost, God had deserted them and the legions of Satan had taken over. It seemed that the Archbishop had come fleeing back, pursued by a mob of Homes and Douglases, and the gate porters had not been able to get the doors closed again in time to keep these out. Alarmed, Davie Beaton hurried in search of his uncle, Lindsay following.

There was no sign of the Chancellor in his own quarters, but another distracted monk directed them to the chapel. And there, amidst much shouting and turmoil, they found James Beaton in dire state, collapsed at the altar, the furnishings of which were part dragged on top of him, being beaten and threatened with swords and staves by at least a dozen mosstroopers, his crimson cape and linen rochet ripped off him and savage hands tugging at the protective breastplate beneath, the better to belabour him.

Drawing their dirks, the two young men ran forward,

shouting to one or two affrighted servants to come and help. Their intervention, if it aided the fallen prelate, had the effect of drawing the fury of the attackers on themselves, and quickly they found themselves back to back, fighting off a rain of blows and thrusts. Fortunately most of their assailants were at least part-drunk and not at their most effective; also they were able to wedge themselves into a corner between the end of the altar and a pillar, which protected them on two sides. Nevertheless, undoubtedly it would have gone ill with them, had it not been for the arrival of more Douglases—but this time of a different status. Bishop Gavin of Dunkeld and another of his brothers, Sir George Douglas of Pittendreich, with their own small escort. The Bishop, taking in the situation, angrily made his presence felt, and succeeded in pulling off the belligerents. Ignoring the two young men, he drew his all but fainting and battered superior-in-God to his unsteady feet, expressing due concern and sympathy—after all, without the Archbishop he would not have had the see of Dunkeld. He solicitously escorted him back to his own quarters, with the others, where Marion, one of the Chancellor's mistresses, and sundry other women had barricaded themselves into the strong vaulted basement kitchen premises—and here they were accorded a reception of emotional relief and touching feminine care.

Clearly however the Blackfriars Monastery was no longer a safe haven for opponents of the Douglas faction, so it was thereupon decided that the Chancellor's party should remove at once up to the security of the castle, Bishop Gavin and company escorting them thither through streets now teeming with riotous men-at-arms. On the way thither they learned from the bishop-poet that Arran and the Bastard had last been seen departing the city in haste and fording the shallow end of the Nor' Loch which lay far below the precipitous castle rock, seemingly heading westwards, both on a single broken-down mount.

Leaving his fellow poet at the drawbridge end, David for one was thankful indeed to hear the heavy portcullis clang down behind them and the rattle of the chains as the bridge rose. Fortresses, however cramping and confining, had their uses.

Marion and Kate fell into each other's arms.

18

So Angus was master of Edinburgh and much of Lowland Scotland—although not of Edinburgh's castle. Also, not of the Homes, who as ever were a law unto themselves and demonstrated it by instituting their own brief reign of terror in the capital for a couple of days and nights when Angus led his Douglases from the city westwards as far as Linlithgow, to ensure that Arran did not muster a force against him in that Hamilton-dominated area, nor possibly come to some sort of terms with Margaret Tudor. In the interim the Homes, led by Wedderburn, rampaged through the town, and made something of a ceremony of taking down the grinning heads of the late Lord Home and his brother from their spikes above the Tolbooth where they had been for over three years, before returning in triumph to their own Merse.

Word of all this reached the castle, in its isolation, gradually. They learned that almost eighty Hamiltons had been slain in that dire street encounter—to which Angus had now given the title of Cleanse the Causeway—fully half the total Arran had had with him. What the Douglas casualties were was not revealed, but were probably not a quarter of that.

News of the Governor, if that term now meant anything, came about a week later, when Angus had returned to his mistress in Douglasdale leaving Greysteel, Bishop Gavin and the Abbot William in command at Edinburgh. A courier arrived secretly by night at the castle, having some difficulty in gaining admittance, with a message from Arran, really from the Bastard. They were at Stirling Castle, secure, and summoning loyal forces. The Earl Marischal was urged to bring the King there just as soon as it was possible, taking of course all necessary measures to ensure the royal safety en route. The visitor added that the Governor had sent a messenger to France informing Albany of the situation and urging his immediate return to Scotland.

It was not so easy, of course, to effect a removal of James and his establishment from one fortress to the other, for the Douglases almost certainly would never permit it. So it would have to be done secretly, by stealth. Fortunately, in Davie Beaton, they had available a past master in the use of stealth and subterfuge; and he it was who concocted the scheme. It now being May and the weather clement, they should send word to the Bishop Gavin, the most reasonable of the Douglases, that the young monarch could do with some country air and space to stretch his growing legs after such long constriction in the citadel. A week or two at Craigmillar Castle would meet the case, where there was excellent hunting and hawking in the royal forest of Duddingston. A safe-conduct would be sought—which even the Douglases could scarcely refuse to their liege-lord—and, to make all seem more innocuous, the Bishop, Greysteel and other Douglas notables could be invited to attend a great royal hunt there one day. This might well appear a wonderful opportunity to snatch the King into Douglas hands, the sort of thing which had happened before to youthful monarchs. Whether or not the Douglases would so attempt was neither here nor there. James in fact would not attend the hunt, on the excellent excuse that his guardians had heard that such a plot was indeed envisaged. The hunt would go on—but, concerned for his royal charge's safety, the Marischal had taken the opportunity to send the King off to Stirling the night previously, under cover of darkness!

This ingenious conception found pretty general favour in the fortress, and seemed reasonably likely to succeed. There were a few doubts, mainly concerned with possible reprisals by the Douglases against any of those left behind, but it was agreed that the arrival of a sizeable force of Lindsays from East Lothian, at the start of the hunt, ought to counter any such development.

All went without any major hitch. A safe-conduct duly arrived from Bishop Gavin, with a reproachful note added indicating surprise that it should have been thought necessary for the sovereign's weal. No time was then lost in moving the royal entourage the few miles to Craigmillar, which Sir Simon Preston held of the crown on condition that he made it available when required. James himself was delighted over the excursion. The womenfolk went along also, meantime.

No incidents took place en route. The hunt was fixed for three days hence, a Monday, with invitations sent out, all to meet at Duddingston village an hour before noon.

On the Saturday David Lindsay escorted Kate and Marion to the Byres, where it was felt that they would face fewer hazards than on a night-time dash to Stirling, although the young women were both loth to leave their husbands. At the Byres, Lord Lindsay promised to bring them on to Stirling when all was signalled as safe; and meantime he would attend the hunt on Monday, with the requisite following, to ensure if necessary that there should be no unpleasantness displayed towards the Earl Marischal and the Lord Lyon.

So, late on Sunday night, a well-mounted party consisting of the Chancellor, the Lord Erskine, the two Davids and Abbot John, with a part of the royal guard, and of course the King, all muffled in cloaks, slipped out of the southern postern of Craigmillar Castle into the half-dark, and turned their beasts' heads west-by-south.

They would have gone more swiftly without the Archbishop who, gross and heavy, was not much of a horseman. But secrecy rather than speed was what was important—and the Chancellor, left behind, could have been used as a hostage, with more effect than could the Marischal or the Lyon.

The route chosen, therefore, was less than direct, in the interests of concealment, keeping well clear of the outskirts of the city, and indeed the villages to the south of it, making for the Pentland foothills where their passage would be unlikely to attract any notice. In May it is never really dark in Scotland, and once their eyes were accustomed to the dusk the horsemen had no difficulty in seeing their way. As far as possible they avoided rough ground and bog, of course. In time they struck the well-defined drove road from Lanark, by Colinton, Currie, Balerno and the Dalmahoy hills. Their liege-lord found it all a most exciting adventure.

By sun-up, and striking ever north-westwards now, they reached the Priory of Torphichen which, besides being a famous sanctuary was the seat or Preceptory of the Order of St John of Jerusalem in Scotland, of which Order the Chancellor was a senior chaplain and the Lord Erskine a knight. So here they could safely wait a while, eat and rest.

Linlithgow, on the main Stirling road, was only four miles away to the north, but with empty hills between. James Beaton was exhausted—as no doubt was the horse which had been carrying his weight.

At midday they were off again, keeping to the high ground of Muiravonside and Redding Muir to the area where Wallace fought the fatal battle of Falkirk. Skirting that town well to the west, they were able to heave sighs of relief when presently they entered the glades of the great Tor Wood, the largest forest in Lowland Scotland after that of Ettrick, which extended almost all the way to Stirling, and where they could feel secure from all eyes. David and Abbot John knew much of its fastnesses reasonably well, having often hunted there, from Stirling.

They came to that town and its fortress as the sun was sinking behind the Highland hills. Never before, so far as he could remember, had David Lindsay taken so long to ride a thirty-five mile journey. But all was well and the Archbishop would recover. James was delighted to be reunited with his papingo, which had been left at Stirling.

After it all, they were surprised to find Arran and the Bastard gone from the castle. They were off to the Hamilton country apparently, raising men.

The Earl Marischal arrived a few days later, having suffered no interference. Not surprisingly, the hunt had not been a great success, with the Douglases much upset and angry, but the Lindsay presence in force sufficient to temper their reactions—Angus himself still being absent, apparently.

So, all seeming to be reasonably settled at Stirling, and a quiet spell likely to develop, David sought leave of absence to go and fetch the young wives, Beaton deciding to accompany him.

At the Byres and Garleton they found all well, and lingered pleasantly for a few days, all glad to be released from duties, as it were, for a while, the Lindsays introducing the Beatons to their area of Lothian, from the bays and sands and cliffs of the fine seaboard to the hills and cleuchs and secret valleys of the Lammermuirs, a carefree interlude made the most of by all four. Davie Beaton, in especial, reverted to perfectly natural and high-spirited good company, the model husband and friend, intrigue and statecraft for the moment forgotten.

Or perhaps not entirely forgotten, for on their fourth day at the Byres another visitor arrived and one of some consequence, the Lord Fleming, a distant kinsman of Lord Lindsay. He it was, it turned out, whom Arran had sent from Stirling to France with the message for Albany. Now he had returned, having taken the opportunity of a passage in a French trading vessel from Dunkirk coming to Dunbar for Lammermuir wool. On his way back to Stirling he called in at the Byres for the night.

Fleming was full of news. Evidently, while the quiet spell had descended on Scotland, there had been major developments elsewhere. The Emperor Maximilian had died and was succeeded, to Francis of France's fury, by his rival Charles the Fifth of Spain. This had precipitated strong reaction from the impulsive French monarch and he had promptly made an extraordinary gesture towards Henry of England, calling for an armed alliance against the Empire, Spain and the Pope and inviting Henry actually to meet him on French soil—or at least on soil which he considered to be French but which Henry claimed was English, in the Pas de Calais. Wolsey, Henry's ambitious Chancellor, pro-French, had favoured this, and the English monarch had gone in great state across the Channel, where he had met Francis between Guisnes and Ardres, to discuss a firm alliance. This had been the situation when Fleming arrived from Scotland; and since Albany had gone with Francis to the meeting, as Lord High Admiral of France, thither Fleming had proceeded also.

Obviously he had been vastly impressed by his experiences there, at seeing this vast assemblage of the pride and nobility of two great kingdoms, each vying with the other in an extravagant display of splendour. For instance, there had been no fewer than two thousand eight hundred great pavilions and tents erected on the plain, many of them covered with gold stuff, and all bedecked with banners and pennons—so that the assembly was being called the Field of the Cloth of Gold. The two monarchs, who had never met previously, had come to terms on mutual support and a treaty of alliance agreed on, with Francis agreeing to Henry keeping Calais but getting Tournai back. In the treaty terms Henry had not failed to involve Scotland, his *bête noire*, claiming it to be under his high protection as Lord

Paramount. Albany, there present, had more or less agreed to these terms—no doubt he had little choice—and ambassadors were being sent, indeed might already have arrived, to convey the details to the Scots Council of Regency. In the circumstances, Fleming's mission to urge Albany's immediate return was scarcely well-timed and to little effect. Clearly, whether Francis would allow the Regent's return, whatever Albany's own wishes in the matter, would depend on the Scots reception of these treaty terms—which were, of course, favourable to Henry Tudor, not to Scotland. It was all highly involved, and boded but ill for the northern kingdom.

All this had the hearers much perturbed, and Davie Beaton particularly so. Ignoring the differences in rank and status, he cross-questioned the Lord Fleming at length and in detail. Then he announced that he must get back to his uncle at Stirling at the earliest. He would leave at first light, whether Fleming came with him or not.

So their brief holiday was at an end, it being agreed that they all might as well go together. What Davie could do in the present situation was not evident, but he could be relied upon to attempt something.

They rode next morning in fine style, for Lord Lindsay himself decided to come with them, for consultation with the Chancellor, and took his usual tail of retainers as escort. With no wish to become involved with the Douglases, who were now in complete control of Edinburgh, they were avoiding the city, skirting to the north of it by the port of Leith. And it was while passing through Leith that they learned that this very morning a French ship was docked, putting ashore a party of French and English magnificoes, ambassadors apparently, who had proceeded with much ceremony up to Edinburgh.

Both Davie Beaton and the Lords Lindsay and Fleming were much interested and eager to learn what would happen now in these peculiar circumstances. They would follow the envoys up to the city—as lords of parliament and the Chancellor's secretary, they were perfectly entitled to do so. But there was always the possibilities of trouble with the Douglases, and it was felt that the women should not be exposed to this. It was decided therefore that David and part of the escort should proceed slowly on their way westwards, with Kate and Marion, and wait at the Priory of St Mary at Queen Margaret's Ferry, till the others came up with them.

In the event, they had some considerable time to wait, indeed were becoming anxious about the safety of their friends, before they perceived the Lindsay colours approaching along the little royal burgh's winding shoreside street. Even so they were doubtful, for this seemed a much larger party than before and there were more colours than the Lindsays' red and blue.

To their great surprise, when the others rode up it was to present to them none other than the aforementioned French and English ambassadors, the Messieurs Lafayette and Cordelle, and Henry's Clarenceux Herald, and their attendants, now it seemed also on their way to Stirling. They did not appear to be in the happiest of spirits.

Davie explained. The envoys had been received with fair ceremony at Edinburgh by Angus himself, who it seemed was back in the capital; but to their bewilderment, despite the Douglas being supported by the Earl of Crawford, the Earl of Rothes and the Lords Glamis, Ogilvy, Kennedy and others, they discovered that these lofty-sounding nobles were not in fact who they had come to see, that Angus was the only member of the Regency Council there, the rest being elsewhere, at this Stirling, and having no dealings with these people. So, although they had explained their business to Angus, the terms of the Franco–English treaty as they affected Scotland and so on, and apparently found him non-committal, they had realised that they would have to travel on to Stirling to see the Governor and the Chancellor and others of the Council. It was at this stage that the Lords Lindsay and Fleming had turned up at Holyrood, where all this was proceeding, and learning that the newcomers were indeed on their way to Stirling had sought their escort thither, Angus scarcely approving but hardly in a position to restrain them. He did, however, curtly refuse to accompany the envoys, to their further astonishment. Clearly they found Scotland a strange country.

The journey was resumed. If the foreigners expected to be presented to King Henry's sister at Linlithgow they were disappointed.

On the way, Lord Fleming, riding beside the Lindsay and

Beaton couples, opened their eyes somewhat to an alternative variety of diplomacy to that practised by Davie—the Bastard of Arran's. For he it was who, in his father's name, had briefed Fleming on his errand to Albany. He had said that the Regent was to be told in no uncertain tones that if he was not back in Scotland by midsummer then the Estates of parliament would declare him not only no longer Regent of the kingdom but unsuitable to succeed to the throne, as second person, and heir-presumptive, in the event of the demise of young James. He would also be declared officially infamous and debarred from any further association with Scotland.

Amazed, the others could scarcely believe their ears, that anyone should so threaten the Regent. Davie Beaton was greatly perturbed, for of course he it was who had all but brought Albany to Scotland in the first place, cherished him as Regent and acted his mouthpiece. He declared that Hamilton must be mad, that such threats were the very last thing to bring that proud man back to Scotland, indeed could almost be warranted to keep him away. Then, as an afterthought, he wondered whether that, in fact, might not be the Bastard's intention? After all, if Albany did not come, and was indeed debarred, then who was heir-presumptive to the throne but Arran himself? Was that it? Arran for king—and the Bastard ruling Scotland for him? In which case, how safe was young James Stewart's life?

Appalled at such possible implications, the others fell silent, until David asked how much of this diatribe Fleming had in fact passed on to Albany, and what his reactions had been? The other admitted that he had indeed toned it down considerably, and the necessary translation from English to French had further modified the message. Even so, the Regent had been less than pleased.

Approaching Stirling, they realised that Arran must be back, for the area to the south and west of the castle rock, around the King's Knot, was like an armed camp with hundreds, perhaps even thousands of men, cooking fires sending up their blue smokes into the evening air, the streets of the town thronged with Hamilton retainers.

They had a mixed reception at the castle, Arran apparently flattered by the arrival of the ambassadors to see him, but less happy to see Davie Beaton back, of whom he was gravely suspicious, probably with reason. Neither did he love the Lord Lindsay. The Chancellor, on the other hand, was greatly relieved to see his nephew, on whom he was being led to rely more and more; but he did not welcome the envoys, recognising that they were not come for the benefit of Scotland. The Marischal, for his part, was thankful to see David Lindsay, as was Abbot John, for the King had apparently been at his most difficult during the interim, refusing to obey anyone and demanding the presence of his beloved Davie-Lin, as he now called him. There was a touching reunion of these two, at least. The Bastard was not present, being away raising more troops in the West.

In theory, the ambassadors had come to see the Regency Council; but this was scarcely practical. Of its six members, Archbishop Forman was now all but house-bound at St Andrews; Huntly was up in his Strathbogie fastnesses and would take at least a week to recall; and Argyll was still conducting what had become almost a private war of Campbell aggrandisement in the Western Isles. The visitors had already seen Angus—which left only the Governor and the Chancellor. At Davie Beaton's suggestion, therefore, a sitting of the old Privy Council, which had more or less fallen into abeyance during Albany's absence, was declared for the next day, which enabled the Earl Marischal and the Lords Lindsay, Erskine and Fleming, all councillors, to attend; and to make it look more authentic still, the monarch should be present for as long as he might stand it. Other members of the Privy Council could be conveniently forgotten.

So something of a round-table conference developed the following noontide, in the castle's magnificent great hall with all ceremoniously rising to bow as young James was led in by David Lindsay and the Abbot. The Chancellor presided, but Davie Beaton was very much at his uncle's back.

From the first, however, the ambassadors made the running, in an odd mixture of French and English, losing no time in stating their terms—since that is what it came to. The most puissant and illustrious Kings of France and of England, they asserted, had come to agreement on many matters of mutual concern for the general weal of both kingdoms, and also that of Scotland happily, for which realm they had much regard. Most of the treaty admittedly little concerned the northern kingdom; but certain aspects most assuredly did.

First and foremost, peace must be maintained between all three kingdoms, in place of the grievous onsets which for so long had bedevilled them. There must be no more armed incursions into each other's territories, either across the Channel or over the Tweed–Esk borderline. The truce presently obtaining between England and Scotland therefore was to be replaced by a permanent state of peace, and any warlike compacts and alliances between any two of the realms were to be done away with.

Secondly, Scotland must make new arrangements for her governance during the remaining years of the minority of her well-beloved but youthful monarch, King James, since by no means could King Francis spare his Lord High Admiral to return to this realm as Regent. However, since His Grace of England's royal sister was King James's mother what could be more suitable than her replacing of the Duke of Albany as Regent, to the satisfaction of all. Especially as this folly of estrangement from her husband, the Earl of Angus, and talk of divorce was to be ended and man and wife brought together again. Thus the so-called English and French parties in Scotland would lose all relevance, including the Douglas and Hamilton factions, and a peaceful and excellent unity would prevail.

Thirdly, the King of France had recently been blessed by God with another daughter, the Princess Madeleine, and she was to be promised as bride for King James, in due course, to the further felicity and well-being of Scotland and the desirable drawing together of all three realms.

Such were the wise and expedient requirements of their Majesties of France and England.

The Scots around the table, whatever their entrenched attitudes and concerns, stared with one accord at the propounders of this astonishing series of statements to the representatives of an independent state—all except its liege-lord, that is who, understanding none of it, was playing with the quill pens he had found on the table before him. All were temporarily reduced to silence—save for Davie Beaton, who quickly leaned forward to whisper in his uncle's ear. Arran looked bewildered and turned helplessly to the Chancellor.

That man cleared his throat. Were they to believe, he wondered, that their excellencies had travelled all the way from France to deliver themselves of this extraordinary pronouncement, this prescription? They made it to sound like an ultimatum—but that was possibly owing to the difficulties of language. Had they come to negotiate on these basic headings? If so, they had not made it sufficiently clear . . .

He was interrupted by Clarenceux, who grimly declared that it was all entirely clear. They had not come to negotiate anything but to inform. These were the parts of the treaty concluded, referring to Scotland. They had been signed and sealed between the two monarchs. Their visit was but a courtesy, to convey these terms.

"Terms!" the Earl Marischal burst out. "Terms, sirrah? Whose terms? Not ours! Who is your Welshman, the Tudor, to make terms for Scotland? Or the Frenchman either? To send you here, with your arrogant decrees!" There were growls of approval for that around the table. Lord Lindsay spoke.

"Englishman—these so-called terms? They were reached by Henry and Francis, them only. They have no references to us, the Scots. None."

"Not so, my lord. They were assented to by your Regent, the Duke of Albany."

"That I do not believe!" the Marischal declared. "Albany is neither so foolish nor so false!'

Arran found his voice. "Besides, the Duke has not been in Scotland for three years. *I* have had the rule of Scotland. If the King of France will not permit him to return here, as you say, how can he assent to anything for this kingdom?"

"He is still your Regent, my lord. While so, he speaks for this young King. Can any of you deny it?"

As shouts arose, the Chancellor sought to control the meeting to something of dignity. "*Messieurs*," he said, careful to address the Frenchmen rather than Clarenceux. "You have brought these informations, which we shall note. As to what you call terms, what if we in Scotland cannot accept them?"

"That is scarcely conceivable, my lord Archbishop," Lafayette said. "The terms are passed, signed, completed. You cannot alter them . . ."

"But we can, and must, reject them!" Marischal interrupted. "And so do, by God!"

"Then you must accept, instead, the consequences, *Monsieur le maréchal!*"

"Which are . . . ?" Lord Patrick demanded.

Clarenceux answered. "Pain of the utmost displeasure of both monarchs and realms, my lord. All measures to be taken to bring about compliance, of the sternest. Trade to be cut off. Hostages taken. No further association with France. And the Princess Madeleine's hand withdrawn."

"All of which we could thole, if necessary!"

Davie was whispering again to his uncle, who nodded. "France and Scotland have been friends for many centuries," he pointed out, reasonably. "The Auld Alliance, we call it. Serving both realms, well, to restrain the aggressions of England. Is all to be thrown over out of one day's talking? Is France so sure that never again will the English invade her soil? That she will not require Scotland's aid, as in the past? Does she trust Henry Tudor sufficiently to throw away Scots friendship? Are the English not still in Calais?" That was perhaps hardly diplomacy as normally practised at Chancellor's level, especially in the presence of a monarch; but as an exercise in driving a wedge between partners it was shrewd and telling, however blatant.

And evidently not wholly unsuccessful, by the expressions of the two Frenchmen and their glances at Clarenceux. They coughed but made no other response.

At this stage, King James yawned loudly, and the Chancellor seized the opportunity to bring the meeting to a close on that note, observing that His Grace had been very patient, and thanking all for their attendance. Even the ambassadors were probably thankful to be done with it.

Next day they departed for Leith again, with an escort of Hamiltons to see them safely past Linlithgow and no interviews with Margaret Tudor—but not to go so far as Leith, in case they ran into Douglases. Lowland Scotland was, in fact, now two armed camps, based on the two great rock top fortresses, with the Queen-Mother sitting exactly in the middle, a peculiar situation which, though she had done nothing to achieve, she might well see her opportunity for profit.

Whether that difficult and unpredictable woman did recognise that her position was now strengthened, and in much more than mere geography, Davie Beaton most certainly did, his acute wits swiftly perceiving the possibilities. He came to David Lindsay within hours of the envoys' departure, where he was playing at the hurly-hackit with his sovereign on the slope above Ballengeich, and whilst joining in the sport on another cow's skull, used his friend as a sounding-board to try out his theories. In between slides down and clamberings up, and with constant interruptions from young James and other distractions, he talked it through, almost as much to himself as to Lindsay, undoubtedly.

In the present dire circumstances, the first priority was to get Albany back to Scotland, somehow. To do that would be difficult, obviously, but surely not impossible. The key seemed to lie with Henry Tudor, of course. His Uncle James had sought to drive a wedge between French and English envoys the day previously— a much greater wedge, between Henry and Francis, was required, for Scotland's sake and for more than Scotland's. That was a large project—but there were various items which might be used in the process. Or, better, personalities. He could think of three—Margaret Tudor herself, Albany and Wolsey. It ought to be possible to use these to play on the weaknesses of the two monarchs—who could not truly love nor trust each other anyway. A fourth, it might be—Pope Leo, who was now said to be dying. Henry sought to use his sister— so could *Scotland* not use her against him?

David, panting his way uphill, dragging his cow's skull, waited.

Margaret was tired of Angus and he with her. She did not want to go back to him; she wanted a divorce. But Henry did not. For his own purposes he required them together again so that he had a further hold on Angus. He wanted the Douglas power in Scotland—it was as simple as that. Now, Albany was seeking to obtain Margaret's divorce, from the Vatican. Why? They had never been friends. But she had written to Albany asking his help, since he now had links with the Medici family to which the Pope belonged. She promised her goodwill if he did this. Henry would know well of that letter, for he had spies everywhere. Suppose that another letter from her to Albany was to fall into his hands—as could be arranged—urging greater efforts while this Pope was still alive, and indicating more than a mere goodwill towards the Duke, actual affection perhaps, or at least the possibility of her favours? Margaret was ever indiscreet and would do almost anything to gain her wishes. What would Henry think of that?

The other wagged his head, lost.

Henry would be furious, that is what. Furious at them both, but especially at Albany. And when Henry was furious, he never failed to act, however rashly. He would attack the Duke in any way that he could. And King Francis was fond of Albany, his friend. That was part of the trouble over the regency, not merely that he was Admiral of France but that Francis wanted him near him. Any attack on Albany by Henry would be an attack on Francis. The first tap on the wedge!

David was perhaps less impressed than he should have been.

The second tap, Beaton went on, in his element, would concern Wolsey. All knew that Henry's ambitious Chancellor was ambitious to be more than just a cardinal—he wanted to be Pope. Equally it was known that Henry was strongly against this, not desirous of losing his clever Chancellor. So, if it could seem that the King of France was working to have Wolsey made the new Pope, with Albany's help—what then?

"But how could this possibly be contrived?" David demanded.

"The same letter, do you not see? If the letter from Margaret was to say that, since Albany and his friend Francis were already seeking Vatican support for Wolsey's bid, surely they could further the much less difficult matter of her divorce? Thus the seed would be planted. It would but require some further watering and nurturing!"

Young James's impatience with all this talk demanded an interval of more active endeavour. On the next climb up, David's doubts erupted.

"These are all but speculations, man!" he objected. "Hopes, not probabilities. And why should Margaret Tudor write such a letter? She is no catspaw, that one."

"I think that I could persuade her. I will go to see her. Assert that this would help her cause. Would bear on Albany. Tell her that I, myself, would be going to France soon and could further pursue her interests, if she thus prepared the ground."

"And would you? Go to France?"

"To be sure. It is necessary, in this pass. I must see Albany. And Francis also. I flatter myself that I have some small pull with that headstrong monarch, for some reason. This letter will, I think, sow the seed, as I said. I needs must go and cherish the growth! I can be of more use to Scotland in France, meantime, than here. Fortunately my uncle's affairs can do without his secretary for a while, I judge. Old Forman will not live another year, and I have been at work amongst sufficient bishops to ensure that he is succeeded as Primate by my good relative. The only real rival is Gavin Douglas of Dunkeld, who covets the position—but I believe that I have his measure. Forby, his fortunes must rise or fall with Angus's, and what I seek to do in France will be to Angus's disadvantage. So I think to serve my uncle's cause, and the realm's likewise, furth of Scotland for a while."

"And you esteem yourself able to effect all this? One man, young and but a secretary at that, no great noble, seeking to change the destinies of mighty realms such as France and England! You have ready wits and a nimble tongue, Davie—but is not this beyond you?"

"It may be, yes—for it is a large matter, a challenge. But not impossible, I think. I will strengthen my hand by having myself sent as ambassador, Scotland's resident ambassador to the French court. Old Bishop Leslie has been there overlong and is of little use. I will replace him, meantime. The appointment is one that my uncle can make, as Chancellor, in the name of the Council. That will aid me, give me greater access to Francis."

David, seating himself on his uncomfortable sled, eyed his friend with a kind of wonder mixed with exasperation. "You have all in your hand, I see! Scots ambassador to France, now. Secretary to the Chancellor and Rector of Killearn. What next, I wonder—for the seventh son of a Fife lairdie?"

The other smiled, shrugging.

"And what of Marion? What says your wife? Does she go to France with you?"

"I fear not. That would be scarcely possible." Beaton's tone had changed. "To my sorrow. I . . . she is with child. It would not serve her, or my mission, to take her to France at this time. Marion will go back to her father's house at Airlie, meantime. It, it is the price I have to pay!"

"And *she* pays! You will leave her, to have her child alone? Is that the honest husband's part?"

"What use is a man, at such time? Better without me, perhaps!" But he did not meet the other's eyes, gazing away towards the Highland Line. "The realm's need is urgent, David. And I believe that only I can meet that need, God willing!"

"God . . . ?" Lindsay acceded to the realm's master's urgency and impatience, and launched himself and the King off downhill, leaving behind a man at war with himself, his heart and his head and his fate.

19

That major hostilities did not break out in Scotland that winter was a near miracle, considering that the land was like tinder only awaiting a spark. There were, of course, minor incidents and clashes innumerable, between Hamiltons and Douglases and their various partisans; but that none of these erupted into outright war was a mercy, and more than interesting to all who considered the matter with any knowledge. David Lindsay, for one, came to the conclusion that it was largely thanks to Angus himself, acting as a restraining influence, out of character as this might seem. It certainly was not thanks to Arran—or, more accurately, to the Bastard, who now so dominated his father, and who seemed to be almost spoiling for a fight with his humiliation over the Cleanse the Causeway incident to wipe out. Time and again Angus could well have reacted violently, and did not. Why, was unclear. Possibly he was lying deliberately low, wary over Henry's efforts to bring about his reconciliation with his wife, which most evidently he did not want. Or it could be merely that as he reached his thirties he was gaining in responsibility. Or just that he was so enamoured and taken up with his Traquair mistress that he did not want to be distracted. Whatever it was, the kingdom had cause to be thankful—although it did have the effect of encouraging the Bastard towards ever more challenging behaviour.

Another aspect of the situation was that the Homes now had more or less a free hand in the East and Middle Marches, for Arran, as Warden and Governor, could not get at them from Stirling and the West without first passing through Douglas-held territory and the Edinburgh vicinity. The said Homes made the most of their opportunities.

Davie Beaton had departed for France in September. Whatever influence he had been able to exert on the French–English situation, if any, was not apparent from Scotland, keenly as David, for one, awaited indications. It was not until May 1521 that news arrived which might imply some activity, or at least some unexpected change on the diplomatic front. It came in a highly dramatic not to say farcical announcement from King Henry—first that Scotland should be informed that the boy taken from Edinburgh to Stirling the previous May was not in fact his nephew King James but a mere low-born substitute, James himself having been spirited secretly to France, there to be reared as a Frenchman, like Albany, with Scotland to become no more than a sub-kingdom of France; and secondly that the said Duke of Albany was seeking to gain a divorce from the Pope for the Queen-Mother, Countess of Angus, in order that he might marry her himself and thus gain complete control of the Scottish succession.

This extraordinary development, however ridiculous on all counts, held profound significance. For whatever else it meant, it indicated a notable split in relations between Henry and Francis, so soon after the Field of the Cloth of Gold. And although the story about the changeling at Stirling seemed too far-fetched to have emanated from David Beaton, the divorce reference and general attack on Albany sounded very much as though he had been at work.

David pondered long over the English monarch's reasons for putting out this absurd accusation about James having been secretly removed to France and a dummy installed at Stirling—which nobody in Scotland was going to credit and which could be so easily disproved there. Assuming that Henry was not actually deranged, then, it must mean that the tale was not designed for Scots ears so much as for others. Whose, then? And why? Who could it impress and what advantage could it possibly serve? It certainly could not advantage France, and would be laughed at in Scotland. So it must be aimed elsewhere, to some quarter little acquainted with Scotland. It might well be believed in England itself, but Henry did not require to foster anti-Scots sentiment in his own kingdom—it was sufficiently strong without such nurturing. Who else, then? The Vatican? Could it be that? The treaty with France had been anti-Vatican and Empire. Why should Henry seek to delude the Pope, or the cardinals concerned with his successor, over the King of Scots? Rome was usually well-enough informed. None of it appeared to make sense.

It was well into summer before David, and others who had puzzled over this problem, obtained a possible explanation, when the sensational news reached Scotland that Henry had in fact made one more of his notorious about-turns, had had a meeting with the Emperor Charles at Gravelines, near Calais, and come to terms with him.

This totally unexpected development of course completely changed the entire international situation, shattering the so-called French alliance and linking the unpredictable Tudor with Spain, the Empire and the Vatican. Could the King James story have been some sort of preparation for this move? To be used as an excuse towards Charles and Pope Leo? A preliminary stab in the back for France and an indication that Henry was prepared to switch horses? If this seemed scarcely credible, it was no more so than the actual volte-face less than a year after all the elaborate charade of the Field of the Cloth of Gold.

Whether the new Scots ambassador to France had had anything to do with it all, it now meant that what Davie had wished for had come about, that Henry and Francis were once again on opposite sides, that Scotland would once more become valuable to France as an ally, and that the Regent Albany might well be able to serve his friend Francis best in the northern kingdom.

The news had a profound effect in Scotland, encouraging the Hamilton and pro-French faction of course, but also most moderate and peace-loving folk, while no doubt depressing the Douglases. There was other news coming from the Continent also to encourage David Lindsay and sundry others, if not the Chancellor and most churchmen— word of ever-growing disillusionment with the corruption and state of Holy Church and the need for reform therein, the German Augustinian monk Martin Luther leading the way with notable courage and effectiveness, with the backing of his Elector of Saxony. Pope Leo had excommunicated him at the beginning of the year, but Luther was not to be silenced. The Church must reform itself, he insisted, or Christ's cause would go down, and Christendom sink into the new paganism; and large numbers of God-fearing people agreed with him—as well they might, when Pope Leo himself, a cardinal at the age of thirteen, had hanged another of his own cardinals on ascending the papal throne, and had made the notorious statement that "truly the myth of Christ had brought much gain!" That gain the Pontiff now was capitalising, by sending the Dominican, Tetzel, on a tour of Christendom, with a long train of pack-mules laden with indulgences and pardons for sale to cover any and every offence whatsoever—save criticism of the Vatican—even assuring release from purgatory, all on an elaborate scale of charges. David and Abbot John had long debates about all this and particularly the shameful condition of the Church in Scotland—which, to be sure, the latter was not in the best position to defend, with himself holding a wholly empty abbacy—empty, that is, save for the receipt of the revenues thereof. David argued strongly for reform, as he had done with Davie Beaton also; indeed he had written a poem on the subject—which, however, he was not foolish enough to let Archbishop Beaton read.

The word they had all been awaiting at Stirling arrived in a letter to the Chancellor from his nephew in September, that King Francis was going to send Albany back to Scotland, probably within the next six weeks, and he would not be coming alone either, but bringing French military advisers with him, along with a consignment of arms and money.

Relief at the first part of this message tended to be a little dampened, for some, by contemplation of the second part, which seemed to strike a warlike note, although hitherto Albany had been little of a warmonger.

About the same time a letter came to Kate, from the Braes of Angus, to say that Marion Ogilvy had been delivered of a fine son and both were well.

It was, in a way, strange that Albany's second arrival in Scotland should be looked forward to with so much satisfaction and hope, for he was scarcely a beloved figure, nor had ever sought to be, no paladin nor brilliant statesman, and still could not speak the language. Nevertheless, compared with the anarchy which had prevailed before his first coming and which had revived since his return to France, he seemed to represent lawful authority and stable government in place of chaos, and by and large the land ached for peace and an end to feuding and bloodshed. And he *was* the second person in the realm, heir-presumptive to the throne, however much Arran and his people might deplore it.

This time, with Dumbarton Castle presently in Douglas hands, it was considered advisable to bring the Regent's three ships to an alternative landfall, although this had to be on the west coast, for similar reasons. So a small craft was despatched to meet the French vessels in the Firth of Clyde and conduct them up through the maze of sea-lochs and isles which penetrated Cowal, the southernmost part of Argyll, and into the Gareloch, near the head of which the welcoming party would wait. If this might seem an odd place to bring ashore the realm's ruler, to his French associates, or even to Albany himself, it was in fact illustrative of the state of affairs prevailing in Scotland, a locality which ought by its remoteness to ensure a safe and uncontested landing and one to which Arran, the Chancellor and the reception party from Stirling, ought to be able to reach without fear of interception by the Douglases or their friends, as this landfall was only a few miles from Finnart on Loch Long, the Hamilton lands which gave the Bastard his title.

So the welcoming group made its way, by quite difficult routes, up the Carse of Stirling, through the hilly MacGregor lands around Aberfoyle and the head of Loch Lomond, and by fierce mountain passes and wild glens to the head of Loch Long and so down to Finnart, a major journey in November weather. David prevailed on the Earl Marischal to let him go along, restlessness strong upon him again. His was not really a suitable temperament for the kind of life he was being forced to live.

It took them nearly three days, halting at the distinctly inadequate monastic hospices of Portanellen and Arrocher. They found Finnart to be a modest square tower-house within a barmkin or high defensive courtyard wall, but surrounded by quite a community of Highlanders' cabins and hovels and a population of herdsmen and fisherfolk. This was no longer the Bastard's home, of course; he was building himself a fine castle at Cambusnethan in Clydesdale, more in keeping with his present status. Here, in less than comfort, they waited for two more days.

On the nineteenth of November they received the information that the three French ships were in sight, and the party crossed the neck of land between the two lochs to Garelochhead and then down the lochside to Faslane where there was sufficient depth of water for sea-going ships to anchor.

Although Albany had been given only four months' leave of absence by parliament, he had been away for over four years—and by his expression when he came ashore was none too happy to be back, even so. His Frenchmen looked still less appreciative, staring about them at the wild and barren mountainous surroundings in something not far from alarm. The Duke's demands as to why they had had to be brought in here—in French, necessarily—rather spoiled the welcoming ceremony, the explanations taking a little time. David had expected to see Davie Beaton there, but was disappointed, and the interpreting had to be done by a little bumbling fat man, who turned out to be Bishop Leslie, lately Scots resident at the court of King Francis and now replaced by Davie—who, it seemed, had decided to remain on in France meantime for reasons of state, despite having a wife and new-born son to bring him home.

The reception party, learning from the last time, had led a long string of spare horses for the newcomers; but these proved to be not nearly sufficient for the numbers Albany had brought and all the baggage they had with them, and some time thereafter had to be spent scouring the neighbourhood for the rough and shaggy but sturdy garrons which were all that were available in these parts. Fortunately there were plenty of these; but it did mean that most of the Scots there, including David, had to ride all the way back to Stirling on these short-legged, broad-backed and saddleless Highland mounts, the proud Frenchmen far too superior to do anything of the sort, requiring their good horseflesh.

On the journey, Albany made entirely clear what he had come for. The establishment of his due authority and rule could be taken for granted, of course; but his primary purpose and duty was the full-scale invasion of England with a large army at the earliest possible moment. Henry Tudor was preparing to attack France, in conjunction with the Emperor Charles, Spain and the Papal forces, and must be forced to look back over his treacherous shoulder to his northern borders and so to divert at least some of his strength. In other words, that Auld Alliance was to be reactivated and put into practice, now that France needed it;

and Albany was here more as Francis's lieutenant than as Scotland's Regent.

There were some long Scots faces arriving at Stirling, David's amongst them. It was, after all, only eight years since the disaster of Flodden, when this French requirement had last been met.

There was news awaiting them at the castle. Archbishop Andrew Forman, the Primate, had at last died at St Andrews, and the way was open for Davie's scheming regarding Church and State to come to fruition—with crown permission, which meant the Regent's acceptance. Albany saw his opportunity and seized it. He would support Archbishop Beaton's translation to St Andrews and the Primacy, and most certainly block the ambitions of Gavin Douglas—in return for a major subvention from Church revenues to help pay for the hire of armed men by the thousand and the adherence of the not inconsiderable numbers of men-at-arms retained by individual bishops, abbots and priors. James Beaton, pained, reluctantly acquiesced.

Neither the Regent nor the Chancellor lost any time in pursuing their two projects. Beaton was off to St Andrews in Fife promptly, to take over the rule and wealth of Holy Church, taking his election by a majority of his thirteen fellow bishops for granted after Davie's careful arranging. And Albany, equally taking for granted that the assembly of Hamilton manpower, now more or less permanently encamped at Stirling, should form the nucleus of his invasion army, went ahead without delay in sending out summonses to all nobles, lairds, chiefs, churchmen and burgh magistrates to muster there also, with their fullest strength, and at the soonest.

But more than armed men gravitated to Stirling, to the surprise of all concerned. The Regent had not been back one week when a small but brilliant cavalcade came riding up to the castle, under, of all things, the joint royal standards of Scotland and England. This proved to be Margaret Tudor, from Linlithgow, demanding to see and welcome the Duke of Albany. Astonished and uncertain, the captain of the guard kept the lady waiting beyond the drawbridge whilst he went to inform the equally unprepared Regent.

The news went round the castle like wildfire, and practically everyone therein hurried down to the gatehouse battlements to witness the scene—although David was careful not to take young James, who had no fondness for his mother.

He arrived in time to see something he could never have anticipated, Albany walking distinctly doubtfully out over the drawbridge planking in wary greeting to the newcomers, and Margaret sliding down from her saddle in ungainly fashion—for she was a heavily built woman—and actually running forward, skirts hitched up, to meet the other, and then flinging herself bodily upon him, not actually into his arms since he kept them to his sides, and in fact recoiled somewhat at the unexpected embrace. But any seeming reluctance on the man's part the woman more than made up for, clasping him to her bosom and planting kisses on both cheeks, in a demonstration never before witnessed by any present. At the Regent's complete lack of response she drew back, but only a little way, running her hands down his arms to grip his wrists, and so to stand gazing up into his eyes as though in near adoration.

The many watchers gasped their astonishment.

That Albany was equally surprised, not to say alarmed and embarrassed, was evident. He could scarcely shake her off, but he did repossess his wrists and arms, and half turned away, a move which Margaret quite cleverly converted into a civil gesture to draw her round and lead her back across the bridge towards the gatehouse pend, she at his side chattering with every appearance of fondness, eyes still on his rather stiff though handsome Stewart features, and one arm still linked in his.

Few there would ever have believed it had they not seen it with their own eyes, nor conceived the arrogant Queen-Mother capable of such play-acting—if such it was—in public, however she was reputed to behave, on occasion, in private. David, pondering, wondered whether Davie Beaton's persuasions, that day, had been even more effective than he had intended?

Everyone was agog, of course, and speculation ran riot. Was there truth, after all, in King Henry's allegations that Albany had only been working for Margaret's divorce in order to wed her himself? If so, he would require a divorce of his own, for his duchess was alive and well in France. But, by appearances, the Regent was taken by surprise in all this affection—which seemed as foreign to his character as it was to the lady's. If so, what did it mean? Was Margaret setting her cap at him, for policy or other reason? Was this a move to try to get back into a position of rule in Scotland? Or merely a means of showing her spite at Angus? Or even part of a device for getting her son under her influence again? There was no lack of theories.

The expected summons to the Regent's quarters came for David that evening; he was to bring the King to greet his mother—despite it being the nine-year-old's bedtime.

They found Albany and Margaret alone in a small sitting room of the palace building, in candlelight, standing before a blazing log-fire, with a table laden with wines and sweetmeats nearby, a cosy domestic scene into which neither the man nor the woman seemed by their natures to fit. The Regent made a more elaborate bow than his usual to the reluctant James, who clutched David's hand and scowled at his mother. Margaret exclaimed in a painfully sweet voice at how he had grown and how good-looking he was. She had not seen him, to be sure, for long. She held out a hand. David gave his charge a nudge forward, but the boy held back. There was an uncomfortable pause.

Albany made some encouraging remark, in French of course; and although James had been taught that language, he did not respond. Margaret frowned, and drummed impatient fingertips on the table top.

"Come, boy—I am your mother!" she said, her tone less dulcet now.

When James actually drew back, half behind David, that man felt that something had to be done. But what? This was the monarch of them all, after all, and himself a comparatively lowly subject. He well remembered being castigated by the Queen-Mother once before for allegedly improper behaviour towards the royal child when James had tripped and stumbled on being propelled towards her at Linlithgow. Yet the other two were clearly not going to make much impression on the boy, who looked as though he might turn and bolt through the doorway by which they had entered. He decided on a device.

"See, Sire—comfits, sweetmeats!" and he pointed. He did not normally address the boy as Sire in conversation, but this was a special occasion. "Come—I am sure that my

306

lord Duke will let us have some." James had a notably sweet tooth.

The boy looked doubtfully from the table to the pair by the fire, and back again, but allowed himself to be led forward. Only he transferred himself to David's other side, to be as far away from his mother as possible.

"You, Lindsay—you have poisoned my son's mind against me!" Margaret rapped out.

"Not so, Madam," David asserted. But he did not elaborate on that, for it was a difficult charge to deny with any conviction; certainly he had never sought to *commend* the mother to the boy.

Albany coughed and looked disapprovingly at all concerned.

Margaret quickly perceived his attitude and changed her own, moving close to him and taking his hand. "Forgive a woman's chagrin over her child's failings, Monsieur le Duc," she said, in French. "I see him so seldom. Perhaps that situation can now be bettered, no?"

The Regent did not comment on that. Instead he nodded towards James. "His Grace may eat, Lindsay," he said. "A little wine, if so he desires."

The King's French was adequate for that, at least, and he reached out to select a confection, but kept a watchful eye on the others as he ate.

"At what studies are you most proficient, James?" the Queen–Mother asked, with a sort of steely patience. "You understand the French tongue?"

Her son, chewing, nodded briefly.

"His Grace is a willing and able scholar, Madam," Davie declared, a little hurriedly. "At French and Latin he is well versed. And at . . ."

"When I require your comments, Lindsay, I shall ask for them!" Margaret interrupted. "James—greet Monsieur le Duc in French."

The boy scowled again, looking at his least attractive, but at a nudge from David, swallowed and muttered, "*Bonne nuit, Monsieur.*"

Albany nodded. "*Merci. Et Madame la Comtesse?*"

Another nudge. "*Et vous, Madame la Comtesse.*"

"I would prefer that you call me Your Grace," the lady said starchily.

That produced another cough from the Duke and an uncomfortable silence thereafter. James helped himself to another cake.

Belatedly recognising, apparently, that her remark might have sounded as much a rebuke to the man as to her son, Margaret Tudor raised a smile of sorts and moved closer still to the Duke, all but rubbing herself against him. "We wish to forget the Earl of Anguish, do we not, Jean? But James is too young to understand such matters. Pray, select me a comfit before this boy eats them all!" That was coy.

Albany did as he was bidden, although glancing ruefully at David.

Thereafter the woman launched into a lengthy discussion with the Regent on the twin subjects of the wickedness of Angus and the progress of her divorce proceedings, interspersed with endearments and touchings, ignoring her son and his Procurator entirely, all embarrassing for David at least even if not for his charge, who made the most of his opportunities with the sweetmeats. It was this, rather than his own desire to be elsewhere, concern that the boy would suffer for overindulgence thus late in the evening, which caused him to catch the Duke's eye, to indicate the need for retiral. At length he succeeded in this, jerking his head from the King towards the door, and Albany perceived, inclined his own head and waved a lordly hand.

Thankfully David bowed towards the pair, tapped his monarch on the shoulder and pointed. Grabbing a last cake, James went with alacrity, in his turn ignoring the others and the whispered instruction to bow to his mother. That princess equally disregarded her offspring's departure, eyes only for Albany.

Heaving a sigh of relief, David got out and closed the door behind them.

Next day the castle buzzed with talk. It had been late indeed before Margaret Tudor had left the Duke's quarters for those allotted to her, so they had been closeted alone for hours. Needless to say, the worst interpretations were put on this circumstance. The lady was the reverse of popular, and although it all seemed strange behaviour for Albany, men being men . . .

To add to the assumed scandal it became evident that the Queen-Mother was not at the castle to pay any brief visit but appeared to be settling in to stay. This was appreciated by few, for her autocratic ways did not help to endear her and quite quickly she was behaving as though she was indeed châtelaine there again. This affected the Lindsays particularly, for although Margaret sought little further contact with her son she had come with only two or three female attendants and Kate was drafted in as a kind of extra lady-in-waiting, to her displeasure. So David heard quite a lot of what went on in the loftier circles of the establishment, as well as the gossip of the groundlings, and wondered the more. He learned for one thing that Albany was intending to make a move to Edinburgh just as soon as he had sufficient men assembled to make it unlikely that the Douglases would contest it. He considered it unsuitable that the country's ruler should not be based on the capital city. And clearly Margaret assumed that she would be going also. Whether they would take the King remained to be seen.

Midwinter was not the best time for the mustering of armed men in tented encampments but the Regent was insistent on at least a token contingent from each magnate and burgh being sent to Stirling forthwith so that a sizeable force would be gathered, over and above the Hamilton array, available for immediate use, even if the main strength would not be able to be marshalled until the spring. This activity was afoot so that Henry's busy spies would report the presence of a major army mobilising; also the projected move to Edinburgh, that much nearer to the borderline, in the hopes that this might deter that aggressive monarch from making his anticipated attack on France in conjunction with the Emperor when the campaigning season started again. All was assuredly for France's benefit, but at least Albany was going to cover himself by calling a parliament at Edinburgh, just as soon after the twelfth day of Christmas as was possible, to approve his plans. Also he was especially summoning Angus to be present thereat to account for his behaviour, and the Homes to answer for the murder of de la Bastie. Kate said that Margaret Tudor was openly asserting that these summonses would in fact ensure that the Douglases and the Homes would *not* attend the parliament but would in all probability flee into England, into her brother's tender care—and Scotland satisfactorily rid of them.

So that Yuletide at Stirling Castle, even though major

war portended, was quite a gay one—not that either Albany nor Margaret was much inclined for gaiety, but the French visitors had to be entertained and the lords who came with their armed contingents kept happy. Whether the Frenchmen were wholly delighted with what they experienced was another matter.

In mid-January the move to Edinburgh was made, with King James and his attendants included, for it appeared that the Regent desired the young monarch to be present at the parliament. To the regret of most others, Margaret Tudor came along also, and was not dropped off at Linlithgow as some hoped. Just before they left Stirling, news came which seemed to support the lady's judgment in one respect at least; Bishop Gavin Douglas, for one, would not be attending the parliament for he had departed for England, allegedly for Henry's court.

This information encouraged the royal party in the belief that there would be no real Douglas attempt to hold Edinburgh and its fortress against them; as they made their slow progress eastwards—and slow it had to be, with a force of almost five thousand men as escort—reports reached them that in fact the Douglases were steadily deserting the capital, and no Homes had been seen there for some time.

So, although the eventual approach to the city on its ridge above the Nor' Loch was made behind an impressive array of armed men, cavalry, foot and even light cannon, no opposition materialised. Admittedly no relieved welcome from loyal citizenry developed either, but that was scarcely vital. The necessary cautious threading of the narrow streets up to the castle tourney ground was uncontested likewise, and at the fortress itself the Regent and his sovereign-lord found the drawbridge down, the portcullis up and a small deputation waiting to hand over the keys to the King or his representative. It was all as easy as that. The said deputation was not very illustrious perhaps, since all such appeared to have fled the city; but the honours were done, after a fashion, by the worthy Robert Logan of Restalrig, the rightful Provost, in the absence of Greysteel of Kilspindie his supplanter in the civil chair, and the provisional deputy keeper of the castle, who turned out to be Sir Simon Preston of Craigmillar. The changeover of command, therefore, was effected entirely without dramatics, almost in anticlimax, with no one in a position to say where Angus was. Albany saw James deposited in his old quarters in the castle, left Margaret Tudor there also with almost visible relief, sent his troops to camp on the Burgh Muir and in the royal forest parkland around Arthur's Seat, and himself resorted to more comfortable premises in Holyrood Abbey. Arran and the Bastard, who had been notably subdued since the Regent's arrival, went off to their former lodgings in Blackfriars Monastery of distressing memory.

That afternoon the castle's artillery, Mons Meg included, fired off a prolonged cannonade of blank shots to inform the realm that order and due royal authority was re-established in the land—to the delight of the royalest individual to hear it, at least, he being of an age when the louder the noise the greater the attraction.

The parliament was held, at Holyrood, ten days later, by which time it was apparent that there would be no immediate Douglas counter-action; indeed, the previous day, word assessed to be reliable was received that Angus himself had now crossed the Border and was residing with the Lord Dacre, the English Warden, at Morpeth Castle, Northumberland, but not apparently accompanied by any large number of his people. Albany could congratulate himself on a successful and bloodless resumption of power.

Despite all this, however, he had less cause for congratulation over the parliament itself, even though much laudatory speech-making was indulged in, much condemnation of the Douglases and Homes, and no actual reminders that the Regent had outstayed his leave of absence by over a dozen times the allotted span. But Albany had made no secret of the fact that the main reason for this parliament was to homologate his plans for the invasion of England on France's behalf, and this the assembly quite definitely refused to agree to. Standing behind the King's throne in his usual position, David Lindsay heard speaker after speaker condemn the venture as inadvisable, unacceptable, dangerous, folly even, the Flodden disaster quoted again and again. There was not indeed a single supporter to speak up for the project after the Chancellor had so obviously disapprovingly read out the Regent's desires. The Archbishop, now Primate of Holy Church and very grand, might be committed to financing Albany's adventure with Church money, but of his reluctance there could be no doubt. With Bishop Leslie translating all for the Duke, that man's handsome features grew darker by the minute. Presently his famous temper took over and, not having a fire available to hurl his hat into, he smashed a fist down on the arm of his chair, jumped to his feet and strode without a word for the nearest doorway to the chancel and out—quite forgetting that he was in the presence of their sovereign-lord and that none must leave before him or without his permission.

Young James did not himself recognise this, presumably, but everyone else did, and was in a quandary. What now? If the King had not been there, then the sitting was over with the Regent departed, and the Chancellor would declare adjournment; but with James present, and superior to Albany, it could still theoretically be in session. There was much muttering and glancing around, until Beaton, concluding that the Duke was not going to return, turned and signed to David, who nodded and whispered to his royal charge. Gladly the boy vacated his throne and preceded David out, grinning, whilst all there bowed.

It was the briefest parliament on record; and nothing had been decided about Angus or the Homes.

Albany's wrath was not readily assuaged on this occasion, with no Davie Beaton there to cajole him, for this of the invasion was what he had come to Scotland to achieve. Too proud to reconvene the assembly and risk another rebuff, he summoned the most important lords and chiefs to his presence and sought to change their minds; but without success. Scotland seemed to have learned its lesson about sacrificing itself for France. Troops would assemble to defend the realm, to maintain the King's peace and to keep such as the Douglases in their places; but they would not cross the Border unprovoked.

For weeks thereafter the Regent was like a bear with a sore head, a problem for all who had to deal with him. And he was not the only one, for news reached Scotland that Pope Leo had died, and without authorising Margaret's divorce. That princess was furious, and all who had any connection with her were made aware of it. Suddenly her extraordinary interest in Albany was over. He was no longer of use to her in that connection, for he had no pull with the new Pontiff, Adrian the Sixth, a Dutchman firmly in the

Emperor's camp, indeed who had been tutor to the young Charles and later became his Regent in Spain. Moreover the Duke had been almost pointedly keeping his distance from Edinburgh Castle and the lady, to her offence. So that odd interlude was over, and Margaret emphasised the fact by promptly removing herself back to her palace of Linlithgow—to the great relief of almost everybody in Edinburgh's citadel, not least her son.

She had barely gone when more news from the Continent informed them that her brother had in fact invaded France in major strength, from the Calais bridgehead. Also it was learned, from nearer at hand, that he had sent the veteran Earl of Shrewsbury up to put the northern counties of England on a war-footing and threat to Scotland, to reinforce Lord Dacre's forces—his reaction to his spies' reports.

This intelligence stirred Albany into action, parliament's views notwithstanding. He exercised his authority as Regent, and commander of the forces of the crown, to order fullest mobilisation forthwith and a march on the Borderland.

David Lindsay would have liked to accompany this expedition, as a change from fortress-life, but the Earl Marischal, much against the entire project, refused him leave, and there was now no Davie Beaton to pull strings on his behalf. All he was permitted was to take King James up to the Burgh Muir to see the vast concentration of men and to watch the Scots host march off southwards, a situation which David found ominously reminiscent of that occasion nine years before when the King's father led a similar vast army from the same mustering place on a similar venture, never to return. Even the numbers were approximately the same, over eighty-thousand, and although this time they were not burdened with those eighteen-foot French pikes, the French presence was very evident, especially in the abundance of light artillery and bombards shipped north. There was a great blowing of trumpets, waving of banners and dashing hither and thither of colourful heralds, and ten-year-old James Stewart much enjoyed it all, and being conducted round the various contingents to inspect all and wish God-speed to his lords. Nevertheless, despite all this flourish, there was an atmosphere of reluctance and foreboding prevalent which certainly had not been in evidence on the previous occasion. David, if not his charge, was very much aware of it.

There was another difference. When Albany came to salute James finally and then rode, under the Lion-Rampant standard, with his French advisers, to place himself at the head of all and lead off, the host marched away from the Burgh Muir of Edinburgh, to the sound of martial music, in a south-westerly not a south-easterly direction, to skirt the flanks of the Pentland not the Lammermuir Hills. Albany at least was showing some discretion in avoiding the Merse and East March approach for his attempt; for Dacre's forces were based on Morpeth, and Shrewsbury was said to have his headquarters in Newcastle, both on the east side of the country, and, of course, in any action, the Homes might possibly create trouble in the Scots rear in this area. So it was to be the West March and Carlisle, in the hope that this would force the English to make a hurried switch across country and so cause them confusion and disorganisation.

Waving goodbye, the little party with the King rode pensively back to the city.

They had almost three weeks to wait for news. When it came, it was both a relief and a cause of shame. The entire affair had been, not a disaster but a fiasco. At Carlisle, the Scots lords had refused to go a step further. They had crossed on to English soil, and, safely behind Carlisle's massive walls, dug in their spurred and armoured heels. This was as far as they would go, for France. Fuming, Albany had been unable to budge them, the Bastard of Arran leading the revolt. Dacre and Shrewsbury had arrived presently with a force not half the size, but still the Scots would not attack unless they were assailed first. This Shrewsbury would not attempt, well content to neutralise the enemy in inaction—which would serve Henry's cause as well as any costly battle. It transpired later that Dacre had been warned by a courier from Margaret at Linlithgow acting with typical Tudor side-switching, that the Scots had in fact no real intention of invading England and were merely putting on a show. So the two sides sat a mile apart and eyed each other, until the English leadership eventually sent heralds to offer a truce, a non-aggression pact—again to Henry's immediate benefit since he could now concentrate on France with an easy mind—and which Albany was forced to accept, if with ill grace, faced by his obdurate Scots lords now anxious to get their levies home for the hay harvest.

So the ridiculous affair trickled to its undignified closure and the Regent's proud eighty thousand turned and marched home intact but inglorious. It was said that the Duke would not speak to a Scot, even in French, all the way back to Edinburgh, confining his few remarks only to Frenchmen.

At least Angus was not in a position to mock and crow, whatever his wife might do, for it appeared that he himself had fled to France, for reasons unknown.

Henry and the Emperor made major progress, and Francis, fighting on two fronts, sustained a serious defeat at Bicocco. Almost immediately thereafter the Regent announced that he had been recalled to France for consultations. Resentful but disenchanted, the Scots could not stop him from going, but there was murmuring that his tenure of the regency was useless and should be taken from him—as undoubtedly would have been attempted had the alternative been anyone other than the spineless Arran. Albany, however, declared that he would be back shortly, and appointed the same Regency Council as before to deputise for him, with the addition of a Frenchman named de Gresolles, in place of the late Archbishop Forman. He also ordained that King James would be safer back at Stirling in the interim, in case of any Douglas attempt against the capital.

So that October of 1522, Edinburgh saw the departure of its monarch westwards once again, and that of the Regent for France, and knew not whether to be relieved or apprehensive.

20

Scotland was blessed with a comparatively uneventful winter that year, with both Angus and Albany out of the country and the Home leaders still in England. Arran was in theory ruling, which meant the Bastard, but with Albany expected to return in a matter of months, that character was restricted in scope; he also found the Regent's watch-dog, de Gresolles, a thorn in the flesh, since being a member of the Council, which Hamilton was not, he ranked as his superior. In fact, Stirling saw little of either him or his father, and since the Chancellor now spent much of his time at St Andrews dealing with the neglected affairs of Holy Church—largely financial, by all accounts—the royal entourage was afforded an unusually quiet interval. This, to be sure, was much appreciated. Yet, human nature being what it is, some began to find life dullish and time to hang heavily. Certainly this applied to David Lindsay, and to a certain extent to Kate also, still not really adjusted to the cramping life of a fortress. When burgeoning spring, therefore, accentuated young people's restlessness, they sought the Marischal's dispensation for a week or two, and escaped. This time they did not head east, to Lothian and home, but north to the Braes of Angus. They would go and see Marion and her child.

They were joyfully received at Airlie Castle, by the grass-widow at least; and even Lord Ogilvy was prepared to tolerate Lord Lindsay's daughter and the King's Usher. Marion was looking blooming, motherhood evidently agreeing with her, and her husband's continuing absence seemingly bearable. The child, called James after his great-uncle, and now eighteen months old, a grave unsmiling infant, all great watching eyes, seemed to ponder life and reserve judgment, a strange offspring it might seem for the lively and mercurial Davie Beaton.

Marion was eager for tidings of the world at large, for up here in the jaws of the mountains even Stirling and

Edinburgh seemed remote, and news therefrom scarcely frequent. Such as did arrive was apt to come by itinerant chapmen and wandering friars, from the former less than reliable, the latter more knowledgeable about Church affairs than other. So the young woman, in fact, knew quite a lot about what went on in St Andrews and other ecclesiastical centres and the new Primate's relations with various bishops, abbots and priors, even that Gavin Douglas was dead— something which the others had not heard of at Stirling— having apparently succumbed to the plague in London, like thousands of others.

Although the visitors were able to tell their hostess considerably more, as it were in bulk, than she could give them, she did surprise them with information affecting the King's future, which they might have expected to have heard first. It seemed that she got occasional private letters from her husband, sent by the couriers who brought Albany's despatches, and the latest of these had mentioned that he, Davie, had at last prevailed on King Francis to make a formal promise, instead of a mere suggestion, of his infant daughter Madeleine, now aged two, to be betrothed to King James, a considerable step in putting the relationship of Scotland and France on an improved footing, one more in keeping with the northern kingdom's dignity and pride. But whenever Henry Tudor heard of this, apparently, he had immediately declared that his nephew should have *his* daughter Mary for bride, now six years, as much more suitable—only he insisted on the condition that Albany's regency should be terminated and in fact the Duke never allowed to set foot in Scotland again.

David asked the obvious question—did Davie's letters give any indication as to when he would be returning to Scotland? Marion sadly admitted that although he wrote that he was longing to see her and hoped that it would not be overlong before he was back, he gave no hint as to when that might be.

Kate confided to her own husband later that she, for one, would not be married to a man who could behave like that and treat his wife as of less importance than any and every other aspect of his life. David protested on his friend's behalf, but with only moderate conviction.

They remained at Airlie for a full week, rejoicing in their

freedom and exploring the exciting glens of Isla, Clova, Prosen, Lethnot and Esk, a world totally different from any they had experienced hitherto, with a people who spoke only the difficult Gaelic and lived not in villages or hamlets but in wide-scattered groupings of turf-roofed cabins which Marion called townships but which bore no resemblance to what that term conjured up in Lowland minds, a cattle-herding folk, with only scratchings of tilth here and there, in marked contrast to the fertile East Lothian farmlands they knew so well. Although snow still mantled the high ground, the valleys were green, quite well-wooded with scrub-oak, rowan and hawthorn, golden gorse glowing its promise everywhere, the rivers peat-brown, rushing and noisy with melt-water, the haughs alive with quacking duck, flitting dippers and grave-stalking herons, as May brought its benison to the mountain land. Thoughts of war and statecraft and intrigue seemed scarcely relevant up here. They saw no sign of the dreaded caterans, the bogey of Lowlanders.

The travellers were loth to return to Stirling sooner than they must, and made a number of brief visits on the way, notably to the abbeys of Coupar-Angus and Abbot John's Culross in Fife, where St Kentigern or Mungo, conceived in their own area of East Lothian and destined to become the patron saint of Glasgow, had been reared by the good Celtic St Serf. Holy Church had become sadly corrupt since those far-off days, but it still did good service by providing shelter and provision for travellers, and work and wealth by the tilling of the ground, the milling of corn, the weaving of cloth and tanning of hides, even the mining of coals at Culross, all of which might just conceivably be deemed a form of practical worship towards the Creator of it all.

Back at Stirling, they learned that the rival offers of a bride for James, from France and England, had been received officially. Needless to say, there was no question as to choice, Henry's conditional overture being not so much as considered, while the French commitment was received with satisfaction. This could be the most useful match for Scotland available, as well as the most prestigious. Davie Beaton's credit was enhanced. Fortunately the prospective bridegroom did not have to be consulted.

Henry's reaction to this rejection, even though he might have been thought fully occupied in France, was not long in being made evident. The Earl of Shrewsbury was with-drawn, as being insufficiently aggressive, and in his place Thomas Howard, Earl of Surrey, was sent north with explicit instructions to burn and slay. This sounded an ominous note in Scotland for this Surrey was the son of that 'auld crooked carle Surrey', now Duke of Norfolk, who had commanded the English army at Flodden where he himself had played no insignificant part.

Nor were the Scots fears unjustified. In great strength, in late June, Surrey and Dacre crossed Tweed and laid waste the land up to and beyond Kelso, which they burned, slaughtering indiscriminately men, women and children, as directed by their master, not sparing the ancient abbey and its inmates, where many of the populace had fled for sanc-tuary. The Regency Council hastily gathered together a scratch force and sent it to the Borders under the Bastard; but by this time the English had withdrawn, leaving behind the message that this was just a small sample of what could be expected if the Scots persisted in rejecting the wishes and authority of their Lord Paramount, King Henry. Any retaliation and they would be back, and in less clement mood.

In the circumstances the Bastard hesitated, for he had instructions not to invade England, remained in the stricken area for some time and then returned to Edinburgh a frus-trated man. There was one small but significant outcome of his effort, however, in that an English messenger fell into the hands of a Scots scouting party, a courier looking for Dacre and not realising that he had retired to Wark Castle. This individual was bearing a letter from Cardinal Wolsey to the Warden, urging still harsher measures against the Scots, and counselling him "favourably to entertain the Homes and other rebels after the accustomed manner, so that they may continue the divisions and sedition in Scotland whereby the Duke of Albany may, at his coming thither, be put in danger; and though some moneys be employed for this entertainment of the said Homes and rebels, it will quit the cost at length". This letter would at least serve to put a halter round the necks of Wedderburn and his colleagues if they should be caught.

The Scots Chancellor thereafter sent an urgent message, in turn, to France, for Albany's immediate return. And a reply was received rather sooner than previous experience had led them to expect. It came from Davie Beaton. The Regent would be in Scotland in the near future, by October, and he would be coming in major strength, at King Francis's command.

The Scots did not know whether to rejoice or to dread.

Presumably Henry's spy-system worked equally efficiently in France as in Scotland, for a new invasion by Surrey and Dacre was promptly mounted, to demonstrate the price the Scots must pay for Albany's return and any French aid. This time, the lower Tweed area being already devastated, the English marched up Teviot and gave Jedburgh, the Middle March 'capital' to the flames, again with its great abbey, together with all the surrounding villages, communities, peel-towers, churches and farm-touns, leaving behind a vast, smoking wilderness and graveyard of what had been one of the fairest regions of the Borderland.

Whether France got word of this projected attack, in turn, or Albany merely was more speedy than anticipated, even as the terror was being enacted over the border the Regent arrived back in the Firth of Clyde. And this time it was not just three vessels but a fleet which came sailing into the Gareloch, to land no fewer than four thousand French troops, with all supporting artillery, arms and munitions, a sign to all of the importance King Francis was now placing on Scots intervention in his battle for supremacy in Christendom. Not even de Gresolles was there to meet his countrymen in their unexpectedly early arrival. Never had Cowal and the Gareloch seen anything like this, such a concentration of shipping and armed men, since the days of Somerled the Mighty, first Lord of the Isles.

The subsequent march of the newcomers through the Highland mountains had to be something of an epic for a Continental army used to campaigning on the level plains of Northern Europe. It took them longer than the journey from France.

Well before they reached the Forth valley, the Marischal got word of it, and in the absence of the Chancellor at St Andrews, and Arran at Hamilton, and the Bastard and de Gresolles off again to the Borderland to see what could be done there, himself led a welcoming party westwards to meet the Regent, the company including David Lindsay

They encountered Albany at Aberfoyle, emerging from the mountains, and in no genial frame of mind. Straggling behind for miles was the strung-out host of weary, unhappy and travel-stained Frenchmen.

The Earl Marischal was no French-speaker, which was one of the reasons why he had brought David, who was reasonably proficient in the language. So the latter found himself acting interpreter. Not that he was overworked in this capacity, for Albany was even less informative than usual and the Marischal had never been a man of eloquence. The journey eastwards was largely a silent one.

The Regent made up for this unpromising start by issuing a flurry of orders at Stirling. Fullest mobilisation was commanded forthwith, no excuses to be considered. All harvesting was over by now and the autumn cattle sales could wait. Horses by the thousand must be gathered; all cannon collected from the fortresses; the Church must produce more monies and provender and forage for the largest army Scotland had fielded for centuries—and quickly, for he intended to march just as soon as his French troops were rested and trained for this new sort of warfare. There was to be no delay, and no nonsense this time about calling an unco-operative parliament.

In a mere two weeks, in fact, so great was the Regent's determination to strike before the winter weather made large-scale campaigning impossible, the march southwards began, belated contingents from the Highlands and Isles to follow on. David went too, on Albany's express orders, since he was supposed to know something about warfare in the East March, as a lieutenant of de la Bastie—for this time there was to be no discreet back-door approach through the West March and Carlisle, but a full-scale assault and retaliation where the English would like it least, and where they had themselves been so recently operating. David would again act interpreter, since old Bishop Leslie was now returned to his native Aberdeenshire and was not suitable for this sort of thing anyway. And though the Bastard spoke better French, having lived in France for some time, Albany did not trust him.

Kate was unhappy, not so much at her husband going off to war as that she could not go with him. But at least she made the parting from young James less difficult for she was now almost as popular with the boy as was David, and so long as one remained, the King was less trying.

Margaret Tudor made no sallies from Linlithgow.

By the time that the vast slow-moving host had passed Edinburgh and picked up the Lothian contingents at the Burgh Muir, it was reckoned that the army, with the French force, totalled no less than eighty-eight thousand men. And a more reluctant legion, despite all its pomp and display, would have been hard to assemble.

Lord Lindsay was feeling his age, it seemed, as well as reluctance, and had delegated the leadership of his retainers to his eldest son John, Master of Lindsay, who was normally based on their Fife estates and not on the best of terms with his father. From this brother-in-law, himself less than eager for the fray, David learned much of the attitudes and feelings of the Scots nobles—by no means all of which he passed on to the Regent. Whilst they were eager enough for vengeance on the English, they were very well aware that this entire venture was being mounted on behalf of France, not Scotland, their strength, resources, even their blood perhaps, to be expended to further the ambitions of King Francis. They resented Albany's closeness to his French commanders, whom he appointed to the most senior positions, and his cold distance from themselves—especially the Bastard of Arran, not used to this relegation. Moreover, they were worried about the Douglases who so very obviously had not responded to this national call-to-arms and who, in the event of a Scots defeat or even a victory costly in casualties, would be in a position to rise behind them and take the initiative thereafter, to impose their will on the land. None knew where Angus was now, whether still in France, in Henry's England, or secretly back home. If he was to join Dacre and this Surrey, and called out the Douglases and Homes in their rear . . .

They marched through the Lammermuirs by Soutra Aisle and down Lauderdale to the Tweed between Melrose and Dryburgh Abbeys, both so far unburned, and turned eastwards towards the Merse. Deliberately Albany led his multitude through the devastated Kelso area, in order to rouse the wrath and urge for revenge of his nobles and lairds. But as they came at length, by Eccles, to the Coldstream fords, and stared across Tweed to the English bank, David for one knew that it would not serve. The lords, the Bastard the most vocal, would challenge the English might here on their own soil and fight if need be, but they would not cross into England for the King of France. That lesson had been too dearly learned.

In vain the Regent argued and pleaded, threatened and raged, language barrier or none. In furious French he named the Scots craven, cowards, spineless dogs, traitors even, to no avail but to their fierce offence. The vast army sat down around Coldstream and would go no further. Albany himself went back to Eccles Priory's comfort for the night. And comfort was called for, in body as in mind, for the weather was grim, driving chill rain and sleet. The disgruntled army had to do the best it could with Coldstream's facilities—to its townsfolk's misery.

The following day Albany, in the hope of shaming the Scots into action, made a great play of parading his French forces and leading them into and across Tweed. He declared that since Dacre's nearest stronghold of Wark Castle was only some three miles away, he and his brave Frenchmen would go reduce it. When the Scots had recovered their courage, they could come on after.

It was not quite so easy as that, however, for the river was already running high with the rains, and it was quickly apparent that only the very lightest artillery could be got across, the heavier pieces merely sinking into the river-bed, indeed the oxen drawing them refusing to take to the water however much they were coaxed and lashed. Such pieces as were got across, like the commissariat, had to be man-handled—and that was a sorry business for all concerned, in those weather conditions with everyone soaked and chilled.

David Lindsay was in a quandary. The Lindsays, under the Master, were staying put on the Scots bank along with the rest. But he himself had come on this expedition on Albany's direct orders and therefore had to consider himself in the nature of a personal aide to the Regent. He did not desire to seem to side with the French against the Scots—yet he could not but feel ashamed of his countrymen's so non-heroic stance, their decision to stand by and let the visitors do the fighting. He went, but unhappily.

They marched, shivering in wet gear, upstream the three

miles on the English side to Wark. They found it to be a strong old Norman-type castle, on a mound, consisting of a massive square keep surrounded by an inner and an outer bailey, each defended by high parapeted walling and the whole surrounded by a moat. The outer bailey was notably extensive. That it would be no easy nut to crack was apparent—emphasised when cannon-fire greeted their approach, and fairly evidently heavier cannon than they themselves had been able to get across Tweed. The situation did not look good.

But four thousand men cannot just turn tail when faced with a few cannonballs, and the Scots left behind had to be shamed into co-operating, if possible. So Albany advanced, despite casualties, bringing up his small artillery, to mass them against one restricted section of the perimeter walling to batter solely at that. They suffered losses in men and guns, but the strategy worked in that the masonry gave way, leaving a sizeable gap through which the infantry charged strongly, the defenders being hampered by the presence of large numbers of the local country folk and their beasts and belongings who had been allowed to take refuge in this outer bailey on the approach of the enemy.

There followed bloody chaos in that confined space, crowded with combatants and non-combatants. The French were not backward in cutting down all in their way, but the cramped conditions made effective fighting difficult and prevented any large proportion of the attacking force from getting within the walling. Admittedly the English artillery-men could not depress their cannon sufficiently to shoot down into this bailey, nor indeed could they use their hand-guns and archery to good effect without endangering their own folk. But the attackers were also largely hamstrung, faced with the high walling of the inner bailey, without cannon to batter a hole in it, and the gates barred against both them and the unfortunate English left outside. Scaling ladders and ropes were called for, and for a while it was stalemate, although the slaughter went on.

David Lindsay, forward with Albany, was sickened at the sight of women and children dead and dying.

Then the defenders in the inner bailey and keep brought in a new weapon—fire-arrows, shooting down shafts with blazing tow attached into the crowded outer bailey. This, as well as the still-struggling combatants and the dead and dying, was full of hay, straw and provisions for man and beast, the beasts themselves, the permanent lean-to outbuildings of the castle's byres and stabling, makeshift shelters for the refugees, carts laden with domestic gear and so on. It was at all this that the arrows were aimed and, despite the sleet, with marked effect. The hay and straw in especial caught fire quickly and the outbuildings were soon ablaze. Choking clouds of smoke filled the constricted area, and cattle and horses went mad with the fire and the smell of blood and rampaged around. That outer bailey of Wark Castle became a foretaste of hell itself.

The French infantry therein were scarcely to be blamed if they now struggled as hard to get out as they had done to get in. Blinded by the dense dark-brown smoke, unable to distinguish friend from foe, charged by crazed animals, tripping over bodies and with no means of getting further into the castle, they fought their way out through that narrow gap—or some of them did, for many would never emerge on their feet.

Furious, Albany and his French commanders racked their wits unavailingly for an answer to the problems. Without heavier artillery which could outrange that of the castle all they could do was to sit down at a distance and besiege the place, seek to starve it out. But in the prevailing weather conditions that was hardly practical, especially for Frenchmen used to a kinder clime than this.

It was at this stage that some of the cavalry scouts, prudently sent out to scour the countryside, came back to announce that Dacre himself was assembling a large body of English troops at Barmoor, barely fifteen miles to the east, and that their outriders were considerably nearer. Albany, faced with a hopeless situation, took the inevitable decision and ordered a retiral to the Coldstream fords—spurred on by the Wark artillery, which had opened up again.

They left an estimated three hundred French dead behind, along with the local casualties.

Even now their immediate problems were by no means over, for the river had risen noticeably in the interim with the continuing rain and sleet, which was no doubt of storm proportions in the surrounding hills. Getting the men back across, especially the wounded, was a dire business and much of the artillery, light as it was, plus stores and munitions, had to be abandoned. Angry, wet and disheartened, they then discovered that many of the Scots contingents had already anticipated withdrawal and had set off northwards for home.

The Regent was a man all but bereft of speech. David Lindsay's one attempt at consolation, to the effect that conditions would be just as bad for Dacre and that the English would not find crossing Tweed any easier than they had done so they need not worry about pursuit, met with only a flood of French cursing.

But the order for a return to Edinburgh was given. It was only 4th November and extraordinarily early for such hard weather as this. They moved off northwards actually in a snowstorm, banners furled and heads down.

21

That was the start of a hard winter, in more ways than one. Men could not remember such consistently bad weather, so much snow and continual gales. And everywhere in Scotland dissatisfaction was rife. Possibly shame had something to do with it, a sort of self-disesteem at the inglorious state into which the realm had sunk, allied to fear for the future. The Regent, by all accounts, made unbearable company, and David was thankful that he did not have to see anything much of him, for he made his base at Edinburgh and seldom came near Stirling. The capital, however, could have wished him elsewhere for, apart from his ill-temper and demands, he quartered his French troops on the city, and since they could not be expected to survive in encampments in the appalling weather conditions, they had to be billeted in houses and premises, even churches, in the town, to the great offence of their reluctant hosts. The Regent was not to be moved by any representations over this compulsory quartering, however lofty the objectors—indeed many of the lords complained that he was requisitioning their town-houses deliberately as reprisal for their refusal to invade English soil.

It all made a sorry Yuletide, for the bad weather disorganised transport by land and sea and shortages were general.

Immediately after that less than festive season was over Albany called a parliament, at Holyrood. On this occasion the young monarch apparently was not required and David Lindsay had no call to attend, but he heard all about it afterwards, for the Earl Marischal and the Lord Erskine, from Stirling, sat therein as lords of parliament. It had been an acrimonious affair from the start, with the Regent at loggerheads with everybody else, even including the Chancellor who was, it seemed, refusing to find any more Church monies for Albany. And that man needed money in a large way—indeed that, it transpired, was the main reason for calling this parliament—for the four thousand French troops had to be kept and paid, unlike the levies of the Scots lords, who had to provide military service as part of their feudal dues. The demand for forty thousand crowns set the tone of the entire proceedings, for it was flatly refused by every speaker there, amidst accusations that the Regent had already bled the Treasury white, and that the two abortive expeditions to the Borderland had grievously impoverished the lords, Church and burghs. There had been a violent scene with Albany promptly losing his temper and marching out.

However, he had been persuaded to return by de Gresolles, who was a fair English-speaker and was on this occasion acting interpreter. But a second session was no more satisfactory than the first, for the resentful nobles, supported by the Edinburgh and other burgh representatives, banded together to demand the immediate repatriation to France of the four thousand visitors who were costing the land so dear, consuming the nation's substance, behaving with arrogant insolence and keeping them out of their own houses. Even the Chancellor, financially concerned as he was, felt that this was going too far, and pointed out that this dire winter weather was no time to embark thousands of men on ships for France or anywhere else. But he was shouted down and a vote demanded. Parliament then decided, and by a substantial majority, that the Frenchmen should go, and forthwith. When the Regent, enraged, jumped up to declare that in that case he would go also, the second session broke up with no more dignity than the first.

Albany flatly refused to attend another sitting and the parliament was dissolved. But later, the Regent called together the members of the Regency Council and some senior nobles and officers of state and told them that he was sick unto death of Scotland and the Scots, that he was indeed going to go back to France to consult with King Francis, and whether he would come back depended on much better behaviour, suitable obedience and firm commitment to solid support by all concerned. When he was asked when this departure would be, and they were told just as soon as the weather was suitable for sea-travel, the councillors, mindful of previous long-delayed absences, wanted a specific date for the Regent's return. This he had haughtily refused to give, and there were protests that this was no way to rule a realm. When this predictably brought this meeting also to an abrupt close, the Earl Marischal managed to get in a quick proposal that if the Duke was not back by, say, the end of August at the latest, then it would be assumed that his regency was at an end, and suitable alternative arrangements for the kingdom's governance made. Although this reasonable suggestion was agreed to by all present except de Gresolles, Albany himself made no response, and left them there.

All this David heard in due course, and feared the worst.

But worse indeed there was to come. News reached Stirling some weeks later that, in accordance with parliament's decision, the French troops had in fact marched, not through the mountain passes, which were blocked with snow, but to Dumbarton on the Clyde estuary, where their vessels, which had been lying the while in the Gareloch, were brought round to pick them up. And bad weather or none, they had all set sail for France. Shockingly, off the Mull of Kintyre a fierce south-westerly storm had struck the fleet, scattering it and driving the ships far off course northwards, where some had been wrecked on the savage Hebridean seaboard and isles, with great loss of life.

So much for the Auld Alliance.

The Duke of Albany came to Stirling in early April, to take his leave of the monarch whom he represented. The worst of the weather was over and a voyage could be contemplated now without major apprehension. It made a strange visit, for although the Regent was still that, and in theory only going on another three-months leave of absence, nobody there expected him ever to come back to Scotland. So the occasion seemed to hold something of the nature of a charade, for he went through the motions which implied a return in a short period, appointing a permanent member to replace the late Archbishop Forman on the Regency Council, none other than Gavin Dunbar, the tutor, now titular Bishop of Aberdeen. He also confirmed various incumbents in offices of state, and so on. Two items did, however, ring a rather different note. These were Albany's surprising nomination of de Gresolles as Lord Treasurer—and when that drew astonished protests, the cold intimation that the Frenchman in that position would ensure that the monies owing to him for the payment of the French force's expenses, much of which he had had to meet out of his private fortune, would be remitted to him in France, notably those from Holy Church; the other that, when the Earl Marischal took the opportunity to declare that he wished to be relieved of his duty of guardianship for the young King, which he had sustained for overlong as it was to the detriment of his other interests, the Regent, accepting, nominated *four* others in his place. One, Lord Erskine, was more or less only a promotion for, as hereditary keeper of Stirling Castle, he had been acting as assistant guardian all along; but three others, the Lords Fleming, Borthwick and Cassillis, seemed excessive, and the explanation that this was necessary so that one was always to be in residence at Stirling along with Erskine for the monarch's security, again gave the impression of a long-term policy.

It was with mixed feelings, then, that the Stirling company said farewell and watched the Duke ride away. There were no tears, nor any real sorrow, for this John Stewart was scarcely a character to attract affection; but there were considerable ponderings.

David Lindsay's earlier ponderings had caused him to write a letter to Davie Beaton, which he besought the Regent to deliver when he got to France. In it, he urged his friend to relinquish his ambassadorship and return to Scotland, especially if the Duke decided not to do so. The country, he declared, grievously needed a firm hand to guide its destinies, and while the Chancellor and Primate should be supplying that, in fact his uncle was becoming progressively less capable or even almost interested, it seemed. As he aged, he was growing ever more heavy in person and lethargic in behaviour. He seemed less and less concerned with affairs of state and more and more so in Church matters, in especial its revenues, and was spending most of his time at St Andrews. Perhaps the endeavour to have him succeed to the Primacy had been mistaken? Anyway, his secretary's and nephew's guiding hand was sorely needed, and he, Davie, would surely serve Scotland a deal more effectively at home than in France, in this pass, however able an envoy he might be. He ended by informing Beaton that he and Kate had been to see Marion and their fine son, and although they were both well, they needed the presence of husband and father.

So the Regent left Scotland once more, and an uneasy period of waiting ensued.

Waiting, during that summer, but no inaction. For one thing, the English kept up their raiding over the Border, not in major fashion, for Surrey had gone south again and Dacre had to probe ever deeper into Scotland to find suitable undevastated areas—although he noticeably avoided the Home territories. This kept the Bastard busy, for he appeared to have become more or less commander of the Scots armed forces, and of course his father was still, in theory, Warden of the Marches. David saw little of him that summer, for he seldom came to Stirling. Indeed the castle there seemed to have become something of a backwater, with Arran at Hamilton most of the time, the Chancellor at St Andrews and de Gresolles remaining in Edinburgh. The Marischal departed too, and David missed him, for he was a strong and reliable character, if lacking in social graces.

There were rumours that Angus was now with King Henry in the Calais area, which sounded ominous. No direct word came from France.

It was a poor summer weather-wise, not what was required for the land after so grim a winter. The crops were late and scanty. People worried about food stocks and forage.

August came, and the Regent's three months were more than up since he had left in April. But that Holyrood meeting had given him till the end of August before the regency would be assumed to be over. Those last weeks, all who had any interest in the rule and direction of the nation held their breaths, for if Albany did not come, nothing was more sure than that a dire struggle for power would follow.

On the Feast of St Augustine, 29th August, a single horseman, dressed in the height of French fashion but ill-mounted on a tired beast, came riding up Stirling's narrow, climbing streets to the castle, demanding admittance in the name of the Regent. He was allowed in—but that would be the last exercise of Albany's authority in Scotland ever, it seemed; for it was Davie Beaton, who had resigned his position at the French court and taken passage on a wine-ship trading to Dumbarton. The Duke, he informed, was not coming. Indeed, he was at present acting Lord Admiral of France and fighting the armies of the Emperor. He had had enough of Scotland, and in Davie's opinion, would never return. But he had sent no message, no formal resignation.

His hearers eyed each other in doubt and perplexity. But not David Lindsay. He preferred that it was Davie Beaton who had returned to Scotland, rather than Albany, any day.

22

Kate Lindsay exclaimed with a kind of delight at what she saw, reining in her horse. The land fell away gently before them, eastwards from this Balrymonth Hill, in great sweeps and folds, cattle-dotted on the higher ground, ribbed with the long rigs of strip cultivation on the lower, now yellow with stubble, until it met the limitless ocean, glittering in the golden October sunshine, a fair and fertile prospect. And in the middle distance, under a faint blue haze of wood-smoke, something of a blunt peninsula jutted into that Norse Sea, a most eye-catching feature, a tight-packed walled city of warm brownstone masonry and red pan-tiled roofs, from out of which rose a host, a multitude of towers and spires and pinnacles, so many in so comparatively small a space as to be scarcely credible, but all as it were supporting and building up to a greater soaring square tower, slender but strong as it was graceful, high above all but not dominant—for the dominance was provided by another edifice, a redstone castle which thrust out into the sparkling waters on a mound at the very tip of the promontory, proud, challenging, yet for all that not contrasting with the mellow serenity of that entire fairytale city by the sea.

"It is lovely," she said. "So fair and—and sure. So . . . what is it? Withdrawn from all else. There. I had no notion that St Andrews would be like that."

"Strange that it should seem so," David told her. "Fair, yes, after its fashion. But sure? I would not say so. And withdrawn only in that it turns its back on all else but itself, the Church and its university. St Andrews cares only for itself."

"Yet all Holy Church is ruled from here, in all Scotland? The realm's seat of learning."

He shrugged. "In name, yes. But its rule is concerned with its own pride and glory, the Primacy's Church, I would say, rather than Christ's! St Andrews looks inward, not outwards. And its learning is like the rest, limited, inward-looking, going only a little way towards knowledge and truth, I think. Here those who would pursue real learning and higher things seldom remain, but go on to Paris, the Sorbonne, Leyden, Padua and the rest."

"*You* came here. And Davie Beaton."

"When I was fifteen, yes. Davie and I were classmates. I stayed for four years and then my father gained me the appointment at court. I am no true scholar—but I learned enough to know why the good Bishop Elphinstone founded his own university at Aberdeen. He said that St Andrews had exchanged both piety and probity for pride! I believe that was why he refused the Primacy."

"I never knew him. He refused it . . . ?"

"Oh, yes. He was the obvious choice. He was Chancellor too. But he would not come here. Abbot John said that even Elphinstone was afraid that St Andrews might seduce him! As it seems to have seduced all the others. Once they become Archbishops of St Andrews they change, gradually turn their backs on the rest, the realm, the needs of the people, and become only lords of this city by the sea, and its treasure-chests. It is happening to James Beaton, as it did to Andrew Forman, William Shevas, Patrick Graham, even James Kennedy. Perhaps it is like the Vatican, the Papacy, spiritual power corrupting even worse than earthly power. Although there is little that is spiritual here, I fear!"

Kate eyed him questioningly. "This is strange talk, Davie! Is this what St Andrews does to you? Were your four years here so grievous?"

"No. Not that. But . . . if I was no great scholar, say that I learned more than my tutors sought to teach me!"

They rode on down past Feddinch towards the metropolitan see and ecclesiastical capital of Scotland.

They had been visiting the Mount, David's inherited property in what was known as the rigging or roof of Fife, the high central area of that ancient land. The King's new guardians were much less strict about attendance on the monarch than had been the Earl Marischal, and when David's old maternal uncle died, who had been stewarding the estate all these years, he had had little difficulty in gaining leave to go and inspect it and to make new arrangements. Situated some three miles north-west of Cupar, the county town, and comprising perhaps one thousand acres around the twin hills of Lindifferon and the Mount itself, it was a pleasant place, with a sturdy tower-house within a court, and a south-facing walled-garden and orchard, plus a hamlet, Lindifferon. Kate had quite fallen in love with it and its surroundings. They had thereafter called in at Pitscottie, the home of David's garrulous far-out cousin, Robert Lindsay, another poet of a sort. Now they were on their way to visit Davie Beaton and Marion, at his uncle's archiepiscopal castle of St Andrews.

It was just five weeks since the end of Albany's regency.

The approach to the city was through levelling land, all carefully farmed, productive and well-tended, the ground notably drained, the barns full, the cattle sleek. If the rest of Scotland was going to go short after a poor harvest, St Andrews seemingly would not.

They entered by the twin-towered West Port, ignored by the guards in the livery of the archbishopric, and rode eastwards along the fine and broad central thoroughfare which led straight for over half a mile to the great cathedral, the magnificent tall and slender tower of which, steeple-crowned so notably overtopped all the other spires and domes and pinnacles of that soaring city. Kate was surprised to see that long broad street, finer than any she had seen in Edinburgh or Stirling, and so unexpected in the seemingly close-packed huddle of the walled town. Remarking on it, she had it explained to her that this was in fact a processional street, and that processions meant a great deal in St Andrews—prideful religious processions, of course, which her husband suggested the good Lord was apt to be offered frequently in lieu of more humble worship. David's disillusionment with Holy Church, always fairly pronounced, appeared to be aggravated by St Andrews.

Certainly there was no escaping the ecclesiastical ostentations of the place. The streets were crowded, and every second person was dressed in a religious habit of some sort, many of them rich, ornate, gorgeous even. And of the rest, a notably large proportion were liveried attendants, retainers and servants, all wearing the cross in various shapes and colours or the sacred monogram, or else men-at-arms with mitres painted on their steel breastplates. Ordinary citizens, as well as being in a minority, were apt to dodge and cringe

335

and scuttle, with due humility, amongst all the imperious churchmen and arrogant servitors. Of students, surprisingly, there were few to be seen—no doubt they were presently at their classes.

As they went, David pointed out the innumerable splendid establishments, chapels, oratories, priories, friaries, monasteries, nunneries, chantries, shrines and the like, jostling for space in that crowded metropolis. Every see was represented, every order in Christendom, every division of the Church—Augustinians, Benedictines, Carmelites, Cistercians, Dominicans, Franciscans, Observantines, Trinitarians and others.

The size and splendour of the cathedral silenced even David for a little, until he was able to point out its more modest but admirable predecessor, hidden at first by the greater edifice, but sited immediately behind it, to seaward, the Celtic Church chapel of St Regulus or Rule, also with its graceful tall tower, but all on an infinitely more humble scale, dating from the times before Holy Church lost its integrity, according to that man.

Their wide street ending here, they turned off northwards along another only a little less imposing. And now they could see, half-right, the castle looming before them and, oddly, behind it, the tops of the masts of shipping in the harbour immediately below its mound.

At the gatehouse in more high perimeter walling, they were challenged by men in handsome mitre-decorated armour, and told curtly to wait, even when David named Master Beaton the Archbishop's secretary as authority. But presently Davie himself came to deliver them from the unhelpful underlings, all smiles, genial welcome and compliments as to Kate's good looks. He ordered men to see to their horses, and led them across the large paved courtyard to the finest of the many towers of that palace stronghold, a square, redstone keep of four storeys below a parapet and attic floor above, over all of which flew a huge flag quartering the archiepiscopal arms with those of Beaton of Balfour. Therein, apologising for the climb, Davie took them up the wide turnpike stair all the way to the very top attic storey, within the parapet-walk, which proved to contain a pleasant suite of four chambers, high above all else and with the most magnificent views. This Davie had taken over for his own, to instal his little family. Here they found Marion and the little boy, in a scene of warm domesticity before a blazing log-fire, with three deer-hounds and two cats, all as though settled here for years.

Given a bedchamber with its own access to the parapet-walk, the visitors were made to feel at home, an ambience they had never before really associated with Davie Beaton. Here he seemed entirely the family-man, playing with his son and the dogs unselfconsciously, affectionate towards his wife and a thoughtful host.

But after an excellent meal, with the young women putting the child to bed and tongues busy, over a beaker of wine with David, Beaton reverted to his more accustomed self. He was full of information, and concerned at what he had learned. His uncle might be retiring into his archiepiscopal shell and losing his preoccupation with affairs of state, but most evidently Davie was not. And if, as Stirling Castle had tended to become, St Andrews might seem something of an ecclesiastical backwater at the tip of its Fife peninsula, its spy-system appeared to be in a healthy condition.

When David remarked, far from critically, on the strange situation in which he found his friend, thus all but banished to a comparatively remote corner of the land for a man used to being at the centre of national affairs and so recently Scotland's ambassador to France, the other assured him that, in the circumstances, St Andrews Castle was an excellent place to be in. He and his uncle were tolerably secure thus. And if by any chance King Henry sought to move more directly against them here, a ship was always waiting in the harbour below, ready to sail and spirit them away to some other retreat, France itself if need be.

"Henry . . . ? France . . . ?" David sounded incredulous.

"Aye, man—it may come to that. Although I hope not. The tide is running Henry Tudor's way now. It will take time before we can reverse it."

"But—you cannot believe that there is any danger *here*, surely? From the English? To keep a ship waiting . . . !"

"You think not? Would that *I* could. Had we not good—or shall we say, well-paid—informants in sundry useful places, even now Henry and Wolsey might well have their unfriendly hands on us. I do not know if you heard, but whenever it was clear that Albany was not to return to

337

Scotland, Henry called for a conference to be held on the Border, to settle amicably, as he put it, the situation between the two realms, that there be an end to bloodshed and raiding. Wolsey would come north in person, Henry being still in France, Angus with him, the Queen-Mother and Arran to be there also. The invitation came to my uncle, as Chancellor, and he would have been hard put to it to make refusal in the circumstances. That is, had we not received information from our spies in Northumberland to the effect that they had intercepted a courier from Wolsey in London to Dacre at Morpeth Castle, carrying a letter which revealed that the conference was no more than a plot to capture my uncle. Arran also. Angus was to effect a forcible reunion with his wife, and they were to take possession of King James and rule Scotland together as a dependency of England. It was to have been happening now, in October. And all Henry's pensioners in Scotland would rise to support it."

"Lord! The dastards! What did you do?"

"We sent warning to Margaret Tudor—who has no wish to be reunited with Angus, whatever her brother says. And to Arran. So—no conference. When the Cardinal-Chancellor of England plans to capture and dispose of the Archbishop-Chancellor of Scotland, at King Henry's behest, it is perhaps time to take modest precautions!"

David wagged his head. "This is beyond all. We heard nothing of it, at Stirling. We hear little there, now. You think that they will try some other villainy?"

"Strange if they do not. And it is not only Henry and Wolsey that we have to watch, but others nearer home. Now that Albany has finally left the scene, there is much activity amongst those left in positions of power. New moves by the old contenders. Margaret Tudor and Arran, for instance. They are in secret correspondence. Both see their ambitions threatened by Henry's. So they are moving together."

"But this is unlikely, surely? They have ever been enemies."

"No doubt. I daresay that they still do not love each other. But they perceive that their causes may be served better, meantime, by working together than by fighting each other. In especial, over the King. We have learned that they are planning to have the Regency Council dissolved, all regency over, and the King declared sufficiently old to rule, themselves of course manipulating him, the power behind the throne."

"James—at twelve years! This is crazy-mad! The boy is no more fit to rule a realm than he has ever been. At twelve, how could he be?"

"To be sure. It is folly, and worse. But he is tall and well-made for his years. Good to look at, likewise. He will serve to *look* the part. And to serve his mother's and Arran's purposes. *They* will rule, through James. They will have little trouble with the Regency Council—for de Gresolles is to be declared incompetent, as a French citizen; Huntly is grievously ill up in his faraway Strathbogie; and Argyll is too busy making himself a king in the Highland West to counter them. That leaves only my uncle and your strange friend, Dunbar, now Bishop of Aberdeen. Arran can get written assent from Huntly and Argyll, and the thing is done, whatever my uncle and Dunbar say."

"And James, in Stirling Castle?"

"His new governors, Cassillis, Fleming, Borthwick, were appointed on Arran's—or his son's—recommendation. And the Bastard is behind much of all this, I reckon. They will not hold out. Arran has got many of the lords behind him, especially those afraid of the Douglases and Angus—such as Lennox, Glencairn, Atholl, Maxwell. He is now, after all, second person in the kingdom. And that is important since—have you heard?—the Duchess of Albany has died suddenly, leaving the Duke with no heir. I judge that he is unlikely to marry again, that one. So, if young James was to die, it would be Arran for the throne!"

"Dear Lord! Fortunately James is healthy, strong."

"Aye—may he remain so! I would say, keep you a sharp eye on our liege, my friend. Only, myself, I would be surprised if you are in a position to do so for much longer!"

"What do you mean?"

"You have always said that the Queen-Mother scarcely loves you. If she gets her son back into her own keeping, will she want *you* along, think you? And is Arran, or the Bastard, so fond of you that they would fight strongly on your behalf?"

"You think that I will be dismissed? Thrown over? James would not like that."

"And do *you* think that the wishes of the sovereign-lord of us all have any relevance or say in all this?"

David stared at him. "I have been with James all his life. Twelve years. It has been *my* life. And . . . I am fond of him."

The other shrugged. "I am sorry. I may be wrong, to be sure. But . . . if I were in your shoes, I would be preparing for a change."

"If the Earl Marischal had not been gone . . ."

"My uncle will do what he can, of course. He likes and admires you. And what influence I have, needless to say, will be exerted on your behalf. But, I fear, the tide I spoke of is against us meantime. We have this little fortress of St Andrews, and Fife, where the Church is strong—strong in power and wealth, if nothing else. And here we must ride out the storm as best we may." That was not like Davie Beaton.

They were eyeing each other a trifle grimly when their wives came back, and although they turned on smiles and suitable banter the young women were not deceived.

"What have you two been saying, that you look so sour?" Kate demanded. "Your faces would have turned the milk! What's amiss?"

"Nothing to worry your bonny heads over, my dears," Beaton said; but his friend was less careful.

"Davie thinks that I may well be in danger of losing my place with the King," he said. "He believes that the Queen-Mother and Arran will take James into their own keeping, and they will not want me there."

"You mean . . . we would have to leave court? Leave Stirling?"

"If they succeed, yes. There would be nothing to keep me at Stirling if James was gone. And if he remained there, but I was not wanted . . ."

"Oh, Kate!" Marion exclaimed. "How sore a trial for you! But—must it be so? It may not. Davie—is this like to happen? How much of it all is but your own overbusy wits at work?"

"Possibly it is but that, my love," her husband conceded handsomely. "Too soon for Kate to be distressing herself, at any rate. All may yet be well . . ."

"I am not distressing myself," Kate denied. "Indeed, in

some way, I would not be sorry. I would win my husband more to myself! I like James very well, but I am a little weary of always playing second to him! And I have had more than enough of being penned in fortresses, always with high walls and drawbridges, like prisons! You, David, cannot deny that, for yourself. No—I would not be heart-broken to leave the royal service for a time. To live in our own house on our own land." She waved a hand to encompass that pleasant room and its domestic atmosphere. "To live like this."

David eyed her thoughtfully.

"Where would you go?" Marion asked. "Back to Garleton or the Byres?"

"A week past I would have said so. But these last days we have been at The Mount of Lindifferon, David's property near to Cupar. It is a fine place. It has been stewarded by his uncle these many years. But he has died, and we thought to find a new steward." She turned to her husband. "We could live there, steward the Mount ourselves. I like it well. No?"

David looked doubtful.

"We would be on our own. No problems with fathers and families. Live as husband and wife should. Work the land—it looked a very fair ground, as good as the Byres. I think that I would prefer that to playing watchdog for a child king."

"Perhaps . . ."

"It might be the best choice," Beaton put in. "You would be near here—safe, in Fife, from much of the troubles which will, I fear, beset the realm. Holy Church can have its uses! And we would be able to see much of each other."

"Yes, yes," Marion exclaimed. "That would be good, Kate. To be near."

David, faced with what looked like a united front, did not commit himself. "We shall see," he said. "It may not come to that, forby."

They left it at that.

The visitors saw little of the Archbishop during their stay at his palace. According to his nephew, who was clearly concerned about him, he was not the man he had been, was drawing in on himself, even talking of resigning the chancellorship—although Davie believed that he had persuaded him not to do that, at least meantime. Certainly he was overweight, seemed preoccupied, and ate and drank too much. In the circumstances, David told Kate, for all Davie's persuasions, poor Scotland needed a stronger Chancellor than this.

After three days, the Lindsays returned to Stirling.

23

If David Lindsay had been inclined to judge his friend's forebodings and warnings as perhaps just a trifle alarmist, he was rudely disillusioned almost on their very arrival at Stirling Castle. For they found Margaret Tudor in residence there, indeed behaving as though she was its châtelaine, and Arran in attendance, apparently almost as much in that lady's favour as Albany had been a year or so before. Young James was the more thankful to see his Procurator and Chief Usher back.

Abbot John was worried. He told David that all the establishment now knew that great changes were on the way. There was to be a council, a Privy Council meeting, held at Edinburgh shortly, not a parliament, and at this Arran and the Queen-Mother were going to propose that the King be declared of age to rule, any regency no longer required, and the court moved from Stirling to the capital. This meant, in effect, that Arran and Margaret would rule, or rather Margaret and the Bastard, for his father was a man of straw. The Bastard it was who was behind it all, or most of it, undoubtedly, and he was cock-a-hoop and scarcely bearable to have around. Inglis feared greatly for the future, particularly their own future.

David, emphasising the folly of pretending that a twelve-year-old could be declared fit to rule a kingdom, said that surely the Privy Council would never agree to this project; but the other told him that the Bastard had been preparing the ground thoroughly and that there had been a stream of callers at the castle these last days, Privy Councillors, no doubt being convinced, bought or threatened—significant figures such as the Earls of Lennox, Glencairn, Atholl, Crawford and others of that order. What they *thought* he knew not, but he was afraid that they would vote as required—for the Bastard seemed entirely confident. And, of course, Cassillis, Fleming and Borthwick, the King's present guardians, were in Arran's faction.

Within hours they had confirmation of all this—and from the highest level. The Queen-Mother herself appeared at the King's quarters that evening, with Arran, unannounced. James, about to go to bed, backed away, scowling, to near the door to his own bedchamber, and so stood as though ready to bolt. Kate, Margaret Tudor dismissed with a flick of a beringed finger.

"So you are returned, Lindsay, from wherever you have been hiding yourself!" she said curtly.

"I obtained leave of absence to attend to my private affairs, lady. After the death of an uncle."

"You will call me Your Grace, sirrah. And you will have sufficient opportunity to attend to your private affairs hereafter, I promise you! You will prepare my royal son to ride to Edinburgh in three days' time, taking all his clothing and personal belongings. We leave Stirling. His Grace will be elevated to the supreme rule in this land thereafter, and his association with yourself and the others here ended. You will bring him to me at the Abbey of the Holy Rood at Edinburgh in three days' time, with all his possessions. You understand? And thereafter you will consider your employment in the royal service at an end. Is that entirely clear?"

David moistened his lips. "Madam—I am devoted to His Grace. All his life we have been close. For his sake, if not my own, I . . ."

"Yes! All his life you have been an ill influence with him! Look at him, there. All but hiding from his mother! *Your* doing, Lindsay. You should never have had the training of the boy. My late royal husband sorely misjudged. But now, that is overpast. The King will be his own governor and will rule. You are no longer required."

"I say that he is! He is!" That was James the Fifth, King of Scots.

He was ignored. "You will inform the others. The man Inglis. And his present tutor, Bellenden, he who followed Dunbar, who is now a bishop. None is any longer in the King's service . . ."

"No! No! Davie is my friend," James shouted. "Abbot John, too. But—Davie Lindsay is mine! Mine! You shall not take him from me—you shall not! If I am King and to rule, I will not let you do this. Davie stays with *me*."

"You do not rule *yet*, James. Mind it! Lindsay goes. You will gain new and better friends . . ."

"No! It is not true!" The boy actually stamped his foot and raised a hand to point at his mother. "You—I *hate* you! I hate you. I stay here, with Davie Lindsay and his Kate." He swung on Arran. "You my lord—tell her. I am the King. She cannot do this. Tell her so."

The Earl spread his hands helplessly and looked unhappy. He said nothing.

"Lindsay—take His Grace and put him to bed," Margaret snapped. "If anything was required to prove the evil influence you have on the boy, this outburst provides it. Take him away. And bring him to Edinburgh in three days." And turning, she swept out.

Arran hesitated, sighed, and sheepishly followed her.

James Stewart flung himself upon David, beating on his chest with clenched fists, babbling incoherently.

It was a long time before either of them slept that night.

For all James's protests and tantrums, and David's reluctance, the one had to deliver the other to Holyrood three days later, with a train of laden baggage-animals. They made a miserable journey of it. Kate came along too, for they were going to the Byres afterwards.

They found that it was Sir James Hamilton of Finnart to whom they were to hand over their charge, with no sign of Arran or the Queen-Mother. The Bastard was amiable and at least superficially sympathetic, conceding that David was the loser by this change but indicating confidentially, if a trifle condescendingly, that he would endeavour to see that some small annual pension should be forthcoming by way of compensation—a suggestion for which the beneficiary appeared perhaps less grateful than he might have been.

The parting from James was grievous for all concerned, and difficult too, for the boy clung to David's person, and since it was *lèse-majesté* to lay hands on the monarch's body, even the Bastard was inhibited from seeking physically to detach him. David himself, much moved, could not bring himself to push the boy away and no urgings from the others present had any effect. It was Kate who eventually solved the problem by taking the King's arm in something nearer an embrace than a grip, and gently easing him away from her husband's and on to her own person, kissing his brow and then holding him at arm's length, whilst soothingly assuring him that they were his friends for always and that they would make shift to come and see him whenever they could—and Sir James Hamilton, she was sure, would facilitate this and look after His Grace well meantime. To which the Bastard hurriedly agreed, asserted entire goodwill as well as his loyal duty and promised that the Lindsays should always be permitted access to the presence, tentatively taking a royal arm as Kate backed away.

He was promptly shaken off, and James stood alone. Hamilton hastily signed to some of the attendants to line up between the King and his friends, at the same time urgently waving the Lindsays away.

Hating to leave the boy thus but recognising that nothing was to be gained by prolonging the misery they raised hands in farewell, David bowed deeply and Kate curtsied, and hurriedly they turned and made their exit, their last sight of their liege-lord standing stricken-featured, desolate, gulping back his tears. Their own vision was not a little blurred thereafter.

They made a silent journey of it to the Byres of Garleton.

The fourth evening of their stay at the Byres, the Lord Lindsay returned—for he had been attending the vital Privy Council meeting in Edinburgh. He came in grim mood and surprisingly, he brought Davie Beaton with him.

It was the latter who did most of the explaining. Much as he loved his good friends David and Kate, he asserted, he was not come on any friendly visitation but practically as a fugitive. Because Lord Lindsay had had his usual tail of armed retainers with him in the city, he had sought his protection and come with him here instead of setting out alone on the long road to St Andrews, unguarded. For the archiepiscopal escort his uncle had brought with him was now disarmed and itself under tight guard in Edinburgh Castle, and the Chancellor himself taken prisoner and confined in Blackness Castle, the state prison near Linlithgow. That Davie was not with him there was only thanks to good fortune and swift preventive action. No least doubt but that he was being searched for in the capital at this moment.

As his friends stared in astonishment at all this, they learned more. The Council at Holyrood had been a disaster. Sundry moderate lords and bishops had been variously prevented from attending, and the Queen-Mother's and Arran's party had had everything their own way. In vain the Archbishop had protested against this device of elevating the twelve-year-old monarch to nominal rule, pointing out that this was a nonsense save in that it gave complete power, without a regency, to those who controlled the child. And who would that be but his mother, not present, but sufficiently well represented? His uncle had been shouted down, but had persisted. Was it sufficiently realised, he demanded, what having King Henry of England's sister controlling the nominal ruler of Scotland would mean, with no Regent? It would mean *Henry's* rule of Scotland, what that monarch had been seeking to achieve all his reign. Already they had sure information from spies in London that Henry was sending up two hundred specially chosen soldiers of his own royal guard to form a close bodyguard for King James, and to this his mother had acceded. Also he was sending a large consignment of gold—no doubt to pay for the bribes offered for a favourable vote in this council! And if that vote should go against him they all knew of his latest threat— that all the property of Scots in England would be confiscated forthwith, and all Scots resident in that realm not only to be banished but to be driven on foot from English soil with no belongings allowed but a white cross affixed to their upper garments, as indication that they were as good as lepers, outcasts of God and man. That was the monarch into whose blood-stained hands they would commit their young liege-lord and his realm if they permitted this folly to be established.

Since the Chancellor presided over this Privy Council meeting, none had been able to silence him. But when Gavin Dunbar, Bishop of Aberdeen, and the Lord Lindsay, sought to support the Archbishop, *they* had been silenced by Arran, at the Bastard's prompting, moving a vote of no-confidence in the present chairmanship, and had it overwhelmingly granted. He then had had himself voted into the chair, as second person in the kingdom, and promptly had put the motion for the elevation of the King to the vote, without further debate. Only three had voted against, the

Chancellor, Dunbar and Lindsay, although there had been two or three abstentions.

The thing was done, the meeting broke up—and the first move of the new regime was to order the apprehension and imprisonment in Blackness Castle of the Chancellor and Primate, and of the Bishop of Aberdeen. Lindsay, learning what was afoot, had wisely left the abbey secretly for the security of his own retinue. Unfortunately, the Archbishop's escort had been rounded up and disarmed whilst the meeting had been going on. So Davie had had to desert his uncle and join the Lindsays, unobserved, and here they were.

Appalled, David and the others listened, comment superfluous.

That night something of a council of war developed. Clearly Margaret and Arran—or his son—had the bit between their teeth now and would stop at little to gain their way, if they could arrest even the head of Holy Church and the realm's chief minister of state, the Chancellor. Undoubtedly those who opposed them were in danger of the same treatment, or worse. All knew that Davie was largely the wits and will behind his uncle and therefore was at real risk. He wanted to get back to the safety of St Andrews Castle just as quickly but unobtrusively as possible, there to do all in his power, and the power of the Church, to gain the Archbishop's freedom. Lord Lindsay was probably safe enough here in his own country, amongst his own folk, with his armed retainers, so long as he did not actively oppose the regime. But David was in a different position, the King's affection for him, in present circumstances, a positive danger. Margaret Tudor hated him, obviously, and although the Bastard was on the face of it on fair terms with him and sought to buy him off with a pension, the Queen-Mother was unlikely to see it that way. He was probably not so much at risk as was Davie Beaton, but danger there was of arrest or other threat. Garleton was too close to the capital for his good, all agreed, and Kate's recommendation of the Mount of Lindifferon as excellent refuge, near to Davie's St Andrews, strongly backed by Beaton, began to look ever more attractive. His father was growing old, but his brother Alexander, at the Barony, was more and more taking over the managing of the property for him, and would not look kindly on David, the older son, coming to supplant him, whilst the Mount required a resident laird.

In the end it was decided that the three of them should indeed make their way secretly to Fife, travelling by night at least for the first part of the journey. It might seem an inglorious business for men who were used to thinking of themselves of some small consequence in the realm, but it was probably good for their souls. They would pay fishermen from Luffness Haven to sail them across the open firth to Pittenweem in East Fife where there was a priory belonging to St Andrews and where they would be able to gain shelter and then horses to carry them on northwards—that way, they ought to run no risk of interception or recognition by enemies.

All at the Byres and Garleton agreed that this was the wisest course both as to the journey and the dwelling in Fife thereafter. Indeed David was a little piqued by the fact that his father and even Mirren seemed less than distressed that he was going off to live far from Garleton and would in the nature of things be unlikely to see much of home and themselves for some time thereafter. Mirren had long settled in at the castle as its mistress, was becoming plump and matronly, and the laird in his old age appeared to rely on her and to be content to be more or less ruled by her. David's presence, not to mention Kate's, probably would have been an embarrassment. And at the Byres itself, although they were very welcome to stay a while, there was no real place for them now, no employment suitable for David.

So, two evenings later, on the Eve of Martinmas, taking advantage of an early frost and therefore calm seas, the travellers made their farewells and rode off down to Luffness, to board a pitch-painted, fishy-smelling coble, just as the November dark was settling on the Forth estuary. It was going to be a cold voyage.

There was little wind, which kept the seas down but which meant that the square lug-sail did not greatly aid them, even though what breeze there was came from the prevailing south-west, the desired quarter since their course was north-east. So the six-man crew had to pull on their long sweeps for the entire fourteen-mile slantwise crossing—although the two Davids were glad enough to take

349

turns at the oars in the interests of keeping warm, being in the circumstances too masculine to take advantage of Kate's offer to huddle with her within the fur wraps she had wisely brought along, even though they would have been delighted to accept.

It took almost three hours to make the crossing, a strange even weird experience for the trio who had never before sailed in a small open boat by night. Their course was never in doubt, at least, for ahead of them all the time, once they had cleared Aberlady Bay's Gullane Point, was the gleam of the blazing beacon on the Isle of May maintained each night by the monks of the same Pittenweem Priory to which they were headed, which isle lay off the Fife coast some five miles—one of the many little-lauded but useful services which Holy Church provided, as Beaton pointed out.

A few miles short of the May, the boatmen changed course to due north, apparently quite sure of their position, and now, calm as the night might be, the swell running in from the ocean began to take them broadside-on, to their increased discomfort. Fortunately there was no lengthy period of this before the loom of the land and the noise of slow rollers breaking on a rock-bound coast, greeted them, and after a little skirting of the shore eastwards, the harbour of what they were assured was Pittenweem opened ahead. All was dark beyond, even though now their eyes were accustomed to the night vision.

Set ashore at a stone jetty amongst moored, bobbing fishing craft, they said goodbye to their boatmen and, stiff with cold, set off uphill in what Davie assured was the direction of St Ethernan's or Adrian's Priory. He knew the area well, of course, and indeed had been here recently, for this was one of the most valuable of the metropolitan see's many daughter-houses. It was nearly midnight, and the little fishing burgh was lightless and asleep. A single lamp did burn, however, at what turned out to be the Priory gatehouse; and when Davie set the great doorbell jangling loudly, it did not take long for a hooded monk to come peering through a grating and demanding to know who dared come disturbing godly men at such ungodly hour? Promptly left in no doubt as to the authority of at least one of his callers, in the name of Archbishop Beaton, he made no delay in opening the postern and admitting them, Davie thereafter demanding the presence of the Prior himself, in bed as he might be. And well aware that the Prior's own house would be the most warm and comfortable in the establishment, he led the way thereto.

An alarmed cleric was presently produced, and a probably deliberate demonstration of the power of the Primate's secretary to achieve results was staged. Soon they were being warmed and restored by a hurriedly prepared meal and excellent wine before a resuscitated fire in the Prior's library, beds were being made up and instructions given as to horses and even an escort to be provided for the morning. This was a masterful Davie Beaton, indicating that the affairs of Holy Church would not be allowed to languish whilst its nominal head himself languished in durance vile.

Kate was interested to hear a female voice plaintively wanting to know what was to do, from the Prior's bed-chamber, as she and David made for their allotted apartment nearby.

Next morning they rode openly northwards, with four of the Prior's armed servitors, through the East Neuk of Fife, by Kellie Law and the high ground of Lathones and Kinninmonth to Pitscottie. Here they had a meal with David's rather odd kinsman, and thereafter parted from Davie, who was turning eastwards for St Andrews, seven miles, while the Lindsays proceeded north-eastwards for Cupar. They promised to forgather soon and to keep in touch always. Davie insisted that they take two of the Prior's men whilst he took the other pair.

They came to Lindifferon as the November day was quietly dying. The twin breasts of its hills swelled gracefully against a pale lemon-yellow sunset, with the tower of the Mount's little castle silhouetted darkly on the flank of the eastern one, surveying all the shadowy, fertile vale of Stratheden. At the sight of it all, they drew rein involuntarily, to pause and gaze, entranced.

"A fair inheritance," Kate said, at length. "A world unto itself. Safe. Secure. Our own. Why did we not come here sooner? Better than palaces and fortresses, courts and intrigues. We shall be happy here, at the Mount, I believe— all three of us!"

"I hope so. I . . . *three*, you say? How three?"

"Three, yes. I have waited to tell you, David, of a purpose. Till . . . now. I am going to have a child, I think. I have wanted it. To be born here, at the Mount of Lindifferon. Oh, Davie . . . !"

"Kate! My dear—you . . . you . . . ! At last—a child! You are sure?" He reined his horse over to hers, hand out—then remembered the escort behind, and moderated his voice and actions, but only a little. "This is . . . joy! Joy! A homecoming, indeed. We have waited so long. Eight years."

"Yes, I am sure enough. So, you see, we start afresh, David Lindsay of the Mount! Come—let us up there and make a beginning."

"With all my heart, my love . . . !"